BROTHERS OF THE SWORD

BOOK 3 IN THE SAXON WARRIOR SERIES

PETER GIBBONS

Boldwood

First published in Great Britain in 2023 by Boldwood Books Ltd.

Copyright © Peter Gibbons, 2023

Cover Design by Head Design

Cover Photography: Shutterstock

A CIP catalogue record for this book is available from the British Library.

Paperback ISBN 978-1-80483-476-3

Large Print ISBN 978-1-80483-475-6

Hardback ISBN 978-1-80483-477-0

Ebook ISBN 978-1-80483-474-9

Kindle ISBN 978-1-80483-473-2

Audio CD ISBN 978-1-80483-482-4

MP3 CD ISBN 978-1-80483-481-7

Digital audio download ISBN 978-1-80483-480-0

Boldwood Books Ltd
23 Bowerdean Street
London SW6 3TN
www.boldwoodbooks.com

For Mary and Peter, for everything.

Hēt þā hyssa hwæne hors forlætan,
    feor āfȳsan and forð gangan,
    hicgan tō handum and tō hiġe gōdum.
Then he commanded each of his men to release their
horses,
    drive them away, and go forth,
    to think on the work at hand and their firm resolve.

— AN EXCERPT FROM 'THE BATTLE OF
MALDON', AN ANGLO-SAXON POEM WRITTEN
TO CELEBRATE THE BATTLE FOUGHT AT
MALDON IN 991AD.

GLOSSARY

Aesc spear – A large two-handed, long-bladed spear.

Burh – A fortification designed by Alfred the Great to protect against Viking incursions.

Byrnie – Saxon word for a coat of chain mail.

Danelaw – The part of England ruled by the Vikings from 865AD.

Drakkar – A type of Viking warship.

Ealdorman – The leader of a shire of the English kingdom, second in rank only to the king.

Einherjar – Vikings who have died in battle and have ascended to Valhalla.

Euton – A supernatural being, like a troll or a giant.

Gafol – The Danegeld, or tax raised to pay tribute to Viking raiders to save a land from being ravaged.

Heriot – The weapons, land and trappings of a thegn or other noble person, granted to him by his lord and which becomes his will or inheritance.

Hide – An area of land large enough to support one family. A measure used for assessing areas of land.

Holmgang – A ritualised duel common amongst Viking peoples.

Jomsvikings – Viking mercenaries based at their stronghold at Jomsburg who followed a strict warriors code.

Nástrǫnd. – The afterlife for those guilty of crimes such as oath-breaking, adultery, or murder. It is the corpse-shore, with a great hall built from the backs of snakes, where the serpent Ni gnaws upon the corpses of the dead.

Níðhöggr. – A serpent or monster who gnaws at the roots of the great tree Yggdrasil, and also gnaws upon the corpses of the dead at Nástrǫnd.

Nithing – A coward, villain, or oathbreaker, not worthy of the glorious afterlife.

Njorth – The Viking sea god.

Norns – Norse goddesses of fate. Three sisters who live beneath the world tree Yggdrasil and weave the tapestry of fate.

Odin – The father of the Viking gods.

Ragnarök – The end-of-days battle where the Viking gods will battle Loki and his monster brood.

Reeve – Administer of justice ranking below a thegn.

Seax – A short, single-edged sword with the blade angled towards the point.

Seiðr – A type of Norse magic.

Thegn – Owner of five hides of land, a church and kitchen, a bell house and a castle gate, who is obligated to fight for his lord when called upon.

Thor – The Viking thunder god.

Thruthvang – Thor's realm in the afterlife, where he gathers his forces for the day of Ragnarök. Similar to Valhalla.

Týr – The Viking war god.

Valhalla – Odin's great hall where he gathers dead warriors to fight for him at Ragnarök.

Vik – Part of Viking Age Norway.

Whale Road – The sea.

Wyrd – Anglo Saxon concept of fate or destiny.

Yggdrasil – A giant ash tree which supports the universe, the nine worlds including our world Midgard.

SOUTHERN ENGLAND, c.1000

N

PROLOGUE

991AD, FOLKESTONE

The *Ormrinn Langi*, the Long Serpent, was a beautiful ship. A drakkar warship built in the east, far from where she sat now in the fish-stinking harbour at Folkestone on England's south coast. Skilled shipwrights had cut her keel from a single piece of oak, and each of her clinker-overlaying planks was carved from wood sourced in the same dark, ancient forests along the banks of Lake Ladoga and the great river which led Vikings south through treacherous waters to far Novgorod and Kiev. She held thirty oars, and it had taken four women an entire year to weave her heavy woollen sail. Olaf Tryggvason stood in her prow and he ran a hand along her smooth sheer strake, the topmost plank from which his picked champions would hang their shields of linden wood when the ship sailed to war. Olaf smiled as the sea lapped at her hull in gentle waves and he looked eastwards, beyond Folkestone's harbour and out to where the grey-green water met the pale blue sky. White-tipped waves rose and fell, and gulls cawed overhead as Olaf remembered the glorious day on the banks of a gleaming river Volkhov when Vladimir the Great of Kiev had gifted him the ship in thanks for his service, back when

Olaf was the captain of Vladimir's army. That was in the days when Olaf's star rose, when the Norns cackled at his dreams from the base of the great tree Yggdrasil, whose branches held the realms of gods, dwarves, nithing-wraiths and men. Those three terrible sisters twisted the threads of men's fates together like so much twine, and they had spun a shining thread for Olaf to raise him up from nothing into a great and powerful warlord.

'Why are you smiling, lord?' asked Kjetilmund, the burly shipmaster of the *Ormrinn Langi*.

'Because spring has come,' said Olaf, tearing his mind away from memories of glorious Kiev, Novgorod and the years he had spent there in Vladimir's service. 'Which means we can leave this place and get back to sea.'

'What is our heading, lord?' asked Kjetilmund, and then raised his gnarled hands in apology, hands that had hefted ship's ropes for twenty years or more. 'I only ask so that I can relay the orders to your captains. We have fifty ships, lord, and our heading must be clear so that we do not lose any. It is spring, but Njorth can still surprise us with a fierce storm to blow us out to sea. Before we know it, it will push stragglers to Frankia and we will lose both ships and men.'

Olaf nodded. He continued to pass his hand along the smooth wood, along where the sheer strake turned upwards into the prow, its curve as smooth as a woman's hip. That prow reared up and snarled out towards the Whale Road, a great spitting serpent with fangs and a forked tongue, with furious eyes to fear. It was Viking custom to remove the beast heads from their warships close to land, so as not to frighten the spirits there, but the ship faced out to sea and, where Olaf was heading, he wanted men frightened.

'We head north around the coast, and we stay in England for the summer,' said Olaf. He had decided that over the long winter, holed up inside a poor hall in Folkestone's town, huddled in fleeces beside the fire. His hall in Kiev had been magnificent, with enough feasting benches to hold one hundred men, luxurious furs for warmth and a hearth fire to warm Valhalla itself. He had debated the merits of leaving England with the captains of his famed Jomsviking warriors, and with his Norse jarls, the powerful earls of Norway and Denmark who had brought their ships to join with Olaf's battle luck and build their reputation and wealth.

'I will pass on the message, lord,' said Kjetilmund, before weaving his way along the deck, ducking beneath seal-hide rigging and around shuffling warriors who brought aboard their sea chests, which doubled up as rowing benches. Beyond the *Ormrinn Langi*, smaller drakkar warships crammed into the harbour, with so many masts that it looked like a great winter forest stripped of leaves. Captains bellowed at each other to keep their distance, using oar shafts to keep the precious hulls from clashing into one another as they prepared to depart from Folkestone. Hull timbers creaked, men bawled orders and protests at one another as they loaded barrels of dried fish, freshly brewed ale, oats and smoked meat aboard the fleet to keep the warriors fed.

'Are you sure you want to stay here?' said a voice with the harsh twang of the Svear men from north of the Rus coast.

Olaf shrugged. 'We have unfinished work here, Burzlief. I am not done with the Saxons yet.'

'We could push north, get you back to Norway, and fight for your title?' said Burzlief. He was a stocky, slab-faced captain of the Jomsvikings, a brotherhood of warriors trained to fight from the time they could walk within the walls of Jomsburg, a walled town in the cold north where warriors lived by *drengskapr*, the way of the warrior.

'There will be time to go north. But we cannot leave Palnatoki unavenged. And we need more men and more silver if I am to become king of Viken like my father, or king of all Norway like my great-grandfather Harald Fairhair.' Palnatoki had been the leader of the Jomsviking order of warriors, a man who had been as a father to Olaf until the Saxons had cut him down.

'I miss Palnatoki as much as you and I hate that big Saxon bastard who killed him. But he died like a warrior and waits for us in Valhalla, in Odin's hall, drinking ale from curved horns beneath its roof made from the mightiest of shields. The Saxons paid us all they could scrape together last year. Their gentle king listened to his black-robed Christ crows and paid us not to fight. So, let's get our silver somewhere else. I don't trust the wyrd of this place. There is ill luck in their nailed god, and we have likely bled the place dry of silver already,' said Burzlief.

Olaf laughed, but part of him believed what men said of the power of the nailed god. He was not a god for warriors, not like Odin, Thor or Týr. He was a god who demanded service, who taught his worshippers of peace and forgiveness. But he also brought the Saxons victory, which spoke of his strength. Olaf shivered with rage as he recalled how Beornoth, the baleful and vicious Saxon warrior, had almost cut him down, and the thunder of hoof beats as the Saxon cavalry snatched his victory away and forced him to accept King Æthelred's payment for peace. 'I make my own wyrd, Burzlief. I am the son of a king, but yet my earliest memories are of living as a slave in the distant east. Driven from our kingdom by usurpers and forced to live like a pig by that bastard Klerkon who sold my mother and I into a horror of suffering and servitude. You have heard the warp of my life a hundred times, of how my uncle Sigurd found me there and brought me to Vladimir in Novgorod. All men know that when I was still but a stripling pup, I found Klerkon and buried my axe in his skull. I rose from the shit of a pigpen to where I am now, the jarl and leader of a fleet of fifty warships. If I can't defeat these cursed Saxons, how can I retake my kingdom in Norway? We must have a victory here. We must defeat their warriors, this jarl-dorman, ealdorman, or whatever title they give to Byrhtnoth, and his champion, Beornoth. They almost killed us last year, but this year we must leave with our hulls buoyed with victory and the bilges of our ships heavy with coin. I need to buy more crews and bring more jarls to my war banner if I am to reconquer my father's kingdom. You say their king listened to his black crows and paid us silver for peace. I say that is because he is weak. If we sail east or north, we must fight strong kings in Frankia or savage jarls in Norway or Denmark to find the silver and men we need. There is more wealth here in Saxon churches and towns, and this King Æthelred does not have the strength to stop us.'

'So, we stay in England, then?'

'We do, and we take our axes and our spears, and we make them suffer. We bring them to battle, and we take everything from them. Their silver, their pride, and their lives.'

'You could be a king here, Olaf. Seems to me it would be easier to kill this King Æthelred than it would be to fight an army of Norsemen for the throne of Viken. We could sail our fleet up the River Thames and take Lundenburg, and from there march on to Winchester. These Saxons have one king, but you need only defeat the warriors in his southern lands of Wessex and Essex. By the time his men in distant Northumbria or even Mercia know we have attacked, the war would be over. It would take months for the Saxon king to raise an army from his entire kingdom.'

'Perhaps,' said Olaf with a shrug. 'But first I want this Essex to burn. I want the warriors of this shire to feel our wrath outside of their own homes. I want their warriors to bleed in their own fields and rivers. They must suffer for the humiliation I suffered last year. There must be a victory here, and then who knows what next? A kingdom to be won with the silver we can rip from the Saxon dogs and their puny king.'

A tall man in a white robe stalked along the *Ormrinn Langi's* deck. He wore his long silver hair unbound, and his beard was the colour of an old cauldron. The tall man frowned at the sailors who shrank from him, for he was a *seiðmann*, or what the Saxons would call a priest of the Asgard gods. In his right hand he clutched a dagger with a wickedly curved blade, and a hilt carved into the shape of a raven's head with an open beak. Behind him two warriors heaved a pitiful figure in their brawny arms, their limbs strengthened from hauling an oar across the surging dangers of the Whale Road. The figure bucked and wailed in their grip, his face a swollen mass of purple swelling. The *seiðmann* stopped a pace away from Olaf and raised his arms to the sky, thin fingers clawing towards Asgard. His eyes turned in on themselves and showed only white, the colour of his dagger's hilt.

'Odin, hear me,' the tall man rumbled in a voice as deep and foreboding as a bear's winter cave. 'With this offering, bring your loyal son Olaf victory. Send your ravens Hugin and Munin to watch his deeds, to witness how he fights and strives for greatness, so that one day he can take his place amongst your Einherjar, to fight alongside you on the inexorable day of Ragnarök.'

Olaf bowed his head in solemn respect and found that he was clutching the silver hammer amulet at his neck. It was a *mjolnir* pendant in honour of the god Thor. Whilst Olaf had always believed that he had forged his own luck, had clawed his own way up from the slave pens, the favour of the gods was not something to be taken lightly or ignored. There was powerful *seiðr* magic in the gods' power. Warriors believed in it, fought harder when they felt Odin was on their side. So Olaf knelt before the *seiðmann* and clenched his teeth as the two warriors pushed the bruised smaller man to the deck before the tall, grey-haired Odin priest. The man was a Saxon slave, a young, thin man with a wispy beard and large hazel eyes full of fear. He wept and begged, writhing on the deck timbers like a landed fish. The pitiless *seiðmann* grabbed a fistful of the Saxon's hair and yanked his head back, and in one fluid motion, he whipped his wicked knife across the man's throat. The slave twitched and jerked in the *seiðmann's* grip and fiery blood spurted from the terrible wound in his neck and splashed across Olaf's face in a hot slap. Olaf resisted the urge to recoil from that blood, and he grinned, the iron taste of it bitter in his mouth, because the blood had struck in the right place and, therefore, the omens were good. The men saw they were good, and that would give them confidence. Viking gods did not demand their followers act with forgiveness, or live in peace and never-ending prayer. They craved war and bravery, rewarded valour and weapon skill. They were unforgiving and vengeful gods, and Olaf prayed that Odin and Thor saw him, and that they would bring battle luck to his campaign against the East Saxons.

1

Beornoth cuffed at his dripping nose, and breath steamed from his mouth like a cloud of dragon smoke. A robin danced across frost-dusted grass amongst fallen, twisted leaves. Its small black eyes watched Beornoth and his men, its head jerking from side to side as though it judged them for what they were about to do. Behind him, a horse whinnied, and the bird flew away, fearful of the beasts and the plumes of air billowing from their nostrils in the cold. Beornoth stroked his horse's powerful neck and leant forward to scratch its ear. The leather saddle creaked as he moved, and he rested his hand on the pommel of his sword. The bird was wrong to fear the horses. It was the men astride them who were the killers.

'Are you sure he's here?' asked Aelfwine of Foxfield, his green eyes shining in the bright spring morning.

'He's here,' said Beornoth, shrugging his shoulders to bring his thick, woollen cloak closer around his neck. It covered the iron rings of his byrnie chain-mail coat of armour and kept out the worst of the chill.

'Let's get it done then,' grumbled Wulfhere. His hulking frame shivered where he sat upon his roan mare, and the bald warrior wore a hood over his scarred head. 'I'm bloody freezing.'

'We are here on the orders of the king,' said Leofsunu of Sturmer, a lopsided smile splitting his ugly face. 'And the royal embrace should warm kings' thegns, even on days like this.'

Wulfhere grumbled to himself, for he was not a thegn like most of Beornoth's riders. Wulfhere was a warrior of Beornoth's hearth troop, but Beornoth, Leofsunu, Aelfwine and the rest of the thirty men gathered at the forest's frosty edge were Saxon thegns of Essex, sworn to serve their Ealdorman Byrhtnoth. The ealdorman was in favour with the king, Æthelred, after years of fighting and killing Vikings, and it was in the name of the king that Beornoth rode out when frost shrouded the country in its icy blanket, and the swallows and wagtails had not yet returned from their winter homes. He should be at home, in Branoc's Tree by the fire on such a day, but the king had ordered him to ride north and punish a traitor.

The ride from Branoc's Tree to Bocking had taken only a day and a half, and the king had received word that the traitor, Æthelric, had returned to his lands to visit his family, and so Beornoth and his men rode north-east. Æthelric was thegn at Bocking in the shire of Essex and was one of several Saxon thegns who had welcomed the Danish war king Sweyn Forkbeard to England's shores the previous summer. The rest cowered under the protection of the Danish overlord, most were thegns in East Anglia itself, but Æthelric was an Essex thegn, a man sworn to serve Ealdorman Byrhtnoth and King Æthelred. An oath-breaker and turn-cloak, a man who must be brought to justice. Sweyn had brought his army of Viking warriors and his beast-prowed dragon ships across the Whale Road from Denmark and found succour in East Anglia from men such as Æthelric who, although Saxon nobles, were descendants of

Viking blood. The Danelaw, a vast swathe of England running north of Watling Street, had only returned to Saxon rule in recent years after living under Viking rule for over one hundred summers. The king wanted every treacherous thegn punished, but to ride into Sweyn's lair and kill them was no simple matter. Yet Æthelric had shown himself, no doubt come to check on his lands, retrieve his family and whatever silver he had hoarded away before Ealdorman Byrhtnoth confiscated his lands, his heriot of estates, war gear and wealth, as punishment for his crimes.

'Do you have the proclamation?' asked Aelfwine.

'I have it,' replied Beornoth. The stiff piece of paper covered with monks' scratchings and a thick red dollop of wax imprinted with the king's seal lay tucked in Beornoth's saddlebag.

'Why would a good Saxon lord like Æthelric want the return of the cursed heathens?' said Wulfhere, blowing into his hands and rubbing them together. 'It's beyond me.'

'For many, the Church here is a foul and greedy overlord, exempt from taxes, swallowing up men's land by royal decree. Fine mills and farmland taken for monasteries and ruled over by fat monks and bishops. For some, Viking rule was fairer,' said Aelfwine.

'Aye, until they take an axe to your family and burn your hall with you in it,' said Leofsunu, and the warriors chuckled.

'It's time,' said Beornoth. He dug his heels into his horse's flanks and clicked his tongue. 'Spear.'

Cwicca, his young face ruddy-cheeked from the cold, reached over with Beornoth's aesc spear. Beornoth took the smooth shaft in his right hand, its broad-leafed blade gleaming in the morning sun, which shone bright despite the cold. His horse ambled from the treeline, frozen leaves crunching under its heavy hooves. Beornoth's men followed from the bare branches and brush, which curled and twisted like the frozen fingers of an ancient *eutun* giant.

Bocking was a collection of thatched wattle buildings with a high gate and a timber church surrounded by a wooden wall. It was the home of a thegn, a warrior lord who held at least five hides, or farms, from his ealdorman in return for his duty to fight for that ealdorman whenever he called. It was, Beornoth thought, not dissimilar to his own home at Branoc's Tree. Smoke floated up from roof-holes to sit heavily above the dwelling and then disappear into the pale blue sky. It was a still spring morning with no wind, as crisp as the ice on a frozen water barrel. Behind the walls, a dog barked, and a small child wailed for its mother. The people inside would wake up to reach for whatever food they had left in their winter stores to break their fasts with bread or milk from animals brought into the living quarters for winter warmth. They would be warm and safe, and unaware of the warriors at their gate.

Beornoth pulled gently on his reins when he came ten paces before the walls. The entrance to the smallholding was double gated, below a high turret, and barred from the inside. There were no guards or sentries on the walls. Beornoth sighed.

'Cwicca, Kari,' he barked to his two youngest warriors.

'Yes, lord,' they both said at the same time.

'Go up there, climb over the gate, and open it.'

'But, lord,' said Kari, his words halting, not wanting to question his superior. 'Won't they hurt us if we do?'

'Do you see any warriors on the walls?'

'No, lord.'

'So, how can they hurt you?'

'Yes, lord.' Kari urged his horse out of the line and, followed by Cwicca, he cantered towards the gate. Cwicca held Kari's horse steady, and the tousle-haired lad stood up gingerly on his saddle, resting his palms against the walls for balance. He reached his hands up to the timber wall and hauled himself over, disappearing behind the dark timber palisade in a flurry of arms and legs.

'Hard to believe they had no sentries,' said Wulfhere, shaking his head.

'Especially with a traitor at home. You would think the bastard would be nervous,' said Leofsunu.

'He will be,' said Beornoth.

Moments later, the gates swung open, and Kari stood in the open space. The bracing spar rested in his hand and Kari waved at Beornoth, a grin splitting his beardless face. Beornoth urged his horse on and rode through the open gate, followed by the rest of his horsemen. Their hooves clattered noisily on the frozen mud inside the walls, and a woman stood before them carrying a bucket of water from a nearby well. She dropped the water, a hand rising to cover her mouth in alarm.

'Æthelric of Bocking,' Beornoth shouted. His voice was loud and deep, carrying on the cold air like the roar of a stag. A clatter of hastily moved furniture came from a high-gabled building and mumbled voices hid behind closed doors. 'Æthelric of Bocking,' Beornoth shouted again. 'I come in the name of the king. Show yourself.'

A priest in a faded smock tied at the waist with a cracked leather belt slid from a side door. He was portly, and the tonsure on his head grown long into a see-through fuzz. The priest raised a hand in greeting and made the sign of the cross.

'Hello, noble warriors,' said the priest, his voice high-pitched and stuttering. 'Welcome to Bocking. How can we be of service?'

'Get Æthelric,' Beornoth said, a frown creasing the scarred crag of his face.

'Regretfully, Lord Æthelric is not here. The Lady Leofwynn is in residence, and I am here in the service of the lord. It is the third hour. Are you here to make your terce prayers?'

'I don't follow the Liturgy of the Hours, priest. I know Æthelric is here, so either he comes out, or I go in and get him.'

The priest's head snapped back as though Beornoth had slapped him. 'You do not make your prayers? What kind of man...'

'Æthelric!' Beornoth roared, and the priest took a step back, wincing at the anger in his voice. Beornoth levelled his spear at the main building, and his horse's foreleg scraped at the frozen earth and shook its head, skittish beneath Beornoth's fury.

'How dare you ride in here, unannounced and uninvited,' came a voice from across the courtyard. Beornoth turned to see a line of ten warriors, two of them wearing knee-length byrnie coats of mail, and all armed with spears and axes.

'Æthelric's hearth troop,' said Aelfwine. They were the thegn's men, warriors he fed, armed and kept within his house to help fulfil his duties as the protector of his lands.

'We come from the king, in search of the traitor Æthelric of Bocking. A man who sides with Danes, with Viking murderers and rapists and invites them on to our land. Are you Æthelric?' Beornoth said, pointing his spear at the warrior who had spoken. He was a big man, his mail polished, his black hair pulled back from his face and tied at the nape of his neck, and over his lip was a long, drooping moustache.

'No, I am not the thegn,' said the warrior, and smirked over his shoulder at the warriors behind him.

'Then you will die for him,' said Beornoth. He was tired of asking, and was not a man known for his patience. He slipped down from his saddle and marched towards the line of warriors.

'Beornoth, wait,' said Godric, a young thegn who rode with Beornoth. But he ignored the plea.

The warrior with the moustache turned his smirk to Beornoth, but it quickly faded as Beornoth's arm drew back and he flung his spear. He grunted with the effort and kept striding forward, dragging his sword free from its fleece-lined scabbard, the cold metal scraping on the scabbard's wooden throat. The warrior swayed aside, and the spear flew past him to thud into the chest of the man behind. The power in the throw snatched the warrior from his feet and he fell sprawling onto the frost-dusted grass. Blood spilled in the bright morning, thick and dark on the hoar frost, and suddenly Bocking erupted into a maelstrom of shouting and screaming.

'Wait, wait...' said the moustached warrior, hastily holding up his hands in peace and shuffling away. Beornoth took a long stride forward, with a speed that belied his size, and plunged the tip of his sword into the warrior's gullet. The moustached man's eyes went wide with surprise at the pain, and at how fast the situation had deteriorated into deadly violence.

'Too late for that,' said Wulfhere, who had leapt from his horse and ran past Beornoth with a long-handled war axe held in both hands. Wulfhere blocked a spear thrust from a stocky Bocking fighter, and back-cut his bearded axe blade into the warrior's shoulder with a wet thud.

'Lord help us, protect us, O' God...' the priest wailed, falling to his knees and clutching the cross around his neck.

'There is no God here, priest. Only the king's justice for a man who invited Vikings to our lands,' Beornoth snarled as he marched past him, the tip of his sword dripping blood. The clang of iron, and the shouting of Bocking's hearth troop subsided as Leofsunu and Aelfwine joined the fray, and with three men down, Æthelric's warriors threw down their arms in surrender. Bocking's thegn, Æthelric, had still not shown himself, and Beornoth was tired of waiting. The blood-fury was on him, and he crashed a heavy boot into the main hall's door, flinging the heavy oak timbers back on their dark iron hinges. Beornoth marched into the gloom, where a fire roared in the central hearth, and tendrils of smoke spiralled up out of the hole in the thatch above it. The place smelled of animals, of sweat and boiled vegetables. Pale faces cowered from him in the corners, a pot left boiling over on the fire as folk shrank back from the huge, vengeful warrior who had stormed into their home.

'Where is he?' Beornoth said, raising his blood-soaked sword to a gap-toothed man in a brown rough-spun jerkin. The sword wasn't just a weapon, it was a warning. A warning to Beornoth's enemies. It was an expensive weapon, just as rare as the chain-mail byrnie he wore. It spoke of a successful warrior, a man strong and deadly enough to hold sword and mail in battle when others would try to rip them from him, it spoke of a man who protected his people from their enemies with his brutality and war skill. The sword told men to be wary, that its wielder was not to be trifled with. He was to be respected and feared. The gap-toothed man pointed a shaking finger toward the shadows at the back of the hall.

Beornoth marched through the old floor rushes, which were dank and soaked from a winter full of spillages. There was a small door on the rear wall, and Beornoth smashed it open with a kick, without even breaking stride. There, in a candlelit room, window shutters closed, and an unmade bed, was Æthelric of Bocking. He was a tall, thin man with a balding head of black hair run through with silver. Æthelric had a lugubrious face, and a close-cropped beard. He stood before a stout woman in her night-dress who wailed and hid her face behind hands thick with rings. Æthelric held a seax before him, its broken-backed blade wavering and his face drawn and pale.

'How dare you enter my home like this? I am a thegn of...' said Æthelric, his jowls trembling as he spoke.

'How dare you provide aid to Sweyn Forkbeard, war king of the Danes? A Viking who had brought blood and death to our lands. I fought his man, Ragnar the Flayer, last year and he slaughtered our people, raped them, and enslaved them.' Beornoth spoke evenly, staring deep into the thegn's eyes. 'I am Beornoth of Branoc's Tree, here on the order of the king to bring you to justice.'

Beornoth pulled a crumpled roll of parchment which contained the king's decree in spidery scrawl and tossed it at Æthelric's feet. He batted the seax away contemptuously with his bloodied sword and grabbed Æthelric by the scruff of his neck. Æthelric grabbed at Beornoth's huge paw, calloused from use of sword, axe and spear, but he was like a child toying with its father and Beornoth dragged him into a savage headbutt. Æthelric's nose mashed against Beornoth's forehead with a crunch, and the thegn went limp. Beornoth dragged him out of the chamber and into his hall, the Lady Leofwynn running behind him, screeching in horror. Beornoth threw Æthelric through the open doors of his own hall, so that the thegn fell sprawling into the frozen mud and sparse grass of his courtyard.

'Not here, is he?' Beornoth snarled at the priest, who still cowered with his cross clutched in soft hands. 'Æthelric of Bocking,' he shouted, loud enough for all in the settlement to hear. 'I am here to punish you as a traitor to the king and your people. Let all witness the king's justice, for those who have lost their lives at the hands of Viking raiders.' Beornoth marched to Æthelric and grabbed a fistful of his thinning hair. He dragged the thegn, who coughed and spluttered as he stumbled behind him, to the palisade gateway, where Wulfhere was fixing a length of rope across the gates' cross-beam. Beornoth grabbed that rope and looped it around Æthelric's neck. Æthelric shook his head and wept, spittle flecking from his lips into his beard. Beornoth handed the rope to Wulfhere, and the big warrior hauled Æthelric up to hang on the rope, his thin legs kicking in the wintry morning air. Wulfhere tied the rope off, and they mounted their horses.

'Burn the hall,' Beornoth snarled. Cwicca and Kari ran into the hall, and emerged moments later with burning timbers from the hearth fire. They tossed the timbers into the dry, cold thatch and mounted their horses.

Beornoth sheathed his sword and led his riders out of Bocking's gate, and towards home. He left Lady Leofwynn on her knees, sobbing beneath the body of her hanged husband, and the burning hall of a traitor. Beornoth hoped that the simple folk who had suffered at the hands of Ragnar, Sweyn and their Viking killers would hear what he had done. Many had suffered and died last summer, people Æthelric should have protected. He was their vengeance, their strong hand against vicious enemies who would put them to the sword. He was Beornoth, thegn of Essex. He recalled all that he had witnessed when the Vikings had raided East Anglia, the flayed skins of honest Saxons used for shield covers, the slaves shackled in pens to be sold in the slave markets of Dublin or Hedeby. Beornoth remembered his own dead children, slaughtered by Vikings years ago, and he felt no pity for Æthelric. He felt rage, and he craved vengeance on the hated Viking invaders. His hate for them was insatiable.

2

'This place is beautiful,' said Cwicca, scampering to keep up with Beornoth's long strides.

'It's the ealdorman's horse-breeding farm,' said Offa. 'Many of the shire's finest warhorses were born and trained here. Maybe the king is here for a horse?' Offa was Byrhtnoth's captain, and commanded the ealdorman's hearth troop, much as Wulfhere was the captain of Beornoth's own warriors. Beornoth liked the old fighter. Beornoth had met Offa when he had first sworn his oath to Byrhtnoth, and they had fought side by side many times since. Offa had a reputation as a steady sword and had been a thegn in Byrhtnoth's household, going back to the time of Byrhtnoth's father. He had a long grey beard, and although the hearth troop looked to Beornoth to lead when it came to battle, Offa was their commander.

'What need would the king have for a warhorse?' said Leofsunu, and the rest of the group sucked in a sharp intake of breath at that cutting truth.

They had left their horses at the huddle of buildings and stables, which made up Ealdorman Byrhtnoth's sprawling horse

farm and breeding stud. The ealdorman's steward had greeted
the band of thegns on arrival, ordered for their mounts to be
cared for, and then pointed up to the distant green fields where
the ealdorman and King Æthelred had gone to spend the
morning hawking. The king's guard of warriors lolled around
the stables, big men in byrnies, leaning on spears adorned with
triangular pennants daubed with the king's writhing dragon
banner of Wessex. They eyed Beornoth and his riders with
indifference as he marched past, but Leofsunu scampered over
to grasp the forearm of a warrior he knew and the rest of
Æthelred's warriors welcomed him warmly. Leofsunu was the
ugliest man Beornoth had ever seen, but he was a stout fighter
and men liked his easy humour, so he was ever popular. He was
also the thegn of Sturmer, prosperous and fertile lands in
Essex.

Beornoth strolled across the pasture, where a fine white mare
cantered around in a circle, her muscled legs and neck shifting as
she moved and her pale mane flowed behind her. A fresh breeze
drifted across a wide pasture at the bottom of the wooded valley,
cool on Beornoth's neck and face. It had been two days since he
had left Bocking, and Beornoth's legs ached from the hard ride,
and he yearned to return home to Branoc's Tree.

'I wish I had my own birds with me,' said Aelfwine cheerfully.
'There is good hawking to be had at Foxfield, perhaps not fit for a
king, but there is game there, Beo.'

'You will be back in your home at Foxfield soon, our work
should be over now until summer,' said Beornoth. It was unusual
for warriors to be called out to fight so early in the year, before
there was proper fodder for horses, and when provisions were
light. But news had come of Æthelric's return to Bocking from
East Anglia where he had hidden in safety with the Danes, and
the king had summoned Beornoth to punish the traitor.

'Ale, lads,' called Leofsunu cheerfully, two sloshing ale skins tucked under his arms, and a loaf of bread in each hand.

'You are more resourceful than you look, Leofsunu, I'll give you that,' said Wulfhere, gleefully grabbing a skin of ale and taking a long drink from its stoppered end.

'We should let the men stay. You, Offa and I will go to the ealdorman,' said Beornoth, and Aelfwine nodded. Offa ordered the men back to the buildings to enjoy their food and drink, and the three thegns continued across the pasture, the dew-wet grass soaking through Beornoth's leather boots as he walked.

'The ealdorman and the king have grown close,' said Offa.

'Now that he is free of his mother's shadow, Æthelred can find his own advisors. And who better than Byrhtnoth?' said Aelfwine.

'The old crone would choke on her soup if she knew,' said Offa, his lined face creased by a grin. Beornoth and Aelfwine laughed. The king's mother was notoriously famous for her deep cunning and plotting. She had killed old King Edgar's heir, Edward, to put her and Edgar's son Æthelred on the throne when he was only twelve years old, and she had ruled the kingdom from behind the throne from that day until last year. She had tried to have Byrhtnoth and Beornoth killed, a plot which they had uncovered and which had seen her banished to a nunnery.

'Hopefully, the king is here to discuss how to rid ourselves of the Vikings,' said Beornoth.

'Olaf has been at Folkestone all winter. He's been nice and quiet. Kept inside the town, no raiding,' said Aelfwine.

'So he should be, with all that silver the bishops gave him last year,' Offa spat. Byrhtnoth had sent scouts to watch Olaf Tryggvason through the winter, and he had behaved himself, even though he remained on English soil despite his defeat. Olaf was a Norseman and leader of the Jomsvikings. He had led an army of Vikings in raids across England's south-east coast the previous summer, and there had been hard fighting to keep his savage warriors at bay, but not so deep enough a victory to force Olaf to sail away across the sea to find another kingdom to attack.

'Which is why they will always keep coming,' said Beornoth, shaking his head. 'The Northmen crave land like this, lush and fertile. They hunger for our land and our silver. They want it enough to sail their warships across treacherous seas and risk their lives to get it. If we keep paying them, then we give them what they want.'

'More will come,' agreed Offa.

'And now we have Sweyn Forkbeard of the Danes with his army in East Anglia, and Olaf in Folkestone. Two packs of wolves, sleeping peacefully over winter, but sure to wake up snarling and hungry once the frosts melt,' said Beornoth.

A wide-winged kestrel soared overhead, its deep black eyes searching the meadow for prey. It seemed to rest in the air, floating there like a ship at sea. Beornoth felt its cold eyes upon him. It was a predator, a hunter of rodents, and he offered the bird a salute as the king's party came into view beyond a small hill, and before a copse where bright green leaves budded on spindly branches.

'Ah, our brave warriors returned from the field,' bellowed Byrhtnoth as he saw the three thegns approach. The ealdorman was enormous and towered over the surrounding men. His great grey spade of a beard moved as he spoke and he raised a hand in greeting. 'Was the bastard there?'

'He was there,' said Offa, and quickly dropped to one knee as the king himself emerged from Byrhtnoth's shadow, a hooded sparrowhawk resting on a thick glove at the end of his outstretched arm. Its hood was tan brown and covered its head save for its golden, curved beak. Its talons shifted on the glove, and its hunter's head twitched from side to side. Beornoth and Aelfwine also dropped to one knee and bowed their heads.

'Rise, please,' said the king. Æthelred was young and thin. He wore a worn leather hunting jerkin with knee-high boots. The king had long auburn hair which caught the sun when he moved, and his face was long and lantern-jawed. 'So, the traitor Æthelric returned to his nest?' He stared at Beornoth.

'Yes, lord. We have come straight from Bocking to bring news of it to Lord Byrhtnoth,' said Beornoth.

'And did you dispense the crown's justice?'

'Yes, lord.'

'Details, man,' said the king. He grimaced at the weight of the sparrowhawk and passed the bird to one of his huntsmen. 'I want to know what happened.'

'Beornoth dragged Æthelric out of his house and hanged him from Bocking's gate,' said Aelfwine. 'We killed some of Æthelric's oathmen and burned his hall.'

'Good,' said the king, and clasped his hands together. 'Now men will know what happens when they side with the heathen over our own people, over their own king. Men should fear the king, and we should have warriors every bit as fearsome as the Vikings themselves.'

'Lucky for us we have Beo, then,' said Byrhtnoth.

'Quite so,' said Æthelred, and he exchanged a furtive glance with Byrhtnoth. 'You have served well, Beornoth, thegn. We will need your sword again this year, I fear. If we are to shake these cursed Vikings off our shores, along with the traitors who give them aid.'

There had to be more fighting once spring warmed the fields and forests of Æthelred's England, the Vikings would be hungry for silver, war and food, and Beornoth would need to bring his sword and his savagery to protect the sheep from the wolves. The wounds he had suffered fighting Olaf and his supremely skilled and organised Jomsvikings had healed during the winter, and as much as Beornoth wanted to return to Branoc's Tree, to be with his wife Eawynn and rest with her in the sun, he knew his duty and he knew what he was.

'Ah,' exclaimed the king, smiling and pointing over Beornoth's shoulder. 'Your kestrel has struck, Lord Byrhtnoth.' Beornoth turned, and the bird of prey swooped away from a line of hedge which separated one field from another. A small mouse dangled from its sharp talons as it beat its wide wings and flew towards the pale blue sky.

'Go, get some food in the house, Beo. Meet me at the stables at noon,' said Byrhtnoth, and he turned back to the king. The two great lords of Saxon England walked and talked together amongst their woodsmen, hawks and the barks of their hunting dogs.

Beornoth sat on a milking stool beside wet and rotting bales of hay. Their stink filled his nose, mixed with the shit and filth piled in a far corner by the stable boys who tended Byrhtnoth's herd. The hay was the remnants of the summer harvest, dwindled to almost nothing now, having fed the fine horses across the cold winter months. He drank cool milk from a tankard, kindly provided by Byrhtnoth's steward when Beornoth refused the offer of ale. Beornoth had once succumbed to drink in the dark times, and these days he did not touch a drop. Byrhtnoth strode into the stable courtyard. He walked on the balls of his feet despite his age. He was tall and broad shouldered, and strode with a fighter's gait, smooth and well balanced.

'Beornoth, welcome,' said the ealdorman. Beornoth smiled. Byrhtnoth was a good lord. He had rewarded Beornoth with a heriot of lands in Essex, and had restored him to the rank of thegn, which he had once lost in his descent into drunkenness. 'The king is hale, don't you think?'

'He looks well, lord. He also looks confident.'

'He does, now that he is free of his mother. I thank God every day for that mercy. She is with the Benedictines at a nunnery she founded, Wherwell Abbey.'

'Do the nuns guard her?'

'No, the warriors do that. The king wisely has six men guarding her day and night. We couldn't have a fox out loose with the chickens, Beo.'

'Just so,' agreed Beornoth. She had tried to kill them both, and snagged them in a plot which threatened to subvert the entire kingdom, and all because she was jealous of Byrhtnoth's reputation.

'So, Æthelric is dead, and you have done your duty once more.'

'There are many others just like him, lord. Forkbeard has rested peacefully all winter in East Anglia with his fleet. Someone is feeding the bastard.'

'Aye, and then we still have Olaf to deal with. He took the silver offered by the bishops, but that only buys us peace until this summer.'

'So, there will be war, lord.'

'There will. It seems to me there will always be war, Beornoth. There is always someone else to fight. But there is a thing I must ask of you, which must be done before the swallows return from across the sea.'

'Yes, lord?'

'The king would know what this king of the Danes plans behind his walls and amongst the fisherfolk of East Anglia. He would have you go to Sweyn Forkbeard and parlay, find out what kind of man he is, who is giving him succour and what he wants. The king fears more fighting, because he fears for his kingdom if men are welcoming warmongering Danes to England. He would rather pay this Forkbeard to sail away than drench our soil with Saxon blood.'

'The king wants me to go to East Anglia?'

'Yes. Take the men with you, my hearth troop. Take them all. Sweyn will meet with you. You are a man of reputation, with a name that must surely have reached his ears after the fighting last summer. Be wary of him, though. Sweyn is no simple raider here for silver and fair fame. Men like him have been invited here, welcomed by some who would have Danes rule in the Danelaw again. It is said he usurped his own father, Harald Bluetooth, and drove him from his kingdom. So he is ruthless and hungry for power. He picked the place to moor his ships well, for he is at Gippeswic, and that place contains a royal mint, where they have the king's seal to forge and issue coin.'

'So he can make his own silver, his own coin?'

'Yes. If he has the iron and silver, he can fashion his own coins to finance whatever it is he has planned. Whether that is to take the money back to his kingdom in Denmark, or make himself a king here on our shores. Why would a king sail away from his own kingdom, freshly wrested from his father in a bloody war? Forkbeard wintered here with forty ships, so they say, which is a long time for a king to be away. Speak with him, Beo, find out what he is up to, and what kind of man we face.'

'He might just kill me when he learns that I cut the legs and arms from his man and made him a heimnar.'

'He might,' allowed Byrhtnoth, with a grin. 'But you will fly the king's banner, so he will listen to you first.'

That news struck Beornoth like a slap to the face. The dragon banner of Wessex. Beornoth's chest swelled with pride.

'You honour me, lord.'

'You have earned it. Take the hearth troop and find out what you can, for there is no news from East Anglia, not even from my old friend Leofric, who is ealdorman there. He was a good man, once. It worries me, and we must know what has happened there, for we have Viking fleets to the east and south.'

'I will go then, lord. But first I must go home to Branoc's Tree, but I will not stay there long.'

'Do that. See your people and then go to Forkbeard. You have fought hard since becoming a thegn of Essex. You are a killer of Vikings, Beo, and we need you. I remember you lost your warhorse last year. So, I have a gift for you.' Byrhtnoth beckoned Beornoth towards a stable door, and Beornoth followed. Ealdorbana had been his warhorse, a magnificent animal, and Beornoth had loved the horse. The wound of Ealdorbana's death was still raw, and Beornoth missed his silent companionship, and also the horse's ferocity in battle.

Byrhtnoth grinned within the spade of his beard, and Beornoth peered inside the darkness of the hay-strewn stall. A huge white horse bobbed its head, munching from a nosebag which hung from the wall.

'He must be fifteen hands,' gasped Beornoth. The horse was monstrous, and pure white except for the darker grey mottling at his lower legs and on his forehead.

'Fourteen and a half,' said Byrhtnoth. 'The horse is all yours, Beornoth. He has been trained for war here on this farm. He will not frighten at the smell of blood nor the clash of arms. He is a warrior of God to be used in our fight against the Vikings. There is a saddle, tack and everything you need. You have earned it.'

'Thank you, lord,' said Beornoth, staring at the beautiful horse and his snow-white mane. 'What is his name?'

'Hríð.'

It was a good name, which meant violent storm, and

Beornoth's heart swelled with pride at such a gift. It was a Lord's duty to reward his oathmen, to be a good ring-giver. But the horse was as expensive as a chain-mail byrnie or a magnificent sword, and Beornoth did not have the words to express his gratitude.

'And there is one more thing, Beo.'

Beornoth raised an eyebrow, recognised in the wince of the ealdorman's eyes that this next thing must be a pig's turd of a request, if it was worse than asking him to ride into the den of a notoriously savage Viking war king.

'What is it, lord?'

'Take Thered with you. He remains with me as a hostage. Come over here, don't skulk in the shadows.' Byrhtnoth waved across the courtyard, and a young man with a long face and short dark hair approached with his head bowed. He was clean-shaven and broad across the shoulder.

'I am truly thankful for your gift, but I am sorry, lord, but could you not keep Thered here, or send him to a burh for garrison duty?' said Beornoth. His hand dropped to the hilt of his sword, and he crunched his teeth, the muscles of his face working beneath his beard.

Byrhtnoth raised a hand and closed his eyes, acknowledging the difficulty of what he was asking. 'I know, I know. His father tried to kill us both and worked with the king's mother in their plots of deep cunning. But he has spent a long winter here with me. He has found the Lord and recognised the error of his ways. He wants to make things right.' Byrhtnoth leant closer to Beornoth and lowered his voice. 'I killed his father, Ealdorman Oslac, as you well know. It had to be done. So, Thered is ealdorman of Northumbria now, or he will be once the king ratifies his succession. Your friend Alfgar is ealdorman in Cheshire, and to have Thered loyal to the throne in Northumbria secures the north. The king wants that. Enemies threaten us from across the sea, so to have the northern shires peaceful, loyal and secure is vital.'

'If he has found God, and seen the error of his ways, then let him go north and take up his seat as ealdorman.'

'Not yet.' The crag of Byrhtnoth's face crumpled into a frown. 'I am not asking. Take him with you, let him ride with the warriors for the summer and learn what it means to fight a war. Let him prove himself, spill some blood. He will join my hearth troop of thegns. Offa is captain, but Thered is your responsibility. I want him experienced and humble, but alive.'

Beornoth nodded his agreement, and scowled at Thered. He had no choice in the matter, but did not relish either meeting Forkbeard or the responsibility of minding a petulant thegn who had tried to kill him less than a year ago. It was only spring, and already war and strife circled Beornoth like crows above a battle-field. He would ride for Branoc's Tree, his home and only haven of peace, but then he must meet a Viking war king in his lair.

3

It rained the day Beornoth arrived at Branoc's Tree. It heaved across the fields in wet gusts from a pewter sky, and the spring chill turned Beornoth's ears to stinging ice. He rode with the hood of his cloak pulled up, but the rain soaked through the wool to drench his hair and trickle its spite down the back of his byrnie coat of chain-mail and the padded leather jerkin beneath. Despite the ill weather, the people of Branoc's Tree turned out to greet the returning riders. They bowed their heads to Beornoth, who was their lord and thegn, and waved and clapped at the rest of the column. The journey to Bocking had kept the riders away for a week, which, after the closeness of living indoors together all winter, felt like an age. Winter months were a bleak time of short days and long, dark nights, where folk huddled indoors and longed for the return of spring and the sun's warmth. Offa had disbanded the thegns of Byrhtnoth's hearth troop to return to their own homes for two days, before they would meet at Leofsunu's lands at Sturmer to ride north-east to talk to King Sweyn Forkbeard.

Cwicca and Kari leapt from their horses to greet their family and friends with grins and laughter, whilst Aethelberga beamed to see Wulfhere returned safe and unharmed. The big warrior swept her up onto his horse, and despite feigned protests, she laughed as he cantered her around Branoc's Tree's courtyard in the rain. Aethelberga ran Branoc's Tree as the lady of the house. She had been married to its thegn, who had died fighting the Vikings, and when Ealdorman Byrhtnoth awarded the place to Beornoth, he had kept Aethelberga in her position. Aethelberga was both clever and capable, and although she could be fussy and pious, Beornoth both respected and trusted her. She had found love for Wulfhere since becoming a widow, and Wulfhere doted on her.

Beornoth handed Hríð's reins to a stable boy with instructions to handle the warhorse carefully, and then marched to his hall, which he had missed on the cold journey to Bocking. The fire in the central hearth crackled, and its warmth washed over Beornoth like a fond embrace. His shoulders slumped in its familiarity, relaxing in the warmth. He closed his eyes and breathed in the smell of old smoke, the smell of the floor rushes, the wood of its beams, and of the place itself. It seeped into his chest, into his pores, and he dragged off his wet cloak and handed it to a serving maid, who gave him a shallow bowl filled with thick soup, and a mug of water. He drank the water and handed her the cup, nodding his thanks, and then clasped the soup in both hands, relishing the heat feeding into his fingers, which were red-raw from the cold. Beornoth walked slowly down the length of the hall, pausing at the fire to let the flames warm his wet clothes. Tiny droplets of rain drifted in through the smoke in the thatch, and singed on the crackling heat from the hearth. Beornoth took a sip of soup. It was thick with parsnips, onions and cabbage stale from being stored through the winter, but which after a week in the saddle tasted like a meal fit for the king himself.

The doors to the hall burst open, and Aethelberga spilled through them, laughing and batting away Wulfhere's wandering hands. She abruptly stopped and recovered her dignity when she saw Beornoth by the fire. Wulfhere shook his head and tucked his hungry fingers into his belt.

'Praise God in heaven that you all returned safely,' she said, fussing at the cross on her chest. Beornoth chuckled to himself, knowing how her piety wracked her with guilt for allowing herself to be happy with Wulfhere.

'Wulfhere talked of nothing but you the entire time,' said Beornoth, which wasn't entirely true but would make her happy to hear it.

'Then he is even more of a fool than he looks,' she said, but flashed Wulfhere a coy smile.

'Where did you get that soup?' said Wulfhere, rubbing his hands together.

'There's some in the pot there by the fire,' said Aethelberga. 'It's from yesterday, and the vegetables aren't the best this late into the stores, but it will fill your belly.' She took the sodden cloak from Wulfhere's shoulders, draped it over a feasting bench close to the fire to dry and ladled a portion of the steaming soup into a wooden bowl. Wulfhere took it hungrily and slurped a mouthful down noisily, which made Aethelberga wince and tut at his rough manners. 'I see we have another guest with us? Last year it was a Norseman, this year it's a Northumbrian.'

'He won't be here long,' said Beornoth. 'We ride out the day after tomorrow, and he comes with us.'

'So soon?'

'We must go to East Anglia. At least this guest is not a

heathen. He is a man of God, or so I hear from the ealdorman. So bring him to our church and let him pray.'

Aethelberga beamed at the news, and she scurried off in search of Thered to bring him to Branoc's Tree's modest church.

'Do you really believe that piece of weasel shit has turned pious?' asked Wulfhere.

'I believe he said whatever it took to make Byrhtnoth happy. He must hate the ealdorman for killing his father, and us for taking him as a hostage. He just wants to go north, back to his own people.'

'The ealdorman won't let him go until he knows he's loyal?'

'No. Which is why we have to bring him with us, and nurse-maid him. Test him, but don't get him killed.'

'As though we don't have enough problems.'

Beornoth grunted agreement. He sat and pulled off his wet boots to let them dry by the fire. 'She seems happy?' He nodded his chin after Aethelberga.

'She's a fine lass. I'm lucky to have her.'

'She won't marry you, though.'

'I know. She's told me a hundred times. She is a thegn's daughter, and the widow of a thegn. Too good for the likes of me. But she seems content to live in sin, which suits me.'

'Nothing like a warm bed to come home to?'

Wulfhere grinned, and his cheeks reddened. 'She is big-lipped, with a tongue which can sting like a wasp. But she has the kindest heart in the kingdom.'

'Watch Thered. He could ride off under our noses. Keep a close eye on him until we can be sure of his intentions.'

'Yes, lord. We don't want another bloody mess like that Viking bastard Brand.'

'I couldn't have known that would turn out like it did.'

'We all warned you... lord.'

Beornoth drained the last dregs of his soup and laid the bowl down on the table. Last summer he had taken in a Viking hostage, Brand Thorkilsson. Brand had ridden with Beornoth, and fought alongside him. Even though the rest of his men disliked Brand, Beornoth had liked the man. He had learned to speak Norse as a boy in the north-west of England where there were as many Viking families as Saxon, so he and Brand could converse easily. Beornoth had enjoyed Brand's company. He was quiet, brave and a skilled warrior. During an attack on Olaf's fleet, Brand had left Beornoth and returned to his Lord, Olaf Tryggvason. Olaf had been under Beornoth's blade during the battle outside Folkestone, and Brand had saved his life.

'Aye, well. Maybe we will cross swords with Brand again.'

'If we fight Olaf again, I'll search out Brand myself. My axe will soon put an end to him. If it wasn't for him, you would have killed Olaf, and we would now be rid of those cursed Jomsvikings.'

Beornoth stared into the dancing flames and accepted that truth. 'Olaf hates me even more now since that fight. You know Vikings just as well as I. That hate will twist at his insides and his pride will sting because we burned his ships, and I killed his foster father, Palnatoki.'

'He will burn for vengeance, lord. That's the truth of it. His gods will demand it, and the defeat tarnished his reputation. His men expect it of him.'

'So, we must strike at him before he strikes at us.' Dreams of Viking dragon ships driving up onto Essex beaches had plagued Beornoth's dreams all winter. Visions of Olaf Tryggvason and his Jomsvikings swarming across the palisade at Branoc's Tree to bring their axes and their malice to bear upon his people. Jomsvikings. The thought of those supreme warriors made Beornoth's shoulders shudder. The Jomsvikings were professional fighters from the island of Jomsburg who lived only to fight and honour their gods. They fought for pay, trained to it by their founder Palnatoki, the same man who had rescued Prince Olaf Tryggvason of Norway from captivity, and raised him to the blade. Palnatoki had taught Olaf all he knew, made him a master of sword, axe, spear and ship. Olaf was a man to fear, a warlord in search of glory and reputation.

'Why does the king want us to go to Forkbeard? We've done our bit. Why can't we have some time here with our people? Let others take up the fight. The king has other ealdormen who should bring their thegns to the fight.'

Beornoth stood and pulled his boots back on. He grunted at a pain in his lower back, and where the cold ached at old injuries in his shoulder and thigh. Beornoth ran his tongue through a gap in his teeth where an arrow had torn through his face in a fight long ago. He wanted to stay in Branoc's Tree as much as Wulfhere. To spend a summer there, working the land and living in peace. Wulfhere had Aethelberga, and Beornoth envied him that closeness, having that hand to hold in the darkness, that feeling of warmth. But that was not his fate. Beornoth was a thegn and a warrior, and it was his duty to do as his ealdorman commanded, and that meant riding to East Anglia to speak with the king of the Danes.

'It is our duty to act on the king's, and the ealdorman's, command. We do not question our orders. We must remember our place, it is an honour to be trusted and to do their bidding. We go because I speak Norse, and the Vikings know me as Byrhtnoth and Æthelred's warrior. So, Forkbeard will talk to me. But you are right. We talk to this Danish king, and then we persuade Byrhtnoth to attack Olaf, so we can rid ourselves of him once and for all. The king would pay them both off, convinced of it by the bishops who believe that if we give them enough silver, they will sail away rich and happy and we will have peace.'

'Silver only makes them greedier. Pay them now and they will just come back for more, like children greedy for honey cakes. Vikings only understand one thing, lord. Violence.'

Beornoth clapped his friend on the shoulder and warmed his hands again on the fire. 'Go to Aethelberga. Spend time with her, laugh and talk together. Then we ride.'

Beornoth left him and strode along the hall's length. He rolled the ache out of his shoulder and went to look for his wife, Eawynn. He wished they could share the closeness Wulfhere had with Aethelberga. They had lived like that once, when they were young, before the Vikings came. They had been young, happy and in love. Beornoth ducked under a door frame in the rear wall and walked down the gloomy corridor that linked the main hall to its adjoining rooms, which served as his living quarters. He trod softly, slowing his pace so that his heavy boots were quiet on the hard-packed earthen floor. Beornoth didn't want to startle her. He wanted to see Eawynn at peace before she saw him. He found her in the small weaving room. She sat with her back to him, working a loom. She spun the wool and hummed to herself, and hearing the light song come from her stopped Beornoth. A warmth encompassed his chest, and he smiled. Her hair shone like copper against the light shining in through an open window shutter. The rain came down outside, its pitter-patter constant through the window and the rhythmic thrum of the loom like music to her light humming. He leaned against the door frame and just watched her. He remembered her as she was, young and beautiful, playing in the field with their two fair-haired daughters. His little girls would always be small and perfect, and the happiness suddenly drained from Beornoth like water from a beached ship. For he could not picture their little faces in his mind's eye, only their soft skin and the fresh smell of their golden hair.

Eawynn stopped her weaving and turned her head to him, the light catching the lurid scar across her neck and face where Viking raiders had cut her throat and left her for dead.

'I am sorry, please continue,' said Beornoth, and moved away from the door.

'No, wait,' Eawynn said. 'You haven't disturbed me. I would have come out to greet you, but there were so many people there, and well... How was the journey?'

He knew how she shunned crowds, preferring to be alone, so he was not surprised that she had hidden away in her rooms. Beornoth had to suppress a smile. Years had passed where they had not talked at all, Eawynn being so damaged by her loss and her injuries, and Beornoth lost at the bottom of an ale jug. Since she had come to live at Branoc's Tree, Eawynn had slowly begun to talk again, albeit in brief moments. But when her eyes met his, and he heard her voice, Beornoth's heart skipped just as it had when they were young together.

'It went well. The king and ealdorman are happy. It's getting warmer. Soon you will be able to tend to your garden again.'

'I miss the outdoors. You look tired. Shall I have the maids prepare you some food?'

'Thank you. Will you take a meal with me?'

'I would love to.' Eawynn smiled and crows' feet showed at the corners of her eyes, while faint wrinkles creased her top lip. The chance to sit with her and share a meal meant more to Beornoth than all the silver in Wessex. 'Do you know it wasn't much later in the year than this when we were married?' continued Eawynn.

'I remember. You wore daisies and pink wild flowers in your hair. You took my breath away.'

'You were so nervous, and so handsome.' She laughed, holding a pale hand to her mouth.

'I suppose I was nervous. Your mother never liked me, even on our wedding day. She fixed me with her look of doom throughout the entire ceremony.'

'She did. They were different times. You were funny, Beo. Remember the time your father's men chased you up the fields when you tied their cloaks together?'

'I don't think I have ever run so fast. They were angry because two of them got into a fight over it. I thought they were going to give me a going-over. And you were watching from a willow tree you had climbed? If I remember it correctly. You told them where I was hiding!'

They laughed together, and Beornoth felt twenty years younger. She joined him in the hall for a meal of fresh bread and fish. Wulfhere and Aethelberga joined them. Beornoth talked and laughed and sat with his wife. They did not live like husband and wife, had not since the terror of that Viking raid so long ago, and Eawynn blanched as Wulfhere and Aethelberga sat close, touching hands whenever an opportunity arose. Beornoth missed that, the closeness of having someone to sleep next to on a winter's night. But Eawynn was happy, and spoke to him again without hate or bitterness, and that was enough.

Two days later, they rode for Sturmer. Beornoth travelled at the head of the column with Wulfhere and Thered, followed by Kari and Cwicca, and then three of his household troops, Maccus, Aelfhere and Wulfmaer. The rest of his men stayed at Branoc's Tree to protect its walls and the surrounding hides. Ragged clouds sat in a still, bright sky. It was early, and the pastures were free of frost. Beornoth sat astride Hríð and the white warhorse picked its way across the cow field. He was two hands taller than the rest of the company's horses and Beornoth had filled a saddlebag with wrinkled carrots and a few oatcakes to treat the horse on the journey.

'You should give him his head, lord,' said Cwicca, grinning at Hrið's huge flanks. 'He'll run like the wind. I've never seen a finer horse.'

'He's a warhorse, not a racing pony,' said Beornoth. He had not galloped the beast since accepting the gift from the ealdorman, but with the power in his huge legs, Beornoth did not doubt his speed.

'You might fall off, lord,' whispered Wulfhere, leaning across his saddle.

'Thered, your horse is Hengist. I rode him before this one. He is a good horse. Take care of him,' said Beornoth.

'Yes, lord,' Thered replied. He rode with his head bowed. He wore a fine byrnie mail coat as befitted his station, and his long face was solemn beneath his raven-dark hair.

'We haven't spoken since you joined my men. Can you use that?' Beornoth pointed to the sword strapped to Thered's belt.

'I can, lord. I just wanted to say, Beornoth... lord...' Thered bit his bottom lip, his eyes locked with Beornoth's.

'Spit it out, lad. You don't need to call me lord. We are both thegns, and you will be ealdorman of Northumbria one day.'

'If you don't get killed fighting Vikings,' said Wulfhere. 'Beornoth will be at the heart of any fighting this summer. You can count on that. You'll need that sword before long.' Maccus and the others laughed, and Beornoth shot them a frown.

'I just want to apologise for what happened last year. My father, he was just following orders. Queen Aelffyrth ordered it. He owed her. He had no choice.'

'It's done now and men died. Learn from it. Be a good ealdorman. Try to make the right decisions for your people and for the crown,' said Beornoth.

'Archbishop Sigeric tells me that God has forgiven me. That if I wield my sword against the heathen I will bask in the grace of God.'

'You have become devoted to God, then?'

'Yes, lord.' Thered reached for the small silver cross which he wore over the chest of his byrnie on a silver chain. 'Prayer has helped me see the error of my ways, of how I was living. When I return to Northumbria, things will be different. I will be a leader supportive of God's will. And I will try to be a good man.'

'A truly good man is a rare thing. We'll see how you fight when we come against the Northmen.'

They crossed an icy ford of the winding River Stour, passing close to the borders of Ealdorman Byrhtnoth's lands until they reached Leofsunu's burh at Sturmer. It was close to the banks of the winding Stour, and sat beside a wide pond. Leofsunu held sixteen hides, and within his walls were a mill along with his high-gabled hall. Beornoth stroked Hríð's soft mane and he thought fondly of the meal he had shared with Eawynn, and how content he had been to see her smile. Riders milled around Sturmer's gate and Beornoth recognised Aelfwine and Offa. He would not dally at Sturmer, the sooner he got to Forkbeard and spoke to the war king of the Danes, the sooner he could return to Branoc's Tree. If he survived the encounter.

4

Byrhtnoth's hearth troop rode to Gippeswic, but Byrhtnoth remained on his lands. The king stayed with the ealdorman for a week, and the two great lords hunted, feasted and talked of the affairs of Æthelred's kingdom. Beornoth rode with the picked thegns of Essex, each one a warrior of reputation. He spent most of the two-day ride with Wulfhere, Leofsunu, Aelfwine and Offa. They had woken on the first morning to a land covered in hoar frost and their breath steamed from their mouths like smoke. The days, however, were warm and clear with a bright sun low in the sky so that on the second day they woke to a warm morning with the singsong of birds ringing around the Saxon countryside.

'Let's test this Forkbeard's mettle,' Godric said to his brothers as the walls of Gippeswic came into sight around the meander of the wide River Orwell. His hand rested on the pommel of his sword, with its hilt wrapped in gold wire. He was a young thegn, favoured by Byrhtnoth because of the power and wealth of the rich lands he and his brothers held in Essex. 'He must surely have heard of the Bloodsworn of Ealdorman Byrhtnoth and our brave deeds.' His brothers nodded, and one of them laughed.

'I don't remember seeing much of his mettle,' whispered Wulfhere, smirking and flicking his eyes towards Godric.

'I remember seeing him chucking his guts up before the battle at Watchet last year,' said Leofsunu, and he made mock retching noises which sent Wulfhere, Cwicca and Kari into peals of laughter. Godric twisted in his saddle to shoot a murderous look at them, but held his tongue when he caught Beornoth's eye.

'The Danes have been long absent from our shores,' Godric piped up again. 'Not since before the time of King Edgar have Danish pirates brought raiding ships here. We have fought men from Norway; Olaf and his black-hearted gang of Norse brigands met our swords last year and know our bravery. The Danes will be surprised to see our strength.'

Beornoth had to agree with Wulfhere, but he kept his tongue. Godric had been there at Watchet, in and around the hard fighting, but Beornoth could not recall the man striking an enemy down. It did not concern him. Most men did not have the courage to stand in the shield wall when swords, axes, spears and knives came for their chest, neck and face. Of those who did, only half of them could hold a shield steady and stand in the battle line. The rest could stand in the rear ranks with their shields held firm, hoping that the warriors in front of them would be enough to deal with the enemy. Some of those rear-rankers would hold firm, they would swing their weapons desperately despite their bone-numbing fear. They would clench their teeth and close their eyes and hope to live whilst their enemies tried to rend and tear at their flesh with hard iron. Perhaps two men out of every hundred were the proper warriors, the lovers of battle. These were the men who sought the front line of battle, the men who soaked their blades in the blood and gore of their enemies and relished the clash of arms. Those men lived for the test of man against man.

They hungered to burnish their reputations bright with the souls of the fallen and did not shirk from the horrors of the shield wall. Beornoth was such a man, as were Wulfhere, Offa, Leofsunu and Aelfwine. He did not hold it against Godric or the others for their unwarlike nature; it was just the way of things, but it was good to know whom to depend upon when the shields came together and enemies came to kill.

Beornoth urged Hríð along the old Roman road towards the fishing port of Gippeswic. Its walls were high and dark-timbered atop a raised bank above what was once a ditch, but was now nothing more than a grass-covered dent in the land. He adjusted the strap of his shield across his shoulder where it chafed him, the shield itself laying heavily across his back.

'We should wait here,' Beornoth said to Offa, and the grey-haired captain nodded and reined his mount in.

'Halt,' shouted Offa and raised his hand to bring the riding column to rest, the horses' hooves clopping on the stone road.

'We should ride up the gate and announce ourselves,' said Godric, looking for support to his brothers, who nodded vigorously.

'Go on then,' said Beornoth. 'But they might fill you full of arrows before you get to the gate, or send out riders to cut you down, so you'd best unsling your shield before you go.'

'But why wait here? They will surely think we are afraid?'

'We wait here until they see us. Then, they will know that we show them respect, and that we come in peace. Riders will come out to talk, and we will go in.'

'But...'

'Enough,' barked Offa. 'We wait.'

Beornoth reached into a saddlebag and fished out half a shrivelled carrot. He leant forward and fed it to Hríð and the stal-

lion munched it happily. Beornoth stroked his ears and watched
the gate. Spear points glinted on the timber rampart and moved
back and forth across the length of the gate wall, one on each
side. After a time, one of those spears halted, and then disappeared. The gates swung open slowly outwards and three riders
came out. The riders let their horses trot at their ease, and talked
to each other, laughing and sharing a skin of ale as they rode to
market.

'What are they doing?' Godric said, fussing with the fox-fur
collar of his cloak. 'Insolent heathen turds. Don't they know we
are thegns?'

'They are showing us they do not fear us, and that they
despise us. They have seen our fine horses, our byrnies, and our
weapons. So they know we are lords of war and not merchants or
priests,' said Beornoth. 'They will exchange some insults with us,
and with luck, they will allow us to enter.'

'Stay calm and let Beo talk to them,' said Offa in his gruff
voice.

The three riders came close and reined in their horses. Each man
wore a shining byrnie, and two wore helmets polished to a gleam.
They wore finely embroidered cloaks with fur thick and warm
around their necks, and each man's arm was thick with Viking
warrior rings. The central rider was middle-aged, with a golden
beard and a scar running across his top lip to his ear. He made a point
of casting his gaze slowly over the Saxons' horses and their war gear,
then tutted and shook his head. The warriors on his flanks chuckled.

'I am Runolfr Eagle Eye,' said the blonde warrior in Norse. He
paused, leaning on his saddle and looking across Offa, Beornoth
and Aelfwine's faces for some sign of recognition of that name.

'I am Beornoth of the Saxons. Come to talk to King Sweyn
Forkbeard.' Beornoth spoke in Norse, and Runolfr turned his

mouth into an upside-down smile of appreciation and sat back in his saddle.

'I have heard of you. You make heimnars. No doubt you have heard of me also, for I am the killer of twelve men, victor of four holmgangs, and have sailed the waters between Jutland and the Frankia more times than any man alive.'

'All men have heard of your exploits, Runolfr Eagle Eye,' Beornoth lied. 'I have made a heimnar. I cut the arms and legs from a bastard named Ragnar the Flayer last year. He killed some of my people, fisherfolk and farmers, and used their skins to cover his shields. He said Forkbeard ordered him to ravage the country like Ivar the Boneless would have done it.'

'Well, Ragnar won't be doing that any more.' The warriors beside Runolfr dutifully laughed again, their thick chests rumbling. Beornoth was surprised that the Danes in Gippeswic had heard of how he had whittled Ragnar, because he had sent the heimnar as a message to Olaf and his Norsemen at Folke-stone, to spread terror in their ranks. But Beornoth dismissed that concern and maintained his hard face to the enemy. A warrior who had fled the fight with Ragnar's men must have watched from the trees or bushes and reported the event to the Danes at Gippeswic.

'I come from King Æthelred to talk with King Sweyn,' Beornoth repeated, and he looked up at the green dragon banner of Wessex which hung from Cwicca's spear. It sat across a spar halfway down the weapon's shaft so that the sigil stood wide and clear even though there was no wind.

'I heard you the first time, but the king does not talk with cowards and turds.' Runolfr grinned at Beornoth, and his two warriors could barely hide their glee at the first insult in what they hoped would be a lengthy exchange.

'And yet he sends three of his whores out to greet me and my men.'

Runolfr nodded in appreciation. 'The king sends his finest warriors to show you Saxon dogs what real fighters look like. You looked like warriors from the walls, but close up I can see you are nothing but a gaggle of shit-eating goat humpers.'

'I killed Palnatoki of the Jomsvikings, Skarde Wartooth, and Einar Ravenhair. All warriors of reputation. I cut your man Ragnar to pieces and left him to live in shame. So, take me to Forkbeard, or I will ride away and you will have to explain to your king why he has not received a message from King Æthelred. I grow tired of your insults.'

Runolfr shook his head in disappointment and turned to shrug at his men. Their sport for the day spoiled, the exchange of insults was over. 'Very well, follow me.'

Beornoth clicked his tongue, and Offa led their band along the road towards Gippeswic. Runolfr rode slowly again, to annoy the Saxons, and Offa turned in his saddle to cast a murderous look at Godric, who grumbled at the delay. They rode in through the high gate, and inside the town was silence. Gulls cawed and soared above the port to the east of the town, and Viking warriors thronged the main path which led through Gippeswic on a slope down to the waterfront. They stood solemnly before the buildings, with muscled arms crossed and hard glares. Beornoth wanted to warn the younger warriors like Cwicca and Kari not to be intimidated and to keep their faces hard, but he could not. The Danes had turned out in force to frighten the Saxons with their numbers and their ferocity. They were hard men all. Their farmers and weavers remained at home with their wives and families and the comforts of Denmark. These men were the adventurers, the warriors sworn to serve King Sweyn Forkbeard and who had taken to the Whale Road, risking everything for silver and reputation. They were killers and fighters, and Beornoth did not look at any of them. He kept his eyes ahead, staring at Runolfr's back, and resisting the urge to meet the gaze of the hundreds of eyes which glared silently at him.

Runolfr led them to a cobbled courtyard, and the horses' hooves clattered on the smooth stones. Boys came running to care for the horses, and Runolfr led them towards a hall topped with grey rotting thatch.

'Wait here,' Runolfr said. He gestured into an open side door on the hall's western side. Beornoth ducked under the lintel and found himself in a small room warmed by a fire, where tables were covered with jugs of ale and platters of fresh bread. 'The king will meet you tonight. We will feast in the main hall this evening. Rest now from your journey.'

Beornoth nodded thanks, and Runolfr closed the door. The Saxon company shrugged and grinned at one another in surprise at the Viking hospitality.

'It's their way,' said Beornoth. 'They offer us food and drink to show that they won't kill us. They extend the custom of welcomed guests to us all.'

'That's a bloody relief, then. Us all herded in here like cattle,' grumbled Wulfhere, staring around the walls of the small room. 'It would be a simple thing for them to charge in here and butcher us all.'

'They wouldn't, would they?' asked Godric, his jaw slack at the thought of it.

'I already said they won't. They haven't even taken our weapons, to show that they do not fear us. So eat, rest. There will be a feast tonight and I will talk to Forkbeard, then tomorrow we will leave. All of us,' Beornoth said. He spoke more harshly than he had intended.

'Don't tell me you have lost your temper with him already?'

said Leofsunu, as the men tucked into the bread and ale. 'It's only been two days.'

'Aye, and the ride to Bocking before that. He's like a mewling infant.' Beornoth caught himself and held his tongue. Godric was a thegn, and it would not do to malign him where sharp ears might overhear.

'His voice is shrill like an old fishwife, and he blusters like a youth with his first belly full of ale, bragging to maidens at a Yule.'

Beornoth laughed at that truth and placed a hand warmly on Leofsunu's shoulder. He sat with Leofsunu, Wulfhere and Aelfwine.

'So, Leofsunu. Tell us, were you born looking like that or did you fall off the ugly tree as a child and hit every branch on the way down?' said Wulfhere, and wagged a finger at Leofsunu's bulbous eyes and sticking-out ears.

'Our Lord Jesus Christ blessed me to be born this handsome, my simple-minded friend. Now, you tell us; were you born with an empty head or were you dropped down a well onto your skull as a babe?'

The men roared with laughter as the two scarred warriors teased each other. Beornoth was glad of the change of mood, it would distract the men from their fear of being at the centre of their enemy's nest. Beornoth watched the Northumbrian hostage. Thered sat at the end of an eating bench, taking bites from a loaf of brown bread, and sipping from a wooden mug of ale. He had barely said a word on the ride north-east, keeping himself to himself and taking the opportunity at any break in the journey to say his prayers. If he was pretending to be a changed man, he was putting on a good mummer's show of it, Beornoth thought. He rose and went to sit with the young man, his long face dropping in surprise as Beornoth sat down next to him with a frown.

'Lord Beornoth,' said Thered, inclining his head in greeting.

'What keeps you in Essex?' Beornoth asked harshly, memories of fighting Thered last summer still bright in his mind. 'You could have ridden away north and nobody would have followed you. You are the ealdorman of Northumbria now, or you will be once the king anoints you.'

'I gave my word to Ealdorman Byrhtnoth to remain as his hostage until such time as he trusts me enough for me to rule my shire.'

'Come now, you were a strutting pup who tried to kill me. Now you are Byrhtnoth's tame pet?'

Thered blushed and stared at the table. Beornoth sighed, he had spoken too harshly, but before he could soften his tone, the Northumbrian fixed him with a steely gaze.

'I am here to atone for what I have done, and to learn from Ealdorman Byrhtnoth. I have found solace in the Lord our God, and when I do return to my shire it will be as a better man who can rule with the respect of his people and the support of Wessex and Essex.' Thered spoke strongly and clearly and met Beornoth's eyes without flinching, and Beornoth could sense no hint of a lie. *Perhaps he has changed.*

Evening came, and Runolfr arrived at the door and asked the Saxons to leave their weapons in the room. Godric complained, asking if the Dane had any idea how much his sword was worth, until Beornoth shot him a glare that would wither an oak, and the young thegn relented. Their weapons would be safe. Vikings might be brutal and murderous, but they followed *drengskapr*, their warrior code, and were men of respect and honour. Runolfr led Beornoth and the Saxons into Gippeswic's main feasting hall. It was a paltry affair, because Gippeswic was a small town, an old fishing port of significance only because of the shelter its harbour offered to ships from the wilds of the seas off the East Anglian coast. The hall wasn't that much larger than Beornoth's own at Branoc's Tree. A fire burned in a central hearth, surrounded by tables for forty men to feast. Beornoth strode into the hall, and instantly felt warriors' eyes upon him, judging him. He pushed his shoulders back and looked from side to side, meeting men's gazes with his cold face. Beornoth was a big man, a head taller than most, and so he looked down at the Vikings with braided beards and plaited hair. Arm rings and byrnies gleamed, and men whispered as he passed their tables. Runolfr showed the Saxons to their places of honour, close to the fire, where a spitted pig roasted. It dropped fat to sizzle in the flames, and the smell of the roasting meat was glorious.

They led Beornoth and Offa to a long table on a raised platform facing towards the wider hall. There were six seats at that table, and all were empty. Runolfr grinned at Beornoth and went to take his own seat at an eating bench further back in the hall. Beornoth sat with Offa, and the grizzled warrior grinned and rubbed his hands together. Platters of roasted fish and boiled vegetables filled the tables. There was hot bread whose smell made Beornoth's eyes water, jugs of frothy ale, and gleaming hot eels. No matter how ravishing the food looked, Offa was a wise man and knew to wait until their host arrived before touching anything.

A drum boomed at the gloomy rear of the hall, a rhythmic music to which the Danes beat their fists on the tables in time. The hall seemed to shake with the thrum, and the hairs on Beornoth's neck tingled. They swung the doors open and a line of warriors marched in.

'Forkbeard! Forkbeard!' the Danes at the table roared between the beats of their fists. The man who led the marching column raised his hand to salute his warriors and they lost themselves in a frenzy of cheering. The lead man was shorter than the warriors behind him. He wore a huge white bear-fur cloak over his byrnie, and a circlet of gold sat on his golden hair. That hair was scraped back from his round face and tied at the nape of his neck. He wore a thick torc around his neck, coiled and twisted like a ship's rope. Beornoth knew the man for the king by his beard, which was long, golden and shone like his jewellery in two long braided forks upon his chest. The men behind him were huge, snarling Danes. Each man's brawny arms were thick with warrior rings, and their hard faces told of wind-whipped sea journeys and brutal battles fought.

Beornoth and Offa rose from their seats to greet the king, and he smiled graciously. The king of Denmark mounted the high dais and his head only reached Beornoth's shoulder. His bear-fur cloak made him seem broad, but the slimness in his neck belied his slight frame.

'Sit, please,' said Forkbeard, his voice pleasant and even. He ducked to wave a hand over his shoulder at a monstrous warrior who had joined him at the top table. Just as the king was slight and round-faced, this man was hugely muscled and broader across the shoulder even than Beornoth. His crag of a face was all hard angles and planes, and his forehead jutted above deep brown eyes. 'This is my uncle, Knut War Raven.' Knut sneered, and Beornoth met his fierce glare with one of his own.

'Thank you, my lord,' said Beornoth in Norse, and inclined his head as a mark of respect. 'I am Beornoth, thegn of the East Saxons. This is Offa, captain of Ealdorman Byrhtnoth's hearth troop.'

'I apologise for the surroundings. We are not at home and must make do with this humble feasting hall. You speak our language well, for a Saxon.'

'I am from the north, lord king. From the edge of the old

Danelaw. There are still many descendants of Danes and
Norsemen there.'

'Just so. Your king has sent you here to spy on me, no?' His
blue eyes twinkled in his round face, and there was a cleverness
there. It was not the face of a warrior, although Beornoth noticed
the lattice of raised white scars on Forkbeard's forearms and
hands, which were the telltale sign of a fighting man.

'King Æthelred seeks to know your intentions, given that your
ships rest on his shores and you have seized his lands.'

Forkbeard ate a mouthful of fish and turned to smile at
Beornoth. As he did so, he shrugged his bear-fur cloak back from
his shoulders and Beornoth rocked back in his chair with
surprise. He had not noticed before, because the chain lay hidden
beneath the folds of his cloak, but the king wore a silver cross
below his breast. Garnets and opals encrusted the crucifix, and it
hung from his neck by a thick silver chain. It was not the crafts-
manship of the cross, or the fine jewels that astonished Beornoth,
but that a Viking king wore a crucifix.

'It surprises you I am a Christian?' Forkbeard said, following
Beornoth's eyes. 'My father worshipped Christ, as do I. But many
of my jarls and warriors are worshippers of Odin, even though I
tell them that God is infinitely more powerful. My father's
brother here is a pagan, a fervent worshipper of Odin and Thor.'
Knut just grunted in response at that. Pork fat dripped into his
greying beard and his mouth was stuffed with food.

'I am surprised, lord king.'

'I have another surprise for you.' Forkbeard waved towards
the rear of the hall, and the doors opened, creaking above the din
of the feasting warriors.

Two men emerged from the gloom of the doorway, and the
crowd hushed to silence as they moved through the hall. They
carried a box between them. It was long, and they struggled

under its weight. They passed the fire, and Offa made the sign of the cross as he glimpsed what lay inside it. The men stopped in front of the raised dais and set the box upright. Beornoth put the handful of roasted pork he was about to eat back onto his platter, and clenched his teeth.

'This is your work, I believe?' said Forkbeard, for in the box was the shrunken torso of Ragnar the Flayer, who was now Ragnar the Heimnar. Ragnar growled and his head thrashed against the box. His ashen face was pale in the dim torchlight, and spittle foamed in his beard as he shook with fury. Two thick ropes across his chest held him in the box and he wriggled there like a salmon out of water.

'He was a raper, a slaver, and a raider,' said Beornoth. 'You unleashed him on my people, lord king. And he got what he deserved.' What Beornoth really wanted to ask was how Forkbeard had Ragnar in his company, given that he should be with Olaf Tryggvason on the south coast.

'You reap what you sow, eh?'

'Something like that, yes. It's my duty as a thegn to protect my people. I am the instrument of their justice and their vengeance.'

'We are Viking,' said Knut, banging his fist on the table. 'We take what we can until there is someone who can stop us. That thing you made of Ragnar is an affront to the gods. You deny Ragnar his place in Valhalla.' His voice rumbled like thunder, and Beornoth noticed that the little finger was missing from Knut's left hand. He had scars crossing the backs of his hands, and his face bore more than one lurid white reminder of battles fought and men slain. 'Why don't you drink some ale, like a man?'

Beornoth instead reached for a small wooden cup of water and took a sip. 'I do not drink ale.' And nor would he, not for Knut, not for anyone. Not after the hurt it caused him following the death of his children. Knut scoffed and shook his head, mumbling something about Beornoth being a Saxon whore, which he ignored.

'Ragnar is sworn to me,' said Forkbeard. 'So I will look after this horror that you have created. Now, before we can talk, you must pass a test. Do you agree? You are under my protection as my guest, Beornoth Reiði, as my men have taken to calling you. Beornoth the Wrathful. So you can leave, but if we are to talk openly, you must pass my test.'

Beornoth sighed. Vikings were always lovers of a holmgang duel, or a wrestling match to test strength and bravery. They gloried in such tests, pitting man against man, cheering their champions and scorning the losers. He had expected such a challenge, but the prospect of fighting one of Forkbeard's Danish growlers was not a prospect he relished. If he lost, there would be shame and humiliation for him and his company, and if he won, the Vikings would hate him even more. Their glares already burned into him, snarls and muttering at feasting benches. Forkbeard's men knew what Beornoth had done to Ragnar, and that was a terrible thing, and they would hate him for denying their man, a jarl, any prospect of a place in Valhalla now that he was not destined to die in battle. But he could not go back to Æthelred and Byrhtnoth without having spoken with Forkbeard and obtained some news of his intentions. Knut glared at him, huge and baleful, a Viking *drengr*, a taker of warriors' souls and a man to fear.

'Very well, lord king. Who must I fight?' said Beornoth, and kept his eyes on Knut's cliff of a face.

'A fight? I think not, Beornoth Reiði. This will be a challenge of riddles.'

The hall erupted into raucous cheers and table banging, for Northmen and Saxons alike loved a good riddle on a cold night. But Beornoth's shoulders slumped, he would have preferred a fight to a test of his cunning. The wily king would not have proposed such a test if he did not fancy himself a man of cunning.

'What do you say, lads?' Forkbeard bellowed, standing and spreading his arms wide to address his men. 'Best out of five?'

5

Benches and tables scraped on the hard-packed earth floor.
Warriors laughed and rubbed their hands and made a makeshift
circle around the central hearth. Beornoth stood still and silent
before the crackling warmth of the fire. His feet wanted to pace,
and his hands itched to wring, but Beornoth fought against his
urges. He had to keep his face cold and show indifference to the
challenge. Any sense of apprehension or fear would embolden
the Vikings, and they were ever a proud and arrogant people.

'I have never known you to be a man of riddles, lord,' said
Wulfhere, standing next to Beornoth but with his face to the fire
and his back to the crowd.

'That's because I'm not,' Beornoth growled through the side of
his mouth. It was a common enough pastime across Saxon
England, as it was in the harsh, cold lands of the Vikings. In the
long, dark winter nights, men would take pride in devising and
testing each other with riddles, to pass the time and challenge
one another. They would subject the loser to ridicule and the
winner could bask in the glory of his deep cunning. Beornoth
had seen more than one brawl break out over a riddling contest

and had always kept away from it. He didn't trust his temper, and nor did he put much stock in his ability to tease out the warp and weft of a well-crafted riddle.

'Maybe let another stand in your place?'

'That would show Forkbeard that I have a head full of rocks.'

'And? Let him have his stinking riddles. If it was a fight, you would fill his belly full of iron faster than a startled weasel.'

Beornoth wasn't so sure about that. He towered over Forkbeard and was wider than him in both shoulder and chest. But there was something about the man. He bore the scars of a fighter and why would a freshly crowned king risk his life on the Whale Road to make war when he could live a life of luxury and ease in his newly won Danish palace? Forkbeard was a fighter and a lover of war. Beornoth could see it in those soft eyes and round face. They belied his ferocity, but Beornoth could sense it on the man like stink off a pig.

The Vikings completed their circle, and placed four stools at its centre, two stools facing each other. They gathered like a pack of baying wolves, faces red from the fire's warmth, seafarers' hard eyes gleaming at the prospect of the contest to come. Their beards dripping with ale froth; horns, mugs and tankards in meaty fists as they huddled to witness the test of wits. Forkbeard shouldered through his men, his white bear-fur cloak still cast around his shoulders despite the heat. He pulled an even shorter man along beside him, a thin man with a tonsured head and a long black robe belted at the waist. He wore a crucifix around his neck like his king.

'Now, let us begin,' called Forkbeard, and he smiled at Beornoth, laughing silently so that the prongs of his beard shook and his warriors roared their approval. 'This is Father Ulf. He will be my second in the contest. You also may select a second, Beornoth Reiði.'

Beornoth resisted the urge to thank the king, or to let the relief show upon his face. He shrugged his indifference and turned to the Saxons who had gathered behind him.

'Anyone fancy themselves a good man for a riddle?' Beornoth asked. They met him with pursed lips and blank faces.

'Men have known me as a bit of a fox for a riddle,' said Godric, and one of his brothers slapped him on the back. The young thegn puffed out his chest and grinned, but Beornoth kept his gaze moving across the huddle of warriors. Leofsunu closed his eyes and shook his head. Wulfhere looked at his boots and Offa scratched at his grizzled beard.

'We need a little more experience, Godric. Aelfwine. Seems to me you are the man for the job. Do you know any good riddles?' The thegn of Foxfield often regaled the men with stories of long ago at evening campfires, and he was both well spoken and respected amongst Byrhtnoth's hearth troop.

'I know a few. I will do my best, Beo,' said Aelfwine, and rubbed his hands across his handsome face to make himself alert. 'Better to be facing Forkbeard in a shield wall, rather than this.'

'I know, but get your thinking head on so we don't make fools out of ourselves.' Beornoth sat on his stool, and Aelfwine eased down next to him. The surrounding Vikings grinned and nodded, slapping one another's backs until Forkbeard cleared his throat, and the hall fell as silent as if a ghostly fetch had floated in through an open shutter.

'I will go first, Saxons. Then you will go and so on. First one to get three correct is the winner. Agreed?' said Forkbeard, his eyes gleaming in his round face.

'Agreed,' replied Beornoth.

Father Ulf leaned over from his stool to whisper in the king's ear, and Forkbeard nodded without taking his eyes from Beornoth's own. Forkbeard stood, and tucked his thumbs into his wide leather belt, which was studded with silver strips around its length. The Vikings stamped their feet in time, creating a rhythm, and the king grinned.

> *'Would that I had now, what I had yesterday,*
> *Find out what that was;*
> *mankind it mars,*
> *speech it hinders,*
> *yet speech it will inspire.'*

The king spoke in time with the beat of the Vikings' boots. 'Ponder that, Beornoth Reiði,' he said.

'I think he starts us off with an easy one,' said Aelfwine.

'Aye, I know the answer to this one all too well,' said Beornoth. He stood and met the king's eye. 'A good riddle, lord king, and one which the men in this hall, and any hall, are all too familiar with. The answer to your riddle is ale, King Sweyn.'

Forkbeard smiled and waved his hand in acknowledgement of the correct answer, and a murmur went around the hall in appreciation. 'Well done, Saxon. Now, your turn.'

Beornoth glanced at Aelfwine, who stood to join him. The Vikings again took up their boot-stamping rhythm.

> *'Lone-dweller I am, injured with iron,*
> *battered by the blade – I've had my fill of battle-works*
>
> *–*
>
> *exhausted by the edges. I have seen warfare,*
> *often perilous fighting. Hopeless of comfort,*
> *respite from the struggle of battle shall not come,*
> *before I should be eaten up entirely among men,*
> *legacies of the hammer should beat upon me,*
> *hard-edged, slicingly sharp, handiwork of smiths –*

they bite me upon the battlements.
I must endure these loathsome moots,
never able to locate a healing tribe
who might in the houses of men
wind my wounds with herbs –
but the gashes become greater
through fatal blows by day and by night.'

Aelfwine spoke in a deep, chanting voice. The Viking faces around them stared, open-mouthed, taking in every word as Beornoth translated each line into Norse.

Forkbeard cocked his ear to his priest, who whispered into it, and the king nodded his agreement. Beornoth had heard that one himself at his own fireside many times, so he expected the king to get the answer.

'It seems we are probing each other with a simple challenge,' said the king. 'Like warriors who face off in the holmgang square. The answer is a shield.' Aelfwine bowed to confirm that the answer was correct, and the surrounding Vikings beat their chests with their fists. 'One correct answer each. A good start. Now, my turn again.'

The priest whispered to Forkbeard again, but the king shook his head, ignoring whatever advice he offered. Forkbeard raised his hands for his men to take up the boot-stomping drum again.

'Who is that shrill one,
who rides a hard road,
has fared that way before.
He kisses hard
who has two mouths,
and goes only on gold.'

Forkbeard's hand rose to finger the jewels on his crucifix as he waited for the Saxons to offer their answer.

Beornoth translated the riddle for Aelfwine, and the thegn of Foxfield screwed up his eyes. 'Two mouths? Only on gold,' he whispered. 'A river has a mouth, but only one, and nothing to do with gold?'

'Kisses hard,' said Beornoth. 'Must be something that hits, like an arrow or an oar into the sea?'

Aelfwine stroked his beard, and then his eyebrows shot up. 'That's it, Beo, it's a hammer. A gold hammer.'

Beornoth repeated the answer in Norse, and Father Ulf scowled, his lips retreating to show a set of brown stained teeth. The Vikings in the hall hoomed their appreciation of the answer.

'Well done, Saxon,' said Forkbeard. 'Your turn.'

Beornoth looked at Aelfwine, and the thegn set his jaw. Any of the riddles Beornoth knew were for children, about milk or rainbows, not fit for a Viking king's mead hall. But Aelfwine looked like he was getting into his stride, and he leant forward to fix the king with his clever eyes as he chanted his next riddle.

>*'Wob is my name, all topsy-turvy –*
>*I am a splendid creature, created in the struggle.*
>*When I am bent, and a poisoned arrow*
>*borne in my bosom, I am entirely ready*
>*to sweep far away that deadly evil.*
>*After my sovereign, who shaped in me that torment,*
>*let's go of my limbs, I am longer than before,*
>*until I vomit it up, a venom, baleful to all,*
>*corrupt with ruin, that I swallowed before.*
>*It is not easily avoided by any human –*
>*none at all – what I have to say in those parts.*
>*If what flies from my womb touches him,*

> *they purchase that wicked drink with their power,*
> *atonement fixed and full for his life.*
> *Unbound I do not wish to obey anyone*
> *unless skillfully strung. Say what I am called?'*

Beornoth repeated each line in the Viking language, and at the end Forkbeard wrinkled his nose in disgust. 'That one is too easy. I heard one similar at the knees of my father when I was but a pup,' he said. 'The answer is bow.'

The king took a swig from his horn of ale and cleared his throat, and the crowd once again took up their stomping rhythm.

> *'Who is that great one*
> *who grasps the earth,*
> *swallowing wood and water?*
> *Bad weather he dreads,*
> *wind, but no man,*
> *and picks a fight with the sun.'*

The king smiled. 'Beornoth Saxon, guess my riddle.'

'Could it be darkness?' said Aelfwine in Beornoth's ear. 'It grips the earth and swallows all, and picks a fight with the sun, but does not dread bad weather.'

'I don't know,' said Beornoth, growing tired of the game. 'What about ice, maybe? Or snow?'

'It could be snow. That would block out the sun, but would not swallow water.'

'Do I have you?' said Forkbeard, grinning.

'Snow,' said Beornoth, struggling to contain his temper.

'I have you! We have found the depth of Saxon cunning,' the king crowed. 'The answer is fog.' The crowd cheered and laughed at their king's deep cunning, and rejoiced at the frowns on the Saxons' faces. 'If I get your next one right, I am the winner.'

'Pick a good one, Aelfwine,' said Beornoth. 'I am at a loss here, and might challenge the king to fight if they laugh at us much longer.'

'I have one that might stump him,' said Aelfwine, after a few moments of head-scratching as he tried to summon up the words from the back of his mind.

> *'Shoulder-brother of nobles,*
> *soldier's comrade,*
> *beloved by my master,*
> *retainer of the king.*
> *His blond-tressed lady*
> *at times lays her hand on me,*
> *an earl's daughter, no matter how well born.*
> *I have in bosom what blossomed in bower.*
> *Sometimes I ride upon a proud courser*
> *before armies – my tongue is forged.*
> *Often I grant the glib talker*
> *requital after his stories.*
> *Good aspect, and dark all over –*
> *Say what I am called.'*

The king listened eagerly to Beornoth's translation, and he stroked at the plaited forks of his beard. The faces of the surrounding Vikings glowed red from their ale, and their eyes grew wide with anticipation. Ulf, the priest, whispered in the king's ear, and Forkbeard turned to him and clapped the smaller man on the shoulder so hard that he stumbled, almost falling into the floor rushes.

'I have it, and I win the contest. The answer is a war horn!'

Forkbeard roared the answer, and his warriors banged their boots
and shouted their acclaim for the king and his deep cunning. The
rafters of the hall shook with their celebrations and Aelfwine
shook his head in disgust that they had lost the contest.

Wulfhere clapped Beornoth reassuringly on the shoulder,
and Offa shrugged. Beornoth hated to lose to Forkbeard, because
he hated Vikings. It was a thing that broiled deep within him, and
although he had been raised in the company of such men, what
they had done to his young family could never be forgiven. So,
even though it was a simple riddling contest, the loss lay heavy on
Beornoth and he forced himself to relax his bunched fists before
Forkbeard saw the white of his straining knuckles and could
glory in his anger. Beornoth swallowed his pride and his hurt and
strode across the open space to where Forkbeard received the
congratulations of his men.

'Well done, lord king. You are a clever man,' Beornoth
shouted above the din.

Forkbeard turned to him and clasped Beornoth's extended
arm in the warrior's grip. 'That was a good contest,' said the king,
and he shook Beornoth's arm warmly. 'Come, let us share some
ale and some food, and we can talk. Our exchange amused my
men, and we spilled not a drop of blood in the contest.'

Beornoth breathed a sigh of relief. Forkbeard would have
been within his rights to refuse to have any further discussions
following his victory, but Vikings seek amusement and the king
seemed happy enough that the contest had adequately enter-
tained his warriors. Beornoth followed Forkbeard through the
throng, and as many Vikings clapped Beornoth on the back as
they did Forkbeard. The king stopped to call a man's name and
smile at him, or remember an amusing anecdote with another,
so that it took an age to return to the raised dais. Forkbeard was
good with his men and they loved him. Their faces glowed

when he spoke their name and stopped to speak with them. That was a thing to be remembered to Byrhtnoth, for leaders who carry the love of their men are hard to fight. Forkbeard's warriors would fight to the death for their king, and there would never be a retreat or surrender unless the king himself ordered it.

Forkbeard sat down heavily on his chair and took a long pull from a frothing horn of ale. 'Now,' he said, wiping the white bubbles from his moustache with the back of his hand. 'What did you come here to ask me?'

'You are with your fleet, lord king. You took Gippeswic by force and unleashed your man Ragnar on the people of East Anglia. Are you here to raid, or take the land for good?' said Beornoth.

'You speak plainly. I like that. Straight to the point,' said Forkbeard. He belched loudly and fished a hand beneath the neck of his byrnie, grimacing until he found what he was searching for and tossed a silver coin onto the table. It was small and ringed with tiny circles and at its centre was a crude likeness of King Æthelred. 'This is what I am here for.'

'For the mint?'

'Just so. I need silver, even if it bears the face of a fool. I am king of the Danes, but to become king, I had to overthrow my father. He is Harald Bluetooth, a man of reputation and a warrior to fear. To do that, I had to turn his own jarls against him, and that takes more than strength at arms. It takes silver and gold, and lots of it.'

'You have been here all winter. Do you not have enough yet?'

'I went home for the winter and only returned to Gippeswic last week. My men have been here all winter, but we need silver to put into the forge to make the coin. We need more.'

'You sailed in winter?' It was dangerous enough in the

summer, but to make the journey north on winter seas was a monstrous risk.

'Aye. It was no jaunt across a still fjord, I can tell you. I am still a new king, and I need to be in my kingdom so men don't forget to whom they owe their allegiance.'

'You think you can come to our shores, kill our people, take one of our ports and steal our silver without repercussions?'

Forkbeard shrugged. 'I have been here for almost a year and nothing has happened. Your ealdorman here in East Anglia is weak and does nothing to stop me. Your thegns here welcome me. I am no heathen. I am a Christian king like your Æthelred. Men here would like me to be king, and to have a more honest Church that does not take their land. I feel like a welcomed guest here, not like the pirate you make me out to be. Maybe I will stay, the soil is good. Sheep and cattle grow fat and crops grow high and strong.'

'There are men here who welcome you, the king is aware. I hanged such a man last week, a traitor to his king and his people.'

Forkbeard smiled and nodded. 'You are a fierce warrior, Beornoth. My uncle Knut would love to fight you, to test his skill against yours. There is reputation to be gained in your death. But we are not barbarians. Well, Knut is, but most of us are not.' He shrugged and cocked an eyebrow at Knut War Raven.

'If it is silver you require, my Lord Æthelred will pay you more to take your ships and return home.' The words spilled from Beornoth's lips, and he had to fight hard to hide the disgust from his face. He wanted to pay the Vikings in steel and blood, not good Saxon silver.

'I know he will. But can he throw me out? Would it be you he sends to kill me, Beornoth Reiði?'

'I hope not, lord king, because you have shown us hospitality and respect. It would be a shame to come here with all the strength of Æthelred's kingdom, from Cornwall, Wessex, Lunden-wic, Mercia, Northumbria and Cheshire. I would regret swarming over your walls and crushing your brave *drengr* with my sword and seax. It would keep me awake at night to know that I cut the heart from my friend King Sweyn Forkbeard and put his head on a spike as a warning to pirates and raiders.'

Forkbeard laughed and fixed Beornoth with his clever eyes. 'We shall see then what happens across this fine Saxon summer, friend Beornoth.'

Beornoth nodded his thanks to the king and rose from his eating bench, and though it was late and the shroud of darkness had fallen to cover East Anglia, he wanted to be away from Gippeswic as quickly as possible. Anger broiled in his belly like broth over a fire, and he did not trust himself to keep his calm amongst the grinning Viking wolves. He stalked along the hall, trailed by the Bloodsworn, the thegns and warriors who had sworn their oath to serve and die for Ealdorman Byrhtnoth. Beornoth set his jaw and met the eyes of the smirking Vikings as he marched, the muscles beneath his beard working as he ground his teeth. He passed Ragnar the Flayer in his coffin-like box. A slave spooned food into his mouth, and the heimnar spat it out so that the moist scraps hung in his beard. His eyes were wide and burned with hate in his wasted, pale face. Ragnar shuddered with fury, and Beornoth winked at him, just to annoy the man he had whittled to a stump.

'It's coming!' Ragnar roared, the noise reaching every nook of the hall so that the Vikings fell silent to listen to the tortured jarl. 'Wrath and vengeance are coming for you, Beornoth. Blood! Blood like a river. Oh, how you will howl with despair as your people die and writhe in pain. I will see you die, I will watch you, Beornoth. It will be slow, and you will weep for your dead loved ones before the end.'

Beornoth snapped. He took three long strides and kicked the heimnar's box, toppling it to the ground so that Ragnar was trapped beneath its darkness. The hall erupted with horrified anger, and Beornoth marched out of the doors before they were roused to violence. He turned for one last glance at Forkbeard, who was smiling and laughing with his men. Knut War Raven pointed at Beornoth, and then banged his fist into his thick chest as though it held a blade. He dragged that imaginary blade across his torso with a snarl, showing Beornoth what he intended to do if they ever met where blades clash and men die.

6

'We should return to the ealdorman with all haste,' said Offa. Despite the spring sunshine warming the riverbank, the old warrior hunched in the saddle, frowning, with his cloak pulled tight. Having spent an uncomfortable night in Forkbeard's camp, and Beornoth unable to sleep because of Knut and the heimnar's threats, the Bloodsworn rode west under a bright sky. The fens and flat woodland of East Anglia showed greens and yellows as the land was reborn from its winter slumber and the clouds shone so white that they were hard to look upon. Larks and warblers called from trees showing green buds and as the sun moved across that shining sky, the day moved from frosty morning to sun-warmed midday.

'You are our captain, Offa,' said Beornoth. 'And I take my orders from you. But Byrhtnoth wants to know why the ealdorman of East Anglia tarries and does nothing to oppose Forkbeard. It will cost us only a day to ride to his lands and find the answer.'

'Aye, well. I just want to follow orders, that's all. As captain, it's me who will bear the ealdorman's displeasure, not any of you lot. Let's stop here. I need to piss.'

Offa called the halt and slid off his horse to relieve himself for the third time that day. The captain had aged a decade over the winter. His hair had thinned and turned white, and the veins in his skin-spotted hands were blue and prominent. Beornoth took a handful of broken oatcakes from a saddlebag and fed them to Hríð. The horse whinnied and the softness of his lips tickled Beornoth's hand. He rested his forehead on the horse's own and they paused for a moment, horse and rider. Beornoth wished he were alone with the beast, just riding across the countryside in companionable silence with no destination, simply a horse and his rider. Hríð nudged Beornoth's head backwards, and he laughed, tickling the horse behind the ear.

'Sometimes I think you like horses more than people,' said Wulfhere. He took a pull from a water skin and handed it to Beornoth.

'Sometimes?'

Wulfhere laughed and shook his head. Cwicca came running over and walked Hríð to a line of rope he had fastened between a crooked willow tree and a briar. Leofsunu and Aelfwine approached, and the thegn of Sturmer threw an old cloak onto the grass for them to take a rest. They sat, and Beornoth groaned at the click in his knees, and the ache of his old wounds.

'If Offa has to keep pissing so much, it will take us a full turn of the moon to get home,' said Leofsunu, and waved at the old captain as he fastened his breeches.

'This might be his last summer at arms,' said Aelfwine, laughing.

'We should reach Leofric's burh before dark,' said Wulfhere. He tore up a loaf of bread and handed a chunk to each of them.

'And the ealdorman is a friend to Byrhtnoth?' asked Beornoth.

'He was,' said Aelfwine. 'They fought for King Edgar, Æthelred's father. And they fought for his son before he died and Æthelred became king.'

'But that was a long time ago,' said Leofsunu. 'Leofric is much older than Byrhtnoth. Older even than Offa.'

'But he has sons?' asked Beornoth.

'Aye, two, as I remember it. From when he used to visit Essex, which he hasn't for some time.'

'You think they have sided with Forkbeard?' said Wulfhere.

'Never!' said Aelfwine, his handsome face stern. 'Leofric is loyal to the house of Wessex. He would never welcome a Viking to our shores.'

'But why hasn't he tried to fight them then?'

'There must be a reason. Perhaps he fought, but was defeated? Who knows?'

'We will find out soon enough,' said Beornoth. 'East Anglia should be able to field as many thegns as the East Saxons. Not to mention the fyrd.'

'Why doesn't the king just order Ealdorman Leofric and his thegns to fight Forkbeard?' asked Wulfhere.

'He did, last summer,' said Beornoth. 'But we were too busy fighting against Olaf and his Jomsvikings at Watchet and Folkestone.'

'So for all we know, Leofric actually fought Forkbeard, or harried him at least,' said Aelfwine.

Beornoth wasn't so sure. He didn't want to give voice to it, but he feared that most of East Anglia had either submitted to Forkbeard, or simply didn't care that Forkbeard was there as long as he wasn't raiding their lands. Forkbeard had let Ragnar the Flayer loose upon the countryside last summer, and perhaps that horror had been enough to keep the thegns at home, with their blades and men close to their families.

'What worries me more, is how that thing you created found its way back to Forkbeard,' said Wulfhere, and he spat over his shoulder and made the sign of the cross to ward off Ragnar's evil *seiðr*.

'Like a turd floating downstream,' said Leofsunu.

'Well, we know that Olaf and Forkbeard have met, or have at least exchanged messages,' said Beornoth. 'Olaf must have brought Ragnar to Gippeswic by ship, so the Norse in Folkestone and the Danes in Gippeswic know one another are here.'

'If they unite, they will create a new Great Heathen Army,' said Wulfhere. 'Just like when our lands almost fell to the Vikings a hundred years ago.'

'Except now they are not all heathens,' said Aelfwine. 'For men once forced to surrender land to abbots and priests by royal decree, maybe a new king would not be so bad, a strong Christian king with no loyalties to the Saxon church.'

'And Forkbeard doesn't need to accept our king and his arch-bishop's offer of silver to sail away. He can make as many coins as he wishes from the mint at Gippeswic,' said Leofsunu.

'So, Vikings surround Essex,' said Beornoth, fixing each man with a stare to make sure they understood the challenges Æthelred and Byrhtnoth – and therefore they too – faced. 'Fork-beard to the east and Olaf to the south. If they can combine their men, they will have ninety ships. Two thousand warriors, not fyrdmen, farmers and millers. Two thousand Viking warriors, each one of them a match for a Saxon hearth-troop warrior. An army large enough to win a kingdom. How many proper warriors can we put into the field, not including the fyrd?'

The question went unanswered, because each of them knew the answer. Not enough. They made the rest of the journey to Leofric's burh in silence, and Beornoth did his best not to think about two thousand Vikings swarming over Essex, over Branoc's

Tree. Forkbeard had not even flinched at the offer of payment to return to Denmark. He was here for more. Perhaps he saw the chance for more silver, or just to burnish his reputation brightly with the blood of Saxon warriors. But Forkbeard would need to be removed from East Anglia by force, as would Olaf from Folkestone. Beornoth was sure of it.

They reached Leofric's burh at Ravenbrook before dusk, and a smiling steward welcomed them through a wide gate in a well-kept palisade atop a ditch and bank. Boys led their horses to stables, and the steward showed Beornoth and the Bloodsworn to a wide hall with an elk's skull above the door, its antlers huge and sprawling. Inside, a fire crackled and a band of six warriors met them with ale and hot broth. The warriors were friendly enough, their armour clean and their weapons well cared for.

'So, no trouble from the Danes over the winter?' asked Leofsunu once they had exchanged pleasantries about the weather and the premature return of greenery to tree and plant.

'No trouble.' A big man, with his two front teeth missing so that he lisped when he spoke, shrugged. 'They stayed quiet enough in Gippeswic.'

'Which they took without challenge?' asked Wulfhere.

The big man took a drink from a tankard of ale, and his eyes flashed with anger for an instant before he mastered himself. 'They will probably sail away with little enough trouble,' he said, dragging a smile on to his face.

'There was trouble last year,' said Beornoth. 'When I attacked one of their jarls who wore the skins of your people on his shield. I freed East Anglian slaves destined for the markets at Dublin or Hedeby.'

'There was trouble last year,' came another voice. A well-built man stood up, one of the few in the hall wearing a byrnie. He had chestnut-brown hair and a beard to match, and wore a thick silver chain around his neck. 'And we did our best to protect our people. Unfortunately, we cannot all be such accomplished Viking slayers as you, Beornoth, or Ealdorman Byrhtnoth. The rest of us must pray to our Lord God and do what we can.'

Beornoth chewed on his beard, for perhaps the East Anglians had fought hard against the Danes. Perhaps they could not hold them back, for Vikings are savage, ruthless warriors.

'I am Wictred of East Anglia,' said the man in the silver chain. 'My father is Ealdorman Leofric. It is late, and you cannot continue your journey this evening. You are most welcome to spend the night at Ravenbrook. Come, sit with me awhile. Then I will take you to see my father.'

Beornoth and Offa thanked Wictred, and the warriors from both sides shook hands in the warrior's grip. Slaves brought food and ale, and Beornoth sat on a high-backed chair carved with whorls and boars and took a drink of cool water. Offa thanked Wictred for his hospitality and for the care the men of Ravenbrook would give to their horses.

'I rode into battle alongside your father many times,' said Offa. He raised a cup of ale to Wictred. 'He was a brave man, and a good friend to Ealdorman Byrhtnoth.'

'Aye, he was. My father has been ill these last years. He is bedridden and has been so for the last two summers. He was once a great man, his wisdom valued by King Edgar, and his sword protected the kingdom. Those days were long ago.' Wictred stared into his ale with a furrowed brow.

'So who rules the shire if sickness confines the ealdorman to his bed?' asked Beornoth.

'I am his eldest son, but cannot be confirmed as ealdorman whilst my father lives. So, my father rules. I do what I can to keep the shire in order, as do my brothers.'

'Is it possible to speak with your father?' asked Offa.

'Yes, if he has the strength. He can still speak, which makes things harder.'

'Because men won't take orders from you?'

'Not whilst they can still consult my father, which is possible on good days.'

'But would he not hand over the shire to you now?' asked Beornoth.

Wictred flashed a wry smile. 'He would, but he has advisors. Men of power and influence. Churchmen. And I fear they speak otherwise. They cling to power, ruling the shire whilst my father lies abed.'

'Can we speak with Lord Leofric this evening? The matter is urgent. King Sweyn Forkbeard of Denmark is in Gippeswic with forty ships, and he has not sailed across the Whale Road with his bloodthirsty warriors to make friends. We are here at the behest of King Æthelred.'

'You can try,' said Wictred. 'Follow me.'

He led them through the hall and across a courtyard. A full moon bathed the burh in a silvery half-light and they strode to a huddle of wattle buildings and under a lintel where Beornoth had to duck to enter. Wictred moved through a darkened hallway, barely wide enough for two men to walk shoulder to shoulder. Beornoth's head almost scraped the beams in its roof and the walls were close, his broad shoulders filling the corridor. After five paces, men appeared. A gaggle of priests stood against the wall. They peered at Beornoth with white faces and beady eyes. They fingered the crucifixes and beads at their necks. Beornoth was so large that his shoulder and cloak brushed against them as he walked. He could feel their sneers, hear their muttering as his heavy boots crunched on the floor rushes. He was a full head and shoulders larger than any of them and he glared down at a weasel-faced man who bustled from a doorway and tutted at him.

The priest flung himself against the wall when he noticed Beornoth's bulk.

'There are a lot of priests here,' Offa hissed in Beornoth's ear.

'Too many. They have their claws in this place,' Beornoth replied.

Wictred guided them into the room. Candles flickered around its corners so that the room seemed to shake with a dull glow. A small fire burned in a hearth at the far wall, and an old man sat propped in a bed swathed in furs. White hair grew from his head, in thin, almost translucent strands, like the fluff on a summer dandelion. His long, gaunt face was ashen and littered with discoloured spots. Two hands rested on the furs draped across his bed, and they were skeletal and trembled in time with the gentle shake of the old man's head.

'My lord father, Leofric, ealdorman of East Anglia,' said Wictred. Beornoth and Offa bowed their heads to the ancient lord. 'Father,' Wictred shouted, and the old man's eyes flickered open, showing a blue so pale they were almost grey. The eyes searched Beornoth and Offa, but the face remained passive. 'These men have come from your friend, Ealdorman Byrhtnoth.' The corners of Leofric's mouth twitched at the sound of Byrhtnoth's name, and his hands lifted slightly.

'There are Danes in East Anglia, my lord,' said Beornoth, speaking just as loudly as Wictred, assuming Leofric was hard of hearing. 'They are at Gippeswic, and must be thrown out.'

The door to the room creaked open and two black-robed priests shuffled in, one of them with a jewelled crucifix around his neck and another with a huge ruby ring on his left hand.

'You disturb the ealdorman. He should be resting. Can't you see he is unwell?' barked the priest with the ring. He was a slender man with a freshly shaved tonsure and a long nose.

'We have important matters, priest,' Beornoth growled.

'What could be more important than the ealdorman's health?'

'Vikings. Here in East Anglia. Men who would kill and rape your entire shire.'

The priest shook his head and looked Beornoth up and down. 'You warriors. Dull-minded brutes. There will be no Viking attacks on East Anglia.'

Beornoth's head snapped backwards as though someone had slapped his face. From the corner of his eye he saw Wictred shake his head slightly at the priest, and the little man licked his lips and raised his hands, fussing with his robes. 'We trust in God that there will be no raids. Our faith will keep us safe. Is not this King Sweyn a good Christian man?'

'A good man? How can you be so sure there will be no attacks?' said Beornoth, stepping closer to the priest so that he towered over the man. 'And how do you know Forkbeard is a Christian?'

'You have no authority here, thegn. Go, leave us...'

'I am here with the king's authority!' Beornoth roared. The sudden deafening shout frightened the priest. He winced and jumped backwards so that he banged into the bedroom wall.

'Beornoth, my father...' Wictred began. But he stopped when Beornoth fixed him with a glare.

'Your father is clearly ill, and not able to rule his shire. You must take control. Do not allow these black crows to dominate you.'

Wictred looked at his boots, and the ealdorman coughed and wheezed in his bed.

'You have no power here. I look after things for the ealdorman. I am in charge and you cannot...' the priest began, surging from the wall in an embarrassed fury.

Beornoth placed a heavy hand on the priest's shoulder and fixed him with an icy stare. 'Do you feel in command now? If I find out that you took Forkbeard's coin to keep the warriors of East Anglia at bay, I will come back here and crucify you. I will kill every priest in his place. Do you hear me?' Beornoth roared again, and the priest shook with fear. Beornoth turned to Wictred and jabbed his finger into the man's byrnie. 'Ealdorman Byrhtnoth will send a messenger here for your warriors. Do not ignore it. Bring your thegns and your hearth troops, and you lead them.'

Wictred nodded and set his jaw. 'We will come, I swear it.'

Offa extended his hand, and Wictred took it, sealing the agreement with the warrior's grip. Beornoth turned and marched from the room, and the priests shrank from his ferocity. He stalked down the dark corridor and out into the hall. Beornoth and the East Saxons spent the rest of the evening away from the men of East Anglia, and the men of Ravenbrook left them alone. In the morning, servants had their horses saddled and Beornoth rode Hríð out of the gates. There were no goodbyes, and no supplies or other offerings of hospitality as they rode away.

'You frightened that priest,' said Offa, smiling, so that his lined face creased around the eyes. 'The Church rules East Anglia whilst Leofric waits to die.'

'Which is why Forkbeard rests unopposed,' said Beornoth.

'Do you really believe the East Anglian priests are taking silver from the Danes and using their power and influence to keep Sweyn unmolested?' asked Aelfwine.

'I do,' said Beornoth. 'When have you known a priest refuse coin? And Forkbeard has the Gippeswic mint. Those priests will be as rich as Lundenwic whores by summer.'

'Maybe they keep Forkbeard at bay with riddles,' said Wulfhere, and the entire company laughed.

'Will Wictred bring his warriors when we call?' said Aelfwine.

'He must. We have Vikings to east and south and the warriors of Essex won't be enough to fight them both,' said Beornoth.

'Why doesn't the king just order them to fight?' asked Wulfhere. Which was a good question, and one that had rattled around in Beornoth's thought cage all winter.

'It's not as simple as that,' said a mumbling voice. Beornoth turned in his saddle and peered past Wulfhere, Cwicca and Kari to a rider at the rear of their company. It was Thered, the Northumbrian hostage. 'East Anglia used to be its own kingdom, as did Northumbria and Mercia. The nobles there still hold on to those memories of when their ancestors were kings. Then there is the Church. Those priests and their archbishops hold swathes of land across East Anglia, as they do in Northumbria. If the king sends an order to rally the warriors of East Anglia, the ealdorman of the shire and its archbishop must support it.'

'Are you saying the men of East Anglia would ignore the king?' asked Godric, his incredulity making his voice squeak.

'They wouldn't ignore him,' said Thered. 'But they would not march without the order from their ealdorman and archbishop. That's all I'm saying.'

The quiet thegn was right, and Beornoth saw it now for what it was. People thought of the king as all-powerful, but in reality England was a country held together by fragile alliances, and by the strength of the swords loyal to him. Before Alfred's time, only one hundred years earlier, England had not existed. There had been Wessex, Mercia, East Anglia and Northumbria, each ruled by its own king, just as Thered said. Men owed their oaths and their fealty to their ealdorman, and would not risk his displeasure by marching against his orders. They held their land at his pleasure, and no thegn or warrior would march off to support the king in Wessex and risk returning to see his wife and children turned out into a ditch.

'We must inform Ealdorman Byrhtnoth,' said Offa. 'He will know what to do.'

As he rode across the flat meadows of East Anglia, Beornoth turned those problems over in his thought cage. Storms of war approached, threatening to engulf England in a bloody war where the battlefields would be Saxon fields and villages. He shuddered as he thought of the brutal Viking wolves and their savage axes and spears descending on the farms and the East Saxon people. Beornoth tried to steel himself against visions of bearded Vikings climbing over the walls of Branoc's Tree, of their brutal violence amongst those he loved and was sworn to protect.

7

'How is the horse?' asked Ealdorman Byrhtnoth. He took a broad-bladed aesc spear from a rack and closed one eye to stare down its shaft. The ealdorman's silver spade of a beard nodded as he showed his approval of its craftmanship.

'He is a magnificent animal, lord,' said Beornoth. 'He made the journey from here to East Anglia with ease and needed no more rest than the smaller horses. Thank you for the gift.'

Byrhtnoth smiled and returned the spear to its place in the tall willow-wood rack. They stood in a long barn made from stones, large rocks piled high and held in place by hardened mud and straw to form its walls, and huge beams topped with grey thatch for the roof. It was an old barn, and the wind blew in where rocks had fallen from the wall to leave gaps filled with spiderwebs and birds' nests, and drips came through holes in the roof amongst shafts of golden sunlight. The spear rack spanned an entire wall of the barn. Above it were timber shelves with sheaves of arrows tied around with thin wool rope. On the opposite side of the barn, shields rested against the wall. Dull iron bosses peered out at Beornoth like the dead eyes of a monstrous spider from between the linden-wood boards. Many of those shields were freshly painted with bears and wolves, and others were old and flaking.

'The men will be out to practise soon,' said Byrhtnoth. He picked out another spear and thumbed its edge. 'I have pushed them hard this winter. Weapons practice every day, no matter the weather. The smith's hammer has not ceased, despite my wife's complaints. We have good spears and shields.'

'We shall need them, lord.'

Byrhtnoth frowned and stared up at the roof for a moment. A robin perched on a beam, watching them with its small twitching head and its red breast. Byrhtnoth smiled at the corner of his mouth, a whisper of a smile appreciating the beauty and fragility of the bird. It hopped on the beam and then flitted away through a tiny hole in the thatch. 'Aye.' Byrhtnoth sighed and turned his enormous fists around the spear shaft until his busted knuckles turned white. 'So, you met the Danes?'

'I did, lord. King Sweyn Forkbeard of the Danes is well dug in at Gippeswic. It's a small fishing port. The burh is well repaired, its palisade tops a bank, and the ditch is overgrown but can easily be deepened by his men. He returned to his own kingdom for the deep winter, with one ship, and only arrived back on our shores recently.'

'So he is a risk-taker, then?'

'Or determined. He returned to oversee his new kingdom and left the rest of his warriors here to maintain his foothold.'

'He must have been sure that Gippeswic would be safe from attack over the winter.'

'He was sure. He has forty ships there, lord. That's a thousand men, maybe more. To keep a thousand men in one town over a long winter takes a lot of food. More than they could fish out of the sea.'

'So, if he felt safe enough to sail north and his warriors were well fed through the cold, he is here as a guest rather than an invader.'

'Perhaps an unwelcome guest, but one whose hosts are too afraid to throw out.'

'The Church should be in an uproar that an army of heathens defile their lands around Gippeswic.'

'Forkbeard is a Christian, lord.'

'A Christian? Are you sure?'

'His father, Harald Bluetooth, became a Christian and had his son baptised. He wears a cross around his neck and is advised by priests. I saw it with my own eyes.'

'So, not a heathen, then. A Christian king from the north with no links or allegiance owed to our own Church here in Æthelred's kingdom.'

'Which would make him a welcome alternative for wealthy men who have lost land to our own Church.'

'Especially those in what was the Danelaw. Half of the bastards in East Anglia and Northumbria are descended from Vikings.'

'He has both Christians and pagans in his crews, and he has the royal mint of Gippeswic. He needs silver for his wars at home.'

'Is it true he deposed his own father?'

'It's true, his father's brother is at Forkbeard's shoulder. Knut War Raven is his name.' Beornoth shuddered at the thought of the monstrous Viking and the thought of meeting him on the field of battle.

'So, what kind of man is he?'

'A man of deep cunning. He challenged me to a contest of riddles, which he won. He is a small man, slight across the shoulder.'

'No offence, Beo, but you are not a man I would put forward
for a challenge at riddles. A duel or a wrestling contest, no better
man. But riddles?'

'Aelfwine helped me, and we still lost.'

'So Forkbeard is a thinker, not a fighter?'

'He's a fighter. He bears the marks of it on his forearms. Sometimes smaller men are savage in battle, you know that yourself,
lord. There was something else as well. Ragnar was there, in
Sweyn's hall. The Viking jarl I whittled to a stump last year and
sent with the fire ships into Olaf's fleet. He was with Sweyn, spitting venom about the end of days for our people. For him to be in
Gippeswic means that Sweyn and Olaf are aware of one another's
presence here.'

'True enough.' Byrhtnoth frowned and rubbed his eyes
between thumb and forefinger. 'The men will be out soon to
practise and it's a fine morning. Shall we work together, you and I,
before they do?'

Beornoth smiled. 'Why not? Go easy on me though, lord.'

Byrhtnoth laughed and selected a spear from the many
racked along the barn wall. Beornoth picked the one closest to
him. He tested its weight and it felt well balanced. He followed
the ealdorman across the barn towards the racked shields. Byrhtnoth hefted one with a snarling dragon daubed across the boards,
and Beornoth picked a plain shield without a leather cover over
the bare wood. He slipped his left hand through the rope which
would hold tight against his forearm and grabbed the smooth
timber grip which spanned the empty bowl behind the boss.

'Are you ready?' asked the ealdorman, and held his shield
before him, forearm tight against the back of the shield and his
left shoulder leaning down into it. He swung the spear around to
rest upon the iron rim of the shield, on its upper edge, and

crouched, poised, and ready to fight. His form was perfect, and the huge ealdorman smiled.

'Aye.' Beornoth set himself in the same position as the ealdorman, and the two warriors circled each other.

'Did you visit Ealdorman Leofric?' As he spoke, Byrhtnoth lunged with his spear, whip fast like a serpent, and the tip banged into Beornoth's shield. Beornoth leaned away just in time to avoid the iron shield rim hitting him in the nose. Byrhtnoth laughed, and Beornoth circled him.

'I did. He is dying, lord. Sorry to be the one to tell you. I know you are old friends.'

Byrhtnoth lowered his shield, and his face dropped at the news. Sadness washed over him like the incoming tide. 'Is he bad?'

'He is shrunken and shrivelled, lord. Priests watch over him, keeping him alive. Running his shire.'

Byrhtnoth growled and lunged with his spear again. This time, Beornoth caught it on his shield boss, turning the blow and bringing his own weapon overhand so that it hissed past the ealdorman's face. They broke apart and circled again. 'So Leofric's archbishop rules East Anglia?'

'Yes, lord.'

'And they won't fight?'

'No, lord. I fear the archbishop and his priests are being paid by Forkbeard to keep the warriors of East Anglia in their burhs.'

Byrhtnoth came on again, jabbing his spear overhand and underhand. Beornoth blocked the strikes with his shield and swerved around others. The ealdorman raised his shield too high as he lunged underhand, and Beornoth stepped around the blow and brought his own spear under Byrhtnoth's shield so that the ealdorman had to leap away before Beornoth's spear struck his groin. 'You almost had me there. So, there is little hope in East Anglia?'

'The ealdorman's son, Wictred. He might rouse the warriors of East Anglia, if you call for him. I told him we would, and if he didn't bring his blades to answer the call, that I would return.'

'Good. I will send for him. They must fight. We will need an army to fight off Olaf, and even more men if Forkbeard rouses himself from his lair. The king will send his men of Wessex. He has gone to rouse them before summer begins.'

Beornoth launched himself at the ealdorman, and they exchanged a flurry of attacks and blocks. Spears went high and low, and they swung heavy shields in defence as if they were as light as apples. But Beornoth's shoulders burned from the exertion, and sweat sprang out upon his brow. They both slipped each other's lunge, and their shields came together in a crash which echoed around the rafters. Beornoth pushed, and Byrhtnoth did the same. They were both big men, seasoned fighters, the finest warriors in Saxon England. Beornoth shoved hard, putting his shoulder into it, and Byrhtnoth matched him. The ealdorman bared his teeth and veins stood out amongst the corded muscle of his neck above the like of his chain-mail byrnie. Beornoth thought of stabbing his spear into the ealdorman's boot, or dropping the spear to grab the bottom rim of Byrhtnoth's shield to tilt it and smash his face with the upper rim. But it was just practice, so Beornoth broke off and danced away, raising his spear to salute the ealdorman, who was every inch his match, but for the savagery which bubbled in Beornoth's chest like a boiling pot, contained for now, but always simmering.

Clapping from the barn's entrance surprised Beornoth, and he turned to see Aelfwine and Wulfhere. Behind them were Leofsunu, Godric, Thered and the rest of the ealdorman's hearth troop.

'A fine display,' said Aelfwine, clapping his fist to his breast in salute.

Beornoth placed his shield back on the rack, leaning against the barn wall, and wiped the sweat from his brow on the palm of his hand. He had enjoyed sparring with the ealdorman. They were well matched. Despite his age, Byrhtnoth moved well. He had bull strength in his shield arm and there was speed and power in his spear work. Byrhtnoth smiled broadly and clapped Beornoth on the shoulder before returning his own shield.

'Good,' said the ealdorman, planting his spear butt on the ground. 'I am glad you are all here. Come in.' The warriors filed in, some coughing and yawning as they cuffed the sleep from their eyes. Boots were heavy on the hard-packed earth, and each of them wore hard-baked leather breastplates or mail byrnies. They were the warriors of Essex, each man a thegn or a sworn man of a thegn. Professional warriors bred to the blade and oath-bound to the ealdorman of the East Saxons. 'Winter is over. Birds return from their distant nests and our crops reborn. Soon there will be lambs and calves in the fields, and our enemies sharpen their swords and axes. As you know, we fought hard last year, but our enemies remain around us. They are like wolves prowling on the edges of a dark forest, their shining eyes hungrily watching the flocks, waiting for the shepherd to turn his back or neglect his duty. Danes are in East Anglia, and Norsemen are in Folkestone. They are not here to trade. They are here to kill, steal and rape. It falls to us to stop them, for we are the Viking hunters. The killers of those whom other men fear to fight.' Byrhtnoth's voice filled the barn, and the warriors' faces became stern, their jaws set and eyes fixed on their warlord.

'Will we have aid in this fight, lord?' asked Aelfwine.

Byrhtnoth levelled his spear and slowly moved its point along his gathered warriors. 'Offa, take three men and ride for

Winchester. The king has promised to send the blades of Wessex
to join us in our fight against the Vikings. Tell him what we know,
that Forkbeard enriches himself with Saxon silver. He produces
coin with Æthelred's very face on to send back to his home in the
hard north. That Olaf Tryggvason and his dread Jomsvikings
loiter in Folkestone like a nest of vipers. Tell the king that Forkbeard rests unopposed because the ealdorman of East Anglia, my
old friend Leofric, rots on his deathbed. Offa, bring those
warriors and meet us at the stone circle west of the Jotunwood.
The forest there will provide shelter whilst we muster our forces.'

'Yes, lord,' barked Offa. 'I will ride this very day.'

'Aelfwine, you will return to East Anglia and summon
Wictred, son of Leofric, to bring his warriors. He is to fetch them
to the stone circle, and wait for you there.'

'Yes, lord,' said Aelfwine. 'And what if Wictred will not
summon his men?'

'Then return to me, and we shall inform the king.'

'What about the fyrd?' asked Godric, striding to stand before
the warriors, his hand on his sword hilt chased with golden wire.

'We will leave the men of the shire for now. They must
prepare their fields for the year ahead. We will need the fruits of
their labour to sustain us if it comes to open war. Summoning the
fyrd is a last measure. If it comes to a pitched battle, then we shall
need their numbers, but not yet.'

'We shall crush these cursed Vikings, lord,' Godric said, and
he shook his fist in the air. 'I swear that my brothers and I shall
fight to our last drop of blood.'

'All here are Bloodsworn,' said Aelfwine. He drew his sword
and held it aloft, striding in front of the hearth troop. 'We all
made the cut on our flesh and swore in our blood to fight for
Byrhtnoth and not to rest until our lands are free of the Viking
scourge. We are blood brothers, bound by that oath to give our

lives for our people and for our lord ealdorman. Are we ready to honour that oath?'

'Aye! Aye! Aye!' the warriors bellowed, each man drawing sword, seax or axe and hoisting them aloft.

'We are the Viking killers. They fear us. We have Beornoth, Byrhtnoth, Wulfhere and Leofsunu. We have Offa, Maccus, Aelfhere and Wulfmaer. Think of the warriors we lost last year to Viking blades, like the mighty Wulfstan cut down in his war glory. What men would stand us against and not tremble? It falls to us to throw the sea wolves back into the surging sea. They will taste our steel and regret bringing their sleek-hulled ships to our shores. Are we the Viking hunters?'

'Aye! Aye! Aye!'

They were red-faced and wide-eyed. Aelfwine had roused the men to the same passion they had shown last summer in an East Saxon hall when each man had cut his hand with a blade and took that solemn oath in blood. Beornoth himself had made it, and intended to keep it. Few knew better than he the horror Vikings would wreak upon the land if they broke out from their winter quarters. Beornoth reached a hand behind his byrnie and pulled free the smooth wooden locket hanging from his neck. He rubbed his thumb over the soft timber, warm from resting against his flesh. Inside that tiny wooden tomb were golden locks of hair cut from the heads of his dead daughters, Ashwig and Cwen. His tiny girls, his joy. He had found them shrivelled and charred in the ash of his burned hall. Their blackened hands holding one another in terror as they died in the flames. Vikings had come to his home in the north, and Beornoth had been away at war. Those raiders had killed his children and laid hands on his wife. Her attackers had cut her throat, but Eawynn had survived. Her body had survived, but her love, her laughter and her soul had burned with their girls and lay buried beneath the cold earth in

Cheshire. The Vikings must be stopped. Beornoth knew the men in Byrhtnoth's barn would fight, that they would stand in the shield wall and trade blows with the savage men who brought axe and murder across the sea on their dragon ships. He had stood with them, bled with them, and killed with them. Those sworn in blood to rid the land of Vikings, and they needed to fight again if the folk of Essex and East Anglia were to sleep safely in their beds, and their children were to survive the summer.

The Bloodsworn clasped forearms and slapped one another on the back. They spoke of the men they would kill and the deeds they would perform, but Beornoth moved away, memories too heavy upon him to join in their boasting, although he knew it was part of being a warrior. A man needed pride and arrogance to live a life by the blade, to risk his life. He did it for reputation and glory, and to honour his ancestors. Beornoth found Offa stood with his back to the men, casting his eye over the line of finely crafted spears.

'So you will go to bring us an army?' said Beornoth.

'Dark times,' Offa replied. His lined face split with a wan smile. 'War is for the young, Beo. A decade ago, you and I would boast with the rest of them, swearing oaths and promising great deeds.'

'Many will die this year, before it's over. And even then, we may not have enough men to defeat Olaf and Sweyn.'

'The men of Wessex will come. And Byrhtnoth will rouse East Anglia. We can win.'

'Beornoth,' the ealdorman shouted across the barn, his arm raised and gesturing for Beornoth to approach. Alongside him was a small man, in a dark cloak stained from travel. The man's face was drawn and his eyes flicked around the warriors nervously. The hairs on the back of Beornoth's neck rose, and he marched briskly through the crowd until he came before Byrhtnoth.

'Yes, lord?' he said.

The ealdorman ran his hand along the silver spade of his beard and shook his head. 'Olaf has set his wolves loose in the shire. The Jomsvikings have attacked towns and villages across the south of Essex.'

'Then it has begun,' said Beornoth, and his stomach turned over with fear. 'I must ride for Branoc's Tree, lord.'

'Go, take your hearth troop. Thered can remain here with me. Remember, though, we muster at the Jotunwood. Help the people, Beornoth.'

8

Beornoth rode with Wulfhere at this shoulder, knuckles white on Hríð's leather reins. Hoof beats drummed in his head like a war drum, and the icy fist of fear clenched around his heart. Cwicca, Kari, Maccus, Aelfhere and the rest of his hearth troop raced behind them in a bowshot of horsemen arcing across a country-side blossoming with fresh greens and yellows after the grim darkness of winter. It was traditionally a time of hope for the people of Saxon England, of ploughing, planting and rebirth, but this year the Vikings had come with blades and savagery to wash the shire in terror. Beornoth cantered with eyes fixed upon the horizon, scanning for columns of smoke, the familiar signal of Viking raiding and burning, but there were only still clouds above a grey-blue sky. He resisted the gnawing urge to push Hríð too hard. The huge warhorse could canter for twenty furlongs before he would need to rest, so Beornoth kept him moving below that pace. A blown horse would not get him home faster. He wanted to race to Branoc's Tree, to charge across the hills and dales of Essex and get to Eawynn and his people, because the hatchet-hard face of Olaf Tryggvason seared into his mind's eye like a red-hot iron brand. The leader of the Norsemen hated Beornoth for killing Palnatoki, the man whom he had loved like a father. Olaf had once threatened to bring his Jomsvikings to Beornoth's lands, and that was a thought to keep a man awake at night and chill his heart with fear.

Beornoth's war band rode through a shallow ford, Hríð's hooves kicking up spume along a boundary hedge which separated the lands at Fox Hollow from Gytha's Dun. These were familiar lands, close to home, where the simple folk lived and farmed and loved their families. These were the people living under Beornoth's protection, whom his oath to Byrhtnoth demanded that he keep safe. His sword was all that kept them from the wicked men, the vicious ones who would come and try to take everything from them with violence and pain.

'Smoke,' called Kari as they urged their mounts up a heather-dusted rise, and Beornoth's heart stopped.

'Where?' he growled, squinting at the land ahead. Along a soil-brown hill, treetops not yet thick with leaves covered a shallow banked valley. The myriad branches clawed at the sky like the fingers of a skeleton bursting from the earth. But Beornoth could see no tendrils of smoke, no signal of Viking destruction.

Kari clicked his tongue and urged his roan mare alongside Beornoth, and pointed between where a sloping field met a clutch of pines above a tilled patch of farmland. 'There, lord.'

'I see it,' growled Wulfhere. 'That's close to home. If they have hurt Aethelberga, I'll...' The big man didn't finish his sentence. His hand fell to the axe haft sheathed in his saddle and a frown creased his brow and wrinkled the top of his bald head.

'On me,' Beornoth said, and he pushed Hríð into a canter. Fear curdled in his belly and his head rang like a church bell. No man had felt the pain and suffering of Viking raids more than he had. The screaming women and dead children, the black ash of burned homes and pale-white bodies cut and slashed with cold, pitiless blades. Beornoth rode with his jaw set firm. He had left warriors at Branoc's Tree and the burh was in good repair. Its palisade was strong and its ditch deep. But it would not be enough if the Jomsvikings came.

An elderly man and woman shuffled along a ragged line of briar, their faces anxious. The old man tugged along a goat, and when he saw the riders, he pointed a bony finger towards the ominous tendrils of smoke. Beornoth rode up along the row of thorns to the crest of a high pasture, and the sound of a war horn rang clear and true across the countryside as though sounded by one of the land's ancient spirits.

'God help us,' Wulfhere said, horror forcing his eyes wide and his lips away from his teeth. They paused in the pasture, and time stood still. A swarm of men clad in leather, furs and ring-mail byrnies flowed around the palisade and gate of Branoc's Tree like rats on a dying animal. Bile rose in Beornoth's stomach and he leant over his saddle to vomit. His worst fear unfolded before his eyes. Viking raiders were amongst his people. Eawynn was in there, and he had sworn to protect her. His love, his wife. She who had already felt the wrath and pain of a Viking assault once before. Beornoth tugged a war axe free of its sheath at his saddle and shifted the shield strapped to his back. He untied the helmet from its fastening next to the axe and pushed it onto his head. The iron of its eye rings sat cold against his face and Beornoth flexed his hand upon the smooth haft of his axe.

'They are inside the walls,' said Kari, the words coming in a ragged whisper.

Beornoth dug his heels into Hríð's flanks and pushed the warhorse into a gallop. The wind rushed past his face, making his eyes water, and Beornoth rode with teeth bared and his axe levelled. There were over one hundred Vikings attacking Branoc's Tree, and Beornoth found himself hopelessly outnumbered with his force of ten riders, but he had to get to Eawynn. The fear inside Beornoth broiled and bubbled and became a white-hot rage, the rage of a man who has seen his children burned and his wife raped. The fury of a Saxon thegn. He thundered down the hill towards Branoc's Tree, giving the mighty warhorse his head. Hríð pounded the earth, his white mane flowing like a snowstorm and his magnificent head rising and falling in time with his powerful gait.

'Please God, let Aethelberga be safe,' Wulfhere said somewhere behind Beornoth. God had deserted Beornoth and his family years ago, and since then Beornoth had looked upon God, Jesus and Holy Mary with disdain, sure that his own soul was lost and his God had thrown him to the wolves. But for a fleeting moment, in the time it took Hríð's forelegs to leave the hillside and rake the air, Beornoth closed his eyes and prayed to Holy Mary, to God and Jesus. Despite the years spent cursing God, certain that he was outside the Lord's embrace, Beornoth searched for hope amongst the horror unfolding before him. He asked God to aid Eawynn, who had led a good and noble life. She had seen enough suffering, he pleaded, and had always prayed to and loved her Lord God. *Just keep her safe until I can get to her, Lord God, I beg you. Grant me this one thing and I will be forever worshipful to you and your Church.* Hríð's forelegs hammered into the heather and Beornoth snapped his eyes open. Ten Viking warriors, hearing the thunder of hoof beats, turned to meet Beornoth's charge. They scampered in front of the gate, bringing shields and spears to make a shield wall. A rider on a smoke-grey stallion barked orders at them, waving a bright sword whose blade caught the sunlight. Beornoth recognised the cruel lines and sharp face of Olaf Tryggvason, the Norse warlord who had brought fifty

ships of Viking warriors to plague England and make for himself
a reputation and a fortune. Next to Olaf was a man in a red cloak,
a man whose muscled arms lay bare within a fish-scale coat of
armour which shimmered like a monster from beneath the
Whale Road. The man had bone-white hair, and he sawed on the
reins of his gelding to bring the beast about, roaring orders in
guttural Norse.

'Be brave, my friend,' Beornoth said to Hríð, leaning forward
so that the horse could hear him above the din of the gallop. 'Use
your strength today, help the people of Branoc's Tree, help me get
to Eawynn, mighty warrior that you are.'

The Vikings dashed to huddle together and bring their
shields up, which was the right thing to do. A horse will not
charge a solid shield wall, and the men would bar entry to the
burh, meaning that Beornoth would need to fight his way in. But
Hríð was fast, and a burly man wearing a dented helmet stared at
the monstrous white stallion with wide eyes. Beornoth swung his
axe around in a wide circle, and before the Vikings could make a
complete shield wall, Hríð smashed into them with a bone-
breaking crunch like the sound of a ship driving on to rocks in a
North Sea storm. Beornoth grunted and kept tight hold of his axe
as the swing brought the bright axe head around to cut into the
dented-helmeted man's chest. There was resistance as the honed
blade carved through leather armour, flesh and bone. It tugged at
Beornoth's shoulder and then came free to leave a ragged Norse
corpse to dung Saxon soil, and the iron tang of blood filled the
air. It mixed with the screams of the dying Vikings as Hríð scattered the unmade shield wall without breaking stride. Wulfhere
howled his war cry and the clash of blade on blade, and the
crunch of shield boards, rang out across Branoc's Tree.

Beornoth glanced at Olaf and his white-haired companion,
and both sprang their horses into action, shouting orders at the

warriors to pursue and kill Beornoth. He ducked low against Hríð's neck as the warhorse pounded through the open gate, and Beornoth's eyes filled with the unfolding carnage within the walls of his home. Vikings attacked his people in groups. Fur-draped Norsemen dragged screaming women through the mud and hacked at the men who tried to protect them. The noise of it was a feral thing, the worst side of men which came to the fore whenever warriors sacked a town. A wild, sadistic fury, which lowered men below the beasts in the ditch; that terrible ferocity which is peculiar to man. Preying on one's own kind, raping and slaughtering for enrichment and gratification. But Beornoth had arrived at Branoc's Tree and he drove Hríð hard towards a group of six Vikings who dragged a milking maid by the hair. They turned at the sound of his approach, and Beornoth swung his axe in a low arc and it scythed the head from a flaxen-haired warrior, sending it spinning through the air in a spray of blood. Hríð reared on his hind legs, and Beornoth clung to the beast with his knees and his left hand wrapped tight in the cracked leather reins. Hríð's hooves beat into the chest of a falling Viking, crushing him into pulp, and the warhorse snapped his teeth at the face of a snarling warrior and ripped his nose away to leave the Viking with nothing but gore and filth for a head. Beornoth parried a spear thrust with his axe and then brought the weapon down overhand to slam its blade into the top of his attacker's skull. The weapon clove through the man's helmet and split his skull open to kill the Norseman instantly. Blood splashed across Hríð's pale white flanks and flecks of it were in Beornoth's beard. He tugged the axe haft, but the blade became snagged in the gore of the dead man's neck so Beornoth let it fall with the corpse. He sawed on Hríð's reins so that the horse turned towards his hall and dragged his sword free from its scabbard.

Wulfhere thundered past Beornoth and launched his spear

overhand. The weapon flew across the courtyard to slam into a
Viking's chest, throwing the warrior from his feet. Wulfhere drew
his own axe and charged at a clutch of Norsemen busy hacking at
a thin Saxon in a worn woollen jerkin who tried desperately to
protect himself with a shovel, his body already carved with red
wounds. Wulfhere reached the Vikings and laid about him with
the axe, bellowing for Aethelberga, desperate to find his love
before the Vikings could lay hands upon her. Beornoth charged
at the largest group of Norsemen, twenty men pushing and
shoving each other before his hall, desperate to get inside the
burh's main building. The hall drew Vikings like flies to shit, for
that was where they expected to find silver, coins, plate, candlesticks and jewellery. Beornoth held his sword low and barrelled
Hríð into the rear of the bunched Vikings. The monstrous horse
tore into them, throwing bodies to the earth and trampling them
with his powerful legs. He snapped his teeth at faces and ears and
the Vikings fell away from the warhorse's terror. Beornoth
stabbed the point of his sword into the neck of a turning warrior
and sawed the blade free to wash the man's leather breastplate in
dark blood. He felt a blow strike the shield on his back with a dull
thud and swung his blade over his left shoulder to strike its edge
into the arm of an axe-wielding Norseman.

The Vikings recovered from the initial surprise of the
warhorse milling into their ranks and turned on Beornoth, blades
bright and deadly in the sunlight. They came for him, and
Beornoth feared for Hríð's life, so he kicked his feet free of the
stirrups and leapt to the ground. He slapped Hríð's rump to send
the beast running clear and parried a spear thrust with his sword
blade. Beornoth punched the attacker in his bearded face with
his left hand and drew the man close. The Viking spat and cursed
through his bush of brown beard, dark eyes beneath a cliff of a
frown and rotten teeth bared. Beornoth held the man close like a

lover and turned in a circle to use the man's body to deflect the blows of his enemies as he slid his shield from his back. An axe blade meant for Beornoth cracked into the Viking's skull, shaving the top corner from his head, and Beornoth let him fall. He brought his heavy shield to bear, slamming its iron boss into one man's face, and then the iron rim into the underside of another's chin.

Beornoth drove forwards, crouching behind his shield and deflecting unseen blows on the linden-wood boards. He clenched his teeth and hacked blindly with his sword, feeling it strike iron and bone alike. Blows thudded on to his back, but the rings of his byrnie mail coat held firm. Beornoth growled and fought his way to the doors of his hall, certain that Eawynn would be inside. She would have locked herself in her rooms, he was sure of it. A huge hand curled around his shield and ripped it wide, revealing a warrior as tall and broad as Beornoth himself and with a fine byrnie and arms thick with warrior rings. He smiled mirthlessly at Beornoth and raised his axe to strike, but Beornoth lunged forwards and crashed his helmeted forehead into the warrior's face and then drove his knee into his groin. The mailed warrior howled in pain and then an axe slammed into the back of his neck and Wulfhere kicked the corpse free of his weapon.

'Shield wall in front of the hall,' Beornoth shouted as more of his oathmen joined Wulfhere to stab and slash at the Vikings. Beornoth raised his shield and turned towards the courtyard where Olaf and his white-haired captain rode through the gate and called to their men, to rally a force drunk on pillage and slaughter. 'We don't have long,' said Beornoth. 'Wulfhere, inside with me. The rest of you hold them there. Once we come out, we run.'

'Yes, lord,' said Cwicca from behind his shield.

Beornoth turned and stepped over a fallen Viking, writhing

upon the timbers beneath the hall doors, and he stamped his boot down on the injured man's throat to crunch his windpipe to ruin. Beornoth strode into the gloom of his hall with his shield at his side and his sword raised. His eyes adjusted to the change from the sunlit courtyard into the shadowy gloom of his hall. Bodies shifted in the darkness, and the flame-red glow of the always lit hall fire glinted off steel.

'Aethelberga!' came a cry. It was a terrible sound. It came from the depths of Wulfhere's soul and the big warrior sank to his knees three paces in front of Beornoth with his hands held aloft as though beseeching God to remove his pain. Beornoth followed his friend's gaze to where a limp body hung from the rafters, dangling from its neck and turning slowly on a rope. As the body came around, Beornoth recognised it as Aethelberga and he roared in pain at his loss. Her face was purple and bruised, her dress torn and bloody where hungry hands had torn at her and used her before hanging her in the hall she called home.

'Bastards,' Beornoth hissed, and he charged forwards at three warriors who knelt digging beneath his high table with their blades, searching for hidden treasure. They rose at the awful keening of Wulfhere's pain, but it was too late. Beornoth slammed the iron rim of his shield's bottom into the first crouching Viking's face, crushing his eye sockets and driving his skull into the hard-packed earthen floor. He drove the point of his sword into the chest of the second warrior and pushed the man backwards on the end of the blade as bubbles of blood frothed at his mouth. He back-cut the blade across the throat of the third man as he tried to rise and then drove the point into the writhing man's belly. Beornoth yanked his sword free and swung it high to cut through the rope at the rafters. Aethelberga fell to the floor and Beornoth knelt next to her. He lay his sword down and placed his rough hand on her swollen face. Her loss was like a knife in his heart and he closed her open, bulging, dead eyes with his fingers.

'She's gone, Wulfhere,' Beornoth said. 'Avenge her, help Cwicca hold the door and kill as many as you can.'

Beornoth picked up his sword and ran across the hall towards the small door at the rear, which led to his and Eawynn's living chambers. A shaven-headed Viking appeared in the doorway. He held a bloodstained axe in one hand and a jug of ale in the other. He saw Beornoth approaching and swung his axe at Beornoth, who took the blow on his shield, the thud of it jarring up his arm. Beornoth jabbed his sword blade at the warrior's legs, but he danced away from the blow and tore his axe free of the shield. He was quick and lithe and he crashed the jug of ale into Beornoth's head, but it smashed on the iron helmet to spill frothy ale over Beornoth's byrnie. Beornoth lunged the tip of his sword at the Viking's chest, but he batted the blade away with the haft of his axe and kicked Beornoth's shield savagely so that it drove Beornoth backwards. The Norseman let out a roar of defiance and swung his axe in two hands at Beornoth, and he had to crouch behind his shield to avoid the powerful blow. The axe slammed into Beornoth's shield, the tip of the bearded blade punching through the boards to land a finger's breadth from Beornoth's face. He wrenched at his shield, but the axe was stuck in the boards, so Beornoth simply let go of his shield and rose to his full height. The Viking tried to lift his axe with a snarl on his face, but the fallen shield made it too heavy to lift and Beornoth drove the tip of his sword into the man's belly and put his left hand around the Viking's throat. He winced and clenched his teeth in pain and Beornoth drove him backwards along the dark corridor which linked the hall to the living quarters. The Viking thrashed on the end of the blade like a landed fish and Beornoth twisted his sword in the man's guts as he ran forwards.

'Eawynn!' Beornoth roared, the sound of his voice bouncing from the walls like the roar of a bear.

'Beo,' came a shriek in response, and Beornoth was overcome with rage.

It was Eawynn, and the Vikings had found her.

9

Beornoth froze with terror and the Viking slid off his sword with a wet sucking sound as the blade pulled clear of his stomach in a rush of fiery blood. It flowed down the sword's fuller and over Beornoth's hand, and he watched the twisted look of hate and pain on the dying Viking's face in a moment that lasted only two or three heartbeats, but it felt like an eternity. Eawynn's cry for help stunned Beornoth, the emotions of it overwhelming. She needed him, just as she had once before. That dark day, Beornoth had not been there for Eawynn and his children. He had almost missed that need again, but he was here now, and he locked eyes with the dying Viking. For a fleeting moment Beornoth wondered why things were not different, why the Norsemen did not stay at home and till their own fields, why it was necessary for life to be filled with so much pain, blood and suffering.

'Beo, please!' Eawynn cried again, and it hit Beornoth like a hammer blow to the skull. He snarled and slammed the rounded pommel of his sword into the dying Viking's nose and stepped over his corpse. War was constant. Beornoth's life was a long tale of death and brutal men who came looking for wealth, violence and reputation, and Beornoth was a killer and a protector of his people. He ran along the corridor, dark and without windows, and his heavy boots crunched on the hard-packed earthen floor. Beornoth's men fought outside the hall doors, outnumbered by the raiders. Beornoth ran along the hall until he came to the age-darkened oak doors of the bedroom chambers. Eawynn's was closed and, before it, a serving man lay curled in a ball. Blood soaked his jerkin and his face, and his killer had slashed his arms and body with terrible wounds, which told the tale of how the brave man had tried to defend Eawynn's door. She was inside, and the door was closed, which meant one or more of the Norse raiders were in there with her. Beornoth did not break stride, and he smashed his mailed shoulder into the thick timber and it crashed open under his weight.

Beornoth stumbled into the room, following the door as it smashed open on its iron hinges. His eyes squinted, adjusting to the bright shaft of light bursting in through the open window shutters. Four Viking warriors stared at him, leering mouths in thick beards, faces dropping with the shock of Beornoth's sudden, violent entry. Their hungry eyes flickered across the Saxon thegn, taking in his height and breadth, his blood-drenched sword and his eye-ringed helmet which covered the top half of his face. They saw a lord of war, a huge Saxon warrior clad in a byrnie mail coat and armed for the fight. They had closed the door to Eawynn's chamber, thinking to take her for themselves without interruption, but she stood quaking by the window. The sun shone in her auburn hair and her face quivered in terror. She clutched a dagger in her two pale hands, its blade reddened where she had fended off her attackers. Beornoth roared at the men who had tried to hurt his love, his wife. His war cry shook the very timbers of the room and every fibre in his body tensed for vengeance. Muscles built across a lifetime of hefting heavy sword, shield, axe and spear bunched, and the Vikings came for him.

The room was too small to swing a sword, so Beornoth reversed his grip on the blade and leapt towards the closest attacker, stabbing the point down into the man's boot to pin his foot to the floor. Without breaking his momentum, Beornoth grabbed the warrior's wrist above where he held a short-hafted axe and punched the Norseman full in the face. In the stunned quiet of the room, the warrior's face cracked and crunched under Beornoth's fist as he crumpled to the floor. Beornoth whipped the seax free from where it hung in a scabbard from two thongs at the rear of his belt. A second warrior came at Beornoth. He, too, clutched an axe and went to swing it overhand, but the blade crashed into the chamber's low roof timbers, fouling the attack. Beornoth crouched and came up low with his seax held in an underhand grip. He punched the tip of the weapon through the Norseman's leather breastplate and rose to his full height, lifting the Viking from the ground so that the seax pushed into the man's gut all the way to the hilt. Beornoth bellowed in his face and threw the warrior across the room to crash into the far wall.

A red-bearded Viking came at Beornoth, cursing and stabbing with a knife. He bore cuts on his arms where Eawynn had slashed at him, and once Beornoth saw those marks, his fury became unbounded. This was a man who had tried to lay hands on his wife, and Beornoth lost himself in his rage. He batted a knife thrust aside with his forearm and surged forward, slicing his gore-drenched seax across the warrior's thighs. Beornoth reached out with his free hand and grabbed a fistful of the Viking's flame-coloured hair at the rear of his skull and pulled the man into a vicious headbutt. The iron of his helmet crunched into the Viking's eye socket with a sickening crack and Beornoth butted him again, four times in quick succession so that his face turned to a bloody pulp. He pulled the warrior's head backwards and shoved the wicked point of his seax into the soft flesh under his chin and drove the blade upwards until it scraped against the top of his skull. Blood flowed down Beornoth's arm like a river and he watched the Viking's eyes as life poured out of him. He felt no pity. This man would have raped and slaughtered Eawynn without a second thought, so Beornoth ripped the life from him with brutal efficiency.

The red-bearded warrior slumped to the ground, dead, and Beornoth turned to the final Viking. He was a young man, tall with wheat-golden hair and a wispy beard. He drove himself back against the far wall and licked at dry lips.

'Please, lord,' he stuttered in Norse. 'I wouldn't have hurt her. That man was my uncle. Please, lord.' He pointed to the dead warrior with the red hair. Beornoth stalked across the small room. He lifted the bed with his left hand and tossed it out of his way as though it were a weightless twig. The young warrior closed his eyes and clutched at a small silver hammer amulet hanging round his neck and whispered a prayer to Thor. Beornoth felt no pity for the lad. He would have taken his turn with Eawynn, and ripped her life away with the approval of his uncle. So Beornoth swept up his seax and drove it hard into the side of the Viking's head. The blade slammed through bone, brain and blood, killing the young warrior instantly and pinning his head to a timber wall stud.

Beornoth turned to Eawynn, and she ran into his arms. He brought her into his embrace, and she nestled her head into his mailed chest. Beornoth stroked her soft hair, the blood on his hands streaking in it. Warmth and relief flooded him.

'Thank God you came,' she said. 'I feared...' She shook her head and sobbed. 'Aethelberga, the others?' Eawynn asked, tipping her tear-strewn face to search Beornoth's eyes.

He shook his head. 'We must go before they kill us all.' He ripped his seax free of the young Viking's head, so that the lad's corpse slumped to the floor, pumping black blood onto the floor rushes. Beornoth held her small hand in his own and pulled his sword from where it stuck still in the foot of the fallen Viking. Beornoth pulled it free, stabbed the tip into the fallen man's gullet to make sure he was dead and ducked under the door lintel. They strode along the corridor and back into the hall. Beornoth recovered his shield and slung it across his back. The long feasting benches were empty, and the fire crackled and spluttered with nobody to feed it. Eawynn wept when she saw Aethelberga's corpse, and Beornoth pulled her close, walking with his arm around her shoulders. The clash of warriors clanged beyond the door and Beornoth steeled himself to it, because beyond it, where the light danced in through the shadows between the movement of the men who fought beyond, was Olaf Tryggvason and his murderous Viking warriors.

'Stay close to me,' said Beornoth, and Eawynn passed her arm around his hip, clinging to him. They emerged from the doorway into the daylight, where his men fought for their lives in Branoc's Tree's courtyard. Cwicca held his shield firm with four others in a tight half-circle with Wulfhere at the centre. The huge warrior fought with an axe in each hand, unshielded and without a care for his own safety. He hacked and slashed at the shields of the Vikings, who came on. Wulfhere drove them back, the Vikings afraid of his wrath. Wulfhere howled as he fought, the high-pitched keening of a madman, lost in the wrathful grief of Aethel-berga's death. The Vikings came at Beornoth's men in ones and twos, testing their bravery in front of their shipmates, but not assaulting the feeble Saxon shield wall with their greater numbers. The greater Viking force massed beyond the battle line, where Olaf sat atop his horse, arms crossed and leaning on the pommel, enjoying the entertainment.

'Cwicca,' Beornoth called, and the young warrior turned to him, face drawn and pale from the exertion of battle.

'Thank God the lady is safe, lord,' Cwicca said, his head turning back to the Vikings and then returning his gaze to Beornoth. 'Bastards are toying with us, lord. They could have killed us all by now.'

Beornoth slipped Eawynn's arm from his hip and unslung his shield. She shook her head, and he smiled at her. She was ever beautiful, ever gentle. He remembered how she used to laugh, what a wonderful mother she had been to their children. He would die to protect her, but better to get Eawynn to safety, if possible, and get her out of the horror of Branoc's Tree. Beornoth swallowed with a dry throat. Escape seemed impossible. Warriors surrounded Olaf. Vikings filled Branoc's Tree and more swirled beyond the walls. Olaf was enjoying his revenge for Palnatoki's death.

'Cwicca,' Beornoth shouted above the tumult of battle. 'Stay with Eawynn. I will take your place in the line.' Cwicca nodded and wiped the sweat from his brow on the back of his arm. Beornoth forced his way into the small shield wall just as Wulfhere chopped his axe deep into a Viking's shield and sent the attacker reeling. Beornoth overlapped his shield with Maccus, the warrior next to him, and glared at Olaf through the eyeholes of his helmet. Olaf pointed at him and laughed. He leaned in the saddle to talk to the warrior with the white hair on the horse next to him. The warrior grinned and slipped from his saddle. He was tall and lean, with hair and eyebrows so white they were the colour of snow. He ambled forwards and the warriors facing Beornoth's men fell back.

'Your man here fights well,' said Olaf in Norse, gesturing at

Wulfhere. He shouted, smiling and staring at Beornoth. 'Let's see how he fares against the White Wolf.'

The white-haired warrior unclasped his red cloak and let it fall into the mud. He strolled towards Wulfhere, slowly drawing a sword from a red scabbard at his belt, and another from a scabbard strapped to his back. He stopped ten paces away from Wulfhere and began to twirl and swing the swords in a flowing pattern so fast that the blades became a blur. Sunlight flashed on the blades and the Vikings whooped for joy at the skill of their champion.

'Lower your shields,' Beornoth said. 'They won't attack us now. They want single combat.' Even though they stood next to each other, Wulfhere couldn't hear Beornoth. Aethelberga was dead, and her loss had broken Wulfhere's soul. He stood with his two axes raised; blood spattered his face and his chest heaved from the exertion of the fight. 'Wulfhere,' Beornoth repeated, but still the bald-headed warrior stared unwaveringly at the White Wolf's dazzling display of swordsmanship. Beornoth sheathed his sword and placed a hand on his friend's shoulder, and Wulfhere's face spun around to fix him with a wild-eyed stare. His lips pared back from his teeth like a snarling dog, and the wet lines of his tears ran through the blood and filth on his cheeks. 'I'll fight him, Wulfhere. You fall back with the others.'

'No,' said Wulfhere. He spoke in a hoarse growl, and Beornoth could tell from the fury in his eyes there would be no argument. Wulfhere wanted blood in payment for Aethelberga's death, and Beornoth would not stand in his way.

Wulfhere strode forwards hefting his two war axes. The White Wolf continued his display of sword twirling, approaching Wulfhere, spinning the twin blades around his shoulders and torso like a dancer. Wulfhere suddenly charged at the younger man, bellowing with rage and swinging both axes

over his head in a wild charge. Without a break in his sword
spinning, the White Wolf danced around Wulfhere, the blades
of his swords clanging as they deflected the Saxon's axe heads.
He turned and brought a sword around in a flashing low arc
aimed at Wulfhere's legs, but the big man anticipated the move
and stepped over the blow. The White Wolf kept moving and
drove the point of his second sword towards Wulfhere's chest,
and the big Saxon grunted as he blocked the attack with the
haft of his axe. The surrounding Vikings cheered for their
champion, and Beornoth worried for Wulfhere. His enemy was
skilled and Wulfhere was too angry to fight with sense.
Wulfhere tried to strike the Viking with the butt of his axe, but
he spun away and as he did so he rested a blade across his
shoulders and flicked the tip across Wulfhere's face and it
carved a slice of flesh from forehead to jaw. Wulfhere stumbled
and the White Wolf turned as quick as lightning and slashed
the edge of his other sword across Wulfhere's back. As Wulfhere
fell to his knees, Beornoth charged forward. Beornoth knew he
should not interfere with the ancient rules of single combat, but
he could not lose another friend that day. He barged the White
Wolf with his shield and sent the Viking flying backwards from
his feet.

'Enough,' Beornoth said, pointing his sword at Olaf. Cwicca
darted forward and dragged Wulfhere back towards the hall and
the line of Saxon shields. 'It's me you want. I'll fight your Wolf, or
you if you prefer.'

Olaf tossed his head back and laughed, and he raised a hand
to stop the White Wolf, who advanced upon Beornoth. 'Be care-
ful, Wolf,' he said. 'For this is the mighty Beornoth. Killer of
Skarde Wartooth and Palnatoki. Beornoth, I will allow you to live
today. I want you to contemplate what you have lost, what I have
taken from you. I want you to live knowing what my men would

have done to your woman, and what we have done to your people.'

'Bastard. Let's just get it over with now.'

'I don't think so. We have your horses ready, and you and your people can ride away. What's left of your people, anyway. We have killed most of them.' Olaf pointed to the great tree which stood at the centre of the courtyard, and which gave the burh its name. From the branches hung the bodies of the men, women and children of Branoc's Tree. Their bodies twisting slowly from the ropes around their necks. 'There is just one more thing, and then you can be on your way. Jomsvikings, forward.'

At Olaf's order, two lines of byrnie-clad Jomsvikings marched forward, flanking his horse in perfect order. Each warrior's left foot and then right foot stomping the Saxon soil in time, their spears levelled at exactly the same angle pointing towards the sky like a moving forest. They came to a halt in the courtyard between Beornoth and the White Wolf, and each man called out a guttural shout in unison.

'See, Beornoth?' said Olaf. 'This work of raiding is not fit for Jomsviking warriors. This is the work for the raiding crews, for the hungry men who have come here for plunder, and for the thrill of the hunt. We keep our blades clean for war, for the shield wall, for true battle. There is just one more thing you must see before I let you go.'

A warrior in a shining helmet with an eagle's feather at the crest dragged forward a cowed figure. It was a Saxon warrior with a wounded shoulder. Beornoth's shoulders sank when he realised the man was young Kari. A lad who had begun as part of Beornoth's household troops, his friend even. The warrior shoved Kari into the dirt and the White Wolf grabbed Kari by the hair and hauled him to his knees.

'This pup is one of yours, I believe?' said Olaf. 'Remember his tears when you scuttle off to your ealdorman, remember his blood and that of these others when you glory in how you have killed Palnatoki and my warriors.' He nodded, and the White Wolf raised a sword and nestled the point in the gap between Kari's neck and shoulder.

'Please, no,' Kari said, sobbing. His entire body shook, and he nodded his head, hand clenched before him in prayer. A dark patch stained the crotch of his trews. 'Beornoth, lord. Please help me.'

Beornoth shuddered with impotent rage, his heart urged him to charge forward and hack into the enemy, to kill and wound and get Kari to safety. But he could not, there could be no rescue, no way back for Kari.

The White Wolf laughed, and with two hands he forced the sword through Kari's neck, chest and body, grimacing and pushing until he buried it to the hilt. Kari quivered, coughed blood, and died.

'See how he begged? Dying like a screaming pig? You Saxons disgust me, your god makes you weak. Bring their horses,' said Olaf.

Beornoth's shoulders burned, and there was a catch in his throat. He was tired, wracked with sorrow for those who had died, those he was supposed to protect. He hadn't the energy to retort to Olaf. The Norseman gloried in his victory, just as he promised he would. Vikings brought Hríð and a mount for each of Beornoth's surviving men. They mounted in silence, Eawynn taking a dappled mare, and Wulfhere slumped over the saddle of a gelding.

'Go, Beornoth,' said Olaf. 'I allow you to live. War is coming. Not gentle like before, but hard and painful. We come for your land, your wealth, and for glory. We shall meet again in the shield wall, Beornoth. Tell your warriors and your king to bring your army to me. The ravens are hungry.'

Only seven riders left Branoc's Tree and Olaf Tryggvason's slaughter. The innocent folk, the women and children all dead. Beornoth, Eawynn, Wulfhere and four warriors left through the gate, riding through the baleful and sneering Viking eyes, Beornoth saw a familiar face. A man with a golden beard and a raven tattoo upon his neck. It was Brand Thorkilsson, the Viking warrior who had spent the last summer with Beornoth as a hostage before returning to his Lord Olaf, only then to save Olaf's life when he was under Beornoth's sword. Brand dropped his eyes, unable to meet Beornoth's gaze. There was blood showing on Brand's axe, Branoc's Tree blood, and Beornoth left his home choking with sorrow and grief.

10

Hríð picked his way across a field of wild grass, stained yellow from the winter frost and a half day's ride from Branoc's Tree. Beornoth slumped in the saddle, limply rocking with the horse's movements, silent and staring ahead, numb with pain. The sun lay hidden behind pillars of cloud in a sky the colour of an old cauldron, and a chill wind whipped Beornoth's neck and the sweat beneath his byrnie and jerkin made him shiver. Olaf Tryggvason's triumphant smirk burned within Beornoth's thought cage, etched there forever like a cow brand.

'We should tend to Wulfhere,' said Eawynn. She trotted her horse alongside Hríð, and Beornoth turned to her, his mouth hanging open. 'His face is badly wounded, and I fear he has lost an eye. The cut to his back broke through the rings of his byrnie and we must see how bad it is. You are still wearing your helmet.'

He reached up and touched the cold metal of his helmet and fumbled with the strap, but his shoulder ached from battle and he hadn't the strength to take it off. Beornoth stared at Eawynn, her face stained with tears, but her eyes bright. She shook her head and turned to Wulfhere; he was lying over the saddle of his horse, limp and unconscious. Cwicca held the reins of Wulfhere's horse and three other survivors followed. All rode in shocked silence at what they had witnessed. Only seven survived Olaf's slaughter, Beornoth, Eawynn, Wulfhere, Cwicca, Osmod, Maccus and Aelfhere.

'Beornoth,' Eawynn said, speaking more firmly this time. 'Pull yourself together. You are their lord, they need you. Wulfhere needs you.'

People always need me. What about what I need? He shook that thought out of his head and took off his helmet. Sweat soaked the leather liner, and the wind blew at his wet hair. He turned in the saddle, wincing at the aches in his back. Wulfhere needed tending to or he would die, and Beornoth had seen enough death to last ten lifetimes. He swallowed at his dry throat and licked cracked lips. *Aethelberga is gone.*

'We'll stop there in that copse. Olaf's men won't follow,' he said, pointing to a clutch of silver birch and hazel trees. Cwicca tied off the horses and Beornoth went to heave Wulfhere down from where he was draped unconscious across the saddle. Beornoth put a hand on Wulfhere's bald head, wanting him to wake up and shake off his injuries, rising hungry for vengeance, but he lay still. His friend was wounded both inside and out, and Beornoth did not want to drag him roughly from the horse to drop on the fallen twigs, branches and soggy leaf mulch of the copse floor. So Beornoth pushed his arms underneath the armpits of Wulfhere's byrnie and pulled him close. He bent at the knee so that Wulfhere's chest leant against his own, and his injured face nestled against Beornoth's beard. There was wetness there, and Beornoth gritted his teeth against the feel of Wulfhere's blood. He shuffled backwards, dragging Wulfhere with him, and as his legs fell across the saddle, Beornoth's knees creaked at the weight. Wulfhere was a big man, and Beornoth blew out his cheeks as he took short backwards steps to where he could sit Wulfhere up against a silver birch trunk. He was determined not to let his friend drop, not to let him suffer more than he already had.

'Let me help, lord,' said Cwicca, running from the horses.

'No,' barked Beornoth. He wanted to care for Wulfhere himself.

'Get some clean water,' said Eawynn, and Cwicca nodded. 'And some clean cloth, a cloak or spare jerkin. You there,' she pointed to another survivor, 'what's your name?'

'Osmod, my lady,' he said, staring at the grass and nervously fingering his belt buckle.

'Osmod, get a fire going.'

Beornoth lay Wulfhere down and gasped as he pulled away to look upon his friend. The uninjured side of Wulfhere's face was as white as a fetch, and the White Wolf had carved the other side wide open. A wound filled with dark blood and ooze ran from Wulfhere's forehead, through where his eye should have been and down to his jaw. Beornoth's hand was dripping with his friend's lifeblood from when he had clutched his back to carry him. So much blood. Too much blood. Beornoth leant in again and let his cheek touch Wulfhere's.

'Aethelberga is gone, my friend. She was a good and noble woman and will be in heaven waiting for you,' he whispered. 'Live. I need you. Please.' He stood and strode away, anger suddenly filling his throat with bile. Beornoth slammed his fist into a tree and kicked the trunk. He cursed and roared and beat at the wood, drawing his sword and hacking at it. 'God help me,' he bellowed, spittle flying from his mouth into his beard. 'Please,

God, help Wulfhere. God help our people.' Beornoth had prayed to the God he believed had forsaken him before the attack, begging for Eawynn's life, and she had lived. He swallowed, wondering if he had been wrong all these years, and that God did actually favour him, and did hear his prayers. But if he did, and watched how his people suffered, how could he allow such cruelty in the world?

Beornoth felt a hand on his shoulder and he twisted, his face scrunched into a savage scowl. He was enraged, distraught and confused. He had lost friends, seen horror brought down upon his people, and God had heard him, the very God he had scorned for so many long years. Eawynn's eyes met his own, and he dropped his sword. She reached up and placed a chilly hand on his cheek.

'You can't save the others, Beo,' she said. 'But you can save Wulfhere. Help me.'

'God saved you,' he said, and pulled her close. She hugged him.

'You saved me.' Something had changed in Eawynn, her fragility washed away by the blood and suffering of Branoc's Tree. Beornoth sensed something of her old self in the way she knew what to do, in how she took command of the dire situation. 'Come, to Wulfhere.'

Beornoth picked up his sword and followed her.

'There was a skin of water on your saddle, lord,' said Cwicca, kneeling next to Wulfhere. 'And I have my cloak, I washed it in a river only three days ago.'

Eawynn nodded. 'Good, well done. Now, help Osmod with the fire. Ask Maccus and Aelfhere to collect some branches and wood.' She reached over to Beornoth's belt and slid his seax free of its sheath. 'Clean this and heat it in the flames until its blade glows red.' Eawynn knelt next to Wulfhere. 'Help me pull off his byrnie,' she said to Beornoth.

They peeled the mail from Wulfhere's body; it was heavy and they had to pry each of his arms free of it before sliding the armour over Wulfhere's head. Eawynn winced as the small iron rings touched the wound on his face, dragging at the flaps of skin around the open wound. Eawynn tore a piece from Cwicca's cloak and pressed it against Wulfhere's face, and then Beornoth helped her roll Wulfhere onto his side. She rolled up his jerkin and tutted at the wound on his back. The mail had taken the worst of the blow, and the cut itself was shallow, but the skin around the wound was already purple and angry. Eawynn pressed her fingers around the wound and all across Wulfhere's back.

'He has broken ribs,' she said. 'He needs proper care, and a warm bed. But we will do the best we can for now.'

Eawynn soaked another section of Cwicca's cloak in the water and washed the wound on Wulfhere's back. Cwicca and Osmod had a small fire made from birch twigs crackling, and Beornoth's seax sat in the flames, its blade heating. Once it was glowing red, Cwicca wrapped a cloth around its hilt and brought the blade to Eawynn.

'You do it,' she said to Beornoth, shaking her head. He swallowed and took the blade. He knelt next to Wulfhere, who was thankfully still unconscious. Beornoth lined up the seax and pressed the red-hot blade into the cut, and Wulfhere's blood and skin hissed. The blade sealed the wound upon Wulfhere's back but left an angry welt of a burn, and Eawynn bound it with strips torn from Cwicca's cloak. They propped Wulfhere up again, and Eawynn removed the cloth from Wulfhere's face. She dabbed and cleaned the wound with water, and bade Cwicca heat the seax once more. Beornoth took the glowing weapon from Cwicca and held it before Wulfhere's ravaged face. He swallowed the lump in his throat and glanced at Eawynn.

'His eye is lost. The burn will be terrible, but it will seal the wound. Infection kills more men than swords,' she said. 'Do it.'

Beornoth pressed the red-hot seax onto Wulfhere's face and grimaced at the hiss of his burning flesh and the smell of his seared skin. But Eawynn was right. The wound was clean and closed, and the blood flowed no more. They left Wulfhere to sleep and walked through the small wood.

'Will they destroy all of Essex?' Eawynn said after a time of wandering in silence, stepping over fallen logs and crunching through the undergrowth.

'Olaf has fifty ships, and an army to crew them,' said Beornoth. 'We will need an army of our own to stop him. We should have finished him last year instead of paying a fortune in silver for an empty promise of peace.'

'I thought I would die. That they had come to finish what they started before, when they killed our girls.'

'These are different men, Vikings yes, but not those Vikings.'

'They are all the same. Will they never stop?'

'No. Not until we put them in the ground and drench our fields with their blood.' Beornoth stopped and turned to her, looking deep into her chestnut eyes. 'I asked God to protect you. I asked the Virgin Mary and Jesus and they answered my prayers.'

'You have cursed God, Beo, many times. You have sinned and denied him. But he is there. You came for me.'

'I should never have left.'

'You have no choice. You are a thegn and you must fight again. The ealdorman will need your sword. We cannot allow the Vikings to do what they did to us today to other folk in our shire.'

'Olaf came for me. He promised he would.'

'If he came to hurt you, it is because you fought him and won.

You didn't ask the cursed Northmen to come here with their ships and their axes. It's a never-ending circle of violence and death. They come here and attack us, try to take what's ours. We defend ourselves against them. Defeat hurts their pride, their precious reputations suffer. So, they bring more warriors to fight us, seeking revenge. It will never end.'

'It won't.' Beornoth sighed at that truth. 'I haven't heard you talk so much since...'

Eawynn folded her arms, and a wan smile creased her face. 'I know. It's been... hard.'

'Eawynn, I...' Beornoth wanted to tell her how much he had missed her and how much he loved her, how sorry he was about how their lives had turned out. How much he missed their daughters. But the words died on his tongue. They were things too hard to say. Too much time had passed, and life had been cruel to them both.

'I know.' She reached for his hand, holding it with one, and stroking the scars across his knuckles and the back of his hand with the fingers of the other. 'Let us not talk of such things, Beo. I have been a prisoner inside myself these long years, locked inside my head by grief. Something today awoke me from that prison. Let that be enough.'

Beornoth nodded and smiled, enjoying the sensation of her gentle touch. 'Aethelberga,' he said.

'She is in heaven now, and we must pray for her, and for the people of Branoc's Tree. Aethelberga was a kind and noble woman. She did not deserve such a fate.'

'No.' Beornoth ground his teeth, the memory of Aethelberga's body burning behind his eyes. 'Nobody deserved what happened today.'

They held hands in silence, remembering Aethelberga. She had been difficult when Beornoth first arrived at Branoc's Tree.

She had lost her husband to the Vikings. And Beornoth himself was not a simple man to get along with. But, over time, a mutual respect had grown between them, and then friendship. Even after Beornoth's arrival, she remained the lady of Branoc's Tree, and she ran the place with a firm but respected hand. The folk liked her, and she was a pious woman devoted to the Church. The Vikings had hacked her to pieces and had their way with her. That was her reward for a life well lived. Beornoth thought of God again. The Almighty, or the Virgin Mother, had granted Beornoth's prayer and saved Eawynn, but how could God then allow so righteous a servant as Aethelberga to be butchered and his own church defiled by pagans?

'I think God has a purpose for me,' he said.

'God has a purpose for us all, but his ways are mysterious and beyond our reckoning.'

'I think he welcomed me back into his flock by keeping you alive until I returned.' The words spilled from Beornoth's mouth, but he was unsure of what it meant, whether he really believed it. But he wanted it to be true. He wanted there to be a God and a heaven.

'Aye, well, you came. That's enough. So, what now? Do we go to the ealdorman?' She fussed at her dress, uncomfortable with the talk of God and his purpose.

'No. We go north to Alfgar.'

'North? Surely you must join the ealdorman's forces. You are sworn to fight for him?'

'I am. But I must get you and Wulfhere to safety first. Alfgar is ealdorman of Cheshire. He will keep you both safe in the north, away from Olaf and his Vikings.'

'We cannot afford the time to go north, Beo. I will be fine. The ealdorman's priests can heal Wulfhere. We must go to Byrhtnoth today. It would take many days to ride to Cheshire.'

'It will take many days to ride to Alfgar, and Wulfhere might not survive the journey. I will return to the ealdorman once I know you are safe. This is how it will be.' He fixed her with a stare and she nodded, although the thin-lipped smile she flashed him made her disagreement plain enough.

They spent a chilly night in the copse, taking turns to keep the fire lit, and to watch for any signs of a Viking attack, no matter how unlikely Beornoth thought that was. In the morning, Beornoth led the company north. He had spent much of that night awake, worrying about Eawynn's words. She was right. His duty was to ride to Byrhtnoth and help the ealdorman defend Essex from Olaf's Vikings. But in his heart, Beornoth was certain that his first duty was to Eawynn. He had to get her out of Essex, and Cheshire was about as far as he could go to find a friendly place for her to stay. Beornoth had helped make Alfgar ealdorman there, and the young man had learned to fight alongside Beornoth. When Alfgar's father, the old Ealdorman Aethelhelm, had first asked Beornoth to take Alfgar under his wing, he had been a callow youth fresh from studying at the Church, his fingers stained by ink and his arms and shoulders unused to the weight and use of weapons. Alfgar was the second son of the old ealdorman, and a bastard. As was usually the case for most second sons, Aethelhelm had steered Alfgar into the Church, but he had failed at his studies, stating that he did not feel close enough to God to preach his word. The ealdorman reluctantly took Alfgar from the Church and gave him to Beornoth to turn into a warrior, which Alfgar struggled with at first, but he was now the veteran of many battles against the Vikings, and had been instrumental in the defeat of Olaf's forces outside Folkestone the year before. Beornoth thought of Alfgar as a friend, and being an ealdorman made him one of the most powerful men in England, answerable only to King Æthelred himself.

Wulfhere remained deep in a sweat-soaked fever on the first day, and through the following three nights spent at a monastery on the shire's northern edge. The monks provided sparse meals of porridge and bread, but they had good fodder for the horses and applied fresh dressings to Wulfhere's wounds, and to the cuts and scrapes suffered by Beornoth, Osmod, Cwicca and Maccus during the fighting at Branoc's Tree. Beornoth feared that they tarried too long within the quiet calm of the monastery buildings, but they needed time to recover and to heal before venturing out on the road again. Beornoth waited by the fire that third night until all had retired to their beds, and then he took a torch from an iron basket on the stone wall and let the thin light lead him to the chapel. There, the torchlight flickered across a painted timber depiction of Jesus on the cross, hanging high above a stone altar. The son of God was thin and the nails at his wrists and feet were ringed with blood, but his face was calm and peaceful. Beornoth knelt before the cross and raised his clasped hands. He thanked God, Jesus, and the Mother of God for keeping Eawynn alive. The chapel was silent, but Beornoth felt a presence in the smell of old wood and the stale-sweet smell of burned incense. Beornoth had spent much of his life doubting God, but he prayed for his long-dead daughters and he prayed for his wife, for Wulfhere and the people of Essex.

Wulfhere awoke the next morning, groggy and confused, sheened in sweat and his skin hot to the touch. The straw cot the monks had prepared for him was soaked through, and Wulfhere's ravaged face was drawn and pale. Beornoth scrambled from his own bed to offer his friend a sip of water, which he took with spluttering gulps. Wulfhere reached up and grabbed the back of Beornoth's head and whispered Aethelberga's name whilst staring at him with a single frantic eye, and then would say no more. Beornoth held his friend there for a long moment, before pulling on his boots and marching along the dark corridor thick with the smell of old timber to find the room the monks had provided for Eawynn to sleep apart from the men. He knocked on a heavy oak door, and it creaked open on leather hinges. Eawynn stood in the doorway, morning light from an open window shutter bathing the small room in a warm glow, her hair tousled from sleep.

'We ride for the ealdorman,' Beornoth said. She nodded at him, her jaw set and a fire in her eyes. The long night at prayer, and the fevered look in Wulfhere's remaining eye, had convinced Beornoth that his duty to his lord and his people outweighed his personal duty to get Eawynn to safety. If he left, then the Vikings would burn and raid their way across the shire without his sword to stand against them. More men's wives would suffer, so that Beornoth could protect Eawynn. 'Wulfhere will rest here at this monastery until he can walk again, and I will send men north with you once we have reached Ealdorman Byrhtnoth.'

'You are doing the right thing, Beo,' said Eawynn. She moved to him, taking his calloused hand in her slender fingers. 'Your duty is to the people, and to the ealdorman. When I think of all those people who died at Branoc's Tree.... The Vikings must be stopped.'

The company set off that day. Beornoth left the monks with one of his silver arm rings to pay for Wulfhere's food and care. They were six riders: Beornoth, Eawynn, Cwicca, Osmod, Maccus and Aelfhere. The sky was low and shifting under a bracing wind as they pushed east towards the ealdorman's lands. The riders kept away from steadings and fortifications, Beornoth fearful that they would run into bands of Olaf's raiders. So they veered away from roads and paths wherever buildings came into view and crossed field and forests, sleeping in the open under whatever shelter they could make from their belongings. The nights were bitter, and each person took a turn at watch and to keep the campfire alive, and after two days they were travel stained and hungry, but alive. Eawynn was reborn, directing the building of the camp each night, organising food and rations, foraging where possible, and helping Osmod with the horses.

On the morning of the sixth day since the fall of Branoc's Tree, they followed a silvery river's meander around a shallow valley basin and up across a pine-covered ridge and the sun made a quarter-turn behind a cover of low, shifting cloud. Cwicca took the lead, and they rode in a single column through the pines towards Ealdorman Byrhtnoth's estates as a ragged line of riders, clothes and faces smeared with the dirt of their journey, and Beornoth thanked God again for allowing it to pass without more pain or suffering.

The sharp, sweet smell of the forest washed the stink of blood from Beornoth's nose, and the chatter of birds was a welcome distraction from the thoughts torturing his mind. The pain of those lost at Branoc's Tree was an open, raw wound. The injured, slaughtered corpses of his friends and people were burned vividly into his mind, like a nightmare haunting his every waking moment.

Shafts of light shone through the heavy pine boughs ahead, piercing the deep gloom of the forest, and Beornoth fished an oatcake taken from the monastery out of his pack and fed it to his horse. Hríð nodded his head and took the cake hungrily, and Beornoth fondly stroked his white mane. He followed Cwicca along the path worn into the forest floor, a brown scar winding through the trees and brush, littered with fallen pine cones and twigs. They came out into the light, and Cwicca reined his horse in.

'God help us,' he said, his jaw dropping in horror. Beornoth followed his gaze and pulled on Hríð's reins to bring him to a stop. Beornoth's stomach lurched, for galloping across the pasture below them was a brown mare, her mane and back burning bright with flames. The horse screamed as she hurtled along the grass, and Beornoth had never heard such a terrible sound. It was a horse from Byrhtnoth's stable. Vikings had brought fire and death to the ealdorman's lands.

11

————

Byrhtnoth's estate, which had once been so beautiful, a haven for magnificent horses with rolling green pastures, was now a ragged thing of mud-churned fields and desolation. Beornoth wound Hríð around the twisted corpses which littered the pasture from the forest down to Byrhtnoth's house. Or what had been his house. It was now a pile of charred timbers, its smell acrid and bitter. A large force of men sat or lay on the ground to the west of the destroyed buildings, and some pushed themselves to their feet. They rose slowly and took short, tired steps towards Beornoth and his riders.

Beornoth prayed to God and the Virgin Mother that the ealdorman was alive, and that Leofsunu, Aelfwine and his other friends had survived. He closed his eyes and whispered to God that he hoped Byrhtnoth's wife and family were safe. This was not the ealdorman's home, but only one of his vast estates, and his favourite. Byrhtnoth loved horses, as did Beornoth, and the sight of the burning beast fleeing across the hills had cut Beornoth to the bone. He saw more dead horses amongst the corpses. A dappled stallion lay on its side, flies already resting on the whites of its eyes. The stench of death was thick in the air, blood and filth, loss and suffering. The warriors who approached were grim things of hunched shoulders and smoke-darkened faces. Cries and moans from the wounded wafted across the battlefield like a grim song of the underworld.

'There is the ealdorman. He lives, thanks be to God,' said Eawynn, making the sign of the cross over her chest. 'There was a battle here, and it does not seem that our friends were victorious.'

'And we missed it,' said Beornoth, swallowing against the sudden burning at the back of his throat, his face heating. The feeling of knowing a terrible thing had happened, which might have been avoided, and the certainty that he should have been there to stand next to his ealdorman in the shield wall, was almost too much to bear. The days he had spent between the ruin of Branoc's Tree in the forest and those in recovery at the monastery had been costly.

The hulking figure of Byrhtnoth stood at the centre of a band of ragged warriors, his grey beard shot through with ash, and his long silver hair blackened by smoke. A filthy mixture of blood, gore and black ash smeared his byrnie, and Beornoth shivered at the overwhelming punch of guilt in his chest.

'My lord,' said Beornoth, coming to a stop two paces away from Byrhtnoth and bowing his head in solemn salute. 'It hurts me to see your lands this way. I am sorry for your loss.'

From a crowd of seated warriors, a short man surged to his feet. His round face twisted into a snarl and his hand was upon the hilt of his sword. He wore a fine byrnie, and though soot smeared his face, Beornoth recognised Godric.

'Coward!' Godric shouted, pointing his finger at Beornoth, snot dripping from his nose and the soot on his face run through with tears. 'Where were you hiding? I always knew you were a good-for-nothing. My brother died today, whilst you cowered from the fight.'

Beornoth's head snapped back in shock at the insult. He had killed men for less. He took a long breath and mastered his anger. Clearly, the young thegn was grieving, and the day had been full of blood and slaughter. Two men hauled Godric away, and he thrashed in their arms as though he wished to attack Beornoth, which was surprising. But men are often brave when their friends stand between them and an adversary.

'Forgive him that insult,' said Aelfwine, striding forwards from the gathered warriors. 'For grief has clearly clouded his judgement. Lady Eawynn, I am glad to see you unharmed.'

'Lady Eawynn,' said Byrhtnoth, bowing his head to her before turning his gaze to Beornoth. 'Olaf and the White Wolf came. They brought their Jomsvikings and cut through us as though we were mewling pups. We did not have enough men to stand against them.'

'I should have been here, lord,' said Beornoth. He kept his eyes fixed on the earth, unable to meet the piercing stare of the most fearsome warlord in all England. 'How many did we lose?'

'Twenty dead, more injured. All fighters. We have not raised the fyrd. We killed many of them in return. It was a hard fight.' The ealdorman winced and rolled his right shoulder, and turned over his left arm to examine a cut on his forearm. The jerkin beneath his byrnie, which covered his lower arm, was slashed and bloody. 'Olaf broke off the fight once the hall was aflame. They killed my horses. That cursed White Wolf was here. A vicious killer, that one.'

'I am sorry for your loss, my lord,' said Beornoth.

Byrhtnoth sighed and rubbed the corners of his eyes with the thumb and forefinger of his smoke-blackened hand. 'Leofsunu, find these men some food. Get the men up. We march to the abbot at Ely. We can find shelter there for now.'

Leofsunu nodded at the ealdorman and winked at Beornoth. He flashed a quick smile, his misshapen face twisted. Beornoth was glad to see his friend alive.

'Walk with me,' said the ealdorman, and marched towards the corpse-strewn battlefield. Beornoth followed. He stepped over a Saxon warrior he recognised from Godric's hearth troop, another from Leofsunu's men. Their chests, necks and faces carved open by wicked Viking blades. It seemed to Beornoth that their dead eyes stared at him, following him as he walked amongst the dead. He could hear their dead voices whispering to him, accusing him, asking why he had not been there.

Byrhtnoth knelt next to a fallen horse, a pony with muscled legs and a long neck. He stroked his mane and ran a hand along its cold, dead neck. 'We waited a day for you at the Jotunwood,' he said. 'And then we marched. Olaf has brought his fifty ships of men into our shire. He kills, raids and burns. Sometimes single crews, sometimes in force to provoke us. We met him here today.'

'They came to Branoc's Tree, lord...'

'I know, and I am sorry for that. I heard about the Lady Aethelberga. Leofsunu and Thered rode there. They told me of the tree hanging with the bodies of your people.'

'I need to get my wife to safety, lord. To Ealdorman Alfgar in Cheshire. I wanted to take her there myself, to make sure she reaches safety, but my place is here.'

Byrhtnoth nodded and rubbed at his soot-stained eyes. 'I will send Aelfwine and Thered north with her, for we must also ask Alfgar for men. We must appeal to every shire in England. Thered will ride today, and Eawynn will be safe, she has suffered enough. I know Thered fought against us last year, but he has changed. You have seen that, he can be trusted with Eawynn's life.'

'Thank you, lord.'

'You should have mustered at the Jotunwood, Beornoth. As you were ordered.'

Beornoth held Byrhtnoth's gaze. 'I know my duty. I dare say there are few who can say they have fought as hard as I for Essex these last two years. Was it not I who broke the Jomsviking line at Watchet? Was it not I who brought Ragnar the Flayer to heel and whittled him into a heimnar? Was it not I who killed Skarde Wartooth with these hands?'

'No man questions your bravery. But you should have been here.'

'I am here now. Had I stood with you on this field, would it have changed the outcome? Would we have defeated Olaf? We should direct our anger at the king, and at Leofric of East Anglia and his timid sons. Why does the king not rouse the fyrd? Why does Leofric or his heirs not raise the swords and spears of East Anglia to fight the invaders?' Beornoth realised he was shouting, and that Byrhtnoth's eyes burned with anger and loss. The two huge warriors stood with chests puffed and shoulders back, each man staring deep into the other's eyes.

'I would have done the same thing, if it were my wife, and my people,' said Byrhtnoth eventually, tearing his eyes away after the awful moment of tension. The ealdorman relaxed and sighed, looking out across the field of slain warriors. 'You must forgive young Godric, he spoke in haste and you will let that insult rest.'

'Did he fight today? For I am yet to see him strike a blow against an enemy, lots of fine words and talk of what he will do, or what he has done in the past.'

'He is a thegn, and his father was my friend. He lost a brother today, but his two other brothers survived. The hostage fought like a lion in the shield wall, young Thered of Northumbria.'

'Then we should be happy to have such brave men to fight at our side. I have not seen him fight. He tried to kill us both in Northumbria, and there was not much bravery in his deeds then.'

'Aye, well, a ragged colt often makes a fine horse. Thered's my man as long as he remains with us as a hostage.'

'I am still your man, and I am here now,' said Beornoth, and he dropped to one knee. He raised his hands, and Byrhtnoth took them between his own and raised Beornoth to his feet.

'Get up, man.' Byrhtnoth pulled Beornoth into a hug, his enormous arms as strong as a bear, and the men held each other for a moment and pulled apart. 'You are here now, and we are in the fight of our lives. You are still the thegn of Branoc's Tree. Olaf has come for us, Beo. He comes to kill us all. He would use his sword to make a kingdom for himself, I fear.'

'And what news of the king?'

'The king fears Sweyn Forkbeard. He fears that if he sends the army of Wessex here to Essex, that Forkbeard will march west, unopposed, and seize Winchester. He is unnerved that Forkbeard is a Christian, and that the men of the old Danelaw might welcome a new king, a Christian king, with no ties to the monks, abbots and priests of the English Church. The Church has taken too much land, I fear, and the king knows it.'

'And the men of East Anglia will not fight?'

'They will not. They too fear Forkbeard. East Anglia will not march whilst he looms in Gippeswic with his mint and his ships.'

'So Forkbeard remains at Gippeswic, he does not raid?'

'He doesn't need to. We hear ships arrive with silver. Other Vikings bring spits, candlesticks and whatever else they have looted from our shores, or from Frankia, and he turns it into coin. They sail away with some of that coin, and Forkbeard keeps more. He grows rich without bloodshed or war, so what need has he of raiding?'

'Vikings are Vikings, lord. They crave battle and reputation. He will need to offer his men more than coin to keep his army happy.'

Byrhtnoth grumbled at the truth of that. 'We need more men if we are going to defeat Olaf. We must go back to the king, and we must rouse East Anglia. Or we are done for.'

'How many men do we have?'

'After today? Maybe three hundred.'

'You have not summoned the fyrd of Essex?'

'No. The common folk are the victims of Viking attacks, and they are busy at the plough, and sowing the seeds which will feed us throughout the next winter. If I drag them away from that, we will starve.'

'If we don't order out the fyrd, my lord, we will all be dead before winter and their farms will be in the hands of Olaf's warriors. It will be here as it was in the north, in the old Danelaw. The Vikings will settle, take over and breed us out. Better to kill the bastard Norsemen and have empty bellies in winter than suffer that fate. We must raise the whole of Essex and East Anglia.'

Byrhtnoth ran a hand down the spade of his beard and shook his head. 'I also did not call them out, because so many of them will die if we are forced to make a stand against the Jomsvikings. The fyrd are farmers, millers and potters. They will be cut down like barley. I do not want to watch my people die. But you are right, and we need their numbers. I do not see how we can call out the warriors and fyrd of East Anglia with its ealdorman, and Leofric lays upon his deathbed clinging to life. His son will do nothing, fearful of fighting a man who could soon be his king.'

'King Æthelred must order the men of East Anglia to fight.

That is our only chance. If the king will not commit the men of Wessex to the war, he must rouse East Anglia.'

'I will send word to the king again. For now, let's summon our own fyrd. Let us call out the East Saxons and see if we can kill these cursed Viking bastards. If we could just fight them with equal numbers, one battle would end it all. One shield wall fight and we might have a chance to crush them. A Saxon defending his home is more than a match for Viking greed.'

'So why don't you and Offa ride across the shire, my lord? Call out the fyrd and send another message to the king. Turn me loose on Olaf. Give me men and I will find his camp. I will harry him at every turn. I will kill his warriors and burn his ships. I will whittle his numbers and hurt his pride, so that when it comes to it, he will yearn for battle as much as we.'

Byrhtnoth clapped him on the shoulder. 'So be it. Hurt him, Beo. He burned your home, and my land. He killed your people and defeated me in battle. I want him hungry for the fight, I want a battle. When we have the numbers, we can meet across the war fence, Olaf and I. Sting him, punish him, give our people their vengeance, Beornoth.'

'As you command, my lord.'

Byrhtnoth chewed the beard beneath his lower lip and cast his eyes up towards the pines. He pulled his sword from his scabbard and examined the hilt. It was a magnificent blade, with gold circles set within its round pommel and gold wire around the crosspiece. 'This is the sword of my house,' he said wistfully. 'Wielded by my father, and my father's father, and back for as long as can be remembered. It was used in the fight against Ivar the Boneless and the Great Heathen Army, and has kept East Saxons safe for generations. Will I be the last of my line to wield it? What will become of us?'

'We will fight to the last man,' said Beornoth, raising a

clenched fist. 'Until there is not a drop of Saxon blood left. Even if our weapons are blunted or lost, we would use our teeth and nails to fight the enemy.'

'We will need your ferocity, Beornoth, your savagery burns just as bright as that of the Vikings. Let us teach them what it means to raid our lands.'

They camped that night in the ruin of Byrhtnoth's burned farm. Beornoth found a place for he and Eawynn to sleep beneath a knotted silver birch tree on the edge of the forest next to the now empty grazing pastures. He spent most of the night holding her close, her head resting on his chest, imagining how different their life could have been if the Vikings had never brought their dragon-prowed warships to England. He let himself dream a fool's dream, of a peaceful life with a family, and then in the morning he left Eawynn asleep and stood, groaning at the aches in his back and leg. Old wounds grinding and grating, a further reminder of whom he was, and of what he was. He sought out Aelfwine and Thered, who were already saddling a horse for the journey ahead.

'Thank you, Aelfwine. Take care of Eawynn for me. Take Maccus with you, and on your return journey seek out Wulfhere from the monastery at Sparrow Downs, north of Branoc's Tree. He lies there injured, but will be fit to ride by the time you are returned from Cheshire.'

Aelfwine took his hand in the warrior's grip, as did Thered, and Beornoth marched mournfully to say goodbye to his wife. They parted with smiles and a long embrace, and though it pained him to watch her ride away, Beornoth had to fulfil his duty. Cwicca saddled Eawynn's horse, and Beornoth went to him, stroking the beast's long nose. He slid the simple locket from his neck which bore the locks of golden hair from his dead children, and tucked it safely into a bag strapped to the cracked leather saddle. Beornoth wanted her to have it, so that she could remember the joy their girls had once brought. Inside the bag was a red light woollen scarf. Eawynn wore it in the evenings to ward off the chill air. Beornoth lifted it to his nose and breathed in her scent, and he felt a catch in his chest. He would miss her, but at least Aelfwine and Thered would see her to safety. Beornoth tucked the scarf inside his byrnie.

With a heavy heart, and fighting the urge to run after them, to march off to a life of peace with Eawynn, Beornoth waved them off. He marched back to the simple camp beneath the silver birch. His chain-mail byrnie hung from a branch, and he lifted it free. Motes danced in the morning air as sunlight shone through the forest in bright shafts and Beornoth sighed at the warp and weft of his life. The byrnie caught the light and shimmered, the cold metal heavy as he shook out the morning dew. He lifted his sword from the forest floor, and his seax, and the thick leather belt that would hold them. He wore only his light undershirt, and slipped on the leather jerkin he wore beneath his byrnie, and it smelled of old wood and other men's blood. Wrapped in an old cloak by the tree sat his helmet, the eye rings dark and malevolent. Beornoth slithered into his byrnie, his second skin, and strapped on his war gear, for it was time for war, death and vengeance.

12

The inside of the house was dingy, the smell of fish thick within the close walls and low thatch. A small fire crackled and spat within a pit carved out of the hard-packed earth floor, ringed with smooth, round stones. A cauldron broiled over the flames, simmering a broth of fish heads and other leftovers. It was morning, rain had soaked the low wattle buildings' thatch throughout the night, and as Beornoth watched from a small open window shutter, thick drips fell from overhanging thatch to plop into a mud-darkened puddle. Dark clouds fringed with lighter patches opened up so that shafts of light shone through onto distant fields, and the faint colours of a rainbow shimmered to the east. A sneeze rang out from a barn across the village, followed by a shushing sound and stifled laughter. Beornoth shook his head. A chicken picked its way across the small village square, pausing to lift a leg and peck at the mud. Beornoth rested his hand on the cold iron hilt of his sword and gave it a gentle tug to make sure it was loose in its scabbard.

Beornoth had scoured Essex with a small war band following Eawynn's departure, and for two weeks he had chased shadows

around farmland and forests, following signs of smoking villages
on the horizon, but unable to catch Viking raiding parties and
bring his fury to bear upon them. Aelfwine and Thered had
returned from Alfgar along with Streonwold and thirty riders to
swell Beornoth's force. Aelfwine had assured Beornoth that
Eawynn was welcome and safe in Cheshire, and Ealdorman
Alfgar had sent his best men south with his captain. Streonwold
was a portly man, and could easily pass for a merchant with his
soft face and balding head. Beornoth, however, had known Streonwold for many years – he was a fierce warrior of reputation and
skill and there were few in the kingdom as experienced or
respected as the ageing captain. Aelfwine sought out Wulfhere
from the monastery at Sparrow Downs on his return journey, and
Wulfhere was a malevolent, hulking mass of raw wounds and
barely contained violence. His ribs were healing, or at least the
warrior did not complain of his injuries. His face, however, had
begun to knit together in a jagged red line across his missing eye,
so that Wulfhere looked like a thing of nightmare.

'Will they come?' Wulfhere whispered in Beornoth's ear
where he crouched beside him in the small building.

'They'll come,' said Beornoth. They had been tracking a crew
of Olaf's Vikings for three days following the capture of a small
band of Vikings foraging for food at the edge of a burned-out
village. Wulfhere had put the captured Vikings to the question
with his whittling knife, and they had revealed the location of
Olaf's camp. Beornoth and his men found that camp and
watched, waiting for it to spew forth Vikings for them to kill. A
band of Norsemen had marched north from that southern base
and had already ransacked one village before Beornoth could
bring them to a fight. The village where Beornoth and his men
now lay in wait, Eofasham, was on the Vikings' road back to
Olaf's camp. Beornoth had led his force of forty riders ahead of

the Viking column, leaving Cwicca to scout the enemy's movements and make sure that Eofasham was indeed their target. Aelfwine had tried to persuade the villagers to flee, and some had loaded their belongings into carts or onto the backs of their animals and fled to the west. More had stayed.

'It's all we have, lord,' a middle-aged man had said. His front teeth were missing and his short black hair cut crudely close to his scalp. 'If I leave here, how will I feed my family?'

The men of the village were frightened, but eager to defend their possessions and their wives and children. Beornoth had tried to scare them into running away, talking of how the Northmen would first rape their wives, and then ship them and their children off to the slave markets in Dublin. The village men, however, had fought in the fyrd before, and with stern faces they shook billhooks, wood axes and scythes in the air and promised to fight just as hard as any warrior. Which they would, of course, but warriors they were not. All freemen within the shire mustered to arms once the fyrd was called out, so these men were no strangers to battle likely fought since before the Viking raids had resumed under the reign of King Æthelred. They would stand in the battle line, and would hack at an enemy, but they were not men to stand in the front ranks and trade blows with the professional warriors of Norway, Denmark and Sweden.

'So, we only come out when the fighting starts?' said the gap-toothed man stood on the opposite side of the window. He licked at dry lips and swallowed hard, so that his Adam's apple bounced within his thin throat. He had provided Beornoth, Wulfhere, Aelfwine and Leofsunu shelter in his home for the night, and fed them a thin fish soup with a chunk of black bread for their evening meal. Now, the morning after, he stood ready to fight and die for his family. His name was Gymi, and his hands trembled around the haft of his wood axe.

'You come out when we start killing. We shall wait until they are deep within the village, and then we attack. Once you hear men screaming and men dying, then you attack. We kill them all. If you are afraid, stay inside your home. Nobody will think any worse of you if you do,' said Beornoth. Which was not true, of course. The men had to fight for the families now they had committed to make a stand. But Beornoth did not want the man to die needlessly. Beornoth's warriors would do the real fighting.

'I'll fight. Don't you worry about that,' said Gymi unconvincingly.

'I hope the White Wolf comes,' said Wulfhere. He would not rest until he had killed the man he held responsible for Aethelberga's death, but the white-haired Norseman was not with the Viking crew. Beornoth allowed Wulfhere his anger. His thirst for revenge would drive him on and make him a better killer.

A whistle rose and fell from the far side of the village, and the warriors inside the low-roofed house straightened, leather armour creaked and feet shifted.

'They're here,' said Wulfhere, grinding his teeth, his one eye shining in the gloom. The whistle came from Cwicca, signalling that the Vikings approached. The Northmen had risen early from their slumber, no doubt excited at the prospect of a day of raiding, thirsty for blood and the thrill of the attack. But instead of panicked Saxon villagers, they would find warriors. Rather than farmers with bent backs and children with dirty faces, they would find Beornoth.

'Follow my orders,' Beornoth said, turning to the men packed into the house. 'Do as we planned, and we will slaughter them all.'

Three horses came thundering into the village square, the Norse riders clad in chain-mail byrnies and swathed in furs. They whooped as their horses stomped and churned the village square.

Behind them came two columns of Viking warriors, spears and axes ready for the slaughter of what they believed to be unprotected villagers.

'Not a shield between them.' Wulfhere grinned. 'I want their souls. I hate them. Bastards. Horrible, murderous bastards.' Wulfhere was shaking, his rage ready to burst out of him like a pot boiling over.

'Wait,' said Beornoth, clapping a hand on Wulfhere's back. Beornoth bent to take his helmet from a small boy who crouched beneath the window. The lad was Gymi's son, and he looked up at Beornoth with large hazel eyes. Beornoth winked at him as he took the heavy helm. He slipped it onto his head, adjusting it until the leather liner was comfortable, and he fastened the strap beneath his chin. The iron nasal in the shape of a horse stretched down his nose and the thick rings which encircled his eyes darkened his face. The helmet made it hard for Beornoth to see on his flanks because of the eye rings and cheek pieces. But the helmet protected his skull and face, which were ever vulnerable to attack. A blow to the nose or cheekbone would blind a man for heartbeats, and a strike to the head could fell a man. It wouldn't kill him, but the spear point or axe blade that followed it would. The helmet also made Beornoth look terrifying, his face hidden and brooding like a warrior from a fireside tale of legend. That, combined with his shining byrnie, his sword and warrior rings upon his arms, told the Vikings that he was a successful warrior. A war leader of reputation. Any man who could kill him would become instantly rich, and his own reputation would shine as bright as a star on a clear winter night. But his war gear was also a warning. It told other warriors that he was a man to fear, a man who made his living fighting and killing other warriors, a man who gloried in the clash of blades. It warned them that to fight him they would need skill, bravery and be willing to risk their own lives.

Beornoth picked up his shield and shrugged his shoulders to get used to the weight. He took his spear from where it rested against the wattle wall and left the house. He ducked underneath the low door lintel and out into the rain-soaked day. The Vikings splashed through the puddles and gathered around the square, their heads jerking from side to side, wondering where their prey was, and why there were no screaming maids or men emerging to protect their families. Two Northmen dashed into a building, bellowing their war cries, but quickly went quiet. Beornoth stalked towards the square, keeping his eyes on the men on horseback. Those men in chain-mail byrnies were the leaders. They were the champions, the men who led other Vikings because of their fighting prowess and reputations. They were the men Beornoth would fight, the warriors he would kill.

'Who is this turd?' said a Viking, pointing his spear at Beornoth. 'Turd, can you understand me? Where are the women?'

'I am Beornoth Reiði,' said Beornoth in Norse, using the name Forkbeard had said that Vikings knew him by. Beornoth the Wrathful. 'Which one of you raven starvers wants to fight with me? Who is the brave one? There are no women here for you to fight, no children. Just me.'

The Vikings stared at him open-mouthed, the entire crew of them fallen silent. Beornoth imagined them waking early that morning, laughing and joking about the day ahead of them. Boasting about the women they would take and the men they would kill. They would have marched in good humour, telling stories of the past, striding with a spring in their step, thinking that this was the best time of their lives, what they had sailed to

England for. And now they would die. Beornoth shifted his feet and gripped the shaft of his spear.

'Piece of sheep shit,' growled one of the mounted Vikings. He leaned forward in the saddle as though he would charge at Beornoth. So Beornoth braced himself. He planted one boot behind the other and dropped his shoulder to heft his spear. It was an aesc spear, long with a leaf-shaped blade. The spear point was perfectly weighted and Beornoth drew back his arm so that the shine of its tip gleamed at the corner of his helmeted view. He grunted as he launched the weapon, taking four quick steps forward and throwing the spear with all of his strength. It flew through the damp morning air and slammed into the Viking's body just below his chest. It struck him as his horse turned and his arms were raised, piercing his byrnie, and the sheer force of the throw launched him from the saddle to fall with a slap into the mud of Eofasham's square.

The Vikings watched their leader fall and then turned to Beornoth, anger quickly replacing the looks of surprise on their bearded faces. They charged towards him, howling their war cries, and Beornoth pulled his sword free of his fleece-lined scabbard and made himself ready behind the linden-wood boards and iron boss of his shield. The Norsemen pounded through the mud, snarling and hefting spears and axes, and Beornoth stood alone. As the fastest of them closed to within five paces of him, a thrum erupted from the surrounding buildings and a hail of arrows whipped across the village to slam into the Vikings' flanks. The first men fell, roaring in pain under the hail of missiles, and Beornoth stepped forward to drive the point of his sword into the face of a Viking who had fallen screaming at his feet with an arrow in his thigh. The sword pierced the man's skull between his teeth and nose and blood spread darkly into a shallow puddle of rainwater.

'Now!' Beornoth called to his men, and he smiled as his warriors burst from the houses and barns of Eofasham's village. Where the Vikings hoped to find milkmaids and frightened farmers, they found the thegns and warriors of Essex. Beornoth strode forwards and slashed his sword across the throat of a Norseman struggling to pull an arrow from his shoulder, felling the man in a spray of bright blood. Another came at him, and Beornoth parried his axe with his shield and punched the tip of his sword through the man's belly, piercing his leather breastplate. Wulfhere thundered past him, axe whirling and dealing death to the enemy. Leofsunu of Sturmer killed a man with his sword and urged his men into deeds of valour. Aelfwine of Foxfield attacked a Viking horseman with his spear and drove him into the mud. The Vikings fought back, and one of Aelfwine's men died with an axe in his chest. The villagers came next, hacking at the Vikings with their scythes and knives.

A third rider charged at Beornoth, his heels digging repeatedly into the belly of his horse, and the warrior came on with bared teeth in a golden beard. He carried a long-handled war axe, and he brought the weapon around in wide circles, its blade catching the sun where it broke through the iron-grey sky. The axe blade cut through the raised arm of a villager, slicing through flesh and bone to sever the arm at the elbow. That villager screamed at the pain of his wound, and then died, because the other Viking he had been fighting plunged a spear into his chest and twisted the point to rip the poor man's life away. The horse picked up momentum and moved from a trot into a gallop, and Beornoth knew he could not stand against the beast. He could slash at the horse's legs or chest, but its weight would knock him senseless and the Viking would hack him to pieces with his vicious axe. If he turned his back to leap out of the way, the axe would smash through the links of his byrnie and carve his back open like a roasted hog. So he knelt and crouched behind the strength of his shield, tucking himself behind the safety of the linden-wood boards. The horse's hooves pounded the earth under the weight of beast and rider and Beornoth tensed his muscles and set his jaw. He was too low and safe behind his shield for the axe to kill him, but the horse's mighty hock smashed into the shield and it felt like a bolt of lightning had struck him. It threw Beornoth backwards, losing his grip on his sword and his shield as he twisted, sprawling in the mud. His heart raced, fear gripping him as he scrambled for the hilt of his sword. A boot kicked him in the stomach, and he grunted, rolling over to catch the next kicking boot in two hands. His attacker was a big-bellied Viking with long moustaches and before he could strike down with his axe, Beornoth twisted the leg in his hands and kicked the man's standing leg away. The Viking fell to the mud with a yelp, and Beornoth clawed his way through the slippery, sodden earth to clamber on top of the man. He grabbed the wrist holding the axe and twisted it savagely. Beornoth butted the Viking, pulping his face beneath the hard, cold iron of his helmeted forehead. The axe came free and Beornoth rose to his knees and sliced the sharp blade across the Northman's throat. A bear-like roar erupted from behind Beornoth and he turned in horror to see a Viking charging at him with a spear levelled at his chest. The Viking ran at full pelt and Beornoth did not have time to bring his axe to bear to deflect the blow. Death drew close, and for a fleeting moment Beornoth saw Eawynn's smiling face and hoped that God would permit him to enter heaven and be reunited with Ashwig and Cwen in the afterlife. Suddenly, the Northumbrian thegn, Thered, leapt in front of Beornoth, turning the deadly spear aside with his sword and taking the force of its charge upon his shoulder. The blow sent Thered spinning, but as he spun, he whipped his sword around and slashed it across the

face of the Viking spearman, carving open his eyes and cheeks
with a terrible wound. Thered grinned and extended a hand to
Beornoth and hauled him to his feet. The Northumbrian hostage
then darted away to continue the fight.

The earth trembled beneath Beornoth's feet and he turned in
time to see the mounted Viking saw on the reins of his horse to
wheel it around and come back to finish Beornoth off. Beornoth
dropped the axe and leapt for his fallen shield, the din of the fight
around him ringing around his skull, screams of the dying and
bellows of the vengeful melded into a deafening roar. He grabbed
his shield in two hands and twisted at the waist, channelling all of
his strength built over a lifetime of weapons' practice and battle
into his shoulder muscles. He hurled the shield on its side, and it
whirled through the air like a skimming stone. The rider saw the
shield too late, and it smacked into his chest with a sound like
chopped wood. The Viking curled over the neck of the horse and
slid from the saddle, and Beornoth picked up his sword. Before
he could get to the fallen Viking, Wulfhere set upon him with his
own axe, cleaving the Viking's skull open.

It was all over in the time it might take a man to shear the
heavy winter wool from a sheep in spring, and more villagers
crept from the safety of the heavily thatched buildings, slinking
towards the injured with knives and makeshift clubs. They
hacked and stabbed at their stricken enemies, finding those still
alive and screaming at them, cursing them to hell, and killing
them with the slow ferocity of the untrained but empowered.

'Take what you can,' said Beornoth, walking amongst the
villagers, clasping forearms with his warriors and talking to the
folk of Eoforsham. 'We cannot win this fight against the Vikings
without you. You are the fyrd of Essex, the army, and the protec-
tors of our people. Look to the fallen, strip them of weapons and
armour and arm yourselves. Those who wish to fight for their

land and their loved ones should march with us. We do not cower from the Northmen, we do not wait for them to come and enslave our women and children. They aim to take everything from us, so let us take it from them first!'

The villagers raised their hands and shouted their acclaim at Beornoth's words.

'But we don't know how to fight?' said Gymi. The villager had taken a slight wound to his shoulder and Viking blood flecked his face.

'You are brave. That cannot be taught. We can teach you to fight. Do you want to punish the men who would ravage your wife and enslave your children?' Beornoth was shouting, looking at each of the villagers as they moved amongst the dead.

'I do,' said one man, raising a Viking axe with a bearded blade. Others joined in the chorus until they were all shouting in unison. The villagers took leather armour, knives, axes, spears and all the war gear they could salvage from the dead Vikings.

'You mean to take them with us?' asked Thered. The Northumbrian thegn wiped the gore from his sword upon a fallen Northman's tunic. Byrhtnoth had been right about the young man. Despite his treachery and low cunning the year before, he fought well, and had proved himself trustworthy in his journey north with Eawynn and Aelfwine.

'Those who can fight will come with us. We need every blade, and the ealdorman will soon raise the fyrd, and these men will form part of that force. From now on, any village we pass through we bring any men of fighting age with us. Help them take what they need and teach them how to use their new weapons.'

'Yes, lord.'

'And Thered,' said Beornoth. The young thegn made to leave, but turned back to Beornoth. 'You saved my life today, and you tried to take it last year. So the path ahead of us is clear, the past is wiped out.' He extended his arm, and Thered took it in the warrior's grip, their eyes meeting and holding each other's gaze for a few heartbeats. Men who risk their lives together, who fight and run the danger of enemy blades together, form a bond of iron. There is a recognition that one would die for the other, and that they have existed in the higher state of consciousness where death is upon a man's shoulder and he evades it with his war skill. Beornoth and Thered now had that bond, and men who were once enemies had become brothers of the sword.

13

Beornoth led his force of warriors and villagers against the Vikings for two full turns of the moon. He went from village to village across the east and south of Essex, rousing the menfolk, arming them and hunting Olaf Tryggvason's warriors. Those farmers and blacksmiths swelled the actual warriors in the war band, most of whom were Byrhtnoth's Bloodsworn and Streonwold's fighters from Cheshire. The Norseman Beornoth had captured in his first skirmish upon his return to Essex had told him where Olaf's camp was, and Beornoth led his fighters across the countryside around its location, never getting close enough to see it, but near enough to hunt the crews Olaf would send out foraging for food. The Saxons camped where they could, within church grounds or at the villages they visited, and as the summer settled in, Beornoth's force had become as wolves. They were things of the forest, hills and dales. Their clothes were dirty and worn, but their blades kept bright and sharp. They found Vikings on riversides, trapped them in the woods, and killed them wherever they could find them.

'Are you sure about this?' said Aelfwine, riding alongside

Beornoth at the head of the war band's marching column. They moved across a patchwork of farmland, following the lay of the land like a great serpent snaking across the countryside.

'I'm sure,' said Beornoth. 'We should be within sight of Olaf's camp before nightfall, and today we shall send three men to find the ealdorman.'

'The fyrd should be roused by now, and with God's help, Byrhtnoth will have persuaded the thegns of East Anglia to join the fight. But Olaf has just short of two thousand men inside whatever fortification he has made, and we can't attack that unless we have a similar sized force.'

'We will not attack it, just sting them. Olaf and his White Wolf must be comfortable, enjoying the summer and living off the fat of the land, our land. I want to piss on that. I want Olaf angry and provoked into making rash decisions.'

'Are we stopping soon?' said Leofsunu of Sturmer, nudging his horse alongside them. 'I don't think I've ever been so hungry. I could eat a pox-ridden pig.'

'Soon,' said Beornoth. 'When we reach the safety of that farm up ahead, we shall stop.' He pointed to a high-gabled barn and farmhouse to the south, and Leofsunu grinned. He was the joker of the war band, always finding a jest to ease the men's nervousness before a fight, and a good friend.

'The churl who farms that land will be delighted to see us. There are only one hundred of us for him to feed and water. Why, the man might think we have answered all his prayers when we stop and eat him out of house and home.'

They reached the farmhouse before noon, and Wulfhere rode ahead with Leofsunu to warn the farmer to make ready for the column's arrival. Beornoth led Hríð along a well-worn track with deep ruts from generations of wagon travel to and from the farm. Leofsunu and Wulfhere stood next to the barn, arguing with an

enormous man wearing a jerkin rolled up to reveal thick forearms. His beard and hair sprang out from his head in tight curls,
so that he looked like a bear remonstrating with the two warriors.
The man showed no fear, despite the warriors clad in mail
byrnies and Wulfhere's one-eyed, scarred face, and the
approaching war band.

'We are here for food and water, if you can spare it,' called
Beornoth to the farmer.

'And who might you be?' said the man, fixing Beornoth with a
frown to darken the brightest day. Despite his rank falling well
below that of a thegn, the man showed a defiance and bravery
which amused Beornoth.

'I am Beornoth, a thegn of the East Saxons. I am here with the
authority of Ealdorman Byrhtnoth.'

'I am Dunnere, lord, and this is my land and we do not have
food for so many mouths. We only have enough food for my
small family, as I have explained to these two lords already.'

'You will find some oats or barley, or whatever you have
stored.' Beornoth crossed his arms over Hríð's neck and leant
forward, his voice no longer tinged with the friendliness he had
spoken with at first.

'Ride on to the next farm. Leave us in peace.' Dunnere held a
staff of ash, longer than he was tall, and his knuckles whitened on
the stave.

'You call me lord,' said Beornoth, losing his patience. 'As you
will those men beside you. You will feed us, or we will raze your
farm to the ground and take everything we require. We are at war,
and you farm this land at the ealdorman's pleasure. We are the
only thing stopping the Vikings from swarming over the farm
and slaughtering you and your family. So, show some respect and
find us some food.'

Dunnere sighed and shook his head. He called back towards

his home, a low but wide building topped with freshly cut thatch which shone like gold in the summer sun. Two lads came running from behind the building, as tall and broad as Dunnere himself. He barked at them to bring what they had from the barn.

'There is water from a river, lord,' said Dunnere, 'but to get it, my boys would be gone most of the afternoon.'

'We can find water later.' Beornoth climbed from the saddle and left Hríð to graze on the grass around Dunnere's home. 'The Vikings are only a half-day's ride from here. You are lucky to have avoided their raiders.'

'We have seen them, lord, and thanks to God and the Holy Mother, they have left us in peace. They look for villages, not single farms.'

'They might come for your women,' said Wulfhere.

'There are none here. My wife died years ago. It's just me and my boys.'

'We are raising the fyrd,' said Leofsunu. 'A big man like you must have fought before.'

'Many times,' said Dunnere, and his face turned ashen. 'I knew this day would come. I beg you though, lords. Please don't take my boys.' He swallowed hard and watched his two strapping sons running from the barn with two wheels of cheese and a dried hock of ham. 'I will fight. I will bring my bow and my staff. Please leave my boys here in peace, because I will kill enough Vikings for the three of us. They have never seen the horrors of the shield wall. They have not killed a man, and I would keep it that way if I can.'

'The boys can stay,' said Beornoth. 'I get the feeling that you are worth more than a normal man of the fyrd.'

'Thank you, lord, I will get my bow.' Dunnere stood and strode to his house, calling to his sons to follow him.

'He's a proud man for a churl,' said Aelfwine. 'Impudent, almost.'

'I wouldn't like a crack around the skull from his staff, though,' said Leofsunu. 'If he fights as hard as he argues, then he is welcome.'

'So, what do we do when we get to Olaf's camp?' said Wulfhere. He sat on the grass whittling a piece of wood with a small knife.

'As you know, we have had the men making arrows and gathering as many arrowheads as we can find,' said Beornoth.

'Aye. We have sheaves of them on the carts back there.'

'Tonight we surprise Olaf. We attack him for a change.'

'Good,' said Wulfhere. He pushed himself to his feet and went to find some food.

'He has become a grim beast,' said Leofsunu. 'He used to be good company, always there with a jest and quick to laugh.'

'The Vikings carved that part of him away when Aethelberga died,' said Beornoth. 'A part of him died that day. All he lives for is to fight and kill Norsemen.'

'And there is plenty of that to keep him busy,' said Aelfwine. 'We are but one hundred men against Olaf's many hundreds. Surely you're not suggesting we attack?'

'We shouldn't lose a single man tonight. This is what we are going to do.' Aelfwine and Leofsunu came close and Beornoth told them of his plan, of how he wanted to kick the wasp's nest and let Olaf know he was in a war.

It was a warm, clear night brightened by a low half-moon. Beornoth stared at the stars, twinkling and distant. He wondered if his daughters were watching him up in heaven, if they were happy there and in God's grace. Such thoughts often kept Beornoth awake at night, even though he knew they were questions whose only answer lay in a man's faith. He whispered a brief prayer to God for his daughters and for Eawynn. The words still came unfamiliar and awkward after so long outside of God's grace. A fox barked somewhere in the night, and the rumble of the war band preparing their weapons rustled like the sigh of the sea. Men hiding in the darkness, whispering to each other, stringing their bows and testing their arrows.

'It's time,' said Leofsunu, placing a hand on Beornoth's shoulder. He nodded, and they strode together through the ranks to the front, where Wulfhere waited with Aelfwine. As Beornoth gently shouldered through the front rank of his warriors, a sickly glow crept over the shadowy rise ahead of them, which came from the ground like a great black humped back to reveal the flickering torches of Olaf's camp. The Vikings had taken the village of Actun and fortified it with a fresh ditch and palisade. Torchlight illuminated the ring of that palisade every ten paces, and the fortification was a marching camp, made quickly and simple to take down and erect again at the next town on their march, with the palisade staves little more than the height of a man. Upon first sight, the organisation required to build such a camp had impressed Beornoth. Each man in Olaf's army would have to cut a stave, sharpen it and bury it within the bank created by a ditch the same man had helped dig. But, with one and a half thousand men, they could build such a camp within a day. It sent a shudder down his spine to think that the Vikings could, if Olaf wished it, march across Essex, Wessex and the rest of England in such a way. March all day, stop and make a fortified camp each evening. Beornoth sniffed and turned to Aelfwine.

'Do we have flame?' asked Beornoth.

'We do,' said Aelfwine after glancing over his shoulder, his grin flashing white teeth in the moonlight.

'Forward,' said Beornoth. He moved off in a low crouch, and the men followed. Beornoth, Wulfhere, Leofsunu, Aelfwine and

Thered led one hundred fighters. Streonwold's men marched with them, the northern warriors having distinguished themselves in the fighting across the early summer. Almost half of their force were thegns and warriors, the professional men of the hearth troop for whom weapons and war were how they made their living. The rest were fyrd-men, the villagers Beornoth had picked up as he harried the Vikings across south-east Essex. They had joined him as fearful, honest folk unused to the ways of war. But, after eight weeks of hunting and fighting Vikings, they looked and acted more like warriors. Many wore whatever armour and weapons they had stripped from dead Vikings. Men who had joined Beornoth wearing jerkins and hoods now wore hard-baked leather breastplates and carried axes and spears. Almost half of them carried a shield.

They followed Beornoth's lead, running low with short, quick steps. The sound of their creaking leather and the jangle of their belts and weapons seemed loud in the darkness, and as they ran over the tip of the small hill and the palisade loomed up before them, Beornoth gritted his teeth. If Olaf's men heard them too early, then his men would pour out of the gates and slaughter the much smaller Saxon force. His heart thumped in his chest and Beornoth led them to a point he guessed was five hundred paces away from the Viking camp.

'Form the line,' Beornoth said. He spoke in a half-whisper and half-shout, wanting to be heard by his own men, but hoping that the sound of his voice would not drift across the flat grassland to the Viking walls. The men shuffled into a long line, three ranks deep, as they had practised over and over earlier that day. They had forty bows with them, scrounged and gathered from every home and village Beornoth and his men had marched through since the campaign against the Vikings had begun. 'Kindle the flames.'

Six men knelt and worked at the bundles of tinder they had carried from the hill. They held the handfuls of dried leaves, wood shavings and bark to their mouths, and after adding the glowing faggots they had shielded so carefully on the dash to the Viking camp, they blew carefully into the nascent flames. One caught fire quickly, casting an ethereal glow on the gap-toothed face of the fyrd-man holding it, and the shoulders of the short man next to him sagged as his own bundle failed to light. The gap-toothed man pulled a burning twig from his bundle and passed it to the other, and so it went until there were six glowing bundles of small flames. Men with kindling aflame moved gingerly through the ranks, using their fiery packages to touch similar bundles at the boots of each man with a bow. The fire spread across the lines until they twinkled and shone as bright as the stars above them, and Beornoth let out a nervous sigh, because they would be as visible to the Vikings now as if they had marched up and knocked on the gate itself.

'Light your arrows,' Beornoth shouted, not caring any more about the carry in his voice now that they were lit up like a line of dragon fire. Each man with a bow pulled an arrow from the quiver at his belt and held it to the flames at his feet. How to get the missiles to light had taken a great deal of discussion, until Beornoth decided everybody was right, and so the ranks had a mixture of arrows doused in rendered animal fat, some tied about with dried hay, some with fish oil and whatever else the fyrd-men could find that would burn. Beornoth leaned over and glanced to his left and right. Some men cursed as their arrows failed to spark, and others lifted their flaming missiles with wide grins as orange flame flickered around the shining arrowheads.

'Front rank,' called Aelfwine, drawing his sword and holding it aloft. 'Draw.'

There was a creak as forty bows stretched, each man nocking

his arrow to his bow and raising the weapon skyward as he drew the tight bowstring back to his ear.

'Front rank, loose,' Aelfwine called, and brought his sword down. The arrows flew into the night sky with a whoosh, arcing high and bright into the stars. Some flickered and burned out, but more sailed across the palisade walls to strike into the Viking camp. The Viking Beornoth had captured weeks earlier had told him that Olaf's walls were built around a small village, a typical place of thatched roofs, barns with dried hay for the animals. Also, before Beornoth sent him to Valhalla, the prisoner had revealed that Olaf had brought the sails from his precious ship to use as tents for his men. Heavy woollen sails which would be dry in the summer heat, the precious lifeblood of his Viking warships and the means by which the winds carried them from their cold northern homes to England's shores.

'Second rank, draw,' Aelfwine ordered again. 'Loose.'

And so it went. Flaming arrows soared across the sky to rain fire and death amongst the Vikings. Each rank sent four volleys into the sky before Beornoth heard the first shouts of alarm carry across the field from Olaf's camp. Small pockets of glowing flame sprang up within the walls, casting dancing shadows against the black sky, the outlines of running bodies and the shouts of leaders trying to order their panicked men to deal with the fires mixed with cries of pain. Beornoth nodded to himself, chewing on his beard, his hand clenched around the shaft of his spear.

'Ready the shield men,' Beornoth said, and unslung his own shield from where it rested against his back. 'Keep the arrows going for as long as possible.'

Beornoth took ten steps forward and hefted his shield. Wulfhere came alongside him, as did Leofsunu, Thered and Streonwold. Aelfwine stayed with the archers to encourage their bowshots.

'Will they come?' asked Wulfhere, the night making his one-eyed face even more frightening to look upon.

'They'll come,' said Beornoth.

'We can't fight them here,' said Streonwold, his jowls quivering as he spoke. 'There are too many. We will all die here in the dark.'

'They won't all come,' said Beornoth. 'Most will be busy putting out the flames, trying to save their sails and their plunder. But some will come, their pride demands it.'

'And we kill whatever comes out of that gate,' said Wulfhere, and if any of the Vikings saw the grim set of his jaw, they would fear his wrath more than the flames within their camp.

The arrows flying overhead flew like flocks of fiery birds, but the number of arrows reduced with each volley as men emptied their quivers. Until the arrows only soared in ones and twos. Aelfwine came running, his shield banging against his back.

'No fire left,' he said. 'Do we stand or leave them to their burning camp?' No sooner had the words escaped Aelfwine's lips than the camp gate yawned open. It was a makeshift thing made of the same staves as the walls, but crossways with vertical pieces nailed together to form a gate wide enough for three men to march through abreast. From that gate came the Vikings. First, just two of them came bare-chested from their beds and clutching axes, shouting incoherently above what was now roaring flame inside the walls.

'We have a few arrows left, lord,' came a shout from behind, and Beornoth turned as the hulking figure of Dunnere lumbered from the darkness. 'We can pin them there.'

Beornoth moved to the big farmer and placed a hand on his shoulder. 'Do it then.'

Dunnere called to the bowmen, and they ran ten paces ahead of the thegns and made two fresh lines. He ordered them into ranks, and the men listened to him. Although Dunnere was one of them and not one of the warrior caste, the fyrd-men respected him. He ordered the ranks to loose, and their arrows flew low along the night-darkened grass. Arrows struck the two Vikings, the sound of their contact lost amongst the panic and uproar within the camp. The two fell, and Dunnere ordered his men to loose again, and arrows thudded into three more Vikings who dared to edge out of the gate.

'Hold them there,' Beornoth ordered. 'Cwicca, my horse.'

The young warrior fetched Hríð from the rear, and Beornoth climbed into the saddle.

'Where in the blazes of hell are you going?' asked Streonwold.

'To let them know who burns them.'

Beornoth led Hríð into a canter towards the walls, and as he drew close, he launched his spear across the palisade walls and drew his sword, holding it aloft so that it shone in the red hue of the burning camp. He galloped Hríð along the front of the walls, sword aloft, and then brought the warhorse to a stop before the gates. The stallion whinnied and rose on his hind legs so that Beornoth had to cling to the reins to stay in the saddle.

'I am Beornoth,' he roared at the Vikings. 'I burned your sails, which take your women years to weave. I have killed your warriors. I curse you, Olaf Tryggvason, and your White Wolf. You are the sons of whores, cowardly turds shat from the arses of your dying gods.' He swung his sword, and Beornoth wanted Vikings to see him. His face twisted into a feral snarl behind the eyeholes of his helmet. The rising flames of Olaf's burning sails and his camp flickered above the palisade to shine upon Beornoth's byrnie, helmet and sword. *You raid my home and kill my people. I burn yours and send your men screaming to hell.*

Vikings emerged from the gate, this time under cover of raised shields, so that Dunnere's arrows thudded into the linden wood. Six of them came forth, one falling with an arrow in his foot and the rest parting to reveal a tall, lithe man with bone-white hair. He wore no helmet, and his long hair unbound, shimmering in the moonlight like a fetch or some other being from the underworld. It was the White Wolf. Beornoth pointed his sword at the man, and kept the point levelled at him as Hríð turned on the spot, raking the earth, wanting to charge at the gallop. The White Wolf's mouth moved, but the raucous noise of the burning camp drowned his voice out. Arrows sank into the surrounding earth, but the White Wolf did not flinch. Beornoth let Hríð ride in a wide circle, and he fought against the desire to charge at the Vikings, and to cut down the White Wolf where he stood. That could wait. For now it was enough that he had caused pain to Olaf and his warriors. It would suffice that he managed to attack Olaf where he felt safe, that the Northmen had felt pain and suffering instead of the East Saxons. So Beornoth rode back to his men who cheered and laughed at the victory. He rode amongst them with his sword aloft and let them enjoy the moment, the delight of hurting and punishing men who have come to kill you. The deeply satisfying feeling of vengeance. But the celebrations were short-lived, because the day after the burning, Offa came from the ealdorman. The fyrd was mustering, and all were to meet on Essex's northern border. Byrhtnoth was preparing an army for war.

14

Offa and the fyrd of Essex awaited Beornoth at the ancient moot mound outside of the town of Celmersford. It was a hill topped by a white speckled standing stone as tall as a man. On the ride north, Aelfwine told Beornoth that the place had been a rallying point for armies going back to the days before the Rome folk came to the lands of the Britons. The mound itself was said to house the barrow of an old king, buried with slaves and treasure and protected by a wyrd woven through with ancient sorcery. Beornoth and his hundred men reached the mound to find Offa, Godric and the rest of Byrhtnoth's hearth troop there with more men than Beornoth could count. Makeshift camps littered the fields around the standing stone, with cloaks held up with branches, more elaborate tents of cloth, and men sleeping out in the warm summer air.

'Must be close to a thousand men,' said Leofsunu of Sturmer, scratching at his balding head in wonder.

'Enough to stand and fight, enough for a battle,' said Wulfhere.

Aelfwine and Thered formed the men into a long column and led them to an empty field beyond the mound. It was a pasture filled with too many sour-faced sheep and cows huddling together. The massing army of Essex had driven the animals off their grazing pastures and into one small field full of yellow-flowered weeds. Beornoth ordered Wulfhere, Thered and Leofsunu to set up somewhere for the men to sleep and to find some food whilst he went with Aelfwine to find Offa. The two thegns left their mounts with Cwicca at the cow field and picked their way through the massed gathering of the farmers and villagers of Essex. Men drank ale and played at knucklebones. They baked bread in the ashes of their campfires and stirred thin broths in small cauldrons or upturned helmets.

They found Offa at the base of the standing stone. The old thegn stood with his brawny arms folded across his chest, shouting at a group of ruddy-faced men in jerkins. Offa spotted Beornoth and Aelfwine through the press of men and waved a greeting. Beornoth was a head taller than any of the fyrd men in the group, and they parted to let him through, hundreds of eyes staring up at him. Beornoth's byrnie and cloak brushed against the soft wool of their tunics as he wove his way between them; many bowed their heads to the warrior and thegn and others just stared with mouths agape.

'Trouble?' said Beornoth.

'Pain in the bloody arse,' said Offa. The fyrd men slipped away from the gathering now that Aelfwine and Beornoth had arrived to support Offa. Their mail and weapons marked them out as leaders and men to be feared. 'Not enough food, nowhere for men to sleep, nowhere safe to shit, nothing to make tents from. A bloody mess.'

'You have done well to gather so many, Offa. It's always this way. That's why the ealdorman waited to call out the fyrd. Too hard to feed, not good enough in the fight, and if we stay here more than a few days, men will fall sick from the ill humours rising from a thousand men's shit. Is there water close by?'

'A small brook beyond this hill. I've warned them all not to piss in it. It's our only source of drinking water.'

'Where is the ealdorman?' asked Aelfwine.

'East Anglia,' said Offa. 'Still trying to gather more men. What we have here is not enough to fight the Vikings.'

'Not nearly enough. We attacked their camp, burned it badly. Bad enough so they will have to march again, anyway.'

'We can't stay here for more than one more day.' Offa rubbed his eyes and exhaled loud and long.

'So we march north tomorrow,' said Beornoth. 'We keep the army moving, live off the land. We meet Byrhtnoth and gather more men as we go. Then, we force the Vikings to fight before we run out of food, or the fyrd melts away to get back to their homes and prepare for the harvest.'

'The fighting will be the easiest thing we do this summer,' grumbled Offa.

'How shall we feed so many on the march?' asked Aelfwine.

'The people won't thank us for it, but we must take what we need. Send a hundred men ahead of the marching column to gather supplies. We butcher cows and sheep, and bring some along for milk. Take whatever wagons we can find,' said Beornoth.

'But then we have to feed the cows and sheep?' Aelfwine shrugged his shoulders.

'One problem at a time. The animals can eat the grass as we march. It's summer,' said Beornoth. There was no gilded answer to the problem, no simple solution. They had gathered a force of a thousand men, who all needed food and water, and would all piss and shit until they could bring the Vikings to battle. That fight had to come quickly.

Beornoth spent a solemn night camped with Wulfhere, Cwicca and his men. Streonwold and Thered came to sit by their fire and they shared a thin broth of vegetables and a few scant pieces of rabbit meat.

'He is a changed man,' said Streonwold, raising his eyebrows towards where Wulfhere sat with his back resting upon the wide trunk of a sprawling beech tree. Its branches were thick and old, and its dense leaves provided shelter for the men as they ate their evening meal. Wulfhere whittled at a piece of golden timber. He sat hunched with a thick woollen cloak pulled close about him and its hood hiding his face. 'He used to be good company around the fire.'

'That was before the Vikings came,' said Beornoth, grimacing at a piece of rabbit gristle stuck in his teeth.

'Was it bad, at Branoc's Tree?'

'It was bad. The Northmen got to the women and killed most, all the men butchered. Olaf and his White Wolf hanged their corpses from the tree which gave the place its name. Wulfhere will never be the man he was. There is too much pain there. He saw Aethelberga's corpse, and what they had done to her. He craves revenge, but few know better than I that vengeance is a thirst which can never be quenched.'

'Will you go back there? To Branoc's Tree?'

'It's my heriot. The lands granted to me by Byrhtnoth. I lost my last one, the heriot of my father and his father before him. I can't lose another. If I don't have a heriot, the land that comes with my weapons, my horse, and how I earn my silver, then what am I?'

'You could go back to recovering lost goats for farmers, or

chucking drunks out of country taverns, or whatever you did before you came to fair Essex,' said Leofsunu of Sturmer. He came and sat beside Beornoth, purposefully barging into him as he sat heavily so that Beornoth toppled to one side, and the rest of the warriors laughed. 'Sorry, Beo, I didn't see you there.' Leofsunu cradled a loaf of freshly baked bread in his arms, along with a thick chunk of cheese, and a skin of ale. 'I scrounged this up from Dunnere and his lot. Only cost me one arm ring.'

'An arm ring for a bit of cheese and some stale bread?' said Streonwold. 'Are you drunk, man?'

'They have robbed you, Leofsunu,' said Thered, laughing. 'Did Dunnere have his face covered and a hood up at the time of this bargain?'

'What, like a robber on the road, you mean?' said Leofsunu after a short giggle. 'No, but he was happy with the trade.'

'You will be a beggar by the time the summer's over if that's how you bargain,' said Streonwold.

'There will be plenty of arm rings to take from the Vikings I intend to kill, so what is one less in exchange for some good cheese and warm bread? And there is ale.' Leofsunu took a long pull at the ale skin, and followed it up with a monstrous belch which sent the men into peals of laughter again. He handed the ale to Beornoth, and he took it, its thick hoppy smell wafting up to his nose, making his mouth water. He had once found solace in the emptiness of drunkenness, and had believed that it brought him peace. But it was not a real peace. It took Beornoth away from his problems, from the difficulties he must face. But the people of Essex needed him, and the answer to the problem of feeding and moving the fyrd did not lie at the bottom of Leofsunu's ale skin. So, with a frown, he passed the ale to Streonwold, who took it gladly. 'Here, take some bread then.'

Beornoth nodded his thanks and tore a piece of bread from

the loaf. It was warm and its smell sent his belly into a churning growl. He dipped the piece into his broth, took a bite, and it was delicious. But once he bit down into it, his teeth scraped and crunched small pieces of grit. 'It's full of bloody stones,' said Beornoth.

Leofsunu laughed. 'What do you expect? They baked it in the ground, over yonder. Not in some clean baker's oven.'

'I'll take some to Wulfhere,' said Beornoth, and he thanked his friend as Leofsunu tore another chunk from the bread. Beornoth filled his bowl again with rabbit broth and went to sit next to Wulfhere. The beech tree was as thick around as four men, and its long branches grew from low on the trunk, so that Beornoth had to duck to reach Wulfhere.

'I brought you some food,' said Beornoth, groaning at the ache from his old wounds as he sat next to the broad-shouldered warrior.

'Thank you, lord,' said Wulfhere, and took the food hungrily.

'Watch out though, the bread is full of stones. We shall march north tomorrow and find Byrhtnoth, then double back towards Olaf.' Wulfhere knew that. He had been at the discussion earlier by the standing stone, but Beornoth found it hard to talk to Wulfhere now, and they were the only words he could conjure to break the silence. Before the raid, Wulfhere had been the easiest person to talk to in the world. Always quick with a jest, loved by the folk of Branoc's Tree. 'What are you carving?'

'It's for you, lord. But it's not finished, so you can't see it yet.'

'I am honoured. When this is over, we shall have to rebuild Branoc's Tree. I will need you, the people will need you.'

'I don't think I can go back to that place.' Wulfhere spoke in a soft whisper, so quiet that Beornoth had to lean in to hear him. 'I am sworn to be your man, lord. But I cannot live in the place where... that happened.'

'Life is hard. But it goes on, you have to live. Aethelberga is gone, but you remain.'

Wulfhere shook the hood from his head and fixed Beornoth with his one fierce eye. The other side of his face was twisted and scarred, the dead eye closed over by taut skin. 'I do not remain,' he hissed. 'The man I used to be died alongside Aethelberga. She was everything to me. A lady, a noble, god-fearing woman with a kind heart. Imagine a woman like that taking an interest in a big fool like me. She was the light, every-thing good in the world. And they took her, they hurt her, lord. Hurt her bad. Where is the justice in that? All that remains of me is this creature, this tortured thing my soul is trapped within. I eat this food to keep my body alive and strong, so that I can kill Vikings. That is all there is, vengeance on those bastards from across the sea. I am render, gouger, slasher and killer. My prayer to God is that I die in battle so that I can join my love in heaven. But not before I cut the head from the White Wolf, and I have killed enough Norsemen to send Olaf howling back across the sea.'

Beornoth sighed and nodded, for they were the thoughts that had lived within his own heart. 'There will always be a place for you at Branoc's Tree for as long as I am thegn.'

'You have changed since that raid. Lady Eawynn was reborn in that slaughter, and because she returned, so did you. You are whole again, and I have nothing. I remember when you came for me, when I was a masterless man. You came to Offa's Crag, a brutal man of fury and strength. You saved me and brought me south with you, and you were a cruel being who lived only for battle and blood. What you were, I am now.'

'I am still that thing. My daughters are still dead. Eawynn is better, but not the same woman she was when we were young.'

Wulfhere shuddered, and his head fell forward so that his

chin touched his chest. He sniffed and cuffed at his eye. 'Does it get any easier, lord, with time?'

'No. Not an hour goes by where I don't think of my girls. Not a day passes when I do not mourn for the life I had when I was young. The pain is always there, but I just learned to live with it, to get through each day. I wish I could tell you it goes away with time, but it does not. All that remains after they have gone is anger and vengeance.'

'So we will kill them, lord.'

'That is who we are, what the people need us for. So, yes. We will stand before their axes and spears, we will charge into the fury of the Northmen and will kill them, you and I. For those we have lost.' Beornoth held out his hand and Wulfhere grabbed his wrist in the warrior's grip. They held each other's arms for a long moment, eyes connecting in understanding. They were brothers of the blade, and each had suffered unspeakable loss, and the only way Beornoth knew how to deal with that was war.

The army marched north the following morning, but it took most of that day to get the men moving. Camp had to be broken down, and packs created from branches and whatever else the men could find to carry supplies and weapons. The thegns and warriors of the hearth troops rode horses, but the fyrd men marched. They carried their scythes and knives, rolled-up cloaks with food tied to branches and hoisted across their shoulders.

Beornoth rode along the line until he found Dunnere marching at the front. The big bear of a man had his bow strapped to his back and walked with his quarterstaff as a walking stick.

'Lord,' said Dunnere as Beornoth slowed Hríð to fall in along-side the farmer. Beornoth recognised the men marching with Dunnere as those who had remonstrated with Offa beneath the standing stone.

'You men are leaders, and the others respect you,' said Beornoth, but did not wait for a response. 'The army is slow on the march, and we need to organise foraging parties to range ahead and around the marching column looking for food. You men will be responsible for that.' They grumbled, and one man was about to splutter an objection until Beornoth fixed him with a frown, creasing the cliff of his face. 'Take twenty men each. Hunt for game, confiscate livestock, take cheese, forage for roots and berries, fill skins with water. At the end of each day, report to Lord Offa with how the work has gone that day so that he can understand if we have enough to feed the men.'

'Yes, lord,' said Dunnere.

Beornoth slipped one of his silver arm rings over his hand and tossed it to Dunnere. The big man's mouth fell open, and the fyrd leaders around him gasped. 'That's for how well you fought against the Vikings. There is one of those for each of you at the end of the march if you do as I say.' They bowed their heads and moved back along the column to pick their men for foraging duty. Beornoth clicked his tongue and urged Hríð forward to catch up to Offa and Aelfwine at the head of the column.

'This lot will stretch across half the shire at this rate,' said Offa, leaning back over his saddle to stare at the long line of men behind them. They spanned the dips and rises in the countryside, crawling slowly like a huge worm.

'The rear could be days behind by the time we meet the ealdorman,' said Aelfwine.

'I have ordered foraging parties to range around the column,' said Beornoth. 'Appoint some of our men, perhaps Streonwold's riders, to stay with the fyrd men at the rear. They are most vulnerable to attack, if the Vikings venture this far north. I will ride ahead with Wulfhere, Thered and Leofsunu to meet Ealdorman

Byrhtnoth. Offa, you are the captain, so you should command the army until the ealdorman arrives.'

'Very well,' said Offa, but the curl of his bottom lip said that he would rather ride on ahead than manage the myriad problems created by the fyrd on the march. But he was the captain of Byrhtnoth's hearth troop of thegns, and leading them was his duty.

'We will march south again once we have met the ealdorman, and the army is fully formed,' said Beornoth. 'So even if the column becomes strung out, it will fold in on itself when we change direction. Watch out for the enemy.'

Beornoth left the marching column behind, and he pushed ahead with Cwicca, Wulfhere, Thered and Leofsunu of Sturmer and twenty of their men. They rode north across the flatlands of Essex, low-lying farmland edged by hedgerow and clutches of forest stretching to the horizon as far as the eye could see. Beornoth's riders pushed hard under a pale sky, where thin clouds raced across the heavens before a warm, blustery wind. The next morning, after a chill night sleeping under the stars, they spied the ealdorman at the head of a line of warriors, riders and men on foot. The column wound around the edge of a wild, dark forest bristling with briar, their spears pointing lazily skywards.

'So few,' said Leofsunu, the colour draining from his face as he made a rough count of the spears behind the ealdorman. Beornoth's heart sank at the truth of that, and they rode in shocked silence towards their ealdorman. Beornoth counted roughly two hundred men. Hríð's traces jangled as he rode, and deep in the forest a murder of crows cawed and cackled. A shiver ran across Beornoth's shoulders. He felt the prospect of victory slipping away.

'Beornoth, well met!' shouted Byrhtnoth, rising in the saddle with his hand held aloft.

'Lord Byrhtnoth,' said Beornoth, bringing Hríð close and falling in to ride alongside the ealdorman. He smiled greetings at the men of Byrhtnoth's hearth troop. Godric and his surviving brother Godwig rode behind the ealdorman, and the young men in their expensive war finery glowered at Beornoth. He flashed them a scowl before turning his eyes back to Byrhtnoth. Godric and Godwig had evidently not forgiven him for missing the fight at Byrhtnoth's estate where their other brother had died. 'Offa called out the fyrd as you ordered and they march towards this position.'

'The Vikings are the other way,' said Byrhtnoth, his iron-grey beard bristling on a jutting chin.

'We wanted to keep the men moving. There are too many to keep in one place. Once we join them, we march south. But Olaf is not the only Viking in England. What news of Forkbeard?'

'Still in Gippeswic, he does not raid nor has he made any attack. Ships come and go, he takes silver and makes it into coins.'

Beornoth leaned over his saddle to peer back at the column behind them. 'How many warriors of East Anglia are with you, lord?'

'Not nearly enough. It is as you said, Leofric is dying and his son fears the Danes. He won't call out the fyrd, nor will he rouse the thegns to fight. He fears provoking Forkbeard, both for the fight it might cause, and in case Forkbeard makes himself king in the shire. A new Christian king would not be unwelcome, especially in the old Danelaw.'

'So, who are these men?'

'The sons and warriors of friends of mine, who were also friends of Leofric. They understand the threat we face, and so these are the few brave men who will join us in our fight. This is it. There will be no more warriors from East Anglia. But there are good men here, and a Saxon thegn is as good as two hairy-arsed

raiders from Jutland. We have stout fighters here, men of reputation. Sitric of Thetford, and Aelfnoth from the fens.'

'So we fight?'

'We fight, and it must be a battle, Beo. No more skirmishing.
We must call them to the shield wall, defeat Olaf once and for all.
He has cursed our shorelines for too long. We must beat him so
badly that we leave him with too few men to crew his ships. We
must send him limping back to Norway like a whipped dog.'

'We burned his camp, lord. Stung him, hurt his pride.'

'Something has him rattled. For the rat is out of his trap. We
saw sails heading northward off the coast days back, forty ships.'

'Olaf's fleet,' said Beornoth. 'So he left Essex?'

'No such luck. The ships came back again two days later, their
sails were spotted off the north-east coast but they raced under
sail and we lost sight of them. Perhaps Olaf looked for easy
raiding or a place to camp, or he went to East Anglia but ran into
Forkbeard's fleet and turned south again. We are a half-day's ride
from the coast here, and Olaf and his army could be anywhere.'

Beornoth ground his teeth at the warp and weft of it. His plan
had worked, and Olaf had sprung from his camp to take to the
sea. But the mobility of his sleek dragon ships, even with some of
their sails burned, meant he could be anywhere along the coast,
or he could easily sail up any of the wide estuaries and be deep
within Essex within days, cutting a swathe of blood-soaked
carnage across the land. Olaf had sailed from his winter camp at
Folkestone to move deeper into Essex, and Beornoth had burned
that new camp forcing Olaf to move once more. So large a Viking
fleet could prey up and down the coast, and without a fleet of
their own to follow or challenge them, the Saxons were reliant on
scouts or fisher-folk reporting sightings of the enemy ships.

'We must find him. Enough people have died.'

'Aye. But first we meet the king. He sent a rider to me four days ago. He waits for us at Hertsford. Offa will keep the army moving south, if Olaf wants to take Essex then he must surely seek the River Blackwater. We shall ride to the king with fifty men. Hertsford is a day's ride west of here, and the king has journeyed far from Winchester to get there.'

15

King Æthelred brought three hundred warriors and twenty priests to meet with the ealdorman of the East Saxons. The king's men erected a tent the size of a feasting hall, which they had brought in a wagon all the way from Winchester. A series of thick poles and ropes held the thing aloft, and woven rugs littered the ground within so that the king would not sleep wet-arsed in the heather as he travelled into his shire beset by the enemy.

Beornoth followed Byrhtnoth as he marched amongst the warriors of Wessex. The ealdorman grumbled to himself, chewing on his bearded bottom lip with his forehead creased like the North Sea under a winter storm. Men bowed their heads to Byrhtnoth, and he nodded greetings to those he recognised from previous battles, of which he had fought many in his long life. Beornoth knew better than to talk to the ealdorman when he was in such a mood, his mind boiling over with the troubles of the kingdom, planning how to raise the important issues with the king, and navigate the slippery but highly cunning and learned bishops and monks who travelled everywhere with the pious king.

'Thank God the mother is no longer part of this nest of vipers, the king now has a voice of his own. Or at least he would if his cloying priests gave him a chance to breathe,' said Byrhtnoth, talking to himself and not expecting a response. It had been just over a year since Beornoth and the ealdorman had fallen foul of the Queen Dowager Ælfthryth's plotting. The king had banished her to a distant nunnery, which was all the better for the safety of his kingdom, and now the king ruled in his own right without his mother dripping poison in his ear. Beornoth could imagine the complex warp and weft inside Byrhtnoth's thought cage as they stalked towards the king's tent. Byrhtnoth had been a loyal follower of Æthelred's father, the great King Edgar who had over-seen a generation of peace. But whilst there had been peace without Viking raids, or fighting between the noble houses of England, there was plenty of political turbulence. Edgar had favoured reform in the Church, and to support the revered and holy Bishop Dunstan, the king took land from the rich men of England and gave it to the Church for monasteries. He took land with rivers, mills, smithies and cattle to drive rents and income into the Church, keeping it prosperous and powerful. When the old king died, Edgar's widow Ælfthryth had the king's first-born son by his first wife, and heir Edward, killed so that her own son by Edgar, Æthelred, could become king. Byrhtnoth had sided with the loyal followers of Edward and the dead King Edgar's wishes and fighting had broken out between those who supported the queen, and those who supported Edward. Once the queen had Edward killed, it forced peace between the two factions, and since then, there was no man in all England more loyal to the throne than Byrhtnoth of Essex. No ealdorman had fought harder or spilled more blood for his king than Byrhtnoth. He was the warlord of England.

Two burly guards came to attention before the folded-back

wings of the royal tent, their byrnies' belts and helmets making a shunking sound as they stood tall with their spears angled forwards. Beornoth stepped over a guy rope and ducked under the low entrance to the tent. It smelled damp inside, like freshly dug mushrooms, and the king sat on a high-backed chair flanked by a gaggle of green- and black-robed priests. They were small, frail men with soft hands and sharp faces. They leaned into the king, whispering and gesturing with ringed fingers, and all stood in sour-faced silence as Byrhtnoth and Beornoth entered.

'Ah, Lord Byrhtnoth,' said Æthelred, rising from his seat. 'My *dux bellorum*, and the mighty Beornoth.' The king was young and willowy, his hair cut short and swept back beneath a circlet of gold upon his forehead. He wore a fine red robe over green trews, and a large golden cross hung from his neck by a silver chain. *Dux bellorum* meant 'Lord of War' in the tongue of the Rome folk, which the clergy of England still spoke as though they were Romans themselves. Beornoth knew nothing of that tongue, but had heard the king address the ealdorman by that name frequently. The title honoured Byrhtnoth, and the king embraced and kissed him warmly on the cheek.

'Lord king,' said Byrhtnoth. 'You look hale.'

'I am tired and vexed. The storm of war is upon us, Byrhtnoth, Vikings beset my eastern shires. But what to do about it? That is the question which keeps me awake at night. What to do...'

'There is but one course of action, my king. We must fight them, send them home so badly whipped that they will never return.'

'War is not so easy as it seems.' The king inclined his head towards his priests as they fussed at robes. Beornoth recognised Sigeric, the archbishop of Canterbury, and Bishop Aelfhere of Winchester. The bishop leaned into the taller archbishop, whispering into his ear, his face pursed like a cat's arse.

'I know the face of war, lord king. And it is not a thing of my choosing. These men have come here to kill our people and steal our lands and wealth. Why, Olaf raided Beornoth's own heriot. The Vikings butchered his people and laid their foul, heathen hands upon the good lady Aethelberga before they killed her. I fought Olaf's men on my own estate, my men killed and house burned on the very fields where we flew hawks together. War is upon us, my king, whether we want it or not.'

'I know all this,' said the king. Æthelred dragged a long-fingered hand down his lean face. 'We have Olaf and his Jomsvikings in Essex, and King Sweyn Forkbeard of the Danes looms in Gippeswic like some sort of fell Grendel monster perching on the edge of my kingdom. I am not stupid, Byrhtnoth, and nor am I a coward. If I call out the fyrd and warriors of Wessex and Devonshire and march on Olaf, we could become bogged down there all summer fighting a war of attrition. Which leaves the land wide open for Forkbeard to march unopposed on Winchester and Canterbury. He could capture my royal seat and the centre of our most Holy Church whilst we trade blows with the Norsemen in the south. Or, we march on Forkbeard and Olaf has the run of the country. I could summon the ealdormen and their warriors from each of my shires, but we are in late summer. By the time my messengers reached the ealdormen in the north and west of our fair island, and they sent word to their thegns to muster, gathered food and other supplies to keep their armies fed, and then marched to support us here in the south east corner of the kingdom, months will have passed. Worst of all, they tell me Forkbeard is a Christian! You met him, I hear, Beornoth. What sort of man is he?'

'He is indeed a Christian, lord king,' said Beornoth, shifting his muddy boots on the king's soft rug. Heat ran up his neck and his face turned red under the gaze of the men in the tent, the men who effectively ran the kingdom. 'Forkbeard is a thoughtful man, clever. He turned on his own father to make himself king of the Danes. He is ruthless and cunning, lord. His are not honourable, god-fearing men like the bishops and gentlefolk in this tent. Forkbeard might worship God and wear a cross on his chest, but he is a brutal man, a warlord and a warrior.'

'There,' said the king, pointing at Beornoth. 'So this Forkbeard is a new kind of Viking, not the bloodthirsty pagan raiders of Alfred's day. This Sweyn is a thinker. We all know how sour the nobles of the old Danelaw are, and how quickly they would accept a new Christian king with no ties to our Church. Why have the men of East Anglia not thrown Forkbeard out? Why?' The king turned around, searching the whole tent with his arms outstretched, and he was shouting, and no man would offer an answer because the king wanted to answer his own question. 'Because calling out the fyrd ruins a shire for years. Crops die, the army eats every animal and grain store in its path, and the men die, leaving the fields unharvested. They don't want to fight Sweyn. He is probably related to half of the bastards in East Anglia! So, what do you advise we do, Ealdorman Byrhtnoth?'

'Everything you say is true, lord king,' said Byrhtnoth, the confidence sapped from his voice so that it came from his enormous frame as more of a tired plea than advice offered with conviction. 'But we must fight. Defeat Olaf first and then march on Forkbeard. We must protect our people, and your throne. We have tried paying the Vikings with a *gafol*, the monstrous payment of silver handed over to Olaf in return for peace. The only peace it bought was through wintertime, when it is too cold and wet for men to fight anyway. Twice we have paid Olaf, and he keeps coming back.'

'Battle is ever the solution for a warmonger,' said Archbishop Sigeric. The holy men around him nodded, arms folded across their chests. The insult of the words hit Beornoth like a slap across the face. 'I am sure that defeating Olaf and Sweyn would burnish your fame even brighter, Lord Byrhtnoth. But we live in a civilised kingdom, where diplomacy and thought carry as much weight as strength at arms.'

'Warmonger?' said Byrhtnoth. The ealdorman shook his head with incredulity.

Æthelred raised a hand to the archbishop to silence him. 'Byrhtnoth is the protector of our realm, and no man has risked more or fought more bravely than the ealdorman of Essex against the Viking threat. And you are right, Byrhtnoth. We must defend ourselves against the invader. So, I have brought you three hundred of the finest warriors of Wessex, led by men of my hearth troop. Wighelm and Wigstan, come forward.' Two big men emerged from the shadows at the tent's rear. They were both broad, with scarred faces and swords strapped to their waists. They were a striking pair, because they were twins. Identical in every way, apart from the scarring across their flat, hard faces. 'These are amongst the finest warriors in all England, and as you know, three hundred professional warriors are as good as a thousand men of the fyrd. I give you men, Byrhtnoth, to defend your shire, but we still support the strategy of avoiding war with the Vikings.'

'Your warriors are most welcome, lord king. But without the fyrds, or full complement of thegns of East Anglia, Wessex and Devonshire, we cannot win a battle against Olaf. He has one and half thousand battle-hardened Vikings in his army. And with all due respect, my lord, what strategy of avoiding war?'

Archbishop Sigeric sidled forward, his long robe slithering across the plush rug like a snake. 'We give them what they desire, we pay them silver in return for peace. It has worked before. They are pirates and brigands, nothing more. If we pay them, they will sail away without another Saxon life wasted.'

'When has it worked?' said Byrhtnoth, laughing with incredulity at the plan. 'You paid Olaf before, and he is still here. You pay him at the end of each summer, and he swears oaths not to attack. He spends his winters nice and safe here in England, and then in the spring he sails his fleet to another port on our coastline and attacks us again with axe and spear. Have you forgotten Watchet? River's Bend?'

The archbishop coughed and spluttered, his lips pared back from his yellowed teeth in anger. Again, the king raised his hands for calm.

'This is how it will be,' said Æthelred. 'Byrhtnoth, you have the fyrd of Essex. You have five hundred men from East Anglia and three hundred of my own warriors from Wessex. With that force you will fight Olaf, for he has broken oaths and is not to be trusted if we offer him another *gafol* payment. We will send messengers to this Forkbeard and sue for peace. We will pay the man to leave and return to his own kingdom. Now, I tire of this bickering. We shall reconvene this evening for supper. I hear we have venison.' The king smiled, and Byrhtnoth nodded in grim acceptance of the king's order. 'And how is the noble warrior, Beornoth?' asked the king.

Beornoth stood with a straight back and picked a corner of the tent over the king's shoulder and fixed his eyes upon that. The king's question surprised him, and he didn't want to stare at his boots like a churl, but nor did he want to lock eyes with the king and seem impudent. The king was not a short man, but Beornoth was still half a head taller than him, so he stared to the right of the king's forehead at a tent pole of smooth wood. 'I am well, lord king,' said Beornoth.

'I am sorry to hear of your troubles at Branoc's Tree. Please pass on my best wishes to your wife.'

'That's very kind of you, my lord. She will be honoured to hear that you have asked after her.'

'So, this Forkbeard is a tricky man to understand, is he not?'

'He is not your normal Viking, lord.'

'Does he fight in the front line with his warriors, or is he more of a thinker, a leader who keeps himself behind the clash of arms to preserve his ability to make decisions?'

Beornoth cleared his throat. It was a slippery question, for the king himself was no warrior, and Beornoth did not want to insult his king with his reply. 'We haven't met across the war-fence, my lord. But he bears the scars of a fighter, and he has the respect of his men. Men who were loyal to his father. Forkbeard has your royal mint at Gippeswic, lord king, and he forges coin of his own, enriching himself.'

'Yes. A man who would depose and banish his own father is both ruthless and ambitious. Which is precisely why we must be wary. If he makes his own coin in the mint, at least he is not raiding and stealing it. Let us face one enemy at a time, Beornoth. Now, farewell until this evening.' The king beckoned to Archbishop Sigeric and walked away with his hands clasped behind his back and his head held low, deep in thought.

Byrhtnoth turned on his heel and strode from the tent, and Beornoth followed. 'Stay here, Beo,' said the ealdorman. 'Talk to the bishop of Winchester and tell him we need silver for the men, and to buy food and iron. See what you can get from him.'

'Me, lord?'

'Yes you, who else?'

'Well, perhaps Aelfwine is better suited to that kind of talk.' Beornoth knew what he was, and what he wasn't. And he was no man for negotiating with a silver-tongued bishop. Breaking a shield wall, yes, but haggling for a chest of silver was best left to a man with a better mind than his.

'He's not here. Go on, you are more cunning than you think. See if you can't rattle his thought cage a little. Whilst I think about how we will fight Olaf Tryggvason and his Jomsvikings with a handful of warriors and a thousand farmers. Because we must stop them. Olaf won't leave our lands whilst he believes our king will pay him off every summer. He makes himself rich whilst our people suffer. I will return to the men and ready our horses to leave, join us when you can. The archbishop is wrong. The only thing Olaf and his Vikings understand is this.' Byrhtnoth rested his hand on the gold-wrapped hilt of his sword.

'Yes, lord.' Beornoth watched the ealdorman duck under-neath the open tent flap and disappear into the sunlight. Beornoth turned and shifted himself awkwardly. Bishop Aelfhere was a portly man. He wore a long robe of purest white covered by a woollen knee-length garment of green, with baggy sleeves. Beornoth waited whilst the various bishops and priests of the king's inner circle talked together in hushed voices. A serving girl with golden hair braided neatly beneath a cloth cap offered him a silver cup of ale, and Beornoth asked her for water instead. She strode briskly away and returned with his drink. Beornoth thanked her and sipped his water, waiting for his moment to approach the bishop. The holy men spoke at length, and Beornoth felt like a mud-caked churl in his byrnie, boots and stained jerkin compared to the clean, crisp finery of the churchmen present. After what seemed like an age, the men dispersed and Aelfhere sidled over to a table spread with cuts of chicken and pork and a dark loaf of bread. Beornoth saw his moment and followed the bishop to the table.

Bishop Aelfhere reached down towards the table, and his chubby fingers hovered over the food, dancing as though he plucked at an invisible harp. Rings of silver and gold shone on his fingers, and he wore a silver crucifix embedded with gems upon his chest. Beornoth came alongside him, and the bishop jumped and made a small mewing sound. He put a hand to his chest and turned to Beornoth, but had to look up to see his face.

'By all the saints in heaven but you startled me,' said the bishop, his voice high-pitched and gentle. 'Do you really need to wear all that iron and leather everywhere you go? There is a stream close by. You should wash yourself, man.'

Beornoth swallowed and bit his tongue. If the bishop had been a warrior, Beornoth would have hit him for such an insult, but a blow from one of Beornoth's fists would likely kill the man of God. Beornoth held his anger inside and resisted the urge to lower his head and smell himself. 'My lord bishop, Ealdorman Byrhtnoth sends me to ask you for...'

'Can you not see that I am trying to eat?' the bishop said, turning to the food and waving his hand dismissively in Beornoth's direction. 'Away with you. Come back this evening.'

The bishop was clearly in no mood to be asked about silver or supplies, so Beornoth admitted defeat. He strode from the king's tent and found the twin warriors of Wessex waiting for him.

'I am Beornoth, a thegn. We ride tomorrow, so have your men ready at dawn,' he said.

'I am Wigstan, and this is my brother, Wighelm,' said the man on the left. They were both big men, only a few fingers shorter than Beornoth himself, and it was unnerving to see two warriors who looked identical to one another.

'How do men tell you apart?'

'I am the clever one,' said Wigstan, and they both laughed. 'He has a broken nose, and half of my ear is missing.' Beornoth looked closely at the men and saw that Wigstan's description was true. They were both heavily scarred, a sure sign that they were no strangers to the shield wall.

'Your swords are welcome,' said Beornoth, regretting the harsh tone he had used when introducing himself. The bishop's cruel words had stung him and his holy vestments protected the little man from Beornoth's anger, which annoyed Beornoth even more.

'The men are hungry to get at the Viking bastards,' said Wighelm. The brothers looked at one another and grinned.

'We've heard how they slaughtered your people,' said Wigstan.

'Heard of you as well. Honoured to fight alongside you, Beornoth.'

He clasped forearms with them both in the warrior's grip. Beornoth liked the twins. They were friendly, and the king was right in that it was more useful to have three hundred seasoned warriors of Wessex than a thousand men of the fyrd.

'Can you hear that?' asked Wigstan. Beornoth cocked an ear, but couldn't hear anything above the hustle and bustle of the king's camp around his tent.

'I hear it. It's horses. Do you have more men coming, Beornoth?' asked Wighelm.

'No,' said Beornoth. He searched the horizon for signs of riders, but could see nothing. He felt the pulse of hoof beats in his chest, and turned, unable to see any sign around the camp of horses approaching. The land itself was flat, and farmland stretched ahead for miles around, interrupted only by hedgerow or the occasional tree.

'The forest,' said Wigstan. The three warriors ran around to the rear of King Æthelred's tent, to where it bordered on a wood where darkness loomed beneath the lush greenery of leaf and branch.

A war horn rang out from deep within the trees, and a roar shook the very boughs themselves. The roar of warriors.

'Protect the king,' said Beornoth through gritted teeth. 'It's the Vikings.' He drew his sword, the blade scraping on the wooden rim of its fleece-lined scabbard. From within the ancient dark of the forest, another eerie war horn blast peeled out, followed by the collective roar of approaching riders, closer now, louder. The twins turned and ran, bellowing orders to their warriors to arm themselves, and to the servants and churchmen to flee for their lives.

Beornoth peered into the darkness, and a rider appeared as though he had sprung from the depths of hell. He held aloft a war axe, and his white hair shone in the blackness. Beornoth clenched his teeth, and hate mixed with the spiteful churn of fear in his belly. The White Wolf had come with a band of Viking warriors and luck was with him, for he had a chance to kill King Æthelred of the Saxons.

16

Riders burst from the forest in a crashing, thundering rush of horseflesh, war cries, and steel. Beornoth planted his feet and gripped his sword in two hands. No time to find a shield or to think about how the Vikings had evaded the army of Essex to reach the king's camp. The White Wolf did not notice Beornoth amongst the terrified confusion of the Saxons, and instead drove his horse around Æthelred's tent. Beornoth's stomach twisted with hate as the White Wolf crunched his axe into the skull of a fleeing man clad in the scarlet livery of the king.

Beornoth counted forty horsemen at least, and a man with crow-black hair charged towards him with a twisted, snarling face. The Viking leant over his saddle as he levelled his spear point to strike at Beornoth. It was a long, wicked blade at the tip of a shaft of ash wood and would punch through Beornoth's byrnie chain-mail armour and rip his chest open. The momentum of the horse would throw Beornoth from his feet, and he would be dead before he hit the ground as the spear point ripped his heart apart. But Beornoth let go of his sword and dropped to his haunches. The spear point flicked down towards his face, but the rider was too slow and Beornoth felt its wind as it passed a finger's breadth from his face. Beornoth snarled and grabbed the shaft with both hands and used all of his strength to yank on the spear. The shaft jolted Beornoth's body, and he twisted, maintaining his grip on the smooth wood and ripping his attacker from the saddle. The Viking toppled from his horse with a yelp to roll on the grass. Beornoth stood and ran to the fallen Viking. The long-haired warrior scrambled in the grass to rise to his feet, and Beornoth kicked him brutally in the stomach. The Viking doubled over, winded, and his eyes grew wide with terror as he saw Beornoth looming over him. Beornoth slammed the spear point into the Viking's gullet so hard that it punched through flesh and gristle and sunk into the earth beyond. Beornoth twisted and tore with the weapon so that dark blood seeped from the dying warrior to soak the grass in thick crimson. He put his foot on the Viking's face and yanked the spear free, turned and threw it at another rider. The spear flew and thumped into the Viking's thigh just as he raised his axe to strike at a cowering Saxon. The Viking cried out in shock and pain, and the Wessex twin Wigstan buried an axe in the Viking's stomach and dragged him from the saddle.

Beornoth retrieved his sword, bent to pick up the fallen Viking's axe, and ran around the tent in the direction the White Wolf had ridden. Blood rushed in his ears, and his heart pumped furiously. Viking riders were everywhere, cutting and slashing at the surprised Saxons. The Northmen whooped for joy at the success of their attack, and the Saxons died under their savagery. Somehow the White Wolf had evaded Æthelred's scouts and launched a surprise attack which placed the king of England himself in dire peril. Also, it meant Olaf had landed his fleet on the Essex coast and news of that had yet to reach Ealdorman Byrhtnoth, so Olaf had unleashed the fury of his Vikings upon the countryside. Men screamed and died, Vikings cheered with joy, horses pounded the earth, and blood splashed bright to wash the summer grass red. Beornoth came around the tent into more chaos. A Viking warrior hopped lithely from his saddle and clashed with one of Æthelred's tent guards. The big Saxon jabbed at him with a spear but the Viking parried it easily and stabbed a vicious-bladed knife into his ribs over and again, in rapid short bursts. The guard slumped to his knees, and the Viking dragged the blade of his axe across the dying Saxon's throat. Beornoth roared at the killer and before the Viking could bring his axe to bear, Beornoth closed the distance between them in three long strides and plunged the tip of his sword into the Viking's gut, driving him backwards and sawing the blade back and forth to rip the man open. He fell to the earth with a surprised look on his face, and Beornoth stepped over the purple coils of his insides to search for the White Wolf.

'The king, the king!' came a cry above the tumult. Beornoth turned towards the call and saw a makeshift shield wall forming with Wigstan and Wighelm in the front rank. Viking horsemen flowed around them, hurling spears and bellowing ferociously, but the Saxon twins held them back. More men joined the shield wall, and at its centre the king's head bobbed, hunched and low into his shoulders, his golden circlet askew and his face a mask of terror. Beornoth ran to join that desperate defence of the king, but then noticed two shapes dashing from the king's tent pursued by an axe-wielding Viking. Beornoth turned on his heel and made for them. One was the portly bishop of Wessex, who had been so rude to Beornoth moments earlier, and the other was the small, pale figure of the serving girl who had brought Beornoth water.

'To me! Run!' Beornoth shouted. The bishop waddled, cheeks puffing and face red, eyes wide with terror. The girl hitched up her long dress and her pale legs showed as she sprinted towards Beornoth. She was faster, and the pursuing Viking was a young man. He had a shaved head save for a long golden braid sprouting from the top of his skull, and his youth made him fast. The Northman reached the bishop before Beornoth, and at full speed he swung his axe so that the blade slashed across the back of the bishop. Bishop Aelfhere tumbled into the grass, screaming in horror, turning onto his back and shielding his face with his hands. The young Viking stopped and grinned at the bishop. He grabbed the golden crucifix from the bishop's neck and ripped it free, and for a glorious moment he was rich. In that heartbeat of glory, the young warrior would think his long journey across the raging seas to England was a success. He had risked everything to join Olaf's crews and go a-Viking. He held his treasure up triumphantly, and for a fleeting moment, a look of pure joy sparkled in his blue eyes, and then he died. Beornoth drove the point of his sword into the young man's unarmoured chest, the lad clearly not yet able to afford leather armour, and certainly not a chain-mail byrnie. His heart burst on the end of Beornoth's cold steel, and he fell dead on top of the yelping bishop.

'Get up,' snarled Beornoth. The bishop held out his soft hands to Beornoth for help, the dead Viking's blood spattered across his jowls and his white vestments. Beornoth turned away, the serving girl clutching his waist. Beornoth drew her close with the arm in which he held the axe and marched towards the Wessex shield wall. Warriors made the war-fence there and pale-faced bishops cowered behind them clutching their crucifixes and praying to God for their lives. The Vikings milled before that wall of linden wood, the horses refusing to attack the massed front of shields. Wighelm cast his spear into the Vikings, and it

sank into the powerful chest of a black stallion. The horse reared
and spilled its rider. Beornoth led the girl to the shield wall, and a
grim-faced warrior lowered his shield to let her pass. The injured
bishop came tottering after her, whimpers escaping his lips as he
rejoiced at reaching the relative safety of the Wessex shield wall.

'Beornoth!' a voice cried out in a heavy Norse accent. He
turned, and there, at the edge of the Viking horsemen, was the
White Wolf. He held a blood-soaked sword in his right arm, the
blade levelled and pointed at Beornoth. At the feet of his horse
slumped one of Æthelred's bishops, a bloody wound had carved
his neck and chest open so that his dark blood soaked the earth
and soiled his fine vestments.

'Riders,' said the warrior who had ushered the serving girl
and the bishop into the centre of the shield wall. Beornoth felt
relief wash over him, because Ealdorman Byrhtnoth came thundering across a field of high barley with his fifty warriors at his
back.

The White Wolf saw them too, and he spat into the dirt with a
shake of his head. The Wessex warriors combined with Byrhtnoth's charging East Saxons outnumbered his Vikings. He
glanced at the shield wall and then back at the approaching
riders, and knew that his chance to kill the king of England had
failed, but there was still a chance for him to slaughter more
Saxons before Byrhtnoth's riders closed in. The Viking leader
wheeled his mount around, calling to his men in words lost to
Beornoth's ears over the din of battle. Viking horsemen peeled
away from where they hacked at the Wessex shield wall desperately trying to kill the king. That most glorious of prizes was now
lost to them, so the Vikings instead swirled their mounts towards
the warriors and people of Æthelred's contingent who had not
managed to reach the safety of the massed Wessex ranks. Those
people, priests, servants and warriors who ran for their lives in

the open ground died screaming beneath Viking axes and spears. The White Wolf leant forward in his saddle and came for Beornoth, his horse bobbing its mighty head and lurching forward into a skittish canter.

A vision of Aethelberga's violated corpse, and of the White Wolf driving his blade into Kari's body, flashed before Beornoth's eyes, and he ran. He ran towards the charging horse, sprinting and snarling. Beornoth charged the horse, and before the beast could bunch its huge leg muscles and drive into a gallop which would crush Beornoth with its momentum, Beornoth reached it. He loved horses; he loved their power and their beauty, and his stomach turned at what he must do. But Beornoth did not hesitate. The horse's head came up, a gust of warm breath blowing from its flared nostrils into Beornoth's face, and Beornoth cracked the blade of his axe into the horse's forehead. He darted out of the way as the animal thrashed in pain, the whites of its eyes wide and terrible. A blow banged on Beornoth's back as he moved, throwing him to roll on the grass. The White Wolf had struck at him with his sword, but the small, interlocked links of Beornoth's byrnie held firm under the blow and it did not break his skin. Beornoth came up from his roll and the horse threw the White Wolf from his saddle as it spasmed and thrashed, blood sheeting from its wound into its eyes. The Viking fell to the earth and Beornoth sprang at him, hatred lending him speed as he closed the distance and brought his sword around in a wide arc aimed at taking his enemy's head off. But the White Wolf was snake-fast, and had kept hold of his own blade as he fell. He brought the weapon up to parry Beornoth's strike and, as the edges met in a clang of steel, the blow rang up Beornoth's arm to shake his very bones. Beornoth brought the axe around to strike at the Viking, who lay with his back on the grass, but the White Wolf twisted away from the strike and came to his feet light and agile, like a dancer. He whipped a second sword free from its scabbard at his back and came at Beornoth in a whirl of shining blades.

The White Wolf swung his blades around him in twirling arcs, just as he had done at Branoc's Tree. Beornoth took small steps backwards, desperately trying to keep his eyes fixed on the flashing blades. One lashed out like a viper's tongue and sliced across Beornoth's forearm in a slash of white-hot pain. He lunged his sword, but the twirling blades batted it aside. Beornoth threw himself backwards as a sword came close to disembowelling him, and he could not react in time as the second blade scraped across his chest, his byrnie again saving him from a killing blow. Beornoth swung his axe, but the White Wolf danced away as though it were the attack of a child.

'You are slow, and old. Where is this ferocious Saxon warrior I have heard so much about?' said the White Wolf in Norse, his voice slithering and lilting with the accent of a man from the far north islands of Norway. He stopped his attack and smiled at Beornoth. 'We shall fight again.'

'Fight me now!' Beornoth snarled, and lunged at his enemy, who danced away laughing. The White Wolf glanced over his shoulder to where Byrhtnoth's riders closed in, and he threw his head back and cursed in frustration.

'Away!' the White Wolf called, and his riders surged past in a thunderstorm of crashing hooves. A warrior with a tattooed neck led a riderless horse and the White Wolf leapt across its back into the saddle in one fluid motion. 'We fight when there are more to see you die. You have reputation, Saxon dog, and I would take it from you with more men to see me do it.'

The White Wolf clicked his tongue and his horse sped away, but the rider who had provided the spare mount remained and Beornoth bared his teeth when he realised the man with the tattooed neck was Brand Thorkilsson. The Viking hostage who had become his friend.

'Do not fight him again, lord,' said Brand in Norse, casting his eyes towards the White Wolf, who sped away, his bone-white hair streaming behind him. 'He fights like one of the Loki brood. He will kill you.' Brand dipped his head to Beornoth and dug his heels into the flanks of his mount.

'Murdering bastards,' Beornoth said. 'Where is Olaf?' he called after Brand, but the Viking warrior galloped away and his words were lost in the thunder of hoof beats. Beornoth's shoulders sagged. They were empty words, but he did not have the strength left to articulate all he wanted to say to the Viking. He wanted to ask the Norseman how he could take part in the butchery of the people of Branoc's Tree with whom he had lived for much of the last year. Beornoth wanted to ask Brand if it was all worth it? All the death, slaves captured, men and women slaughtered, all in the name of glory and reputation.

Beornoth dropped to his knees as the ealdorman pounded by. His chest heaved from the exertion of the battle. The blow he had taken on his back throbbed and his forearm wound leaked warm blood down onto his hand. The White Wolf was breathtakingly fast. Beornoth had never fought a man with such speed. And Brand, a man whom Beornoth had fought beside, who had lived amongst Beornoth's hearth troop, had been at Branoc's Tree on that fateful day, and now he rode with the White Wolf. Bile rose in Beornoth's throat, and he got to his feet. Byrhtnoth had warned him to kill Brand last year, when Olaf had broken his oath of peace bought with Æthelred's silver. But Beornoth had kept Brand, the Viking hostage, alive. Which had been a mistake. A mistake which had cost the lives of his people on that terrible day. Beornoth could still see the corpses swinging from the great tree at the heart of Branoc's Tree.

'Thank you, lord,' said the serving girl. She stood before
Beornoth, her cheeks ruddy, and tears rolling down her face. 'You
saved me, lord. So many dead, so much pain.' Beornoth followed
her gaze across the carnage of King Æthelred's camp. Wounded
men writhed and wept in the dirt. More lay dead.

'Help the wounded,' Beornoth said, and she smiled and ran
towards Æthelred's tent. The construction sagged on one side
where the Vikings had cut its guy ropes. The warriors around the
king ushered him towards the baggage train of wagons and
horses, keen to get moving back to the safety of Wessex. Beornoth
dropped the axe he had taken from the fallen Viking and wiped
his sword blade free of blood. He slid it back into its fleece-lined
scabbard as the priests and bishops emerged from the protection
of the shield wall and fussed around the carnage, some praying
over the fallen, more weeping and clawing at their faces with
terror.

'Get off me, get away from me,' shouted the king, his voice
shrill and cracked. He pushed away his guards, the men who had
protected him from Viking blades from within the shield wall.
Æthelred fussed with trembling hands at the dislodged circlet
upon his brow. The burly warriors fell back from their raging
king. 'I want them dead! How dare they attack me in my own
country, I am the king!' Æthelred wiped his mouth on the sleeve
of his fine jerkin, and he lurched from one foot to the other, stag-
gering and clearly shocked at the surprise attack.

'Come, lord king, let us get to safety,' said the archbishop,
clutching his crushed mitre in trembling hands.

The king's eyes landed upon Beornoth, and he pointed a long
finger in his direction. 'You are our killer, Beornoth, punish them
for me. Do to them as they would do to us. Kill them, Beornoth,
crush their very bones and drive their bloody corpses into the
sea. My ships are in Lundenburg to protect its waters, and if his

cursed Vikings can attack us here, then Olaf has clearly landed somewhere in Essex, either in the River Blackwater or close to it. I will send my fleet west, out of the Thames, so Olaf will sail no further south than that. If he wants to take Essex, then he must bring his fleet to shore north of the Thames and south of Gippeswic. Find him, Beornoth, rid us of their plague.' Æthelred allowed himself to be ushered away, and Beornoth just stared after him, wondering at the difference between the mighty kings of old, like Alfred and Aethelstan, and how pride must have burned in men's hearts to fight alongside a warrior-king. Æthelred spoke like a warrior-king without his priests in his ear, in his anger he spoke the truth; for if the King's ships were in the Thames and Olaf did not want to trouble Forkbeard in Gippeswic, then Olaf could be brought to a fight in Essex. Olaf would not want to challenge the king's fleet for fear of losing too many of his own valuable warships, and he could risk sailing to Forkbeard, but the king of the Danes might not take too kindly to a Norse fleet threatening his newly captured mint. The attack had stirred the king to anger. He had brought the warriors of Wessex to join Byrhtnoth's army, and the twins seemed like good men to have in the shield wall, and now he would send his precious ships to cut Olaf off. Those ships had spent the last two years protecting the south and west coasts from Viking raids howling down from Ireland and beyond, and the Saxons were neither shipbuilders nor renowned for their sea-faring skills, but now those ships were in the Thames estuary and would help keep Olaf north of that wide river, preventing him from sailing along its meandering bends to Lundenburg, further south to Folkestone, or around the south-east coast and on to Wessex itself.

The serving girl came back with a wooden pitcher of water and grey linen cloth draped over her hand.

'You are injured, lord. Let me help you,' she said, reaching out

for Beornoth's injured forearm. He let her take his arm, initially
wanting to object, to send her to help those in greater need, but
he did not have the strength to do it. He just sighed and watched
as Wighelm and his brother ordered the warriors to break camp
and riders to support Byrhtnoth in pursuit of the Vikings.
Beornoth winced as the girl poured cold water over the cut on his
arm, its chill making him shiver. She bound it tight around with
the linen to stop the bleeding and then tied off the bandage. 'That
should stop the blood,' she said, smiling up at him. 'Keep the
dressing clean, if you can.'

She scampered away, towards a warrior sitting upright
clutching at his wounded shoulder. Beornoth wondered what his
own daughters would have looked like had they lived. They
would have been of an age with the serving girl by now, full of life
and beauty. Ready to be married and to start families of their
own. But that could never be, because Vikings had snatched their
little lives away in the flames of their bloodlust and savagery.
Beornoth opened the fingers on his wounded arm and curled
them into a fist, the pulsing pain from his wound focusing his
mind. Olaf had to be stopped. Whatever force Byrhtnoth now
had under his command, it would have to be enough. They
would have to catch Olaf and his ships, to bring them to battle
and stop them for good. Beornoth sucked at his teeth as he
recalled his clash with the White Wolf. The Viking was fast and
lethal, a warrior in his prime and desperate for reputation. He
could have killed Beornoth with his twirling swords, and
Beornoth was not an easy man to kill. The White Wolf had let
him live to fight again, craving more eyes to see the fight, more
people to see how the Norseman made his reputation with the
death of Saxon warriors. He had to be stopped too. They all had
to die, every Viking, every man who had dared the white-tipped
waves of the Whale Road in search of silver and glory at the

expense of innocent Saxons. Beornoth made the sign of the cross, as strange as it felt, a thing long forgotten, but he felt drawn to it. His hands moved across his chest. *In the name of the Father, the Son, and the Holy Spirit. In your name, Sacred Virgin Mother, give my sword arm strength so that I may protect our people. Please, God, grant me vengeance, give me the strength to slay my enemies in your name, Lord God.*

17

A brisk sea wind whipped Beornoth's face. It swirled and lashed the Saxon coastline with the fury of an angry sea god. There was no rain in the sky, but the wind blustered with the sea's salt water and it pulled his skin taut. Beornoth pressed his lips together, squinting as he stared into its eye-watering chill. He shifted in the saddle as Hríð lowered his head to crop at the coarse grass on the clifftop. Days in the saddle had left him with a dull ache in the muscles of his arse, and the inside skin of his thighs burned as though singed by fire. Beornoth's hair blew across his face as the wind gusted, and he pushed it behind his ear, forcing himself to stare down at the churning, white-tipped waves below. The waves roared and crashed in a constant surge, battering the shale beach, which curled away far below into a curving crescent as the cliffs tapered into hard rocks to meet the beach, sharp like the walls of a dark castle forged by the lords of the underworld.

Beornoth and his riders had followed Brand and the White Wolf for three days, the tracks of their horses easy to follow. They left a scar across the pastures and meadows of Essex, churning them to mud littered with horseshit and the detritus of their overnight camps. Following the attack on the king, Ealdorman Byrhtnoth had been livid with rage that the Vikings had managed to get so close to killing Æthelred. Byrhtnoth marched with the warriors of Wessex to join Offa and take command of the army consisting of the men of East Anglia and the Essex fyrd and to begin the march south to try and bring Olaf to battle. That fight must happen soon as Olaf would be too tempted to sail into the wide River Blackwater, and the ealdorman would meet him there with his army. Byrhtnoth ordered Beornoth to bring his surviving men of Branoc's Tree, Aelfwine of Foxfield, Leofsunu of Sturmer and their own hearth troops, Thered of Northumbria, Streonwold and his horsemen of Cheshire, along with Godric and his brothers, to follow the White Wolf. So Beornoth rode with a force of fifty men. In his black rage, the ealdorman had roared that the Wolf must return to his master, and so lead them to Olaf's fleet.

'God save us,' said Godric, his words snatched away by the wind so they came as a stuttering shout. 'So many.'

Byrhtnoth had been right, for fifty ships raced across the wilds of the Whale Road below them. Beautifully crafted, clinker-built dragon ships. Their sails bore designs too distant for Beornoth's ageing eyes to make out, but he knew snarling animals emblazoned those sails: boars, bears, eagles and writhing dragons. They would show crossed axes, skulls, or spears, the sigils of war and death, designed to strike fear in the hearts of men. The ships sliced through the green-grey surge of crashing waves like blades, their shallow-draughted hulls dancing on the malevolent sea; they looked too flimsy, as though the fury of the Whale Road would swallow them up and smash their timbers to kindling, but they rode the water like a stick dropped into a galloping brook by a child, racing on the flow and propelled by its force. They were east of where the Wolf had attacked the king's camp, overlooking a hook of high cliffs where the River Blackwater curved north-east towards Mersea Island.

'Even looking at them makes me want to cough my guts up,' said Leofsunu, his ugly face grimacing down at the enemy. His cheeks glowed red from the wind, and he wore the hood of his cloak pulled tight around his head. Leofsunu's horse skittered on the clifftop, whinnying and scraping its forelegs. Leofsunu shushed the beast, stroking its powerful neck. 'They won't come ashore in this storm.'

'No,' agreed Beornoth. 'But they will come ashore. The White Wolf bastard has gathered supplies for Olaf's men. Olaf searches for a safe place to land his fleet, he can't go to the Thames and he is avoiding Gippeswic. So he seeks a safe port to bring his warriors ashore. Until he finds one, his men must be brought supplies.' He jutted his chin to where a band of Vikings waited on a similar hilltop further along the coastline.

'The Wolf is no fool,' said Godric. 'He surely knows we are here. He won't leave himself open to an attack whilst his men load supplies from the shallows into Olaf's ships. Why would he leave himself so vulnerable?'

'Because he despises us,' said Beornoth, through gritted teeth. 'He can see us just as we can see him, and he fears we shall attack him whilst he brings his looted supplies to his master. But he wants it, craves combat. He is a lover of Odin and Thor. He does not care how many of his men die for his glory. The White Wolf would love nothing more than to fight us on the beach in front of the entire Viking fleet. With fifty ships crammed with men to see his prowess as he builds his reputation on the ruin of our corpses.'

'But the Vikings are ever cautious about losing too many men,' said Aelfwine, which was true.

'They are,' allowed Beornoth. 'The clever ones, the ones with sense. Kings and jarls like Olaf and Forkbeard. They fear losing so many warriors that it leaves them unable to crew their ships and so must abandon their campaign. They can only call upon the warriors who dared to make the journey across the sea, to replenish their numbers they must return to their homes in Norway, Jutland or the Vik. But this Wolf is not such a man. I saw it in his pale eyes, the eyes of a feral beast. The man is driven by reputation. He lives for battle. He wants to make a name that men will speak of across the world. The Wolf doesn't want to be a king, or a wealthy jarl or lord, he wants a reputation that will burn bright enough to earn him pride of place in Valhalla, to give him a place in the front ranks of Odin's Einherjar when their gods will fight against the monster armies of the trickster god Loki at the end of days.'

'So you think he waits up there knowing that we are watching him?' asked Godric.

Beornoth raised an eyebrow and stared at the young thegn, his gold-studded belt and sword shining even under the sunless iron-grey sky above them. He held short of rebuking the man in front of the others. Godric already despised Beornoth, but it gained Beornoth nothing to humiliate him. His only focus was killing Vikings. 'Yes, he knows.'

'There is a cove beyond those rocky cliffs,' said Aelfwine, pointing south where Brand and the White Wolf sat on horse-back atop a sloping escarpment. Their figures were blurred by the distance, but clearly, they waved and signalled to Olaf's ships. 'I know this coastline. They will head for that. The water will be calmer there, and Olaf can get close enough to shore to take on whatever food and ale his riders have scoured from our people.'

'Then that is where we shall attack them,' said Beornoth. 'But we won't engage them in a standing fight, the Wolf has between thirty and forty men. We stay on horseback, ride in, hurt them, and ride away again. The Wolf won't expect us to attack, not whilst our numbers are so evenly matched. Now that we have their fleet in sight, we can follow them along the coastline and try to discover where they plan to land.'

'Aye,' said Streonwold, his jowls quivering in the wind. 'We should send a rider to find Ealdorman Byrhtnoth. A man should ride now each day between us and the army, so we each know where the other is.'

Beornoth nodded at his old friend. 'Choose a man. Now that we have the fleet in sight, there will never be a better chance to lure Olaf into a battle. And we must have that battle before the ealdorman loses the fyrd.'

'The bloody fyrd will do as they are told,' said Godric. The tight curls of his fair beard and hair blew about his round face, the sneer of his lips angering Beornoth.

'The fyrd can only fight so long as they are fed and watered,' said Aelfwine, saving Beornoth from losing his temper. 'Another week at most. Then, they will return to their farms for the harvest. So if there is going to be a fight, then it must be now.'

Streonwold sent a young warrior with a fast pony west in search of the ealdorman, and Beornoth's riders followed the cliff's curve down its bank and out of the worst of the wind. They rode along a wide field of long, heavy grass interrupted here and there by tall yellow flowers. Wulfhere rode beside Beornoth, baleful on his dark horse, his scarred face set to a permanent scowl. They were fifty riders, as much as the ealdorman would spare, and an equal match for the White Wolf's numbers. A gull soared over Beornoth's head, its caw harsh and undulating on the wind. He thought of fighting the White Wolf again, and a pang of fear stabbed his belly. The man was whip-fast, skilled and a man to fear. But he had to be fought. Like a rabid dog, the Wolf had to be caught and killed.

'Did you see Brand amongst them?' said Aelfwine over Beornoth's shoulder.

'I saw him,' said Beornoth.

'He is our enemy now.'

'He was always our enemy,' Beornoth lied.

'Could you kill him, if it came to it?'

'I'll kill him. Always knew he was a Viking bastard. He was never one of us,' growled Wulfhere without turning to look at Beornoth or Aelfwine.

Beornoth leant forward to stroke Hríð's ear and ran his hand down the horse's neck. He hoped he would not come face to face with Brand Thorkilsson, because he would have to kill a man he liked. Brand was a Norseman, he thought, and acted like a Norseman. He loved battle, the gods, horses and hunting. He was a simple man, and Beornoth liked him. Brand did not speak the Saxon tongue, so whenever he had wanted to talk, it was with Beornoth, the only Norse speaker at Branoc's Tree. Brand had only ever wanted to talk of simple things, of his family, to tell the tale of a boar he had once killed, or of a daring voyage he had made. He was a stout fighter, and a good man to have on your left in the shield wall. But he had returned to Olaf Tryggvason and was now Beornoth's enemy. There had been blood on Brand's blade at Branoc's Tree, and for that he would die.

The riders cantered around the wide sweep of the cliff to where Aelfwine knew of a pathway into the cove. Soft grassland gave way to harsher scrub, and rolling hillsides became dunes of wild grass pitted with golden sand. They slowed to a trot, and Beornoth called a halt. He and Aelfwine rode ahead slowly and cautiously to scout the cove, down into a gully flanked on one side by thick grass, and the other by sharp, sloping rock. Hríð did not like the ground, his ears pinned flat against his neck, and he snorted, picking his way down the treacherous terrain.

'Easy, boy, easy,' Beornoth said to the horse, patting his flank to calm him. As the gully widened, the cove revealed itself to be a sharp bend carved into the curve of the cliffs, cutting back behind a jutting headland before opening out into a long beach of dark yellow sand, broken here and there by sprawling patches of shale and pebbles. Where the beach cut behind the headland, five of Olaf's ships rowed toward the shore, the waters there much calmer in the shield of the curved headland around the cove. Whilst Viking warriors took tremendous pulls on the oars, others busied themselves furling the huge sails as the ships grew closer to shore. The rest of Olaf's fleet had spread along the sea, facing the beach. Many had drawn close to drop anchor, and their sails dropped amidst the distant shouts and orders of bellowing ship-masters.

'There,' said Aelfwine, pointing towards where the beach turned into a clutch of large rocks surrounded by deep pools left there to ripple in the wind by the retreating tide. The White Wolf and his horsemen were there, dismounted and gathering piles of food, drink and plunder held within bundles of cloth. They secured their horses against a sandy hillock behind them, bordering on the dunes where the animals cropped at the over-hanging grass. The Vikings were without their shields and spears, busy preparing the plundered supplies for the ships.

'I see them,' Beornoth said. The White Wolf stood atop the largest of the rocks, his long hair flowing in the wind like Hríð's mane. His fish-scale armour shone and his bare arms rippled with muscle, a red cloak billowing behind him. The Wolf pointed and shouted orders to his men, whilst waving with his left hand to the men on board the approaching warships. Two Vikings stood between Beornoth and the Vikings further along the beach, no doubt placed there by the Wolf to watch for any Saxon attack, having been aware of their presence on the hilltops. Without thinking, Beornoth's hand fell to reach for the axe held in a sheath on Hríð's saddle. The shield on his back slid to one side as he leaned, and Beornoth clicked his tongue and urged his warhorse forward, sliding the axe free and gripping the smooth haft.

'Wait!' called Aelfwine. 'Wait for the others, Beornoth. Make a wedge formation!'

The words died on the wind, and somewhere deep inside, Beornoth knew Aelfwine was right, and that he should wait and form an attack wedge to cut into the Vikings whilst they were unprepared. That would provide the greatest opportunity to destroy them, to plunge into them like a monstrous arrowhead of horseflesh and steel and drive them into the sand to die in the shallows. But Beornoth was beyond reason. The thirst for vengeance mixed with his hate created a fury which rose within him like an unquenchable fire and he charged towards his enemies with his axe held low. The warhorse lurched across the heavy, wet sand exposed by the ebb tide. The two lookouts spotted Beornoth and Aelfwine emerging onto the beach, and they turned and ran to warn the Wolf. Beornoth kicked his mount towards them.

Aelfwine roared orders at their riders to follow; and they would come, Beornoth knew. But he could not wait to kill those who had butchered so many of his people. They had to die now. The king's words echoed in his head: the Vikings must die. Hríð pounded along the sand, throwing up its dust like a thunder-cloud. Beornoth let the warhorse have his head, the power of the beast raging beneath him like a storm at sea. In ten heartbeats he was upon them, his approach drowned out by the roar of the sea, and the flailing arms of those aboard the Viking ships pointing at him looked like waves of greeting to the Northmen on the beach, so the White Wolf and his men were unaware of his approach.

The first Viking to hear Beornoth's charge was one of the running lookouts, and he turned with a look of horror on his long face. He saw an armoured Saxon warrior charging at him on a monstrous warhorse with a shining war axe and the Viking scrambled to turn and run in the sand, but it encumbered him and he could not escape his fate. Beornoth let Hríð ride the Viking down, his hugely powerful chest slamming into the Northman and propelling him backwards onto the wet sand. The man tried to scramble away, and he mewed like a kitten just before Hríð crushed his skull with his forelegs and trampled his ribcage. Beornoth yanked on the reins, pulling Hríð around and allowing the monstrous white stallion to stomp over the fallen Viking again, the crack and grind of his bones and limbs sickening as Hríð crushed the fallen Viking like so many rotting vegetables. Beornoth held his axe aloft and let out his war cry, a bellow of white furious rage from deep inside him. The second lookout screamed at the Wolf and his men, and more Vikings turned to stare at Beornoth, and he was glad. He wanted them to see whom it was who came to kill them. The fear and shock on their faces made his heart race, and he became a master of death, a Saxon warlord come to avenge his king and his people. He dug his heels into Hríð's flanks and charged at a short warrior with a bull neck; the man tried to run but Beornoth swung his axe and laid open the back of the Viking's skull with a spray of blood which flecked Hríð's white face and neck.

The Vikings on the beach left their bundles of plunder and dashed across the sand to where their weapons and shields lay stacked against the hulking boulders closer to the cliffs. They were shouting at each other in panic, and the warriors aboard Olaf's ships watched on helplessly. Beornoth urged Hríð into a canter and the stallion's hooves clipped and clopped, the horse whinnying in protest at the tiny shale stones beneath his hooves before he reached the sand and found enough purchase to pick up the pace. Beornoth tugged on the reins and guided Hríð into the space between the Northmen and their weapons. He glanced at the shore, where Viking warriors leapt from the ships, over the bows and into the surf to wade ashore and join the fight. If those crews came ashore before Beornoth's riders arrived, or were able to get behind Beornoth's men before the attack was over, then the Saxons would be slaughtered. His heart raced, death felt close, its hand heavy upon his shoulder. Bile rose in Beornoth's throat, had he led his men to be butchered by Viking axes? The Norsemen on the beach slowed, dragging axes and knives free of the loops at their belts. A shaven-headed warrior charged at Beornoth, a brave man come to kill the Saxon warlord. He swung his axe, his eyes wide with fury, and Hríð barrelled into him mid-swing. The horse knocked the Viking off balance and Beornoth chopped down with his own axe, the blade thumping so hard into the meat of the man's back that Beornoth had to wrench and pull at the blade to drag it free of his twitching body. Hríð surged forward again, his teeth snapping at a warrior who came too close, and Beornoth swung the axe over his left side to crack the blade into the top of that man's skull, cracking it open like a gore-filled egg. Blood seeped into the sand, Vikings were dying and Beornoth swept his axe around in a wide arc to fend off two Vikings who came to attack him from the rear. They ducked under the flashing sweep of the axe blade, and Beornoth yanked on Hríð's reins to twist the enormous animal around, blocking the two men with its hind flanks. As the horse wheeled around, tossing sand into the air and snorting from his flared nostrils, Beornoth locked eyes with the two men. One had a tattooed face and two missing teeth, and the other wore his beard long and braided, with a knot of greasy hair atop his head. Beornoth swung his axe at them, and they

ducked away again but could not bring their axes to bear against
horse or rider.

'Saxon bastard!' came a cry in Norse, and Beornoth turned
just in time to see the unnaturally white hair of the White Wolf
flowing where he stood atop the large rocks. He had leapt across
the boulders, from the grey rock where he had waved to the ships,
across to a jagged black rock next to it, and then to the top of the
smooth, round boulder, higher than a man is tall and against
which the Vikings had stacked their weapons. The White Wolf
leapt from the rock, flying with his arms outstretched and his
teeth bared in a snarl. Before Beornoth could bring his axe to
bear, the White Wolf slammed into him. The momentum of his
leap dragged Beornoth from the saddle and the two enemies
crashed into the sand and Beornoth fell hard on the haft of his
axe so that the wind rushed out of him. He gasped, desperately
sucking air into his lungs, blinded by the sand which covered his
face and beard, its tiny grains stinging his eyeballs. Beornoth
surged to his feet, doubled over as he tried to breathe. His hands
flailed for his axe, but could not find it, and a terrible surge of fear
blossomed in Beornoth's chest. A boot kicked him in the shoulder
and he fell onto his back with a grunt. He could not open his eyes
against the coarse sand scratching them, but shouts, snarls and
curses were all around him like a flock of hungry ravens come to
peck and strike at him. Another boot thudded into his back. He
dragged the back of his hand across his eyes and his left eye flickered open just in time to see a knife coming for his throat. He
blocked with his forearm, connecting with the attacker's hand
and driving it wide. With his other hand, Beornoth grabbed a
fistful of the attacker's beard and dragged him into a headbutt
and clasped both arms around the Viking. Beornoth pulled him
close to shield himself, and blows meant for Beornoth rained
down on the Viking, axes and knives cut at his torso, weapons

aimed to rend and tear at Beornoth's chest and guts. The Viking roared in pain, a gust of his fetid breath washing over Beornoth's face. They locked eyes for a terrible moment, as death came for the Viking under the flurry of blows and the fear of it poured from his eyes in thick tears, but Beornoth did not pity him. He was a man of the Whale Road. The Viking had left his home in far Norway and sailed to England to risk all. He was a killer and an adventurer, and now he had found his fate.

Blows continued to thud into the corpse, and Beornoth slipped one hand free of it and twisted in the sand so that he could pull his seax free from its sheath at the small of his back. That blade was a wicked thing the length of his forearm, its blade broken-backed and perfect for stabbing and rending. Beornoth snarled and jammed its tip into an attacker's black boot inches from his face. His right eye flickered open, and he threw the dead Viking from his chest and came up in a spinning, growling crouch. He cut and stabbed at the surrounding Vikings, and they leapt back from his fury. A man swung a short axe and Beornoth swayed back to let it pass in front of his face and stabbed the attacker in three short bursts to his ribs, then Beornoth spun and punched another Viking in the nose and all was blood, pain and chaos. A horn rang out, as clear and bright as a spring morning, and Beornoth smiled because his riders had come. The surrounding Vikings fell away, and it surprised Beornoth to find himself laughing loudly, like a drunken father at his daughter's wedding. He wanted the Vikings to feel fear and pain, and he wanted them to die. But as the Vikings scarpered to escape the charging Saxon horsemen, they revealed the baleful figure of the White Wolf, his two swords held low at his sides and his pale face long and framed by white eyebrows. Beornoth swallowed hard, and he pulled his sword free of its scabbard to meet the dreaded White Wolf.

18

Beornoth's sword was a simple thing. He did not believe in giving his weapons names, although plenty of men did. He sharpened the blade himself, never entrusting that job to a servant or one of his oathmen. Beornoth always put a fresh edge on it himself before battle, and though enemy blades often nicked its long edge, he worked out the worst of them with a whetstone. It was his tool, how he earned his livelihood, what made him a thegn of England. The sword, warhorse, spear and shield he owned were part of the Branoc's Tree heriot, and when Beornoth died, they would pass back to Ealdorman Byrhtnoth as an inheritance to be passed on to the next thegn of Branoc's Tree. Beornoth flexed his right hand around the supple leather wrapped tight around two pieces of willow wood riveted to the blade's tang. It was a comfortable, well-balanced blade. The fuller along the sword kept it light and allowed blood from the men it killed to run along the blade and keep it free from gore. The crosspiece was heavy, a simple steel bar, and its pommel was a round ball of heavy iron, which gave the weapon its balance. Beornoth raised the tip of that sword and beckoned the White Wolf on.

The fight on the beach raged around Beornoth, but it appeared to happen behind a curtain or tapestry, in a place far removed from where he actually faced the white-haired Viking. He was aware of a sickening crunch as Aelfwine and the wedge of Saxon riders crashed into the Vikings, their horses crushing men and their blades cutting and slashing at their enemies. There were cries of pain and war, but the noise was dull, like the sound a shell makes when held close to an ear. The White Wolf paced before him, twirling his swords around him in a blur. Beornoth shifted his feet in the sand, seax in one hand and sword in the other. The White Wolf came on, his blades scything through the air, coming to carve Beornoth open and spill his insides onto the sand. Beornoth tried to keep his eyes on the swords, to track the path of each flashing arc, but he lost them in the blur. To sit back and defend that whirling attack was to die, so Beornoth swallowed his fear and threw himself at the White Wolf, charging with his weapons raised.

An unseen shoulder cannoned into Beornoth, sending him sprawling into the sand again. He cursed and leapt to his feet, muscles bunched and weapons ready, but his mouth fell open when he realised that the Viking he faced was Brand Thorkilsson.

'This bastard is mine,' growled Brand, standing between Beornoth and the White Wolf.

'No,' said the white-haired warrior. 'He has reputation. I have waited for his death. I want him, for Odin, for Valhalla.'

Brand ignored his fellow Viking and came at Beornoth wielding an axe. Beornoth parried it with his sword and whipped his seax towards Brand's belly, but the Viking pivoted at the waist to avoid the blow. Beornoth leapt back and set himself, preparing to kill the man who had once been his friend. The Saxon charge had carved open the Vikings on the beach, and they were a scattered mess of men fleeing for their lives. A horseman came towards where Beornoth fought, a spear held low, one of Streonwold's men. The White Wolf cursed and went to fight that man, and Beornoth and Brand circled each other.

'I warned you not to fight him,' said Brand.

'I'll fight you instead then, bastard,' said Beornoth.

'No, lord. I will not cross blades with you. I only wanted to keep you from the *seiðr* of his swords.' Brand lowered his axe, and clasped a fist to his chest, offering a bow of his head to Beornoth.

'Fight, you piece of goat shit. I saw you at Branoc's Tree with blood on your blade. You killed my people, the people who fed you and gave you shelter. Fight me!' Beornoth raised his sword and held it a finger's breadth from Brand's throat. The Viking simply smiled and opened his arms wide.

'I am ready for Valhalla, if that is your choice. But I did not kill anyone at Branoc's Tree. I killed a pig to blood my blade, but that is all. I swear it on the honour of my ancestors.'

Beornoth let his sword fall and spat into the sand. Another blow of the war horn rang out, and the horsemen cantered across the sands to form up again away from the shore, closer to where they had first entered the beach. Wulfhere rode towards him, his mail and face sheeted in Viking blood. He held Hríð's reins and let the horse go when he saw that the Viking Beornoth faced was Brand.

'Treacherous filth!' Wulfhere said through gritted teeth. He hefted his axe and came for Brand, but Beornoth leapt between them, raising his arms to warn Wulfhere away.

'Not him,' Beornoth said, confused by his own actions, but certain that he did not want to see Brand dead. 'Let's go.' He climbed onto Hríð's saddle and met Wulfhere's baffled expression.

'He's a traitor, a murderer and a Viking. Kill the bastard.'

'I said no,' said Beornoth, and they locked eyes. For a moment, Beornoth thought Wulfhere would hit him. But the big man grimaced and spat at Brand. He sawed on his reins and wheeled his horse around to gallop across the beach.

Beornoth nodded to Brand and followed Wulfhere across the sands. He reached the Saxon horsemen who whooped for joy at their victory, men clapping one another on the back, their faces creased with smiles and laughter as they rode away, the warriors from the anchored ships still stumbling ashore through the waves. Viking corpses littered the beach, and they had lost but two men. One of them was Streonwold's man, Sicga, the young man who had attacked the White Wolf.

'A glorious victory!' said Godric, a bloody-tipped spear gripped in his hand and his cheeks flushed with exhilaration.

Beornoth felt their eyes upon him, waiting for words of encouragement, of recognition of the slaughter, of what to do next. Beornoth looked over his shoulder. Vikings came from the surf, ungainly in the tide's ebb and flow. Northmen armed with shields, spears and axes. They came from Olaf's ships, thirty or forty men, Beornoth guessed, with more following behind them. The Saxons had killed or wounded half of the White Wolf's men. It was a victory. The raiders had met Saxon justice. Beornoth ground his teeth and slid his sword back into its scabbard. His encounter with Brand left a sour taste in his mouth. He should have killed the man, or let Wulfhere do it. But Brand had likely saved his life, for to fight the White Wolf surely meant death, and despite the victory the Wolf yet lived.

'We should leave this place,' said Aelfwine, two horses away, shouting to Beornoth over the heady celebrations.

'We want to lure them to battle,' said Beornoth, more to

himself than to Aelfwine. He rode Hríð towards the rising sand
dunes which fronted the gully along which he had entered the
beach. Beornoth leaned over and tore a leafy branch from a
thorny bush within the coarse grass. They had killed a few
Vikings, and stung the White Wolf and his master, but it would
not win the war. It was not enough to send Olaf and his warriors
back to Norway. To see those feared dragon ships with sails filled
by a northerly wind, sailing for Norway, broken and so badly hurt
that they could never return, would take more. It needed the
shield wall, the dreaded war-fence where men kill and rend in
the press of blade and shield.

'What are you doing?' asked Aelfwine, nudging his horse
away from the others to face Beornoth.

'I have to talk to them,' Beornoth said. 'To find out where they
are going. We must force them to battle soon.'

'Olaf hates you, and that white-haired killer is there. How do
you know they won't simply cut you down?'

'I don't, but we must know their intentions. We can follow
their fleet all we like, but if we can't use the fyrd whilst we have the
army assembled, then there will be no battle. Which means their
raiding and killing goes on and on. We must end it.' Beornoth rode
ahead, holding the branch out before him to show the Vikings he
came in peace. Some of them surged towards him with shields
and spears ready to strike him down, faces twisted in hate, but a
man in a byrnie waved them down. Brand. Another mailed
warrior strode forward to join Brand, a tall man dripping wet from
wading through the shallows. As he drew closer, Beornoth recognised the blue eyes and sharp-angled face of Olaf Tryggvason.

Beornoth pulled Hríð to a halt twenty paces away from the
ever-increasing mass of Viking warriors, men stumbling from the
sea like the fetches of the drowned, emerging from the depths to

swell their ranks. Three Viking warlords strode forth to meet him: Olaf, Brand and the White Wolf. The Wolf walked as though he did not have a care in the world, still clutching his singing blades but with one resting upon each shoulder. He looked calm for a man who had just seen half of his warriors slaughtered on the beach.

'You have killed more of my men, Beornoth Reiði,' said Olaf, a frown creasing the cliff of his angular, youthful face. He used the same name by which Forkbeard had addressed Beornoth in Gippeswic, which was alarming. Olaf had never used the byname before.

'Men who have been slaughtering Saxon women and children for months,' said Beornoth.

'Have you come to gloat? I should kill you where you stand. I could have my men cast their spears and you would be dead in an instant.' Olaf was shouting, his hands curled into fists. Hríð shifted sideways in the sand, and Beornoth let him move. The horse turned slowly and Beornoth waited until Hríð came around to face Olaf again. The Viking leader had lost his temper, and was normally a man at pains to maintain a calm exterior, despite the war raging around him. Beornoth smiled, leaving as long a pause as possible, which is as annoying as a slap in the face to a man who has let himself fall into a rage.

'I come to talk, instead of kill. I can bring my riders back though, if you like. We killed this one's men as though they were toothless grandfathers, unable to defend themselves. Not one of them is worthy of Valhalla. You should have brought your Jomsvikings ashore so we could have a proper fight.' Beornoth pointed at the White Wolf as he spoke in Norse, noting a twitch in the warrior's smirk.

'I will fight you here and now, old man. You are a stinking

piece of seal shit. You don't have the skill to face me,' said the White Wolf, with the lilt of the men of the far north.

'I am a thegn of the East Saxons. I killed Skarde Wartooth, Einar Ravenhair, and Olaf's foster father, Palnatoki. A man of reputation does not fight with untested pups like you. I saw you kill a soft-faced lad of my hearth troop when he was unarmed. And, I saw you kill women and children at my home. But it's best if you leave the real fighting to the warriors. Go over yonder and give us a show with your dancing blades. I have seen jugglers and mummers do the same thing. It will amuse us whilst we talk.'

The smirk fell from the Wolf's face and he took a step toward Beornoth before Olaf stopped him with a hand on his chest.

'Not now,' Olaf said quietly. 'The man you disrespect is the champion of the men of Hålogaland in Norway. He has killed many great champions. His name is Orm, the White Wolf.'

'He is a nithing son of a whore, and next time we meet, I will kill him and take his head. I will put it on a spear in one of my fields to scare the crows away.'

'Did you come back to insult us, or do you have something to say?' said Olaf, pushing the Wolf away and back to his own warriors. Beornoth laughed then, because he knew he had wormed his way into the Wolf's head. The man hated him now, and few knew better than Beornoth how that can cloud a man's judgement.

'I came back to ask you if you have brought your famous Jomsvikings to England to raid like common pirates, or if you have the courage to test your spears in the shield wall, in battle where the warriors of reputation fight? Why are you here, Olaf? Do you want to make yourself a king? To make yourself rich?'

'I will be a king one day,' Olaf said wistfully, turning his head to gaze at the churning sea. He tucked his thumbs into his belt and ambled towards Beornoth. Olaf's anger fell from him like an old cloak, and he smiled at Beornoth. Olaf walked slowly towards him and Brand followed. Beornoth held Hríð still until they came within reach of his bridle. Beornoth's guts twisted as fear curdled within him. All it would take was for Olaf to reach up and hold the bridle whilst Brand dragged him from the saddle. The Vikings would pounce upon him, and he would die under their blades before he drew his sword. 'A seer told me so when I was a child in the east,' Olaf continued. 'I was a slave once. Did you know that? I am a descendant of Harald Fairhair, the first king of all Norway, and my father's enemies chased my family out of our own country. They hunted my mother like a dog across distant shores. She was a queen and became forced to go as a beggar to halls of rich jarls seeking protection. Eventually, cruel men captured us and cast us down. When I was still a boy, I killed the man who enslaved me. And, whilst they held me awaiting punishment, a dark-skinned woman with burned-out eyes told me my future. I will be a king one day, Saxon, and my name will live on forever. So yes, I am here to make myself a king. But in Norway, not here. To become a king, a man must have silver, victories and reputation so that men will flock to his banner. So, I am here with my Jomsvikings.' Olaf spoke calmly. He ran his hand across Hríð's muzzle and smiled as the horse pushed the soft skin around his mouth into Olaf's palm.

'To kill women and children like a raven-starving nithing?' Beornoth shouted. He roared to startle Olaf, trying to taunt him, and the Northman's head snapped up. 'If you want to fight, let's fight. Bring your army ashore and let us have the shield wall. Fight me, Olaf. Bring your Jomsvikings to the front. I will be there. Make your reputation fighting in the war-fence, not on the burnt backs of children.'

'Who are you to shout at me? I should kill you where you stand,' Olaf roared, his calmness as fleeting as the show of pebbles dragged up by the sea's lull before the tide washed them away again. 'I am Olaf Tryggvason, prince of Norway!'

'So bring your ships south and meet us, army against army. Fight our warriors, and not the wives of our farmers. Let us see the mettle of the prince of Norway!'

'Begone, Saxon, before I drag you off that pale horse and piss down your dead throat.'

Beornoth laughed and pulled on Hríð's reins, expertly walking the horse backwards so that he could keep his eyes on his enemy. 'Bring your ships south, Olaf. Let us do battle, make your reputation or return to your own country as what you are, a nithing pirate too afraid to stand in the line of battle.'

Olaf turned on his heel and stalked back to his warriors, fists bunched at his side, and Brand took two steps towards Beornoth.

'Wait, lord,' he said, holding his palms up as Beornoth's hand fell to his sword. 'There must be a battle. But I beg you, as my friend, Beornoth. Go to your wife, leave this place. There can be no victory for your people this time.'

'A Saxon warrior defending his home is worth two of your Vikings.'

'And you will need many, for King Sweyn Forkbeard has left his fortress at Gippeswic with forty ships.'

Beornoth rocked back in his saddle, unable to disguise the look of surprise upon his face. 'He sails to join Olaf?'

'He sails south, lord. That thing you made of Ragnar the Flayer, that heimnar, rouses the hearts of Sweyn's warriors. They come for blood. They smell the chance for victory, there is a chance for us to take all of East Anglia and Essex, like in the time of Guthrum back when the Danelaw was forged. A Viking could be king in England once more.'

'You lie. I met with Forkbeard. He seeks only to enrich

himself, and he sits like a dragon on a hoard of gold with his mint in Gippeswic.'

'Sweyn Forkbeard is a war king. He is a true Viking, lord. He is ruthless and daring. The song of war rouses Forkbeard, and he will lead his warriors against your Saxons. The day of the Saxon is over. I tell you this when I should not. A victory here would make me rich. I would have lands, silver and glory. But I tell you this because you are my brother of the sword. You saved my life once. So go, ride to Alfgar in the northern shires.'

'You should not have returned to Olaf,' said Beornoth. He spoke softly, still reeling from the news that Sweyn had lurched from his stronghold like some great monster from the tales of old.

'I had to, lord. I am oath-sworn to him.'

'You should not have returned because if we face each other in battle, I will have to kill you.' Beornoth sawed on Hríð's reins and left Brand standing on the sand, his eyes burning into the back of Beornoth's head. For a fleeting moment, Beornoth thought he had rattled Olaf, had poked and jabbed him enough with the defeat on the beach and his cruel words so that the warlord would bring his warriors to the field of battle. He rode towards his men and blood pounded in his ears, the noise of the sea drowned out by the rush of dread flooding his senses. The news that Forkbeard was at sea changed things: goading Olaf to battle now seemed foolish, and Beornoth feared for the fate of his people.

'That seemed to go well,' said Leofsunu, his misshapen face grinning as he leant over his horse's neck. 'They didn't kill you, anyway.'

'We must ride to the ealdorman,' said Beornoth. 'Forkbeard has sailed. If he joins his warriors with Olaf's, we could face over two thousand Viking warriors.'

'Lord God protect us,' said Leofsunu, the colour draining from his face. 'We cannot stand against such a force.'

'Two Viking armies,' said Thered, his jaw dropping at the impossible odds faced by the warriors of Essex.

'We must fight Olaf before Sweyn arrives. We must present our army to Olaf and offer battle, and it must happen soon,' said Beornoth.

They rode west, leaving five men to follow Olaf's ships. Beornoth ordered those men to keep track of the Viking fleet, watch for Forkbeard's ships, and for one of them to ride to locate the East Saxon army each day. One messenger had already departed to Byrhtnoth, and Beornoth rode in silence. His head ached with problems. Of the importance of knowing at all times where Olaf's fleet was. Of anticipating where Olaf would land to take on board food and drink for his vast army. Of getting the fyrd and warriors of Essex to that place and arraying the army in time to draw Olaf into a fight. Hríð ran at a canter, the jangle of tracings and his shield banging at Beornoth's back, a dull sound lost somewhere in his consciousness. He stared ahead at the flat farmlands of Essex as they rolled away before him, carved into pastures and fields for crops, bordered by hedges and brooks. If the East Saxons lost touch with Olaf's fleet, if the Northman could come ashore and replenish the vast amount of food he needed to feed fifty ships filled with Viking warriors, and sail away before battle was joined, then Brand was right. The day of the East Saxons on the windswept island of Britain was over. Olaf and Forkbeard would join their armies together and crush the army of the East Saxons under their boots like ants. They would carve up the old kingdoms of East Anglia and Essex into their own fiefdoms, making themselves kings on the island. Beornoth licked at dry lips, tasting sea salt. He was thirsty. The future of the Saxons rested on a knife edge. He had to get to Byrhtnoth and move the army south in time to head off Olaf and force battle. But he needed a drink first, just a horn or a small mug of ale. To take the edge off, to settle his fear. Then he would be ready to fight, ready to defend the kingdom against Olaf and Forkbeard and their fearsome Viking armies. He thought about what Brand had said, of riding north to Eawynn in Cheshire. He would have a home there, should he wish it. Alfgar would welcome him, he would be comfortable and could live in peace. It was tempting. He could just keep on riding, turn Hríð north and leave the maelstrom of war behind. Turn his back on the East Saxons and leave them to fight off the Vikings. He could simply ride away and leave Wulfhere, Leofsunu, Aelfwine and Byrhtnoth to the great shield wall battle which must come. Beornoth remembered that horror like a knife in his thought cage. The blades, arrows and spears. The champions and killers, the torn flesh and screams of those who suffer the wound that does not kill. The wound that festers and robs a man of a glorious death. Some would die weeks later of infection, but worse was to live on as a cripple, completely dependent on others for food, shelter and silver. The fate into which Beornoth had thrust Ragnar the Flayer when he had whittled away the slaver's arms and legs. Thoughts of that butcher work visited Beornoth in the deep of night, the blood and torn flesh, horrific and an unworthy act for a warrior. Not something about which he could talk to Eawynn with pride. Creating the heimnar had been a mistake. Beornoth's intention was to provoke Olaf into a fight, but the creature had also forged the Vikings will, become a reason for them to fight the Saxons. Better if he had just killed the slaving bastard. The Vikings would not pity Beornoth if he fell into their hands, and they would know him as the creator of the heimnar. Would it be the famous Blood Eagle torture for him, or would they make him into a heimnar as an act of vengeance? These were the risks for a warrior such as he, pain, death, wounds, capture, enslavement or torture. That was war, and perhaps he could leave it all behind him. But he was Beornoth, and he was born for war. He was oath-bound to fight for the ealdorman of the East Saxons, and had also sworn an oath in blood to fight alongside his brothers of the blade. So, he must fight.

19

Ealdorman Byrhtnoth drove the East Saxon army south, the men strung out in a long, sprawling line with half a day separating the vanguard and rearguard. Beornoth and his riders, which comprised Byrhtnoth's hearth troop and Streonwold's men of Cheshire, formed the vanguard, ranging ahead of the lines to scout for any Vikings who might have come ashore looking to spring a surprise attack upon the ragged, crawling thing that is an army on the march. The warriors of Wessex and Essex marched with the fyrd men, urging them onwards, keeping the men moving amidst the endless small groups peeling off to piss or shit, of twisted ankles and broken supply wagons. The ealdorman himself took up the rearguard that day, along with Offa, Godric and the warriors he had managed to prise from East Anglia.

For two days, Beornoth rode at the head of the army, riders coming to and from the coast with news of Olaf's ships. The White Wolf had abandoned his horses on the beach following the fight with Beornoth's riders and had boarded his ships to sail with the army. Olaf sailed his fleet south, stopping at Mersea Island to resupply: that same tidal island in a mud-banked

estuary off the east coast of Essex where Beornoth had tricked
and fought Skarde Wartooth two years earlier. That supply stop
had been too far for Byrhtnoth's army to reach in time to line up
for battle, and Olaf had taken to the sea again that same day, with
his sails filled by a southerly wind.

Beornoth rode with Aelfwine, whilst Wulfhere, Leofsunu,
Thered and Streonwold took a small company of riders each to
ride out in different directions, over hills and around woodland,
so that Byrhtnoth knew at all times that the army was safe from
Viking attackers howling from trees or hidden valleys to butcher
the men of the fyrd. The sun shone high and hot in a sky so blue
it was almost white. Even the clouds retreated from the heat,
leaving only wispy trails to show that they had ever existed at all.
A bead of sweat trickled down Beornoth's back, coming to a stop
to join the larger pool that soaked into the jerkin, which lay
beneath the leather coat he wore under his chain-mail byrnie.
Beornoth took a hand from the horse's reins and grabbed a fistful
of the iron rings at his chest, pulling the thing away from his body
and trying to blow downwards to cool himself. The iron rings
were hot to his touch, and he gave up, turning to frown at
Aelfwine, who grinned at him from beneath a wide-brimmed hat
he had bought from a farmer that morning with a few scraps of
hacksilver.

'It's nice and cool under here,' said Aelfwine. 'You should
have picked one up for yourself.'

Beornoth ran a hand through his hair, which was tied back by
a strip of leather at the nape of his neck. 'It suits you,' he replied.
'Next, you'll be telling me about the virtues of planting barley
early, or the best method for milking a cow.'

'It would be beautiful today at my home in Foxfield. The children would swim and play in the lake, and we would sit in the
shade and enjoy the fine weather.'

'Hopefully those days return, my friend.'

'They will. You should visit me in Foxfield next summer, with Eawynn and Wulfhere, if he ever recovers from his grief.'

'I would like that,' said Beornoth. He smiled, imagining sitting and eating under a shaded canopy with Aelfwine and his wife. Listening to the sound of children playing and laughing. 'Just don't ask me any cursed riddles.'

Aelfwine laughed and shook his head. 'Do you think Wulfhere will ever return to his old self?'

'I hope so. I have prayed for him,' said Beornoth, which was true. 'There will soon be enough Viking blood to slake his thirst for vengeance. But that won't take the pain away. I know that more than most. It will always be with him. But he must learn to live with it. May God help him overcome the pain.'

'It's good to see you have returned to the embrace of the Lord.'

'Aye, well, I prayed, and God answered. I asked Eawynn to be spared the attack on Branoc's Tree, and she was. So now I pray for Wulfhere, and you and the others. I pray for peace and I hope God hears me.'

'He hears you. Look, a rider.' Aelfwine pointed to where a figure raced along a line of hedgerow, and Beornoth had to squint to see under the sun's glare. The man pushed his horse hard. He reined the animal in before Beornoth and Aelfwine in a dusty scramble of hooves and clods of dry earth. The horse was a chestnut gelding and its flanks were thick with white lather. The man gasped for air, his face red, and he swallowed and coughed at a parched throat.

'Out with it, man, what is it?' said Aelfwine, tossing the rider the small skin of water from his saddle.

The rider took a long drink, rivulets of the water running into his dusty beard. 'The Vikings, lord,' he said in quick gasps. 'They went south towards the River Crouch, but the king's fleet came out of the Thames on a strong wind and frightened them off. The wind is as dead as my dear old granny now, lord, so the Vikings are at their oars. Their sails are useless.'

'Where are they now?' asked Beornoth, waiting patiently as the rider took another swig of water with creased eyes and a gulping throat.

The rider tossed the skin back to Aelfwine and flashed a gap-toothed grin at Beornoth. 'The king's ships did not leave the Thames. And the Vikings are coming around towards the Black-water Estuary, lord.'

'That's only a half-day's march from here,' said Aelfwine.

'They will sail as far into the estuary as they can to avoid the rapid tide. They'll come right up the River Pant,' said Beornoth, his heart quickening. 'Go, tell the ealdorman. We'll ride ahead to the burh at Maldon and meet him there.'

'Yes, lord,' said the rider. 'To Maldon.'

The burh at Maldon sat on a small hill, perched upon a wide bend in the River Blackwater. That river rose deep within the shire itself, beginning as the freshwater River Pant flowing south-east through Bocking, where Beornoth had hung the traitor Æthelric earlier that very summer. At the turn around Maldon Hill, the river emptied into the Blackwater Estuary before joining the heaving grey vastness of the sea. Beornoth and Aelfwine summoned the scouts with three bursts on the war horn, and then horsemen rode for the burh ordering men at every farm they passed through to gather food, milk and ale and leave them for the army to gather on the march towards Maldon. The river itself was thick with small fishing villages, nets spread to dry across ancient timbers, wicker traps filled with fish and shellfish, enough for the army to feed itself whilst it mustered.

The thegn of Maldon, a swarthy man named Hodard, rode

with the army and ordered the gate opened and sent men for miles around to secure as much fish, bread, barley, wheat and ale as they could muster. Beornoth paid a boy a battered silver coin to take Hríð and find fodder for the animal, to rub him down and find him some shade. Beornoth himself found shade in the late afternoon beneath the burh's walls. It was an old fortress, built two generations ago by King Edward, and had seen Viking blood spilled many times, perched as it was at such an inviting entryway into the lush farmland of Essex. Many a Viking fleet had dared to sail their shallow-draughted dragon ships around Maldon's hill and found themselves attacked by a ferocious Saxon defence. The burhs were King Alfred's network of fortresses, built at strategic locations such as Maldon, to ward off Viking attacks: to shore up the rivers and estuaries of his kingdom against the bloodthirsty Northmen; to deter them with ditch, palisade and high walls against attack; to send them looking for easier pickings in Frankia or beyond.

Beornoth ate whitefish from a wooden plate, along with a chunk of fresh golden bread. He washed it down with cool water drawn from a well beyond Maldon's southern wall. He sat alone whilst Aelfwine and Leofsunu busied themselves, ensuring the men had places to sleep and food to eat. Beornoth watched the sun come down in the late summer afternoon, shadows grew longer, crawling across the land like dark, sprawling fingers. The Vikings were out there somewhere, fifty or more ships crammed with warriors, axes and shields. He watched a pair of black-feathered lapwings peck and pull at the riverbank mud left bare by the tide.

'Here you are,' said a gruff voice. Beornoth looked up to see Wulfhere standing over him, clutching a small barrel under one arm and two horn cups in his other hand. 'I brought ale.' He plonked the barrel down onto the grass beside Beornoth and sat next to it. 'I know you don't drink, but these are desperate times. So, have a drink with me now.'

Beornoth wanted to say no, but Wulfhere had been so angry and distant lately that he didn't have the heart to refuse. He smiled and held out his hand, and Wulfhere filled one of the horn mugs with frothing ale. He half smiled through the ruin of his face, his missing eye a scarred mess of ridged flesh and pain.

'The ealdorman says we won't stay within the fortress,' said Beornoth, after a few moments of silence. The words did not come easily. It was still hard not to think of Aethelberga whenever he saw Wulfhere, hard not to mention it or say he was sorry. Which had been said enough.

'Olaf won't attack a burh,' said Wulfhere with a shrug. 'Easier pickings elsewhere.'

'There is an island along the bank, towards the sea. A tidal causeway links it to the mainland, like Mersea Island, where we fought Skarde. We'll try to meet Olaf there and force battle.'

'Seems as good a plan as any. I hope there is a fight.' Wulfhere took a long drink from his cup, then rested it on top of the barrel and fished for something in the pouch at his belt. 'I made this for you.' He handed Beornoth a crucifix carved from two pieces of golden wood and tied together with a thin strip of leather. It was like the carving the big man had once made for their friend Alfgar. 'You have found your faith again, and I thought you could use it.'

'Thank you,' said Beornoth. He slipped the leather thong over his head and tucked the carving behind his byrnie. 'I have returned to God's grace. I feel his warmth again. But you have lost sight of it.'

'I feel now as you once did. How can God love us, his children, and yet allow such cruelty into his world? How can men like Olaf and his White Wolf be allowed to harm us? To kill good people, people who have loved God for their whole lives?'

Beornoth gazed out upon the river, the sunset twinkling upon the soft, flowing waters and the call of gulls floating on the light evening breeze. There was no answer to that question. He had asked it himself often enough. Wulfhere refilled their cups, and they drank in companionable silence for a time, the silence only available to old friends, with no awkward talk required to fill its space. The ale flowed, and Wulfhere filled Beornoth's cup again.

'What happens if we don't defeat them?' Wulfhere said eventually, after each man had drunk two more cups. Beornoth's head felt light.

'They take Essex. The king will either need to make peace, with a monstrous payment or a gift of land. But the people will suffer.'

'The people always suffer. Where is God when they need him?' Wulfhere's words slurred as he spoke, and Beornoth wondered how much his friend had drunk before coming to him. 'We should have been there.' Wulfhere's voice dropped to a whisper, his glassy eyes staring out at the estuary.

'We can't be everywhere, and we go where the ealdorman commands.' They were empty words, Beornoth knew. The thoughts plaguing Wulfhere's mind were the same poisoned pools of regret which sat within his own soul. Of not being there when those he loved needed him most. When the wicked men came, when those who cannot defend themselves need the warriors to protect them from those who come with black hearts and sharp blades. They finished their ale and returned to the cramped space within Maldon's burh in companionable silence, the weight of the battle to come heavy on their shoulders.

Beornoth lay down in his quarters that night to a fitful sleep. Faces came to him in the darkness: Olaf's sharp, angular face like

an ice-covered mountain; Sweyn Forkbeard and his eyes of deep
cunning, laughing at Beornoth in the darkness. Men he had
killed, Skarde, Osric and Einar Ravenhair came to him as addled
corpses, discoloured skin hanging in patches from their skele-
tons. He woke drenched in sweat and splashed his face in a bowl
of cool water by his bed. Beornoth sank back into the cot of dry
straw and stared at the rafters. Sleep came for him again, but this
time haunted by the weeping fetches of Aethelberga, Blaedswith
and his dead daughters. He woke again and rose to push open the
wooden window shutters. A light breeze drifting in from the
estuary kissed the beads of sweat upon his chest. The nightmares
were too much, wrenching and tearing at his soul with painful
memories of a life filled with loss and pain. His mouth dry from
drinking too much ale with Wulfhere, Beornoth took a drink
from a pitcher of water and pulled on his jerkin.

Men slept and snored in every room, corridor and cranny of
the Maldon burh. Beornoth walked softly amongst them in bare
feet. The earth, parched by the summer sun, scratched the soles
of his feet and as he came out of the burh's central hall, Beornoth
made his way to the palisade and climbed to its top. Across the
water, and around the wide bend of the River Blackwater, the sun
came up in a wash of red and orange across a pale grey sky, like a
fire kindling on the horizon. There was warmth in its heat
already, comforting on Beornoth's cheeks after the grim visita-
tions he had experienced through the night. It was low tide, and
dunlins and oystercatchers picked their way through the
mudbanks, their beaks searching for food within the riverbeds
left exposed by the ebb. Beornoth reached up to grasp the crucifix
hanging at his neck. It was a fine piece of woodwork. Wulfhere
had worked on it through the summer, the golden wood etched
with the nailed figure of Jesus Christ smiling despite the terrible
wounds in his wrists and ankles. Beornoth thought about that, of

the suffering of Jesus and how he had sacrificed his life for God's people. God had heard Beornoth's prayers once before, and so he knelt on Maldon's rampart and prayed again. He prayed for the people of Essex , but most of all for Wulfhere, so that the big man could find peace once more. Beornoth left the rampart and went to wake Wulfhere and the rest of his warriors, because the Vikings were coming, and there must be a fight to determine the fate of south-east England.

20

Before the red-tinged sun rose fully from its slumber, riders galloped beneath Maldon's gate, their horses lathered and the riders desperately calling for Ealdorman Byrhtnoth. Beornoth could not make his way through the throng of warriors in time to hear the news first-hand, but he found Leofsunu of Sturmer leaning against a timber post which propped up an awning outside a smith's workshop. Inside, bellows pumped and sparks flew in the shadowy darkness, a hammer rang out from the smithy's dark interior, beating its song into a blade or spear point.

'They are here,' Leofsunu said simply, his misshapen face busy examining the edge of his seax. 'Olaf and his ships are here.'

'What, in the estuary?' asked Beornoth, stunned that Leofsunu could be so calm in the face of the oncoming fleet.

'Aye.' Leofsunu thumbed the blade and stroked his hand along the seax's antler hilt before sliding it back into a small scabbard at his belt. 'Worrying about them won't make them go away. Come, let's see the enemy.'

They pushed through the crowds, men jostling each other to get a look at the Viking ships in the river. Beornoth shouldered past men who turned in anger as he moved them aside, but then melted away when they met Beornoth's mailed chest and looked up into his grim face. He and Leofsunu reached the top of the palisade and gazed out upon the river beyond. The river swelled as the sun rose, the flood tide now covered the mudbanks where Beornoth had watched birds digging for food. Beornoth's eyes fixed on the glistening river where, in the distance, a dozen Viking dragon ships rowed lazily with the tide, and the sun glinted off the steel of their warriors' blades. The morning sun created a haze upon the water, but even at the distance from the burh, along the river, and into the estuary beyond, Beornoth could make out the rise and fall of oar blades. The ships snarled at the shoreline, their masts furled and their beast-headed prows threatening and formidable.

'Olaf must have sent just twelve of his ships to take a look at us,' said a wiry man next to Beornoth. He spoke with the slight burr of the men of East Anglia and wore a hard-baked leather breastplate. 'Came and saw the burh, all of our men camped here, and thought better of it.'

'I hear the king's fleet sailed from Lundenburg and scared them out of the Thames. They won't try to sail up this river with all of us in this fort,' said another man behind them.

'Looks like they might stop at Northey Island,' said Leofsunu. 'It's right there, in the middle of the estuary. As good a place as stop as any if they want to come ashore and find food and water.'

'They won't come ashore now that they know our army is here,' said Beornoth.

'They don't fear us,' said Leofsunu with a shrug. 'They'll stop at Northey. Maybe they want to fight just as much as we do.'

Ealdorman Byrhtnoth led the East Saxon army out of Maldon's burh on a balmy morning. With bellies filled with baked fish and fresh bread, a thousand men marched along the banks of the Blackwater, their spear points bristling and helmets catching the sun like the gleam of a spider's web heavy with dew. They were the fyrd of Essex, farmers, millers, potters, blacksmiths and woodsmen. Alongside them rode the warriors of Cheshire, led by Streonwold, and the warriors of Wessex, led by the twin brothers Wighelm and Wigstan. Byrhtnoth rode at the head of the men of East Anglia so that the army of over one thousand fighters left the safety of Maldon's fortress to coax a larger Viking army to battle.

Beornoth rode with Wulfhere, Thered and his household troops. Cwicca had taken Beornoth's byrnie in the morning and polished it to a sheen with river sand, and despite the heat, Beornoth rode to battle like a lord of war. He wore his bright chain-mail byrnie, his sword belted at his hip, and his seax sat in a sheath at the small of his back. Beornoth carried his helmet with its eyeholes and cheek pieces tied to his saddle, and his shield strapped across his back. He carried a long leaf-bladed aesc spear, and a war axe hung low in a sheath upon Hrið's saddle. They rode south-east until Byrhtnoth called the halt before Northey island, the low, flat hump which sat like the arching back of a sea beast in Blackwater Estuary.

The ealdorman called his men to a council on the riverbank, and Beornoth climbed up a grass-covered bank beyond where thick reeds and dark green leaves stretched away into the dark tidal waters. Byrhtnoth turned to Beornoth and smiled, the iron-grey spade of his beard moving with the gesture.

'Tide's in,' said Byrhtnoth, and gazed out at the water rippling gently under the sun. 'The rest of their ships are out there somewhere.'

There were twelve Viking drakkars moored off Northey Island. They bobbed on the flood tide, beast heads carved into growling bears, glaring ravens and snarling wolves. The men from the ships were ashore, watching the Saxons from the island's beach.

'They are looking to take on more supplies, or grow sick of rowing against the flood and await the ebb. When the tide goes out,' said Byrhtnoth, 'there is a narrow causeway which links the island to the shore. Wide enough for three men to walk abreast.'

'Do you want to fight them here, lord?' asked Beornoth.

'They aren't all here. We need the whole of Olaf's fleet here. We need to fight them all, Beo.'

'So, what do we do?'

'Wait until the tide goes out and then talk to them. See where the rest of the bastards are and then pick a fight.' The ealdorman turned and fixed Beornoth with eyes as cold and pale as a freshly forged sword blade. Byrhtnoth ran his front teeth over the beard below his bottom lip. The two men held each other's gaze, and although there was silence, there was also an understanding. Two men who had stood and fought in the shield wall many times would need to do so again. Poets and skalds sang of battle, of the war-fence and its glory, and their stories flooded men's hearts with pride and admiration for the men who fought in the clash of swords and spears. But, for those who knew it well, it was not a thing for song or rejoicing. The Saxons would make a line of shields, and Ealdorman Byrhtnoth and Beornoth would be at its centre. In the front rank, where brave men fought and died. The Vikings would make a similar line, and the two armies would throw spears at one another, and arrows would fill the sky. Men would die, or fall injured screaming between the lines, and then the shield walls would come together. Beornoth saw the horror of that clash behind Byrhtnoth's eyes, the crunching, crashing noise of battle, the screaming of pain and the stench of shit as dying men voided their bowels. The enemy would be close in the press of shields, close enough to smell their ale-stinking breath, and both lines would shove and heave, trying desperately to push a blade into the soft flesh of the enemy opposing them. Those blades were cold and wicked sharp. They would rip a man's flesh, tear at his face and eyes, pierce his heart and stomach and spill his blood on the battlefield. And at the end, one army would flee, and that was when the real killing would begin. In the shield wall itself, the shields protected warriors, each man overlapping his with that of the man next to him, creating a locked and solid barrier against enemy blades. But once men ran, when they showed their backs, then the blood frenzy took over and the victors would chase them down, hacking into those unprotected backs with spear, axe and sword. Beornoth and Byrhtnoth saw that horror in each other's eyes, but knew it must be done. They must not flinch from it, and good men would die. Friends, brothers in arms would die squirming in the filth of a blood-churned battlefield. They were warriors, and this was their fate. Olaf and his savage Vikings must be stopped.

'Lord Byrhtnoth,' said a man behind them, and Beornoth sighed, recognising Godric's whining voice.

'Godric,' said the ealdorman in greeting.

'Forgive me, lord,' Godric continued. His brothers Godwine and Godwig flanked him, each of them resplendent in fine byrnies, and Godric's hand rested upon the golden hilt of his sword. Their fourth brother lay buried on Byrhtnoth's estate, killed by a Viking blade. Behind them stood Offa, Aelfwine, Thered, Streonwold and the rest of the army's thegns, along with Dunnere, the farmer who came to represent the men of the fyrd. 'But why did we leave a perfectly defendable fortress, one of Alfred's burhs designed precisely to help us defend our country against the Northmen?'

'You can ask your questions, Godric, no need for forgiveness,' said Byrhtnoth. And he raised his voice for the others to hear. 'We left the safety of the burh precisely because the Vikings would never attack us in such a stronghold. Our presence there stops them from sailing up the Blackwater, into the Pant and deep into our shire, but they will simply sail away and inflict themselves upon another part of our land. To stop their raiding, we must fight them, and here is where we shall make our stand.'

The thegns muttered between themselves, faces drawn and anxious at the prospect of battle.

'But there are only a dozen of their ships here,' said Godric. 'There are forty more out there somewhere.'

'They will come. They must come.'

'If they don't come, lord,' said Dunnere. The thegns turned their heads to stare at the bear-like farmer, the commoner who dared speak amongst the warrior class of thegns and men of the hearth troop. 'If they don't come, when can we return to our farms?'

'If the rest of the ships don't come, then we must disband the fyrd within days and you can return to your homes. But know this: if the ships don't come, you will return home to an uncertain future. If we do not fight them, if we do not stop them, they will sail up a river just like this one and let their warriors loose in our shire. Then, the fight will be in your fields and before your door, with burning thatch, butchered corpses, and plundered farm-steads across Essex.'

Men pulled at their beards and examined each other with furtive glances, and the ealdorman stepped down off the river-bank to walk amongst them. Dunnere scratched at the bush of his beard and nodded slowly at Byrhtnoth's hard truth.

'Many of you here swore Aelfwine's blood oath. The rest of you are the finest warriors in the kingdom. You all knew our aim was to bring Olaf to battle, and there will be a battle. So, steel yourselves to that. Have your men make ready, sharpen blades and test the boards of your shields. We shall have our war here, men, and we must prevail. It falls to us to stop the sea wolves. It is our responsibility to meet them in the shield wall and put a stop to their raiding and raping. Some of us will die, but more of them will surely fall to our swords, the keener blades of men defending their homes and their country. Go now, take a meal, talk to your men. Prepare yourselves for war.'

'We swore that oath,' said Aelfwine, raising his hand to show the scar left there by the blood oath. 'We thegns of Byrhtnoth's hearth troop, the warriors of Essex. Now is the time to fulfil that oath. Are we ready for war?'

The warriors pumped their fists into the air three times. A clipped roar accompanied each fist, and the men strode away with chests puffed and shoulders back. They were brave men, but that would be put to the test if Olaf and his Jomsvikings came to Maldon. Beornoth waited by the riverbank, and Wulfhere joined him. They stood together for a while, watching the river and the Vikings milling about on Northey Island's beach.

'What happens when the tide goes out?' said Wulfhere, as a gull flew overhead, hanging in the air with his wide wings stretched, floating on the warm breeze.

'When the tide goes out, a causeway will rise from the shallows, and Byrhtnoth and I will walk across it to talk to the Northmen,' said Beornoth.

'A causeway like the Strood at Mersea Island?'

'Just like the one we crossed when we killed Skarde Wartooth.'

'But this time we won't attack them?'

'No, we won't. This time we offer battle.'

Then, when the sun reached the height of its journey across the sky, the tide ebbed again. It shrank back from reeds and exposed the slick, dark mudbanks for the birds of the riverbank to return and hunt for the tiny animals who lived beneath the slime. The tide moved faster than Beornoth expected, faster than he wanted it to, and the rock and stone of the narrow causeway appeared from the water as though raised by *seiðr*. First, it came as a shadow beneath the rippling water, then it poked through the grey waters like the tail of a mighty monster. But the tide was as relentless a force as Olaf and his Vikings, and they were both inevitable.

'It's time,' Beornoth said, smiling wanly at Wulfhere, and he stepped away from the riverbank and waited for Ealdorman Byrhtnoth who came striding from the depths of the army. A thousand men cooked food over small campfires. Hundreds of horses grazed on the grass and brush of the land, butting into the River Blackwater. The noise of the army was a constant undulating murmur, the melting pot of all of those voices, the clanking of their pots and weapons, the smells of their food, sweat and excrement. That army was a living thing, powerful and huge. The men of Essex forged together on the anvil of Byrhtnoth's will. And from that heaving throng came the ealdorman, hulking in his byrnie, his golden-hilted sword on his hip in a red scabbard, and a green cloak hanging from his shoulders.

'They tell me the tide has revealed the path,' said Byrhtnoth.

'The pathway to what, though, lord?' Beornoth said, adjusting his belt and resting his hand on the pommel of his sword.

'To victory, by God's grace. Come, let's kick the beehive together, you and I.' Byrhtnoth carried his helmet, a beautiful thing with a boar carved upon a strip of iron traversing the forehead and a white horsehair tail running from the top so that it flowed down to the back of his neck. Beornoth retrieved his own helmet where it lay with his shield and spear and placed it upon his head. Its leather helmet liner stank of old sweat, but it was supple and soft over his hair. The dark iron rings which circled his eyes were cold upon his cheeks and he left the cheek pieces open at the side of his head. The helmet was heavy, but it made a warrior fearsome, and told his enemies that he was a man of reputation to own such an extravagant piece of war gear. Beornoth and Byrhtnoth, two warriors, strode towards the causeway, and men clapped fists to their chests and bowed their heads in respect as they passed.

Beornoth reached the stones of the long causeway and stepped onto the uneven rocks. Although the tide fled from the strip of stone, a thin film of it remained and the cold water covered his boot and sent a chill along his foot. He strode forward, Ealdorman Byrhtnoth at his side, two men approaching Northey Island where twelve crews of Vikings awaited them. There would be close to four hundred men on the island, or aboard their ships which the Northmen had moved to the deepest part of the river to avoid running aground. Four Vikings ventured onto the causeway to meet them, marching confidently with their thumbs hooked into their belts. One walked with a spear rested across his shoulders and his arms hooked over each end, strolling as though he had not a care in the world. The fourth man, however, had two swords scabbarded across his back, and as they drew closer, Beornoth recognised the bone white of his hair, his fish-scale armour and his languid gait.

'It's the White Wolf,' he said, his knuckles whitening as he gripped the leather-bound hilt of his sword.

'He speaks for Olaf?' said Byrhtnoth.

'Aye, he's the bastard who has done most of Olaf's raiding. Olaf himself hangs back with his Jomsvikings, too proud for raiding.'

'They want this battle as much as we, Beo. So let's give it to them. You speak their tongue. Draw them out.'

The Vikings came to a stop ten paces from the two Saxons,

and the man with the spear hawked loudly and spat a gobbet into the river. The White Wolf grinned at Beornoth, his pale face long and lean under his snow-white brows.

'Ho there, great champion,' said the Wolf in Norse, with an elaborate bow. The warriors with him chuckled, smirks creasing their bearded faces. 'Have you brought your churls to throw sods at us? Or do you want to fight?'

'We have assembled the army of the East Saxons,' said Beornoth in Norse. 'But not to fight you. You are a pirate and raider, a raper of women. You are not worthy of fighting in the shield wall, where the warriors of reputation and honour clash, and where the Valkyrie seek the glorious dead. Run along and fetch Olaf and his Jomsvikings and let us have a battle between warriors.'

The White Wolf laughed and turned to his fellow Vikings. They shook their heads and enjoyed the jest.

'What are you saying?' asked Byrhtnoth, his brows creased like thunderclouds in a winter storm, frustrated at not understanding the exchange in Norse.

'I told him he is a raider and a coward, and that he should fetch Olaf and the Jomsvikings.'

'Good, bait them, Beo. Get all the bastards here in one place.'

'What does your master say?' asked the Wolf. 'He is afraid, isn't he? He wants to pay me to go away, so that I don't hurt him again. Like I hurt your people. I enjoyed that. Olaf did, too. Watching your hall burn and your people die on our blades. Odin saw how we trampled Christians under our boots like so many ants. Do you remember it, champion? That snivelling boy at the end who cried like a mewling pup when I drove my blade into his body.' He laughed again, but Beornoth remembered. He remembered it all.

'I remember. Are there enough men here now to see you

fight? Last time we met, you ran away. That is why you are here, is it not? To make your reputation? So let's fight now. You and I, here on this strip of land, yielded up to us by Ran, your water god.'

The humour drained from the White Wolf's pale face, and he pointed at Beornoth, his eyes peering along the arrow of his finger. 'I'll fight the grandfather next to you. He is a great jarl, is he not?'

'He is the ealdorman of the East Saxons, but he doesn't fight nithings like you. He only fights men of honour, men who have earned their reputation in the war-fence. Not pieces of stinking weasel shit like you who kill only children and women.'

'Watch your tongue,' the Wolf hissed.

'I challenge you!' Beornoth roared, startling the Vikings alongside the White Wolf. 'Fight me now, or your men will know you are a coward, unworthy of a place in Valhalla. Send one of your ships and bring Olaf so that he can see you die. Fight me now, or scurry back into the hole you crawled out of, you son of a thousand fathers.'

'We shall fight then, you and I. You will suffer for the poison of your tongue.'

'What's happening?' asked Byrhtnoth.

'I am going to fight the bastard. He will send a ship to bring Olaf, so that his lord can witness his victory.'

'Can you beat him?'

'With God's grace, maybe.' But Beornoth swallowed a ball of fear away, the fireball which kindled in his belly and rose up to his chest and throat. His mind pumped blood around his ears, screaming at him not to fight the Wolf, that he could never defeat the man with greater sword skill than any Beornoth had ever seen, that he would be butchered in front of his men. But his heart bellowed like a bear. *Be brave*, it said, *be strong. Avenge your people, avenge Kari, Aethelberga and all of your people this Wolf has put to the sword.*

'I will fight with spear, sword, and shield,' said Beornoth, taking a step forward to look deep into the Wolf's pale blue eyes.

'You can fight with whatever you like, I have my two swords. They were forged in the mountains of...'

'I don't give a wet shit where your swords were forged, or what childish name you have given to them. I will go and collect my shield. Send your ship for Olaf and we meet here before the tide comes in.'

Beornoth didn't wait for the Wolf to respond, he turned on his heel and marched towards the Saxon army. He had to steel himself, overcome his fear, for he had to stand toe to toe and trade blows with the White Wolf, champion of Hålogaland in the far north, a vicious Viking, a murderer and Saxon slayer.

21

Beornoth's heart thumped in his chest like a war drum. Thirty Viking warships rowed up the River Blackwater, coming in ones and twos so they could keep to the deepest part of the river and avoid running aground on the ebb tide. His heart pounded because the White Wolf waited for him halfway down the long strip of rock covered with lichens and seaweed, which linked Northey Island to the mainland. The news of Beornoth's impending fight against the Viking had rippled through the Saxon army like fire crackling along a dried-out log. The men clamoured behind him, held back by a line of Byrhtnoth's thegns. They shouted encouragement, beat their spears on the earth, but the noise of a thousand men was dulled to a distant sigh by Beornoth's focus. He stared ahead at the man he must face, knowing that one of them would die. It would be a painful death, a body ripped open by a heavy, sharp blade. The victor would be triumphant, and the victory would buoy his men. The loser would groan and suffer as the pain of his wounds overcame him, his last thoughts the shame of defeat by the hated foe.

Wulfhere stood alongside Beornoth, as did Leofsunu and

Aelfwine. They spoke words of encouragement, meaning well, trying to lift his spirits and give him confidence for the fight. But he could not hear them. All he could hear was the slicing sound the Wolf's swords made as they sang through the air in the elaborate twirling arcs as the Viking made a war dance only the most skilled swordsmen could conjure. Beornoth had never possessed such skill, and the Wolf was the greatest champion Beornoth had ever faced man to man. Where the Wolf was lean and fast, Beornoth was huge and strong. But he had speed of his own. A man did not live as long as Beornoth, fighting as much as he had, without having a quick arm. Suddenly, Beornoth stopped breathing, the realisation hitting him that he might never see Eawynn again. That he may have spent his last moments with her. Beornoth closed his eyes so that he could vividly recall the shine of her eyes, the smell of her hair, the way her cheeks creased when she smiled. She was beautiful, and he was a lucky man to have her in his life, a life that could have been so different were it not for the cruelty in the world. If the Vikings had not come for his young life, ripping it away in a welter of blood and fire. Beornoth allowed that memory to blossom, recalling the sight of his burned hall and the shrivelled, charred corpses of his daughters. A memory of Eawynn came to him, hurt beyond understanding, throat slashed, and left to die. Beornoth's chest rose and fell like a wild beast, strength flooding his arms and shoulders. He turned and stared at Wulfhere, took in the scars of his face, his lost eye and the pain in the remaining eye.

'Tide will be in soon,' Beornoth growled. 'Olaf is here. Looks like we will have our war. Spear.'

Wulfhere handed him the spear, its smooth shaft warm in Beornoth's right hand. Beornoth bent and picked up his shield, rolling his left shoulder under the weight. He wore his helmet, despite the heat, and his byrnie shone in the summer sun.

'He took my eye. Kill him, lord. For her,' said Wulfhere.

'Vengeance,' Beornoth said. He strode onto the causeway, the shouts of encouragement from Aelfwine, Leofsunu and an entire army roaring behind him. He strode forward clad in iron and armed with shield, spear, sword and seax, to meet the Viking champion.

The White Wolf turned towards Olaf's approaching ships and raised his twin blades in salute, and their shouts of acclaim rolled across the river like thunder. They beat their boots against the hulls and the dragon ships came ever closer, oar blades slicing through the rippling water. One and a half thousand Vikings come to watch Beornoth fight the Wolf in his shining fish-scale armour. Beornoth marched toward his enemy as the Wolf turned to his men on the island, and swung his swords around in two arcs, and those men bellowed acclaim for their champion.

Beornoth quickened his pace, taking long strides across the rocks, making sure not to slip or slide in front of so many eyes. His byrnie, helmet, shield and weapons were heavy, but Beornoth welcomed the weight. There was reassurance in it, a familiarity. The Wolf basked in the glory of thousands of warriors shouting his name and saluting his bravery. Beornoth snarled to himself. *He has the reputation he so craves, but now I am here to rip it from him.* A rock moved under Beornoth's boot, cracking against the stone next to it, and the White Wolf turned. His mouth dropped open, alarmed to see Beornoth so close, for he was only five paces away. The Wolf mastered his surprise, forcing a smirk on his lean face.

'You didn't run away then...' the Wolf began, believing that another round of insults would precede the fight. But the time for words had passed, and Beornoth struck out with his spear as he strode forwards, its tip banging against the Wolf's shoulder, sending him spinning. He pivoted as he fell and came up in a crouch, one sword held high and another low, both poised to strike like the fangs of a serpent. His pale face flushed with anger, the Wolf grinned and showed his teeth. He wore his byrnie coat of overlapping metal scales cinched at his narrow waist by a belt, and the scabbards of his twin swords strapped to his back. He wore no helmet, his muscled arms bare, and his bone-white hair fell in a thick braid down his back. Beornoth kept moving and brought his shield around, aiming to crash it into the wolf's face, but the Viking leapt away. As he jumped backwards, the Wolf brought his two blades down hard on Beornoth's shield, and the force of the blow jarred up Beornoth's left arm. He put his shoulder behind the shield and bullied the Wolf backwards, stabbing low with his spear but finding only air. The Wolf kicked Beornoth's shield, stopping his forward momentum, and then stabbed at Beornoth's face with the point of his sword. Now it was Beornoth's turn to move backwards, rocking his head back to avoid the strike. Another blade whipped around and slammed into Beornoth's shield, knocking him sideways, and that blade scraped along the shoulder of Beornoth's mail, but the links of his byrnie held firm against the sharp edge.

Beornoth sucked in a gulp of air, labouring from the exertion and the weight of his war gear. He lunged with his spear and the Wolf brought his two swords together faster than Beornoth thought was possible. Their blades crossed, coming together below the iron tip of Beornoth's leaf-shaped aesc blade, and the Wolf twisted his wrists and wrenched the spear from Beornoth's hands so that it fell with a clatter upon the causeway's grey stones. Beornoth cursed and dropped his hand to his sword hilt, but before he could draw the blade, the Wolf came on with an assault of such speed and ferocity that his blades moved with a blur of iron. He swung them around his body, pivoting at his wrists, and the edge of his swords hammered Beornoth's shield.

He shuffled backwards under the assault, each blow smashing into the linden-wood boards, sending chips of wood into the sea air to bang off Beornoth's helmet. Beornoth reached down for his sword again, but a sword blade whipped low and clanged against the pommel. Beornoth only drew his fingers back at the last moment, or he would have lost his hand to the flashing blade.

The Wolf took a pace back, crouching low and bringing his swords to rest on the causeway. He grinned at Beornoth, a knowing smile. He was faster and had greater skill, and Beornoth saw the confidence in the champion's face. But he was Beornoth, and sword skill was not the only way to win a fight. Beornoth hurled his shield at the Wolf, and as he let go of the timber grip which spanned the cave of the shield's boss, he reached behind his back and whipped his seax free of its scabbard. To draw his sword was awkward and would give the Wolf time to recover, but the seax came free with the smooth speed of a fish darting through a river. The shield battered through the Wolf's guard as he raised his swords and clattered into his chest. The Viking grunted under the blow and fell backwards from his crouch to land on his arse, looking up at Beornoth with wide-eyed surprise. Beornoth darted forward and stabbed with his seax, and the Wolf parried the broken-backed blade with his sword and sprang to his feet. He shouted in anger, snaking out with his second sword, but Beornoth let that blow strike him. He twisted, so the sword scraped down the hip of his byrnie, and ground his teeth as the sword tore open the wool of his trews and sliced his thigh open. But to make that strike, the Wolf had leapt forward onto his foreleg and was off balance.

Beornoth was inside the Wolf's reach, and he was a brutal man, not a dancing swordsmith. Beornoth was a big, vicious killer, and his fear and desperation at the Wolf's skill and speed fell away. This was his fight now, close and savage. Beornoth grabbed the Wolf's sword arm and clamped his huge hand around the smaller man's wrist, twisting as hard as he could. The Wolf grimaced and dropped the sword, whose blade now ran with Beornoth's blood. Beornoth drove his knee into the Viking's gut and slashed his seax blade down the Wolf's pale face, laying open the skin in a terrible red gash. He tried to skip away, but Beornoth grabbed a fistful of his fish-scale byrnie with his left hand and dragged his enemy close. Beornoth glared through the holes of his helmet at the White Wolf, close enough to feel the blow of his breath, and there was fear in those ice-blue eyes, the same fear Aethelberga and Kari must have felt in the moments before their deaths.

The Wolf swung his remaining sword, but he was too close and the blow fouled on Beornoth's shoulder. Beornoth grunted and lifted the Wolf from his feet with his left hand, the tips of the Viking's boot scrabbling for purchase on the rocks, and Beornoth sliced open the Wolf's forearm with the point of his seax. He drove the wicked blade deep, and it scraped off bone and the Wolf shrieked in pain. His remaining sword fell from the wounded arm and fiery blood seeped over Beornoth's fist and arm. He brought the seax back, and then slammed it into the meat of the Wolf's thigh, twisting the blade, tearing it so that his enemy grimaced and roared in pain. Beornoth threw the Wolf to the causeway and took off his helmet, the sea air cool on his sweat-soaked brow.

'Saxon bastard,' the Wolf said through gritted teeth, clawing himself away from Beornoth and leaving a smear of blood on the causeway rocks. Beornoth took a long step forward and swung his helmet, crashing it into the Viking's face with a sickening crunch. The Wolf's head snapped back and hit the rocks, and his face turned from lean wolfishness into a mashed-up mess of crushed nose and split lips. He spat broken teeth into the river. The Saxon army exploded, cheering and shaking weapons at the victory, and the Vikings fell silent. Their man was beaten, and Beornoth knew Northmen. He had grown up amongst them in the Danelaw. They would pray to Odin, Týr and Thor for an honourable death, hoping that their champion would take his place in Odin's Valhalla, or Thor's Thruthvang, the halls for dead heroes. The Wolf wouldn't be going to any hall for heroes.

Beornoth strode and picked up his fallen spear, grimacing at the pain in his wounded thigh as he bent. He turned and took long strides towards the Vikings, stepping over the Wolf who winced as he passed.

'I curse you all to the Corpse Shore,' Beornoth shouted across the causeway in Norse, so that the warriors on Northey Island's beach, and the Jomsvikings and all the warriors on board Olaf's ships, could hear. 'With this spear, I curse you all to Nástrǫnd. With this curse I promise your souls to Níðhöggr. You shall wallow with the corpses of other murderers and oath-breakers. The great Hel-serpent will gnaw on your rotting corpses for eternity. I curse you. I am Beornoth!' He was roaring, red-faced, spittle flying from his mouth. He took two quick steps and launched his spear towards the beach, aware of the terror in that curse. Níðhöggr was the corpse ripper, one of the Loki brood whose lair lay at Nástrǫnd in a hall woven from serpent spines, and was the destination for those who died guilty of such crimes as those Beornoth had listed. A great moan went up from Olaf's ships, the first half-dozen of which had reached the island, and her men spewed forth into the shallows to join their fellow Vikings on the beach. He had beaten their champion and laid a curse upon their souls, and so Olaf would have to fight. Faced with such insults, and of a gathered Saxon army, there was no way the Viking leader could sail away and remain a war leader of reputation. Beornoth had done his work, but he was not finished with the White Wolf yet.

Beornoth turned and strode back to the stricken Viking. He hammered his helmet twice into the White Wolf's face and stamped three times on his injured thigh. The Wolf whimpered through the bloody stream of snot and tears on his ravaged face.

'You asked me if I remembered what you did at Branoc's Tree,' Beornoth growled. 'I remember it well. And this is the price of your murderous thirst for reputation.' Beornoth ripped his seax free of the man's thigh and flipped him over. He cut the leather ties at the back of the fish-scale armour and cut away his scabbards and belt. Beornoth ran the seax blade down the Viking's jerkin and through his trews until he left the White Wolf sobbing and naked. The Wolf was pale and thin, all lean muscle and long limbs. 'Now I have taken everything from you. No Valhalla for you. No glorious death with a blade in your hand. You can pray to my god for forgiveness and redemption if you wish. Your own gods have turned their back on you. But you must hurry, for death is upon you.'

Beornoth slid his seax carefully back into the sheath at the small of his back, and slowly dragged his sword free of its fleece-lined scabbard. He held the blade up for the Wolf to see, but the Viking turned away, curling himself into a bloody ball as he tried desperately to hide his face, as though that would also hide his shame. Beornoth hacked into the man with his sword, shouting Aethelberga and Kari's names with each strike. He hacked until his arm grew tired and the Wolf was a headless thing of torn flesh and bloody ruin. Then, he retrieved his weapons and marched back along the causeway towards the Saxon army, forcing himself not to limp whilst the Vikings could see him, despite the burning pain from the wound in his thigh.

The Saxons cheered and clashed their arms to salute

Beornoth's victory. He raised his shield to show that he was their champion, and the army of the East Saxons let out a roar to shake the riverbank itself.

'That was for Aethelberga,' Beornoth said as he reached the end of the causeway and Wulfhere came to meet him with an outstretched hand. They clasped forearms and Wulfhere helped him clamber up the bank.

'She is avenged, lord,' said Wulfhere, before he noticed the wound on Beornoth's thigh. 'That needs wrapping, or it'll sap your strength.' Wulfhere turned and went to find clean cloth to do the job.

'I think you have annoyed them enough now, Beo,' said Ealdorman Byrhtnoth, grinning and pointing across the water. 'We will have our battle, after all.'

'Why don't they just bring their ships to the shore on this side?' asked Thered. The Northumbrian hostage stood with one boot on the bank watching Olaf's ships row around Northey Island, forty or more looking for a place to drop anchor so that their warriors could wade ashore.

'Their ships will run aground, lad,' said Leofsunu. 'Does the tide not go out up north?'

'It does, I see it now.'

'They can't row to this side, so they pile on to the island and will cross the causeway to come and kill us. If they kill us, then Essex will be theirs, so we have to kill them instead. That's about all you need to know.'

Beornoth stood with Byrhtnoth as the Viking army gathered on Northey Island's beach. The water between them shimmered in the heat and more men joined the battle line as the dragon ships spewed forth the warriors of Norway, and Olaf's fearsome Jomsvikings. They would try to cross the causeway and the ealdorman would let them, for he craved battle as much as Olaf did. Byrhtnoth wanted to finish the Vikings once and for all, and part of Beornoth saw the gleam of glory in the ealdorman's bright eyes, the chance to defeat a Viking warlord, to face the great enemy in a shield wall battle whose tale would live on down the ages along with the names of the leaders and heroes. Byrhtnoth saw a chance of immortality, as well as a chance of crushing his enemies and freeing Saxon Britain of the cursed Vikings.

'Send the horses away,' Byrhtnoth barked. 'We stand or fall on this beach.'

'But, lord,' said Godric, his round face appearing through the throng of warriors. 'Without the horses we have no way of riding away if things go awry. We are outnumbered, Lord Byrhtnoth, and every man in the Viking army is a warrior. We have only our thegns and the fyrd.'

'We stand and fight to the last man,' said Byrhtnoth, fixing the young thegn with an icy stare. 'If the horses remain, it allows the thought of running to fester at the back of men's minds. When the fight is at its hardest, when we are wading in our own blood and that of our enemies, men will look to that line of horses as a way to escape, to run and to live. But the only way we are leaving this beach, Thegn Godric, is if we have crushed our enemies and trampled their bloodthirsty lust for our land and silver beneath our boots.'

Godric just stared at Byrhtnoth, his round face reddened and his tongue flicking out to lick at dry lips. His eyes wandered to the massing army of Vikings, and then back to Byrhtnoth. He turned to his brothers and fellow thegns and they melted back into the throng that was the Saxon army.

'Send the horses away,' repeated Byrhtnoth, 'but first bring my horse to me. It's time to organise this rabble for war.'

22

Ealdorman Byrhtnoth sat astride his warhorse, a black stallion of fourteen hands and a beast every bit as formidable as Hríð. Where Hríð was pure white and shone like fresh snow on a winter morning, Byrhtnoth's horse was as black as the dark of night during a waxing moon. The ealdorman rode up and down the massed Saxons, barking orders, pointing and arranging his men for battle. Across the river, the Vikings themselves massed for war, and a line of the enemy had ventured halfway along the causeway. Beornoth's brutal killing of their champion had silenced the Vikings for a time, but now the Norsemen were all braying war horns and great rumbling hooms as war songs peeled out from their ranks.

Byrhtnoth arranged the thegns in the front ranks, the professional warriors of Essex and the men of his own household troops. Beornoth would stand with those men, at the front and centre, where the fighting would be its most vicious and brutal. Æthelred's men, led by the twins Wigstan and Wighelm, would stand in the centre with Byrhtnoth's own men, which was a place of honour. Streonwold's men held the left flank, and the warriors

Byrhtnoth had brought from East Anglia would take the right flank. The men of the fyrd then stood in ranks behind the thegns, armed with billhooks, scythes, wood axes, and, if they were lucky, a spear or shield. Dunnere had brought together any man with a bow and quiver of arrows to form a company of archers, and those men lined up behind the centre.

Beornoth sat on the riverbank. The grass, though trampled by hundreds of boots, was soft and warm under his palms as he braced himself against the pain. Aelfwine poured clean water over the gash in his thigh and wiped the edges of it with a clean square of cloth. Beornoth sucked air in through his teeth every time the cloth touched the lips of his wound.

'Come now,' said Aelfwine, tutting and smiling. 'Surely the great champion of the East Saxons is not going to weep at this little wound?' Beornoth flashed him a murderous glare and hissed through gritted teeth. Aelfwine bound the wound tight with a strip of cloth and helped Beornoth to his feet. 'Can we win?' he asked, staring across the river at the Vikings, who continued to sing and trumpet their war horns, working themselves into enough of a war frenzy to attack the Saxons.

'We have to,' said Beornoth with a shrug.

Byrhtnoth bellowed at the men of the fyrd. He rode up and down the battle line on his black stallion, calling to them, ensuring that he had each man's attention. As he rode, men brought every spare shield and spear they could find, every weapon carried as spare by thegns or brought on the wagons along the southward march. They handed the weapons to the men of the fyrd, who held them at curious angles, marvelling at the weight of a shield and the sharp steel of the spear points. Byrhtnoth shouted at them, instructing them how to hold the shield. To grab the timber crosspiece, which spans the empty bowl at the shield's centre, to brace their shoulders against it when the shield wall clash raged. That they should push into the back of the warrior in front of them, to heave against the monstrous force of the Viking war-fence. They stared at the ealdorman, some slack-jawed and in awe of the noble warrior, some with stern faces and set jaws, but more with wide eyes and shocked looks warping their features. They were simple men, family men, and they must stand and face the professional warriors of Norway and trade blows for the fate of their land and loved ones. Byrhtnoth told them they could win, that they were men of Essex, and that they would wade in the blood of their enemies before the sun went down. They found courage in the ealdorman's words and roared their defiance at the Vikings across the narrow strip of water.

'Here they come,' said Wulfhere. He held his long-hafted war axe and hefted it to point across the river, where three Vikings marched out ahead of those massed on the causeway. Leofsunu called to the ealdorman, and he rode towards them and slid down from the saddle.

'Looks like they want to talk again,' said Aelfwine.

Byrhtnoth growled and inclined his head at Beornoth to follow him as he stood on the causeway. They marched only ten paces and waited for the three Norsemen to approach. The leading Viking was Olaf Tryggvason himself, resplendent in shining mail and a green cloak hanging from his shoulders.

'So you want to fight?' Olaf called in Norse across the distance between them.

'We want to kill you, Olaf, and drive your bones into the soil. We want to burn your ships and mount your skulls on spikes along the coastline to warn the rest of the Northmen not to return to our shores,' said Beornoth, before translating the words for the ealdorman.

'We have our ships here,' said Olaf, and feigned a yawn as

though he was bored with the Saxon army and the impending battle. 'We can sail away, tell that to your lord. If we fight here today, many men will die. Good men. Fathers, sons, bloodlines... gone. We have more warriors than you, and we will win. All we want is rings and silver. Bring that to us, and we shall leave England.' He waved his hand eastward. 'Pay us tribute, and I will take my men to Frankia and find glory there instead.'

'Tribute? Tell him we have paid him before,' said Byrhtnoth after Beornoth had translated. 'There won't be a payment this time. The only payment he will get today is our spears and swords. Tell him that, the arrogant bastard.'

Beornoth relayed Byrhtnoth's words to Olaf. The Viking chuckled, the hard planes of his face shifting as he smiled, like a mountain shifting its rough-hewn rock under an avalanche.

'Just so,' said Olaf, and he bowed to Byrhtnoth. 'We shall kill every one of you, Beornoth. My men heard your Nástrǫnd curse. That was a foul deed. They fear you and your reputation and now they fear dying at your hand, that it will deny them their place in Valhalla.'

'You should fear me,' said Beornoth.

'I fear no man. When we slaughter you all today and I have your ealdorman's head, you will bow to me and call me lord. I shall keep you as a slave in a cage, great Beornoth, and men will wonder at the once-famed warrior of Essex, who I keep on a rope to dance before my guests.'

'I will look for you on the field of battle,' said Beornoth, and he turned his back on the Viking leader and his horde. That was the end of the talking and of the waiting. Now it was time for red war, and Beornoth's guts squirmed as the time for the shield wall drew closer. They reached the Saxon riverbank and Byrhtnoth had a man lead his horse away and they took their places in the

front rank, ready to meet the Viking charge when Olaf poured his
warriors across the causeway.

Beornoth turned to Wulfhere on his left and he nodded
silently at his friend. They would protect each other with shield,
spear and sword and fight like brothers until the last. He
grimaced and lifted his shield and made ready for the horrors of
the shield wall. War horns blared across the causeway and the
Saxons beat their spears upon their shields so that the estuary
shook with the terrible war music. A rider suddenly appeared,
galloping along the Saxon line of battle, his small pony's flanks
flecked with foamy white lather and the rider's face drawn taut
with alarm.

'Lord ealdorman, my lord ealdorman,' he cried as he dragged
his mount to a halt. 'More ships, lord, many ships.' He pointed
behind and to the north-east where Beornoth could see nothing
but the curling headland of the coast and the grey haze of the sea.

'The king's ships?' barked Byrhtnoth, stepping out of the front
rank and shielding his eyes with his hands as he searched the
distant horizon.

'I... I do not know, lord. A fisherman came and told us, and
the local reeve sent me riding to warn you, lord.'

Byrhtnoth dragged a hand down his broad face and glanced
at Beornoth. He did not need to speak for Beornoth to understand the dilemma swirling in the ealdorman's thought cage. If it
was Æthelred's ships, then they had a chance to trap Olaf in the
estuary and make a great slaughter as the tide came in, but if they
were Viking ships, then all the Saxons massed along the riverbank would die.

'We must see for ourselves,' Byrhtnoth said. 'Aelfwine, ride
and see with your own eyes the nature of these ships. Return with
all haste.'

'Yes, lord,' said Aelfwine, and because the ealdorman had

already sent away their fine warhorses, he took the messenger's horse and set off at a gallop towards the north-east.

'We cannot commit to battle if there is any risk of an enemy force on our flank,' said Godric, standing before the ealdorman with his hands on his hips and a belligerent look across his round face.

'For once, Thegn Godric, you have the right of it,' said Byrhtnoth. He stared at Olaf's Vikings, chanting and blaring horns, working their courage up to attack the Saxons. They edged along the causeway, axes and spears bright and coming for slaughter. 'I need some brave men who can stand on that narrow strip of rock and hold the Vikings until Aelfwine returns.' He frowned down at Godric. 'Not you, Godric. You and your brothers are sons of a man I loved like a brother, and I tolerate your impertinence for that reason alone. I need warriors, men to stand and hew with the champions of Norway and keep their army back.'

Godric spluttered, and for a moment Beornoth thought he would draw his sword and attack the ealdorman, but he shook his head and marched into the lines, flanked by his brothers and elbowing the warriors out of his way.

'I will do it,' said a familiar voice. Wulfhere. 'I will keep them back until Aelfwine comes back.'

'No,' said Beornoth, alarmed that his friend would nominate himself for the task, which meant death as sure as summer follows spring.

'I can hold them,' Wulfhere said, and he placed a brawny hand on Beornoth's shoulder. 'I am ready to go, Beo. It's my time, I can feel it. The pain is too much. She waits for me, and I yearn for her smile and her laughter. Let God see what I do for my people so that he may forgive me my trespasses, and grant me access to heaven to live forever at her side.'

'Then we shall hold the causeway together and fight shoulder

to shoulder,' said Beornoth. Wulfhere was smiling, and for the
first time since the attack upon Branoc's Tree his face relaxed, as
though his sorrow melted away in this chance to be avenged
upon his enemies and then to join Aethelberga in heaven. His
good eye blazed, and the scarred side of his face stood as a
reminder of the pain of that day, where part of Wulfhere had died
alongside Aethelberga.

'I need you for the battle, Beornoth,' said the ealdorman. His
lips drew back from his teeth in a sad smile. 'Aelfwine will return
soon, but we cannot commit men to battle until we are sure
whose fleet approaches the Blackwater. If you fall, our men's
hearts will fall with you. With you at our centre, our men share
your courage and your strength. Wulfhere, pick two men and
hold that causeway. The king will hear of your bravery, Wulfhere,
and men will remember your name.'

'We will stand with you,' said Maccus, striding to stand alongside Wulfhere. Aelfhere joined him, and they were Branoc's Tree
men. They had been born and lived amongst the people of the
burh and its environs long before Beornoth became its thegn.
The two warriors had seen their people butchered, their cousins,
sisters, uncles and kin, and they saw a chance now to strike at
those who had committed those atrocities and a chance for their
names to be remembered.

Beornoth shook his head and stared at the Viking horde. 'If
you go out there, you will die. And you are my oathmen, so I am
sworn to protect you, just as you are sworn to protect me. I won't
let you march out there alone.'

'And I am the ealdorman of the East Saxons,' said Byrhtnoth.
'And I free these three brave men from their oaths.'

'All but one,' said Maccus, holding up his palm to show all
present the scar across his hand. The men of Byrhtnoth's and
Beornoth's hearth troop had sworn an oath in blood the previous

summer to fight, and if necessary, to die in the ealdorman's service and to throw the Vikings out of the kingdom. 'Now, let us show these Norse bastards the strength of a Saxon warrior's arm!' The warriors roared in response to Maccus' war cry, they clashed spears against shields, and the entire Saxon force took up that din, even those who could not hear Maccus' words. So that the three Saxons marched into battle with the thunderous, pounding war music of iron and timber ringing in their ears. Beornoth's heart soared. If there was a way for a warrior to die then it was this.

Wulfhere hefted his shield, holding his axe in the same hand tucked in behind the handle where it spanned the boss' concave bowl. He pushed a conical helmet of dull iron down over his bald head and lifted his spear. Maccus and Aelfhere went similarly armed, and they marched towards the causeway where Olaf's horde came on in a mass of blades and Viking war chants to shake the very ground.

'Wulfhere!' Beornoth called after him. The big man turned and glanced over his shoulder. He smiled and raised his spear in salute and went forward. Beornoth set his jaw and clutched his own spear. He could not find the words to say to his friend at that moment, the man alongside whom he had been through so much. Who had stood beside Beornoth as he rose from ale-sodden reeve to thegn of Branoc's Tree, to wealth and reputation. He owed Wulfhere his life, and Beornoth rested his shield against his leg so that he could pull out the small wooden cross his friend had carved for him. Beornoth held it tight and whispered to God to grant Wulfhere strength and speed, and to wing his soul to heaven, for he fought against pagans, and against savage Northmen who had killed good Christian folk.

Wulfhere, Maccus and Aelfhere strode from the riverbank and marched three abreast along the uneven stones which crested the rippling water as though raised there by magic, held there by God or some unseen *wiccan*, or witchcraft. They marched against an impossible enemy. A hundred Vikings came across the causeway towards them in ranks of three, and countless more herded on Northey Island's beach to follow them. It was like a scene from a poem sung at firesides by scops, poets who kept the tales of great heroes alive.

'How can we just wait here whilst they march to their deaths?' asked Cwicca, standing at Beornoth's elbow. A thick tear ran down his youthful face and his bottom lip trembled. 'They are our friends, our blood brothers.'

'We must follow our orders,' said Beornoth softly. 'The ealdorman is right. We cannot commit to battle until we are sure there is no threat to our flank. In battle, most men die when the shield walls break, when men's hearts fill with fear and they turn and run from the field. If an enemy attacks us from our rear, or our flank, then the men of the fyrd will run like scalded cats and our blood will run thick and flood the land. So those three brave men buy us time to understand what we face, and let us hope Aelfwine returns with that news soon.'

A great, burly Viking strode ahead of the advancing Norsemen. He brandished a huge, shining war axe and wore a long mail coat. He was a champion, and he quickened his pace, eager to be the first Viking to strike a blow and kill a Saxon warrior. He came to make his reputation, and he shook his war axe over his head, basking in the shouts of encouragement from his shipmates. Wulfhere took two quick steps and hurled his spear. It flew along the causeway and the shaft seemed to wobble in mid-air with the force of Wulfhere's throw. The huge Viking tried to block the spear with his two-handled axe, but the leaf-shaped blade slammed into his chest, breaking through the links of his byrnie to sink into the flesh and bone beyond. The Viking flew backwards, sprawling dead upon the causeway, and the Vikings behind him paused in disbelief at their fallen hero. He died five paces away from the pale white corpse of the Wolf and now the Northmen had to step over two of their own dead warriors to get at Wulfhere, Maccus and Aelfhere. The three Saxons stopped their advance and brought their shields together to make a wall which spanned the width of the causeway. To either side of them it fell away sharply, and men would fear wading so deep into the river water for fear of being dragged into its icy depths to drown in their heavy mail or leather armour.

A great war horn blared from Northey Island, and the Vikings on the causeway charged. They came on in a howling press and met the three Saxon shields in a crack of iron on wood like the sound of a summer thunderstorm. Beornoth gripped his spear and held his breath, resisting the urge to charge forward to Wulfhere's aid, to disobey the ealdorman and stand with his friend in glorious combat. But he held, and watched as the three Branoc's Tree men were forced backwards, edging along the causeway. But then Wulfhere ripped his axe free, and Maccus struck with his spear and suddenly it was three Saxons against three Vikings, for the enemy could only stand three abreast. Wulfhere struck, and the Vikings died beneath his vengeful fury. Aelfhere stabbed with his spear and a Viking toppled into the river water to sink beneath the depths, but then a Viking axe hooked Aelfhere's shield and yanked it down and a spear flashed forwards to pierce his belly and the Saxon fell to his knees. Wulfhere tried to protect the fallen man with his shield, but the Vikings dragged Aelfhere into their ranks, and a cheer went up as Norse blades hungry for Saxon blood tore and rent his body. Wulfhere and Maccus lashed out with their blades like wild men, cutting and slashing at the enemy. But then the Vikings fell back, and there were ten of their number dead or writhing in pain between the lines, men who had fallen to Wulfhere and Maccus' blades. Those fallen warriors created a grisly obstacle for the attackers to fight across, and the causeway ran red with their blood. A surge of men shoved through the Viking horde and filled the front rank, forming up into ranks of three. They moved in unison, spears held at the same level, and each wore the same mail and helmet. Beornoth's heart froze because they were Jomsvikings come to kill. The six men each launched their spears, and they flashed across the short gap to thump into the two Saxons' shields. Maccus fell to one knee with a spear through his leg and his shield weighed down by Viking spears. Wulfhere dropped his shield and drew his seax and stood over Maccus like a hound protecting its master. The Jomsvikings came on behind their shields and Wulfhere held them. He fought like a man possessed, beating at their shields with his axe and slashing at their legs and faces with his seax.

The thunder of hoof beats tore Beornoth's gaze from the fight. It was Aelfwine galloping along the riverbank with his cloak billowing behind him. He sawed on the reins and brought his horse to a stop as he slid from the saddle. The beast gasped for air, moments from being blown, and it stood streaked with white foam on unsteady legs. Aelfwine ran to Byrhtnoth and Beornoth, his face drawn and pale.

'Viking sails, lord. Coming this way,' he said, pointing across the estuary.

Beornoth's jaw dropped, for on the edge of the shimmering horizon the sea was thick with Viking sails, square and filled by the wind, racing towards shore. Sun glinted off blades and mail and Beornoth saw the fate of the East Saxons in those approaching dragon ships, as though their doom approached in the snarl of the longships' beast-headed prows.

'But all of Olaf's warriors are on the island?' said Cwicca, his voice high-pitched and disbelieving.

'They are. It's Sweyn Forkbeard and his army of Danes,' said Beornoth, and all that seemed bright and glorious, a chance to rid themselves of the hated enemy, turned to ashes. A great moan went up from the Saxon army and Beornoth turned just in time to see a Jomsviking axe blade plunge into Wulfhere's chest. His friend fell, and the Vikings swarmed upon Wulfhere and Maccus, stabbing with axes and spears until their bodies became lost amongst the enemy horde. Beornoth sagged, the pain of his wounds like that of a splinter in comparison to the horror of seeing his friend cut down. Wulfhere, so brave in war, but a man who could be so gentle. Beornoth fought the urge to charge forward and hack into his killers. His head reeled. His blood brother slaughtered before him, and a new enemy coming in overwhelming numbers from the sea. Beornoth's chest tightened, he wanted to pull off his byrnie to make some room to breathe, the horror and pain of Wulfhere's loss was almost too much to bear.

'Wulfhere... the stand he made there will be remembered, will be sung by bards for eternity. If we ever get out of this bloody mess. An enemy in front and one behind,' said Leofsunu, taking off his helmet to run his hand through his hair and down his ugly face.

'Too many to fight,' said Aelfwine, out of breath from his furious ride along the shore. 'Forkbeard's ships, added to Olaf's fleet, gives the Vikings over ninety ships. That's over two thousand warriors.'

Ealdorman Byrhtnoth strode forward and glared at the Jomsvikings on the causeway, and then out at Sweyn Forkbeard's fleet in the estuary.

'We let Olaf cross,' he said. 'We fall back and let him form up on the beach here on the Maldon side of the causeway and we fight him. We can defeat his men before Forkbeard comes ashore.'

'What then, lord?' asked Offa, the ealdorman's grizzled captain. 'We cannot fight two battles.'

'We must. We are all that stands between the Vikings and our homes, our wives and children. We must stand and we must fight them.'

'We must stand,' said Beornoth, going to stand at Byrhtnoth's shoulder. The death of his friend still ringing in his ears, and clenching his heart like a fist. 'We don't have to beat them, but we must fight them hard enough so that they fear losing their army. We must fight like demons, like warriors of legend, and we must kill so many Vikings that Olaf and Forkbeard will see their strength bleeding away into Saxon soil. The king of Denmark is nothing without his army, and what is Olaf Tryggvason but a bloodthirsty adventurer? He is finished without his warriors. So, we fight and we die if we must, but we will give them such a fight that their armies will die here at the battle of Maldon.' It had to be that way. That was the warp and weft of their fates on that warm summer's day, and the realisation of that grim fate dawned on the faces of the warriors of Byrhtnoth's hearth troop. Olaf's Norsemen poured across the causeway, and the Saxons did not hinder them. They could have attacked them as they came up the riverbank, but that fight would rage all day until the tide came in, and if they were to fight two armies, then Olaf must be fought in the shield wall. In the great war-fence where warriors die amidst the horrors of axe and sword.

23

On a sun-baked afternoon in the month of Þeōdmōnaþ, the weed month so called because it is the time of the year when those plants grow in force – or Augustus, as the Romans called it – Beornoth watched the Viking army cross the Blackwater Estuary. The Saxons did not harry the Northmen as they marched across the causeway from Northey Island to the dark, wet sanded beach beside the river. The Vikings blared their war horns and banged their battle drums so that the river drowned in war music. They came swathed in fur and iron, armed with spears, axes and swords, the boards of their shields daubed with the sigils of the jarls, wolves, bears and eagles.

Ealdorman Byrhtnoth paced along the Saxon front line, glaring at the Vikings, and all the while his men drank ale to find bravery in the face of so many of the hated enemy. The Saxons sang their own war songs, battle hymns of legendary warriors to stir a man's heart to battle.

Olaf Tryggvason stood in the second rank of the Viking army, which he lined up in ranks of fifty men. The Jomsvikings formed the front ranks: organised, fearsome and deadly. Beornoth stood in the front rank of the Saxon army, who also lined up in ranks of fifty men to match the enemy's position, despite being outnumbered. The thegns and hearth-troop warriors were in the front ranks and the men of the fyrd in the rear. Byrhtnoth sent men to watch Forkbeard's ships and send word of where, and when, they came ashore. Beornoth stood with the cheek pieces of his helmet closed, armed with spear and shield. His sword and seax strapped to his waist and his byrnie mail coat reassuringly heavy. The sun sat high in a pale sky, and Beornoth sweated beneath his skin of metal and leather.

'Are you ready?' said Ealdorman Byrhtnoth at Beornoth's shoulder. He too wore his fine helmet, byrnie and the weapons of warlord. His spade of iron-grey beard bristled on a firm jaw, and he fixed Beornoth with his fierce eyes.

'Aye,' said Beornoth simply. Wulfhere had died with honour, a warrior's death to ring down the ages, and Beornoth stood ready to join him. The death of his friend hurt like the cut of a knife, but Beornoth had to force such feelings down. Push them away like an enemy shield. There would be time for mourning afterwards. If he survived. Eawynn was safe in the north with Alfgar, and he was a thegn of the East Saxons, ready to hold true to his oath and fight alongside his ealdorman to whatever fate lay in wait for them. 'Olaf attacks even though he can see Forkbeard's ships have arrived?'

'No doubt the bastard knew all along, they have joined forces. Olaf knows he traps us now between his hammer and Forkbeard's anvil. He believes I am a prideful fool to have let him cross the causeway to fight us in battle formation. But what choice do we have? If we wait until the tide floods, then Olaf can simply sail across then butcher us whilst we fight Forkbeard. So, we fight. No time to wait, no time for speeches or drums to give the men courage. Forward. Spears and archers ready,' barked Byrhtnoth.

The Saxon line shuffled forwards, silently at first, with small, nervous steps. Then Leofsunu ran out of the battle line and shook his shield and spear at the enemy and bellowed a war cry of such ferocity that the entire Saxon army took up the call. They shouted and raised their shields, each man overlapping the heavy linden-wood boards ringed and bossed with iron with that of the man next to him. They banged their spears, seaxes, knives, scythes or billhooks together and created a great rolling thunder of clashing arms. Beornoth shouted his own war cry, bellowing at the enemy. He marched with his shield up and his bright spear resting on the top rim of his shield. He glared through his helmet's dark eyeholes and bared his teeth, a heady mix of fear, anger and hate churning inside him.

'Archers!' Byrhtnoth bellowed above the din, and a lad who stood at the ealdorman's shoulder, ready to relay messages to the captains, scuttled through the lines of shields to pass on the order. Dunnere led the bowmen and took up a position behind the fourth rank of warriors. The order to nock, draw and loose was lost to Beornoth's hearing by the war din, but a thrumming twang rattled his ears, and suddenly the sky flashed dark for a heartbeat as a hundred arrows soared above him, rising high against a sky the blue of a mountain thistle. Blaring horns and pounding war drums deep in the Viking lines ceased as the flock of arrows flew. The cloud of iron-tipped missiles reached the peak of their arc, seemed to hang in the summer sky, and then raced as they descended towards the Norsemen. Arrowheads thudded into shields, chests, faces and sand and its sound was like an iron rain falling upon the land. The screaming started then, and across the sand a golden-bearded Viking clutched at an arrow buried in his cheek while blood spilled across his mouth and mail. Another hail of arrows flew, and more Vikings suffered before they released a volley of their own and Beornoth tilted his head to allow himself to see above the rim of his helmet. He tensed his muscles and forced himself to keep his eyes open, ready to raise his shield if the arrows came for him. They whistled overhead, peppering the men of the rear ranks, and their screams rattled around Beornoth's helmeted ears. He glanced over his shoulder as Gymi, the villager in whose house he had hidden to ambush a band of Vikings, died with a Viking spear in his face.

'Spears!' Byrhtnoth bellowed. 'Pick up the pace.' Beornoth lengthened his strides, as did Byrhtnoth to his left and Offa to his right. Short, fearful steps now became long, loping strides, and then a run, checked only by the knowledge that they must keep their shields together or die on the end of a Viking blade. Beornoth had fought in great shield wall battles before, and it usually took most of the day for each army to drink enough ale to find the courage to charge. Even then, more time became wasted as the two opposing forces would shout and roar insults at one other, champions would come out and challenge each other to fight and die before the masses of eyes there to witness their skill and bravery. But that day there was no time for posturing, or for the men to drink themselves into bravery. If they did not want to have howling Vikings in front and rear, then the attack must be now, and it must be brutal and fierce.

The third and fourth rankers hurled their spears over the shoulders of the front rankers, and Beornoth's head involuntarily sank into his shoulders as they whistled past his head. The enemy were only ten paces away now, and the spears slammed into the enemy front rankers. Most of the spears stuck into their shields, and that was good because it made them heavy and dragged them down to expose the vulnerable faces and necks of the men behind. Some made it through the shield wall, and men crumpled with steel in their shoulders, legs or chests.

'Kill them!' Ealdorman Byrhtnoth roared, and Beornoth's guts squirmed. Five paces now, the man opposite him was a tall, broad-shouldered Jomsviking. A man who had trained his whole life to kill. He stood with men he loved like brothers, just as Beornoth did, and he glared at Beornoth with bared teeth, his shield raised and his spear poised to strike.

Beornoth set his left shoulder behind his shield, and in the last instant before the two enemy shield walls came together, he leapt forward a half-pace so that he crashed into the Jomsviking shield opposite him with his left knee braced against his shield. Beornoth smashed into his enemy. Opposing shield walls crashed together like the sound of a falling oak, and the iron bosses rang like church bells. The Jomsviking snarled and spittle spattered Beornoth's cheek. They were close, so close that Beornoth could see the broken veins and blemishes upon his enemy's face. The shield of the man behind shoved into Beornoth's back and drove him forward. And so it was along the line. The Vikings and Saxons pushed and heaved at one another, too close yet for blades to strike and kill. It was all hot breath and curses. The ground churned beneath their boots and Beornoth let go of his spear and it stuck there, pinned by the crush, resting upon his shield and his shoulder. Somewhere around him a man wept, and the acrid smell of piss filled his nostrils as men wet themselves with fear. Death was close. Men felt it beside them and it terrified them. The light of the world gone forever, to never see one's wife or children again, to never feel the soft warmth of a lover beneath the blankets, enjoy the laughter of a child or the feel of summer sun on one's face. Death as a Viking blade ripped a man's throat out and crushed his corpse under a thousand boots. Beornoth, however, felt his heart quicken. He let his anger overtake him and gave himself over to what he was, what the people needed him to be.

Beornoth let go of his spear because he knew it would stay there, held by the press of men. He darted his fist forward and punched the Jomsviking opposite him hard in the nose and then drove his thumb deep into the warrior's eye. The Jomsviking screamed and shook his head, but he was stuck, trapped by his own men and unable to twist away from Beornoth's savagery. The eye was warm and wet and Beornoth scooped out its jelly with his thumbnail and the Viking roared with unspeakable pain. Beornoth drew back his fist and punched the Northman again and again until his face was pulp and Beornoth's knuckles sang with pain. The man went limp and Beornoth clutched his spear again and as the pressure of the enemy shield gave way, he drove the point forwards to punch into the gullet of the next Jomsviking in line. Byrhtnoth saw the break and leaned into the gap, his size twisting the Jomsviking opposite him, and then the ealdorman leaned back so that his enemy fell forward slightly, exposing his flank on Beornoth's side. Beornoth dragged his spear back and slashed the sharp edge across the man's neck beneath the rim of his helmet. He let go of his spear again and reached out to grab the rim of the enemy's helmet and yanked it down over his eyes; the Viking snapped his teeth at Beornoth but missed and Beornoth pulled his shield towards him so that Byrhtnoth could slide his spear point into the man's neck. The warrior next to Offa, a young man of the Wessex company, died with a Viking spear in his mouth and all around Beornoth was the slaughter and carnage of the shield wall. The men in both front ranks were the vicious ones, the ones who came alive in the clash of arms where other men dared not to stand. Men died there at close quarters, not in glorious combat, but savagely and badly.

The Jomsviking line fell back a pace, and there was a space between the lines. Wulfmaer, a man of Byrhtnoth's hearth troop, toppled forwards with a face full of blood and the man Beornoth had killed fell backwards into his own lines to be replaced by a bigger man, broad in the shoulder and with a tattooed face. Olaf shouted at his warriors and urged them on to the attack, for they did not move back out of fear, but to make space for the real killing to begin.

'God is with us!' Byrhtnoth called, raising his chin like a cock crowing at first light. 'God wants you to kill!'

An enormous man leapt out of the Viking battle line, a Jomsviking with a broad, scarred face. He came at the ealdorman and Byrhtnoth went forward to meet him, dragging his shield away from Beornoth's own. They came together, those two monstrous warriors, and spears jabbed and lunged, shields crashed, and all along the line similar fights erupted as the battle proper raged along the beach at Maldon. The Jomsviking held a speed that belied his size, and he feinted low at the ealdorman but came up high and his bright spear point tore across Byrhtnoth's cheek and blood misted the air around his head. The ealdorman roared with rage and pain and brought his shield around to trap the enemy spear and drove it down so that the spear shaft broke. Byrhtnoth then struck out whip-fast with his own weapon and such was the ealdorman's strength that it passed through the Viking's neck as though it were made of butter. The man quivered and blood poured from his mouth before Byrhtnoth ripped his spear point free, and then in a blur of power and aggression he thrust it forward again to punch into the chest of the Jomsviking opposite Beornoth. The spear scraped above the shield rim and tore open the links of the man's byrnie to punch into the muscle and bone of the warrior's chest.

Byrhtnoth's spear became trapped in the dying man, and the ealdorman threw his head back and laughed with grim delight. 'The Lord is with us!' he called. 'God guides my hand.'

Then a spear flew from the enemy lines, and time seemed to

stop. Olaf himself launched the weapon, and it flew across the narrow space between the lines of battle before piercing the ealdorman's unprotected thigh. He had let his shield drop wide as he praised the heavens and Olaf's spear stuck hard in his thigh. Byrhtnoth let out a cry of pain. Beornoth darted forward, as did Offa at his side, and they crowded around the ealdorman with their shields, but in doing so the shield wall broke and the Jomsvikings poured into that gap and began to hack and slash at the Saxon second rank with spears and axes. Beornoth took a spear blow on his shield and killed his attacker with a spear thrust to beneath the armpit of his extended arm. Blows rained down upon them and the Jomsvikings came on, desperate to kill the ealdorman, who crouched on one knee. Byrhtnoth drew the spear out of his thigh in a roar of pain and the young Northumbrian thegn, Thered, snatched the bloodied weapon out of the ealdorman's hand and hurled it at the Jomsvikings and it slammed into the stomach of the warrior next to Olaf. Beornoth took an axe blow on his shield and the strength in the strike jarred up his arm like a hammer on an anvil.

The Saxons surged forward around Beornoth, driving the Jomsvikings back again. Beornoth glanced over his left shoulder to where the Wessex twins Wighelm and Wigstan cut at the Vikings with axes of their own, moving together in fluid, practised motions, and the Jomsvikings shuffled backwards from their wicked blades. Byrhtnoth rose from his crouch and drew his sword. The hilt wrapped in golden wire shone like the morning sun amongst the blood, iron and leather of the battlefield. He barged Beornoth out of the way, his face twisted with rage, and cut at the Viking closest to him, but the man's blade held. Byrhtnoth swung his sword again, but an enemy blade snaked out and sliced into Byrhtnoth's arm in a spray of blood. The ealdorman dropped his sword and a great cry rang out from the Saxon forces.

Beornoth dropped his spear and grabbed Byrhtnoth, dragging him backwards behind protecting Saxon shields. They had wounded the ealdorman in arm and leg, and his face ran white with the pain. Beornoth wiped his hands on his own trews, horrified at how much of the ealdorman's blood covered his hands and forearms.

'We are not done,' growled the ealdorman. 'Fight on, Beo. We must push them back.'

Offa knelt with him, as did Leofsunu, and Beornoth left them there, long faces gaping and hands desperately trying to stop the blood flowing from the ealdorman's wounds. Beornoth marched, returning to the line of battle where the slaughter raged along the beach. Men died, screamed and roared, and Beornoth thought this must be what hell is like, where those who are denied heaven will suffer for eternity. He stepped over a Saxon warrior who knelt, curled up in a ball like a newborn child, sobbing at the sheer horror surrounding him. Just as he hefted his shield to enter the fray again, Beornoth was driven backwards by a force of warriors. The sheer power of the onslaught threw him off his feet, and the wind gusted from his chest like a sea gale. He scrambled on his knees sucking in huge mouthfuls of air and watched with horror as a swine-head of Vikings drove into the Saxon line and enveloped Byrhtnoth and Offa. A Jomsviking axe smashed into Osmod's face, and the Branoc's Tree man died instantly, another young life wasted and snatched away by Viking bloodlust. Beornoth set his jaw, another friend dead and the horror of it all was everywhere, pressing down on him, suffocating him. The swine-head was a spear point of warriors, led by one man with two behind, then three, and so on, so that they formed a wedge of unstoppable steel and muscle. Olaf's Jomsvikings used that tactic now, bursting forward in a wedge-shaped terror of blades and pain. The Vikings punched into the Saxon ranks, the weight of the attack driving men backwards. They burst into the Saxon ranks, and Beornoth gaped in horror as the ealdorman disappeared within the surging swine-head. Beornoth coughed and a howl of pain and despair died in his throat as he sucked in huge gulps to fill his winded lungs. That air reeked with the iron tang of blood, and Beornoth could not believe the toweringly powerful figure of Byrhtnoth was lost. Hands dragged Beornoth backwards, and he scrabbled in the filthy sand, which had become a heavy mix of sand, blood and piss loosed from the bladders of the dying. Leofsunu scrambled next to him, his face a drawn rictus of horror. They rose to their feet and saw with terrible sorrow that Ealdorman Byrhtnoth, the *dux bellorum* of Saxon England, had died under a welter of Viking blades. Offa had died too, as had four other men of Byrhtnoth's troops. Offa, the stalwart warrior, captain of the ealdorman's hearth troop and veteran of a hundred battles. Beornoth cried out, part rage and part heart-rending sorrow. Byrhtnoth, his lord, a man he both loved and respected, killed by the hated Vikings. He charged them, barging with his shield and slashing with his sword in a blind fury. Leofsunu of Sturmer fought beside him like a feral beast, cutting and slashing, and men joined them, fighting ferociously to force the Vikings backwards. Thered howled like a madman and hacked into the Jomsvikings with an axe. Beornoth caught a spear point on his shield and cut his sword across his attacker's helmet. Leofsunu stood over the corpse of the ealdorman and chopped his sword at the hand of a Viking who tried to grab Byrhtnoth's gold-hilted sword. The Vikings drew back, whooping for joy at their victory, and Beornoth glimpsed Olaf's sharp face amongst the Jomsviking beards and helmets. He and Leofsunu stood before the ealdorman's corpse like wolves defending their cubs, and sorrow washed over the Saxon army like the flood tide during a full moon. Numbness fell upon Beornoth, too much loss for him to comprehend: Wulfhere and Byrhtnoth were dead.

The Vikings pulled back, and there was a break in the fighting. Olaf was there, grinning like a madman, his face soaked in blood. The Viking leader had threatened vengeance for the death of Palnatoki at Watchet, and had brought his warriors to England in search of glory and silver. Now he was on the verge of a victory to ring down through the ages. Beornoth wanted to sink to his knees in despair, but he forced himself to stand on shaking legs burning with fatigue. Thered stood behind him, and it had been the hostage who dragged Beornoth away from the Viking swine-head charge. Beornoth and Leofsunu shared a desperate look. Everything they knew and loved had been ripped away by Olaf and his Norsemen. Long faces stared at Beornoth, looking for orders, for leadership, but he looked away. Offa too was dead – he had been Byrhtnoth's captain, and men needed a leader. Beornoth knew it, felt that the army was a hair's breadth from destruction and slaughter. But he was too shocked to act, hurt by the loss of men who had died already on that grim day. A warrior shouldered through the crowd, and Beornoth reached out to clasp his arm with a bloody hand. It was Aelfwine, clever and dependable, and Beornoth hoped he would help him lead the army and fight back. But Aelfwine's face was pale and his eyes wide with panic.

'Forkbeard's men come ashore,' he said, looking with horror at the surrounding carnage. 'The Danes are behind us.'

Beornoth shook his head in disbelief. The ealdorman was dead, Olaf stood before him ready to crow his victory, and now Forkbeard's war-hungry Danes came from the rear. He remembered suddenly Brand's warning. *The day of the Saxon is over*, he had said. Beornoth felt that: his arms were heavy; his shoulders burned from the furious fighting; his wounds throbbed with stinging pain.

'What shall we do, Lord Beornoth?' said a voice, snapping Beornoth from his thoughts. He stared at each of the faces, brave men all. They were all that stood between the Vikings and the fall of Essex. He sighed and clutched at the crucifix around his neck.

'We fight,' he said.

24

'You hold Olaf's men here,' said Beornoth, glaring at Leofsunu and Aelfwine. 'I will take the men of Wessex and Streonwold's men to fight Forkbeard.'

'But if we split our forces, the enemy will overwhelm us?' said Thered. The Northumbrian was no coward. His mail was bloodied, and he had fought as hard as any other man in the front lines. But he spoke the words and fears which laid as heavy as ballast stones in each man's mind. Norsemen and Danes surrounded them, two Viking armies converged to slaughter the East Saxons. They were outnumbered and their leader was dead.

'If we let Forkbeard's men amongst the fyrd, then we are dead anyway. What choice do we have?'

'I will stand with you then. We strike for Forkbeard, if he dies then his army might fold,' said Thered, and it was a desperate and unlikely hope, but Beornoth was too weary to argue that to get to Forkbeard they must cut down his personal bodyguard of picked Danish champions. Beornoth limped, grimacing at wounds and aching limbs. They marched grimly, swords, spears, seaxes and shields clanking, towards the riverbank where forty

Viking ships dropped their anchor stones and battle-hungry
warriors came ashore in the rippling waters. Beornoth called to
Wighelm and Wigstan, and the twins brought the men of Wessex,
their numbers reduced by those who had already lost their lives
in the desperate fight against Olaf's men. They flew the dragon
banner of Wessex, the wind caught it and the dragon snaked out,
as though it growled at the Vikings. It was the old banner of
Alfred and Aethelstan, and to see it stirred men's hearts. Thered
brought Streonwold, and the Cheshire thegn strode alongside
Beornoth, his jowls shaking as he stepped around the dead and
the dying, his sword red-tipped and notched by enemy blades.
Beornoth glanced at his old shield mate, and a moment of silent
recognition passed between then, a knowing look between old
friends who had fought together many times, an understanding
of trust and respect.

'Find Dunnere and bring him to me,' Beornoth said to
Cwicca, and the young warrior scampered towards the men of
the fyrd. The bravest of those men had already joined the fight,
picking up the spears and shields of the fallen and joining the
East Saxon warriors in the forward ranks. Most, however, held
back. They clutched their billhooks, scythes and clubs and hoped
that the fight would be over before the slashing Viking blades
reached them, and they were not alone in that. Beornoth growled
at a clutch of warriors clad in good leather breastplates and
armed with spears. They were unmarked by battle and had
drifted to rear ranks to escape the welter of death that was the
Jomsviking attack. They had seen their ealdorman fall, and
feared defeat. They feared death, pain and suffering, but they saw
Beornoth, Streonwold, Thered and warriors who had already
fought hard in the thick of the slaughter, and shame drove them
to follow. Of every hundred men, only twenty had courage and
skill to be a real warrior: a man who could stand and trade blows

with the professional warriors of Norway and Denmark. Of those twenty, only two or three were the lovers of the battle, the men who sought out the enemy and rejoiced in the heightened senses and heart-thumping thrill of battle where a man's existence was fleeting and danced on the ethereal line between life and death. But Beornoth growled at those cowering warriors to follow him, for he would need every spear if they were to survive that grim day.

The Danes came wading through the shallows encumbered by their soaked clothes and armour like plodding things from a nightmare. Fierce men clutching axe and spear, their beards and armour dripping with water, and malice in their eyes. They came to kill a force already half-beaten by Olaf's warriors and the hunger for slaughter pulsed from them like an animal's scent.

'Kill them before they reach the beach,' Beornoth growled to his men. 'Don't let them form the shield wall.' If the Danes were able to get ashore and form up, the Saxons would be hacked to pieces between two shield walls. The Danes came from the water in ragged formation, fresh from their ships and eager to join the fighting.

Beornoth ran towards the water's lapping edge and hammered his shield into a black-bearded Dane before he could raise his shield from the water. The Dane toppled backwards and landed on his arse with a splash and then died with Beornoth's sword in his throat. He turned and roared to the men of Wessex, Cheshire, and the East Saxons, and they responded with a battle cry and charged in with him. Streonwold followed, splashed into the water with great strides and the ageing warrior killed a much younger Dane, parrying an overhand axe lunge and stabbing his sword into the Viking's belly with all the sword skill of a man with a lifetime of experience fighting in the front rank. A war horn peeled out across the estuary, long and sonorous, and the Danes let out a clipped roar of ascent. A huge warship crashed its bows between two smaller vessels, and those ships surged aside before its hull rising from the water like a cliff of riveted timber. A man leapt from the prow of the monstrous warship, clutching two war axes. He came up waist deep in the water and waded towards the Saxons, axes held aloft and his long beard braided into two forks. Beornoth knew the man, for it was Sweyn Forkbeard, king of the Danes, come to join the fight. His round face, which had seemed so calm and thoughtful in Gippeswic, was now twisted into a snarl, feral and savage as he came on roaring and brandishing his axes. Beornoth stepped forward to meet the king and try to kill him, to snatch their leader away before that second battle in the shallows had even begun, but a commotion behind him caught his attention and Beornoth turned in horror to see the Saxon army running away.

A warrior in fine shining mail called to the Saxons from the top of a small hill where the riverbank rose to form a slanting meadow of long, lush grass. He wore a magnificent helmet and held a beautiful, golden-hilted sword aloft, and he looked like a king, glorious in his war gear. He called the men of the fyrd to flee, to run for their lives, to live to fight another day. He waved his sword, and his horse skittered beneath him so that he turned on the hilltop like a beacon to the fyrd men, whose hearts shrank at the prospect of exchanging blows with the Vikings, men they had been taught to fear, men whose business was death.

'Treacherous bastard,' growled Thered. Beornoth's sword and shield arm dropped to his sides and his shoulders sank in despair. The man on the horse was Godric, son of Odda, thegn of Essex. He sat upon Ealdorman Byrhtnoth's warhorse, flanked by his brothers. Riding the ealdorman's horse, and waving a golden hilted sword so similar to Byrhtnoth's that the same smith could have forged them, many would think that Godric was, in fact, the

ealdorman himself. The rear rankers would not have seen Byrhtnoth fall, and in their fear would convince one another that the
news of his death sweeping through the army was a mistake. The
men of the fyrd, the simple folk of Essex, did not need to be asked
twice to flee the beach where men died and warriors fought. They
ran, and once men saw others escape the Viking onslaught, they
followed until the fyrd melted away in a panicked roar. Beornoth's
jaw fell open and he just stared at Godric as the thegn wheeled
his horse around and cantered away from the battlefield with
more than half the Saxon army trailing behind him. Godric had
betrayed them. Beornoth stared across the battlefield and there
were only four hundred Saxons left to stand and fight against two
thousand Vikings. Those remaining warriors, however, were the
heart of the East Saxon fighting force, the picked warriors of
Wessex, and Streonwold's men of Cheshire. They were the
veterans of a lifetime of war, warriors of Ealdorman's Byrhtnoth's
hearth troop who had sworn to fight to the death against their
enemies.

A splashing sound brought Beornoth to his senses, and he
tore his eyes away from the fleeing traitors to see Streonwold
trading blows in the shallows with the king of Denmark. Streonwold ducked under an axe swing and lunged with his sword, but
Forkbeard caught it with his second axe and brought his first
weapon in an overhand strike so that the bearded axe blade
smashed through the chain-mail byrnie and carved Streonwold's
chest open. Beornoth had known the Cheshire man since they
were young warriors together. He was a good man, cut down
before Beornoth's eyes. Streonwold fell to his knees, his mouth
opening and closing silently like a landed fish, and Forkbeard
pushed past him as the Cheshire man toppled face first into the
water. Edward the Tall, one of Streonwold's men, flung himself at
the king, but Forkbeard sidestepped his attack like a fleet-footed

youth and cleaved Edward's neck open in a spray of crimson. Beornoth roared and charged at Forkbeard, anger welling within him like a storm. Godric's treachery and the death of too many of his friends washed the aches and pains of his body away. Forkbeard grinned at him, a terrible smile, and Beornoth remembered the king as he had been in his hall at Gippeswic, short and gentle-faced, cunning and clever. He was a different man now, a savage warrior bent on death and glory. Beornoth swung his sword at the king, but Forkbeard was fast and he leant away from the blow and brought his axes down together hard upon Beornoth's shield, splintering the boards and driving Beornoth to his knees. He surged forwards, punching the rim of his shield into Forkbeard's chest and he slashed with his sword and the edge cut across the king's belly, but his expensive mail held and Forkbeard gaped at Beornoth, sure that he should have died from the blow. Another enemy came at Beornoth, hacking at him with a huge long-handled war axe. The Dane roared and spat and drove Beornoth backwards, hammering into his shield and pushing him away from the king. The Dane was huge and Beornoth recognised him from Gippeswic. It was Knut War Raven, the king's uncle and brother of the former king of Denmark, Harald Bluetooth. Beornoth caught another blow on his shield, and the linden-wood boards cracked and splintered, and he fell to his knees in the water. Knut swung his axe again and the enormous blade smashed through the shield boards, jarring Beornoth's arm like a hammer blow so that he could see Knut's terrible face snarling at him through the hole carved by his axe.

'Saxon turd!' Knut shouted through the splintered hole in Beornoth's shield.

But the broken boards tangled Knut's weapon, and Beornoth felt the Dane's monstrous strength tugging at his shield arm as

Knut tried to yank his blade free. Beornoth drove the point of his sword through that gap and it punched through Knut's mouth, smashing his teeth into white splinters, slicing through his tongue until it scraped on the back of the Dane's skull.

Beornoth rose with a grunt and ripped his blade free of the dying man. A warrior came at him, golden-haired and wielding a sword. The man was quick and Beornoth was tired and before he could raise his shattered shield to defend himself the point of the Dane's sword drove into his hip, through mail and leather and into his flesh, burning and ripping. Thered appeared, killing the golden-haired Dane with a sword cut to his neck. He dragged Beornoth back, out of the shallows, and from the corner of his eye Beornoth saw Wigstan of Wessex die, swarmed by five Vikings who hacked him down into the water. Those Vikings came towards Beornoth, hungry and searching for Saxons to kill. They died under a hail of arrows, and Beornoth laughed because some of the fyrd had not fled. Dunnere led those men to the water's edge and fifty of them, armed with bows, poured their arrows into the Danes as they struggled to wade through the water from their ships. It was no time for laughter, but Beornoth laughed anyway because the Danes were dying. His warriors, the men of Cheshire and Æthelred's warriors of Wessex, fought like bears and the Danish dead were thick in the river, turning its murky waters red with their blood.

Thered laid Beornoth down on the sand and he grimaced, the wound on his side burning. His hands were swollen where he had gripped sword and shield and he had taken other wounds to his face, arms and legs but had not noticed in the hard fighting. Those wounds pulsed as he lay there, watching the finest warriors in Saxon England drive the Danes back into the estuary. His lifeblood leaked away to join that of countless others injured or dying on the battlefield. Those warriors who fought on had

been betrayed by Godric. Godric was an East Saxon thegn, a
warrior who had taken the blood oath, and was sworn to fight to
the death for Byrhtnoth. His order to flee had broken the Saxon
shield wall and driven the fyrd to flight, but the brave men who
remained were still alive and Thered bound Beornoth's wound
with a torn cloak and lifted him to his feet. The young Northumbrian's nose was broken, a cut across its bridge, and his long face
was filthy with blood and sweat.

'We must form a circle, or we will all die,' said Leofsunu,
limping over to Beornoth, a bloody gash across one knee.

'Do it,' said Beornoth. They fell back and formed a circle of
shields, warriors and thegns on the outside with Dunnere's
remaining fyrd men on the inside.

'We won't give our land up to these bastards,' shouted
Dunnere, and his men loosed their shafts between the shields,
harrying the enemy and killing men who came to attack their
shield wall. When his arrows were spent, Dunnere fought with
his staff and cracked the skulls of any Vikings who came within
its reach.

'They must all die!' came a shrill voice across the battlefield.
'They are the spawn of hell. God demands their deaths. Kill them
all!'

'What in all hell is that?' said Wighelm, the surviving Wessex
twin, pointing to where four Danes carried a coffin upright, in
which Ragnar the Heimnar spat and shouted curses. A huge
crucifix spanned the coffin and held him in place.

'Forkbeard's men are Christians,' said Beornoth. 'And that
thing was Ragnar the Flayer until I whittled him down to that
stump of a man.'

Ragnar roared at his men, and the Danes came on howling at
the Saxon circle. Beornoth stood with a shield taken from the
hands of a dead man, finding the strength to stand despite his

wounds, and next to him stood Wighelm and Thered. On the opposite side of the circle, Aelfwine and Leofsunu urged the Saxons on to bravery, to fight with honour for their dead lord.

'We swore a blood oath to fight to the end,' Aelfwine reminded them. 'We shall avenge our Lord Byrhtnoth. Make them pay for our ealdorman's death and let us take ten Vikings for every one of us they kill.'

The fighting then became brutal and savage. Olaf's men attacked from one flank, and Forkbeard's from the other. Beornoth's small square of shields stood like a rock beneath a crashing sea in a storm. Norsemen and Danes died in their dozens, and every fresh attack saw more Saxons die. The Saxons roared in horror as Leofsunu of Sturmer died with a Jomsviking's spear in his chest, but not before he took his killer's life with his sword. Beornoth felt Leofsunu's death like a wound, a stabbing, stinging cut to his heart. Wighelm of Wessex killed three Danes who broke the Saxon shield wall before he too was killed by an axe in his face. Dunnere, the simple farmer, fought like a warrior of legend with his staff. When a Norseman took that from him, Dunnere fought with a broken spear before the Jomsvikings trapped him between their shields and killed him with axe blows to his chest.

Beornoth stood with Thered and Aelfwine at the end, and he roared with pain as young Cwicca fell to a Jomsviking sword.. The Saxon youth had fought like the greatest of champions, and in another life he could have lived a life of peace. He would have made a fine husband and father, yet now he was dead. Sitric of Thetford, who had ridden south from East Anglia with Byrht-noth, died fighting to protect Cwicca's corpse. Beornoth had never known such a slaughter. The bodies piled high around him, blood slicked the earth and with every blow he cursed Godric the traitor, and the Vikings who had come to kill them.

They stood and fulfilled their oaths. Aelfwine's handsome face was cut, bruised and swollen so that he could only see out of one eye. Beornoth could barely stand. Those last moments came in a haze of pain beyond reckoning from countless wounds. By sheer will, Beornoth kept his shield up and struck at the enemy. Even after his sword shattered upon a Danish war axe, he fought on with his seax. Aelfwine fell with a Jomsviking's sword in his belly and a spear in his chest. Beornoth wanted to drop and hold his friend, to give up and let the Vikings kill him, to die beside such great friends as Leofsunu, Aelfwine, Cwicca and Streon-wold. But he did not fall. Beornoth swallowed at the ball of pain in his throat and fought on. The Saxon circle grew smaller as warriors succumbed to the Vikings' overwhelming numbers. The Norse and Danish dead piled high around them and Beornoth could hardly move as a spear flew past his head to kill Gylfi, man of the fyrd and a villager who fought as hard as the bravest thegn. Beornoth's seax was ripped from his hand and a blade punched into his guts; cold iron ripped and burned his flesh with pain. He fell to lie amongst those men, his friends, brave warriors who had given their lives for Saxon England. Beornoth closed his eyes and grasped beneath his byrnie, clutching the red scarf he had taken from Eawynn as a token. He wanted to feel close to her as he died. Rough hands tore at his mail and helmet, clawing to rip the wealth from him.

'I want that one, the big one is mine!' he heard Ragnar scream somewhere in the darkness. They had lost the battle, undone by betrayal and by the sheer number of Norsemen and Danes, who had joined forces at the last to overcome Ealdorman Byrhtnoth. Beornoth waited for death, but he could not hear his daughters' voices over the groans of the injured or the exultant shouts of the victorious Vikings. A tear rolled down Beornoth's cheek and he sobbed. He shuddered and wept for all they had lost and for the men who had died. Good men. Warriors. Most of all, Beornoth cried because heaven did not open for him, he was afraid that he would never be reunited with Ashwig and Cwen and that he was falling down into darkness, towards the pit of hell to spend eternity away from his daughters, never again to see Eawynn, even in the afterlife.

But he was not falling. Darkness gave way to light between the slits of his bruised and swollen eyes. There were rough stones beneath his back, and then soft grass. Beornoth could only open one eye, the other hidden and closed behind his smashed and swollen face. Pain wracked him, white-hot and pulsing across his entire body. He was alive. Whatever force dragged him came to a stop and Beornoth coughed thick blood from his mouth. He curled into a ball, doubled up with suffering, the tear in his guts like a rod of iron searingly hot from the forge inside him. A figure loomed over him. A golden-haired man with the tattoo of a raven upon his neck.

'I can't let that cursed heimnar have you, lord,' said the man in Norse. Brand Thorkilsson lifted Beornoth over his shoulder and draped him over the back of a horse. The Norseman climbed into the saddle and carried Beornoth from the battle of Maldon. His head rattled with panic at not knowing who of those last few fighters had lived or died, Thered amongst them, but Beornoth was alive. As Brand carried him away from the terrible defeat, wounded countless times, Beornoth clung to life, he fought against the pain of his wounds, and the overwhelming mountain of grief upon his soul. They were all dead, his brothers of the sword, but Beornoth was glad that he had survived, for he was not yet finished with the world of men. The Vikings had won. There were betrayers to punish, and the dead to avenge.

HISTORICAL NOTE

The two books already published in this series have led us to the Battle of Maldon, fought on a day in August in 991 when an East Saxon force of warriors lost a pitched battle against an army of Viking raiders. The series will continue, for Beornoth has not yet finished his adventures, but the battle is the tragic event at the centre of his story. The Battle of Maldon is important not only as a historical event but also as the subject of a famous poem from the 10th century. The poem is heroic, and honours the brave men who died fighting to protect their land from the Viking invaders. It glorifies the fighting, but also gives us a sense of the shock which rang around England in the aftermath. That shock would lead to changes in King Æthelred's policy which would stop the Viking invasion, for a time at least.

Byrhtnoth, the ealdorman of the East Saxons (of Essex and the east of England) died in the fighting, as did many of the nobility from his shire. The first page of the poem is lost to history and the reader is therefore thrown straight into the action as Byrhtnoth makes arrangements for the battle, riding up and down the battle lines instructing the men how they will fight in the shield wall and what the tactics for the battle will be. The Vikings did land in the River Blackwater and came ashore on Northey Island, which is connected to the mainland by a tidal causeway. The poem refers to the exchange between the Saxons and Vikings where the Vikings called out to the Saxons asking for payment to avoid the battle, which Byrhtnoth refused. The causeway was indeed held by three brave Saxon warriors who slew many of the invaders, and then the poem describes how the ealdorman allowed the Vikings to cross to the beach and fight a pitched battle. The poem refers to Byrhtnoth's *ofermod,* his pride, in allowing the Vikings to cross, but I have preferred to make it a necessity. Byrhtnoth was an experienced war leader, and is described in the sources as a huge grey-haired man, and I doubt he would have been foolish enough to let Olaf's men cross unless forced to do so.

The poem goes on to describe how Byrhtnoth was wounded in the fight and how his golden-hilted sword fell to the ground before he was killed by the Vikings. I have tried to keep the battle as close to the description in the poem as possible, including the betrayal by Godric and his brothers which caused the collapse of the Saxon shield wall. The surviving Saxons fought to the death, and swore vengeance upon the traitors, but then the poem ends abruptly, its last pages lost to the mists of time. Many of the characters in this book appear in the poem: Godric, Byrhtnoth, Olaf, Sweyn, Leofsunu of Sturmer, Aelfwine of Foxfield, Offa, Maccus, Aelfhere, Dunnere and Wulfmaer. The poem also refers to an unnamed brave Northumbrian hostage, who I have made Thered, the man who tried to kill Beornoth in the book preceding this one. Beornoth is a fictional character, as is Wulfhere, but it is through their eyes that we see the war unfold, and hopefully get a sense of the life of a thegn and his oathmen in 10th-century England. It must have a been hard life, full of violence and loss.

There has occasionally been some dispute between historians over the location of the battle. The presence of the tidal causeway and surrounding topography which matches contemporary descriptions have settled that dispute and it can only have been at Northey Island, a mile away from the Saxon burh and existing town at Maldon.

The Vikings were led by Olaf Tryggvason, and his invasion with ninety-three ships is referenced in the Anglo-Saxon Chronicle. As we have seen in this book, and the earlier novels, Olaf landed at Folkestone and plundered the countryside there before moving on to Sandwich and Ipswich, and finally Maldon. The chronicle also references Sweyn, who I have interpreted to be King Sweyn Forkbeard of Denmark, who fatefully returned to England later in Æthelred's reign.

For any readers interested in learning more about the Battle of Maldon, I highly recommend the book on the topic by Mark Atherton. J. R. R. Tolkien, of *Lord of the Rings* fame, wrote a verse on the poem for radio, which was also published in book form in 1964. Tolkien's work is *The Homecoming of Beorhtnoth Beorhthelm's Son*, and that name was the inspiration for the main character in this series of novels. Tolkien's work talks of the heroic way of life, the bravery and loyalty of Byrhtnoth's men, and there are echoes of his fantasy works in the bleak aftermath of the battle.

There are traitors to punish, and Vikings still to fight, and so Beornoth must recover to pick up his sword again...

ACKNOWLEDGMENTS

Thanks to Caroline, Nia, Claire, Jenna and all the team at Boldwood Books for their belief in Beornoth's story, and for their unwavering support along the way. Special thanks to Ross and the editing team at Boldwood for all their effort and amazing eye for detail.

MORE FROM PETER GIBBONS

We hope you enjoyed reading *Brothers of the Sword*. If you did, please leave a review.

If you'd like to gift a copy, this book is also available as an ebook, large print, hardback, digital audio download and audiobook CD.

Sign up to Peter Gibbons' mailing list for news, competitions and updates on future books.

https://bit.ly/PeterGibbonsNews

Explore Peter Gibbons' Saxon Warrior series...

ABOUT THE AUTHOR

Peter Gibbons is a financial advisor and author of the highly acclaimed Viking Blood and Blade trilogy. He comes to Boldwood with his new Saxon Warrior series, set around the 900 AD Viking invasion during the reign of King Athelred the Unready. He lives with his family in County Kildare.

Visit Peter's website: https://petermgibbons.com/

Follow Peter on social media:

twitter.com/AuthorGibbons

facebook.com/petergibbonsauthor

instagram.com/petermgibbons

bookbub.com/authors/peter-gibbons

Boldw⊙⊙d

Boldwood Books is an award-winning fiction publishing company seeking out the best stories from around the world.

Find out more at www.boldwoodbooks.com

Join our reader community for brilliant books, competitions and offers!

Follow us
@BoldwoodBooks
@BookandTonic

Sign up to our weekly deals newsletter

https://bit.ly/BoldwoodBNewsletter

Printed in Great Britain
by Amazon

27411336R00175